The Voyage

Book 1 of the Sorceress of Selvast Forest Series

EK Dobbins

Apellez Dreams Publishing

USA

Apellez Dreams Publishing
5343 Belleville Crossing Street
PMB 75
Belleville, Illinois 62226
www.apellezdreamspublishing.com

Book Layout © 2017 BookDesignTemplates.com

The Voyage/ EK Dobbins. – 3rd ed.
ISBN 978-0-9896487-7-6

Contents

CHAPTER ONE

Port of Churn

The cry of many seabirds permeates the gentle breeze as the sun peaks over the horizon. The stale and pungent night air is replaced with the fresh scent of the ocean. The smell of the fish is soon swapped by the strong odor of hard-working men. Robust voices from sailors of all origins fill the void as the day gets underway. Their curses and swears are almost drowned out by the movement of cargo from one of twelve docked ships. A large number of extra ships put down anchor a short distance from the pier, impatiently awaiting a turn at the bustling ports.

The spray of the seawater is felt throughout the entire village. It leaves a persistent reminder upon the pock-marked houses closest to the churning water as salt and time wear away their defenses. Clear sunny skies beckon both residents and visitors to wander the marketplace in search of the elusive bargain. Several streets of this lower port town, Churn, buzzes with the hawking of merchants as they bark welcome to patrons shopping their wares. The bickering of two men over a tool proves that the bartering way of life still dominates the streets.

A group of tall, stocky women squawks with laughter entertaining the gossip of the day as chickens scratch around their feet. Cobblestone streets click with the hooves of the horses ridden by the city watch. The large men, ripe with muscle, eye all with suspicion as they parade through the crowd searching for anyone who brings trouble. The high-pitched laughter of children mixes with the sounds of the boisterous voices and large animal sounds of the marketplace.

The small gang, consisting of young boys, weaves through the various shoppers with ease and skill in their game of chase. A few surefooted children manage to nab a coin pouch or purse as they enjoy their game. Everyone in the marketplace takes in the gorgeous late summer day, one of a few left for the year. Many elders sit on a tavern porch, discussing the weather with some advising that the season turned from summer to autumn much faster than in recent history.

The joyful cheers of a caravan boost the bustle and excitement as they walk through the gates and into the marketplace of the port town. It is a long, dangerous road to Churn by land, especially with the many wars waging upon the planet, Bri'al. Those roads once safe and secure are now filled with petty thieves and bandits cautioning those that travel alone to do so at their own risk. Townsfolk monitor the arrivals with quick glances then continue their business, noting that there is no threat from the weary nomads so far.

A woman and her daughter pull away from the rest of the caravan and take a slight left in the street towards the ports. The group of gossiping women stops talking as the mother and daughter are quick to pass with a hasty word of greeting. The gossips take note of the woman's long red hair and start to speak in excited yet quiet tones. This prompts the chickens to hasten the scratching adding their own chatter to the noise.

The woman and her daughter continue down the street and turn to walk past the elders causing them to pause and take note of the adult's strong yet very feminine body. Their eyes lock on the swaying of her hips as she disappears down the street. She visits Churn often, usually dresses in a flattering dress, yet today is not her normal attire. She is clad in trousers and a matching vest with a long sleeve shirt underneath it to protect her arms.

Her boots are a little worn yet still very functional, evident when she digs in her heels and turns yet another corner, her child keeping stride with her easily. They take another twist around an oval-shaped home and greet another set of townsfolks as they hone in on their destination. Several of the witnessing locals gawk before speaking in hushed tones among each other, the name and title of the woman and child that they just brushed past. The woman is the legendary Sorceress of Selvast Forest; her name—Milea Sirus.

The girl is her daughter, Sonja, and rumor has it that although she is not a mage, she excels in abilities unknown or unmatched by any man, woman, or beast known to them. The girl stands at least a foot and a half shorter than her mother, with her light brown locks tied back into a single braid. A few strands dangling on the left of her delicate face brought attention to her eyes, the left is blue while the right is golden brown. She dresses like her mother but lacks a shirt under her vest; instead, her left arm is protected by a large leather armband that covers the forearm snuggly. The mayor of the town tries to call to the sorceress and her daughter to stop her for a chat or favor. Milea waves back but does not stop; her mind is on her mission.

Less than an hour ago her twin sister, Maya, contacted her via a mystic mirror with disturbing news. The Temple of Light in the Boiling Seas was under attack by a massive army of dragons. The temple itself is defended by dragons and their kin yet many turns on their fellows due to a strange melody. Milea knits her brow as she recalls the last words of her sister. She said to hurry to her before the mirror went into sudden eerie silence. Milea found trying to reestablish communication with her twin unsuccessful. It is as if someone or something is deliberately preventing communication. Trying to reach the Temple of Light with mystical means would not work either, as whoever blocks the communication extended it to any means of teleportation into the temple. This is a great concern to Milea since teleportation is her usual way of transportation.

An earlier attempt to travel landed her in a dangerous and uncharted swamp known as Wild Territory. She managed a return home to ponder the situation. A dragon, although the fastest means next to teleportation, is out of the question since Maya has a deep-rooted fear of dragons. Her panic can cause a massive amount of uncontrolled dark magic to unleash from within. Winged horses and gryphons are extremely rare if they exist at all.

After exhausting her options, Milea concludes that to get to the Boiling Seas, she will need to take a boat. Yet even the fastest vessels known on Bri'al would take months to reach the secluded seas by any known post worldwide. Milea did not have months to get to her twin and pleaded with the Guardian of Selvast Forest, Keela, for a vessel that would get them there in days.

The Guardian bestowed the gift, creating the craft from one of many trees within Selvast Forest. With a seaworthy ship in hand, Milea must face her second dilemma; she will need a sea captain who knows the way to the Boiling Seas since the ocean path is not very familiar to her. Milea hopes to find a captain that is not already bound to a crew in this city of sailors since her enchanted vessel has no need for a crew.

The duo returns to the marketplace near its end with the pier in sight. Sonja let out a little sneeze causing Milea to pause and turn her attention to her daughter. Sonja opts not to have a shirt since she did not have any to mess up if the need to fight someone arose. Milea smiles at the memory of her daughter's simple explanation then approaches the small booth filled with clothing of all kinds and scans it with her enchanting brown eyes. Sonja also surveys it and is able to keep her objects silent about the various prices that are in her view as she runs her hand through her hair.

The large man behind the table beams a bright smile at the sorceress and girl, a gleam of greed crossing his eyes. Milea meets his gaze briefly then shifts to look at the fine silks and furs he had for display with a slight twist about her lips. She did not want to purchase anything too expensive, especially after Sonja's realistic explanation. Milea turns her attention to a shirt that is made from cheaper silk and dyed deep green.

"Mom," Sonja addresses, "what's the matter?"

"We must find you something a little warmer, Sonja," Milea explains gently to her child in her naturally seductive voice.

The merchant's smile brightens even more after hearing her speak as she continues to examine the silken shirt. Several men hesitate to admire the woman and vie for her attention. They are ignored and move on. One unfortunate soul is scolded and smacked on the back of his head by his wife. Disregarding the activity, Milea holds the shirt against Sonja. A warm smile touches her lips when the girl spreads her arms out for good measure. Just the right size for her daughter, Milea approves the shirt and turns to the excited merchant.

"How much for this green shirt, my good man?" Milea asks, holding up the item.

"One hundred coins and you won't find a better deal," boasts the pot-bellied merchant as he pats his stomach with a bright smile, he continues, "These fine wares are made from the finest material in the Northwest. Spun from the discarded wool of mountain dragons, they are warm, comfortable as well as naturally waterproof. King Randolf of Helbavor guarantees it."

"I see," Milea says with some calm in her voice before turning to walk away, much to the merchant's surprise. "Let us make haste to the Lucky Dragon. I think we will find something of better quality in the next port."

"Hopefully cheaper as well," Sonja adds, relieved that her mother did not pick up the overpriced item that she knew she would tear apart during a mild scuffle. Milea smiles as they continue their path toward the piers.

A large group of horses snorts aggressively as they are led down the street past the mother and daughter team. The beasts grunt in protest of the way their handlers treat them with a few kicking out in spite. Their breath and odor mingle with the rest of the port town's unique smells and the body heat from the animals causes some localized humidity. Sonja makes a sound of displeasure and waves her hand in front of her nose. She makes a small grumble noise when she thinks of the situation, perhaps the horses just got off a ship. Milea pays no mind to the grunting animals as she leads the way turning a corner to continue down a sloping street. Sonja jogs a little to catch up with her mother then matches her stride.

It did not take long for the two to locate their destination. A sign with a dragon sitting on a four-leaf clover hung above the door. The dragon itself appears to have had one too many drinks. His green scales are painted with a hint of purple in spots. The color is deeper on the cheeks and stomach, indicating he is in good spirits both inside and out. His middle section is swollen, eyes and mouth wide with a hardy welcoming call. His arms are wide with greeting. The pictured dragon holds a tankard of ale in one hand, a large jewel in the other.

The tavern sits proudly upon the ports of Churn as a means to meet and carry on any business associated with the docks. A nice two-mast schooner floats on the gentle waves a few feet away basking in the rays of the sun as it awaits departure. The door opens, spewing forth several uninviting odors from the tavern. Both Milea and Sonja take several steps to one side, allowing stumbling regulars to exit. They did not appear to see the two, which is perhaps a good thing. Judging from their mannerisms, Milea deduces that they are pirates. From experience, Milea knows that there are no sailors upon the seas of Bri'al more adventurous than pirates, some to the point of foolhardiness. Milea takes a deep breath and reaches for the door, much to her daughter's surprise.

"We are really going to go in there? Sonja asks, glancing at her mother with curiosity on her features. Seriously?"

"To save your aunt, we have no choice," Milea turns to her daughter. "Stay close to me. I don't think I want to cause a riot by beheading one of their more prominent members."

"I don't want to break their arms either," Sonja counters. "I'll be aware," she continues in the hopes of reassuring her mother.

"Good," replies Milea.

Muffled laughter from inside the tavern is followed by a brief moment of silence. Milea turns to the now-closed door and takes a deep breath. She opens the door to be greeted with a wave of hardy cheers and sharp stench which causes Sonja to squeak and move back several paces. Milea grins at her child's reaction, enabling her to contain her own. With another deep breath, the sorceress bravely enters the establishment, disappearing in the thick smoke a few steps in. Sonja follows her mother, keeping close as the cheers die down.

The music of a mandolin fills the smoke-laden air to capture the attention of those in the room. A voice rings out garnishing participation from the crowd, yet its speaker is not clearly seen. Several drunken cheers answer the proud and boisterous male voice that echoes from the stage. The unseen man then launches into a song, using the thumping of his boot on the stage as a drum. Milea scans the audience, noting that the Lucky Dragon bustles with all sorts of activity, much of it illegal. She is familiar with the tavern's reputation, visiting it numerous times in her past when searching for a dear friend who happens to be a pirate.

Unfortunately, that friend is not among the audience today, which would have made her quest much easier. A series of life circumstances have kept Milea's pirate friend from the seas for many years now. Several men turn from the stage to take gaze at the two visitors who have appeared in their domain. Milea straightens and meets their gaze, unflinching. The men sit back a little then to turn and face the stage once more, determined to avoid any conflict with the sorceress. Milea focuses upon the room and notes a table near the back of the room.

"This way," Milea says and pushes toward her destination.

Sonja keeps close to her mother as they make their way toward the last empty table in the establishment. The smoke thickens as does the stench of alcohol as the two near the center of the room. Sonja inspects the patrons, her curiosity keeping her eyes scanning the entire room. All are sailors of one sort or the other, heralding from the various regions of Bri'al. Sonja's eyes fell on the one person she felt seems out of place. The girl's gaze is met with the curious sea-blue eyes of the elfin stranger. His vest and trousers resemble more of a woodland warrior than the looser clothing of the local sailors. His long, dark hair is tied back at the moment.

An expensive, sharpened sword hung at his waist. Its handle is encrusted with gemstones, yet no one seemed to want to take it from him. From the wear on the handle itself, Sonja suspects the elf is an expert sword master. Milea meets the eyes of the elf, causing him to avert his gaze back to his drink. The sorceress and her daughter walk past the stranger as they continue to the table. He waits until they are several steps away then turns and studies them. Afterward, he stands and walks to a door on the left side of the stage.

A small group of men seems content to watch the woman and child wonder by. The leader of the men sizes up Milea as she continues her way, then speaks to his cohorts. The large group splits into two with the majority of them leaving the tavern while a handful stays with the leader of the group. They disburse into the crowd to blend in as Milea finally reaches the back table without incident. The small, square table is short and squat, with room for just one person. A single chair accompanies the table with the back against the wall. Milea adjusts the table, so two sides are against the corner walls and pulls over an additional chair. Sonja sits down to study the people of the tavern. Many of them openly stare at the newcomers. Milea sits in the second chair.

"This place is not comfortable," Sonja says in hush tones to her mother.

"It isn't," Milea agrees. "However, we will not be here long," she continues turning her focus to the stage.

A man and a woman stand on the large, raised floor that covers a good part of the left wall. They appear to be bickering after which the woman tilts back her head and barks loud, boisterous laughter. The patrons also laugh loudly either from what they hear or because the laugh itself is a bit infectious. Sonja focuses on the stage as well and sees both actors are L'vane like her. She leans forward to try to distinguish them through the smoke. They are adventurers, perhaps sailors as they have similar complexions to those who roamed the waves—the same as that of many of the patrons occupying the Lucky Dragon.

"So, what say you, my fine pirate woman?" the man asks loud enough for his audience to hear. His low tenor voice echoes in the large room. "Do you surrender, or will you face my blade?"

The man puffs up his chest to exaggerate his height of five feet and five inches tall. The flames from the nearby fireplace dance with the dark sand color hair upon his brow and perhaps his chest. A nice ponytail clung to the back of his head, proudly riding from the lower part of his neck down. Auburn eyes sparkle with good humor as he attempts to express anger at the woman. He is wearing a black vest with nice, loose-fitting trousers. The top shows off the strong muscle of his arms and chest. Worn black boots complete his ensemble.

"Oh wait, let me give you my response again," the five-foot eight woman counters. She places her hands upon her hips and throws back her head in a hardy belly laugh. "My, but you are a humorous person."

A grin masks her pretty features. Ginger hair rains down her shoulders, reaching her middle back. A golden band held a portion of her locks in place to keep it out of her face. Her outfit is like that of her cohort at least on the front. She turns her back on the audience to show that her vest is graced with the golden embroidery of a dragon holding a rose. Her body is fit and nicely proportion, garnering the attention of most of the room.

"I see," the man growls holding up his sword. He steps toward the woman who has yet to move. His body language indicates that he is upset at his opponent's lack of concern. "Then, you leave me with no choice than to give you my sword so you may face him," he says while pointing behind the woman.

"What?" the woman asks.

The rush of feet causes the woman to turn and utter a few very unkind words as she pulls her brother's sword and blocks her previously unknown assailant. Sonja notes that the swordsman is the elf that she spied during their walk to their location. Lucky for the actress, he stands just a few inches taller than she; else this could have turned for the worse. The woman locks swords with the elf twice more then she takes a couple of steps back. She places her hand upon her hip to study the elf then turns to her brother as she holds the sword coyly.

"Hold up. How in Ublivorion did that happen? I thought I am supposed to be facing you, brother. Not our traveling buddy," the woman said, annoyed.

"I'll have you know that Brion here is a top-notch Sword Master of his home country," the shorter man introduces. "Besides, one of us has to sing the song, sis. I figure since you're portraying Ra'jil so well, I'll sing while you fight."

"Lovely," the woman says, rolling her eyes. "Thanks, brother."

"Hey, that's what younger siblings are for," the man retorts as he jumps up onto a table. He stomps out a beat and begins to sing, his voice clear and crisp.

The patrons of the tavern clap to his beat as his sister and her opponent battle on the stage. The song fills the entire room along with the ringing of metal. Milea sits back and watches the entertainment of the mock battle. The actress takes several steps back as her opponent presses forward. She then places the blade between her teeth, jumps over the elfman, flips, and lands, facing his back. Her sword appears to jump to her hand. The elf casually holds his sword to cover his back, blocking the woman's swing. She drops a few well-versed swear words and backs up as he turns toward her again, a crooked grin on his own handsome face.

Milea laughs from the antics and Sonja cheers on the woman playing Ra'jil. At the same time, a serving wench appears, snorts in distaste, and places two tankards of ale on the table along with the house special. Some of the slop spills out of the bowl and splatter across the table. It drips down the sides of the containers for a moment, creating small piles of the mess. Milea and

Sonja both eye the offerings then the sorceress is slow to turns her gaze up to the woman that put it there.

"What is this?" Milea motions at the bowl with a slight nod.

"It's free food and ale," the serving wench snaps. "Ye can eat it or toss it to the floor. No bother to me either way." She walks away to serve the next table.

Sonja cautiously studies the contents of the bowl as she takes a whiff. The pungent odor causes her to gag, and she pushes the bowl away in a show of displeasure. There is no way she is going to eat the slop no matter how hungry she is. She turns to see several of the patrons digging into the offerings as if they hadn't eaten in days. The thought causes her stomach to flip a little, but she manages not to get sick from the sight. Milea sits back and breathes a little, calming herself down from the predicament.

"Yes, I think we need to get out of here before I cause trouble. Innkeeper," Milea hails a passing man. He stops from her voice alone, causing Sonja to snicker. "I seek a captain that is adventurous enough to go to the Boiling Seas. Is there such a person here?"

"There be a captain, milady," the innkeeper assures. "His name is Dresden. But he's not sailed in years not even sure if he has a ship now."

"Point me to this Dresden. I will worry about the ship," Milea replies.

The Innkeeper meets her eyes briefly, then ganders toward the stage. She follows his gaze. The mock battle is over with, and the woman is now singing a powerful, high-energy song. Her brother, the one the innkeeper is directing Milea to, sits on the table strumming his mandolin to the song his sister is singing. His fingers dance over the string instrument just as fast as his sister's voice ranges up and down the scale. The elf is now out of sight, but Milea figures he won't be far from his friends. The sorceress's focus once again goes to the man with the mandolin noting that even though he is engrossed with the music, he seems well aware of what is going on around him.

"Thank you," Milea acknowledges the innkeeper. "Tell him I wish to speak with him," she says as she hands the man a few coins.

"Of course, milady. Right away," the innkeeper says with a bright grin. He focuses upon the stage and heads straight for it.

The stage vibrates as the woman does a shuffle dance back to her brother with her hands behind her back. Many of the men whistle and shout for more. Her brother stands and, with a flourish, hands the instrument to his sister. He lets out a cheerful sound as he shuffles center stage. The woman sits down and strums the instrument a little, tuning it to a different pitch for another song. The man laughs and leads a small 'pirate' cheer, which humors his audience.

"Who wants to hear another pirate song?" the male bard's voice rings out. Many of the men raise their glasses with loud hails. "How about another round of our great Mistress of the Seas? Eh?" Loud agreement thunders. The innkeeper walks over and whispers something to the bard. "I see..." he mutters to the man. "Ah, well, duty calls! As well as my curiosity," he addresses his audience.

"Can we at least watch the woman dance?" asks one of the patrons. Verification echoes among his peers.

"Sorry, boys, I have a headache," the actress feigns pain holding her head. "Perhaps another day," she says as she and her brother exit the stage.

The air in the tavern begins to clear up as many of the patrons left much to the relief of the newcomer. Sonja takes a larger breath to keep from passing out, causing her mother to smile a little. The serving wench who had brought them their meal retrieves the bowls and ale as she cleans the table in haste. She then replaces them with large cups of fresh water. Milea watches the woman and notices her features are dark with anger; perhaps she has been given a good scolding by the innkeeper or his wife. The serving wench finishes her chore and leaves without a single word.

Milea picks up the cup and peers at it as the door left of the stage opens. She sees that the contents are fresh and free of any foreign debris. She ponders as she sniffs the contents and signals her thirsty child. Sonja returns the nod and picks up the tanker. She takes a whiff from it before cautiously sipping it. The water is clean and refreshing, causing a sigh of relief from the girl before downing her drink. Milea attention goes back at the stage when she hears a heavy thump of a door closing.

Several of the customers cheer or call to the trio exiting the stage door. Sonja watches their approach and makes a soft sound of acknowledgment to her suspicion with her mother about the two bards. They are indeed l'vane, the shape of the ear tips betraying their heritage. They are, like hers, in the shape of a waning crests moon. Milea studies the trio as they approach, they did not have the gait of novices. All three of them know how to use a sword proficiently. The captain of the group pulls a chair from a now-empty table and brings it over with him. He sat down across from Milea and analyses her a little. The sorceress sips upon her tankard of water, focusing her eyes on those of her guest. She saw that his eyes are bright and alert, indicating that he and his company are sober.

"It is rare to find one of such beauty in this rundown place, milady. And here are two," the seated man says with gentle grace. "I am Neil Dresden," he says and then nods to his left. "This is my older sister, Vicki. To my right is Brion Kaiser. I'm told that you want to make a dangerous and very foolhardy trip."

"Foolhardy but necessary, Neil," the sorceress agree and places her tankard down. "I am Milea Sirus, and this is my daughter, Sonja. I need a sea captain who is willing to guide my ship into the Boiling Seas."

"Ok, wait," Neil shook his head and focuses on the red-haired woman. "You are the Sorceress of Selvast forest. Why do you need a sea captain to get to the Boiling Seas? Can't you use your magic to get you there? And why did you want to go?"

"I need to get to the Temple of Light located at its core. My mystical transportation is not working at this moment, and neither is the communication," Milea answers in short, feeling her patience slipping away.

"You guys were wonderful on stage, I loved your performance," Sonja interjects, hoping to defuse the situation a little. "I am curious though and wonder. Do you have a voice canon?" she asks, tilting her head and focusing on Vicki.

"A what?" Vicki raises an eyebrow.

"Sonja," Milea turns to her child. "Not every songstress or bard we come across will have such a gift. It is a very rare one. The performance on stage was phenomenal. I'm sure Vicki has many talents that make up for the voice canon."

"Your mother speaks the truth on hidden talents," Brion assures. His rich, bass voice causes the girl to jump a little. "And there are always surprises," he says, smiling at the girl.

"Wow," Sonja blinks her shock. Vicki chuckles at the girl's expression.

"I said more than that when I first heard him talk," Vicki assures. "But I think we need to return to the conversation at hand. The Boiling Seas," she clouds up as unpleasant memories race through her mind. "That place is difficult to find and hit, to say the least."

"Full of monsters, poisonous gas, big bugs," Neil recalls swatting his neck as he from a distant yet very clear memory. "And the path itself is dangerous. I don't know."

Neil appears to contemplate, his features twisting as if he is trying to figure out a puzzle. The sorceress inspects her guests for several moments, taking time to finish off her water. She places her tankard back down and glance at all three of the travelers and shook her head as she places her hands upon the table.

"Very well, I will just have to find another brave soul," Milea said as she stood, her chair scooting back. Sonja follows her example.

"Believe me, milady. No one in this port is as temerarious as I..." Neil assures, leaning forward with a challenge in his eyes. "We will guide you, but it will not be cheap. The journey to the Boiling Seas is treacherous, let alone the destination."

"As long as we get to the Temple of Light in haste," Milea focuses her gaze upon Neil's eyes. "I'm willing to pay you whatever I must. Within reason." Sonja shifts a little as the tension rose in the room. Brion leans back, focuses on the client and his friend. Vicki clears her throat.

"Um, Neil. We need a ship," Vicki points out the obvious, catching her sibling's attention. "The last one we had was taken by a storm, dear brother." She places one hand upon her hip, the other on her brother's shoulder.

"That has been some time ago during a foolish part of my life," Neil says, leaning back. His eyes went back and forth a little as he calculates his options. "Well, the *Sea Dragon* is docked outside. I'm sure her captain is not going to let me borrow her cheaply..." He places his hands together and leans on the table a little, fingers on his chin. "I might have to take the ship."

"Don't worry about the ship," Milea says catching the attention of the sibling bards. "I am gifted with one. I only need a guide." She sits back down and casually crosses her legs. "The ship is called *Lady of the Night*. I'm sure it will attract some attention when it sails." Sonja exercises a little caution as she retakes her seat. "You will be well compensated upon our safe arrival at the Temple."

"The Boiling Seas is difficult to encounter," Vicki informs with a shake of the head. "It took Neil several attempts to find it the first time. Then he ran into it while avoiding a rival pirate."

"It smells so bad that I'll always remember the way," Neil assures. "Alright, Milea, you have yourself a captain and crew.

Meet us at Dagger's Point." He stood, pushing the chair back. "With a ship," he concludes and turns to walk toward the door, his companions following him.

Milea watches as the trio left the tavern. A moment later, she stands along with her child. The sorceress smiles when Sonja offers to beat him up with an innocent grin about her features, the girl's rationale, she is unsure if she likes him or not. Milea assures her child that such behavior is not necessary right now, and they need to concentrate on the journey to rescue Maya from the temple. Milea places a small bag of coins upon the table while she walks to the front of the tavern. She takes firm note along with her daughter when several men stand as they pass them and follow them. Milea stops roll her shoulders and face the oncoming men.

"Are you missing something," Milea asks, "perhaps late for an engagement? If not, you will be very shortly."

"No, no, nothing like that at all, milady," the leader of the group assures. He, unlike many in the tavern, is sober. "Good day, miss," he bobs his head to the two and exits. His entourage did the same.

"We're not coming back here, right?" Sonja hints as she and her mother exit the tavern.

"Not as long as it can be helped," Milea replies with confidence.

Milea and Sonja exit the tavern as the girl promise not to cause any mishaps with the new captain and crew. The girl grins when her mother promises that she too would behave so that they could at least give the man a chance. If he turns out to be incompatible, they would drop him and his

companions off at Lybrinthia Bay and find a different sea captain. She hopes it did not take long to find out if he has ill
intentions. Maya's life depends upon the speed at which she can
get there. There is no time to trifle with anyone that makes false
claims about his abilities. Sonja changes the subject to Brion and
his voice, expressing her surprise by it. They head towards the
marketplace as Milea laugh and gave her word to her child that
Brion is indeed an elf, not one of their kin-the car'laden. She
even offers to compare the voices once they meet with their
car'laden friend, Justin, in the future.

Several chickens flap out of the way as they walk down the
street with traveling vendors calling to them. Apparently, Milea
knows what she is searching for, and they aren't selling it. Neil,
Vicki, and Brion keep eyes on the duo as Milea travels with her
daughter deep into the marketplace. Sonja pauses and glances
around, sensing she is being watched.

Milea's eyes fell on the trio she hired a few steps from the tavern and toward the docks. The sorceress acknowledges the
group with a tilt of the head and return to her shopping agenda.
They need supplies to make the trip on the open seas. The curiosity she saw in Neil would lead them to Dagger's Point within
the hour. Neil observes the woman then focus his attention toward the docks to see that the *Sea Dragon* sways in the breeze.

"What are you thinking?" Vicki asks.

"I'm thinking I should take the *Sea Dragon* in case she's lying,"
Neil answers. "I'm not convinced she's Milea Sirus of Selvast
Forest."

"Always the seadog," Vicki chuckles at his denial. "It would be
a stroke of good luck if she is," she continues while placing a

hand upon her hip. "I would have the opportunity to study her a little bit. We can have a little fun with her stories and poems as well as Ra'jil's."

"Oh, come on, Vicki," Neil rolls his eyes. "She's not even acting like what those same poems and stories say."

"Exactly," Vicki agrees.

"Hm, I think I believe her," Brion folds his arms and grins. "Not many claims to be Milea Sirus without bursting into a fit of maddened laughter." He stares after the woman, noting she had disappeared into the crowd. "There is no madness about her. She is very serious and appears anxious to get on with her journey. One, I'm sure I'll not enjoy."

"Yeah, that's right, you don't like boats," Vicki pats his shoulder. "Well, you could stay here."

"And miss an opportunity to travel with a legend," Neil asks, dramatically. "He would never forgive himself."

"You're right. I wouldn't," Brion agrees.

"I'm going to see if I can keep an eye on her," Vicki offers. "I want to make sure she doesn't spontaneously burst into flames before she provides us our payment." She left her brother and friend to follow Milea into the marketplace.

"Let's go to the docks. I want to check on something," Neil says as he walks toward the *Sea Dragon*. "I've never heard of her ship."

"The *Lady of the Night*," Brion says and smiles at the name. "It's catchy. She's right about it bringing attention to itself. I wonder if the figurehead is A'drianis."

"Shadow Eltis, eh?" Neil rubs his chin. "I'm sure that, just like A'drianis, this ship is nothing but a shadow." He continues his way. Brion walks with him, taking in the beauty of the ships that surround them.

Clouds float lazily about in an otherwise perfect blue sky. Sailors, some legitimate, others pirates, stomp around, blasting each other with well-practiced bad language as they prepare their ships to set sail. Seagulls squawk and cry as they circle about, seeking out an easy meal. A large barrel of fish breaks open on the docks, causing the fisherman who dropped it to cry out as his catch either escapes back into the sea or is taken by the waiting gulls, cats, and beggars. Neil dodges a few swift children while studying each vessel in port, stopping his gaze upon a beautiful two-mast ship that caught his attention. He'd never seen it at any dock that he has visited upon the continent of Bri'mor.

As they walk, Brion takes a deep breath in and exhale it slowly as he came to terms with his current situation. He hates ships with good reason. Every time he sails aboard one, he got sick for his efforts. A grumble escapes him as he remembers he must take a ship when he decides to go back home. Brion sidesteps a beggar, taking note of the ship, they are heading toward.

"Neil, why don't you believe she is Milea Sirus?" Brion challenges. He dodges a man as they approach the ship. The sailor grunts a word of thanks.

"Milea is rumored to be an enchantress as well as a sorceress, seductress, and mysterious guardian of Selvast Forest," Neil points out. "I've seen a lot of enchantresses in my travels, and this redhead is one of the most beautiful I've laid eyes on, but I highly doubt if she is *that* legendary sorceress." He shook his head. "What about you?"

"My gut tells me that she is," Brion says as he steps over a moving rope. "I've seen paintings of her back home, though the artist did not do her justice. If I recall, the painting is of a partially nude woman standing in front of a stream. Small, winged children are flying around her for some reason. Mother never liked the painting but left it up anyway. It should still be there unless Eryn took it down. Milea is painted as an elf, naturally."

"In Cathalian, it doesn't surprise me," Neil remarks. They pause at their destination, and Neil turns his attention up. "Ahoy! I've come to ask the name of this beautiful ship."

"Ahoy!" a man shouts back and glares down. He is human. His bald head captures the light of the sun and bounces it right back out. "Her name is *Duchess*! Finest craft on the twelve seas to date," he says while studying the two men. "Do ye wish for passage? We are sailing to Cathalian in a few minutes!"

"Nay, I am just curious," Neil calls up. "I have not visited the port in a while, and your ship is new to me. Tell me, who is her captain?"

"Don't know his real name," the man answers. "We call him Cap'n Res." He glances behind. " 'Ere he comes now."

The docks shake as several large and smelly cows are herds by, mooing in protest of their backsides being smack by a whip to keep them moving. Seabirds circle above as Brion and Neil wait until they see another man glare down at them. The first man departs to continue his work.

The captain wears a flamboyant black and red coat with a matching hat where they could see salt-and-pepper hair flowing from beneath. The edges of his hat are lined with red feathers. Coarse, black hair covers half the man's face and neck. The captain snorts and spits to the side, then once again focus on the men.

"Who are ye' to be interruptin' my men?" the captain demands, his voice gruff.

"I am the bard from the Lucky Dragon tavern," Neil answers. He shields his eyes from the sun as he studies the man. "With me is my bodyguard. I can't be too careful." Neil motions his head at Brion with a slight smirk. Brion folds his arms and made a scoffing sound. It went unheard by the man on the ship. Neil regards the captain once again. "Cap'n Res, can you tell me if you've heard of a ship calls the *Lady of the Night?*"

"I ain't heard no such ship," Res snorts. "And I've been sailing these seas since I was old enough to be a cabin boy. The *Lady of the Night* does not exist." He leans forward to get a better viewing of the two. "That's the truth, else me soul belongs to the ocean below," he snorts

"I see. Thank you," Neil says as he turns along with Brion and starts walking away. Cap'n Res grumbles as he turns away from the side to go back and finish up his own chores.

"So, the conclusion," Brion requests. He sidesteps a mess left by the cows. Several sailors, however, are not keen enough to do the same.

"What the man says. No such ship," Neil shrugs. "This Lady Milea may be pulling our legs. I'm not surprised. Most who claim to be that legendary woman are either wanting attention or insane." They made way for several horses being disembarked from a vessel.

"And we are going to Dagger's Point to tell her she's insane?" Brion asks. "To tell a sorceress she's insane. Even if she is not the legend, she is still a magic-user. You are one brave man."

"I've been in worse situations," Neil grins with confidence. "Besides, didn't my sister warn you that I am impulsive?"

"I held a hope that you wouldn't live up to the denotation," Brion remarks.

More large beasts and freight are moved off the ships and toward their final destination. Brion and Neil exit the ports then decide to take the closest exit since neither wants to enter the marketplace and risk running into Milea. If she is pretending, it is best to confront her outside the village where she could not harm many people. Several women call for the attention of Neil and Brion as they continue to the exit, passing by a brothel.

A few of the ample-breasted women revealed their cleavage and shakes them vibrantly to catch the attention of anyone who shows interest in their antics. Brion ignores the women with practice ease, continuing his quick pace towards the gates. Neil hesitates, causing one of the women to smile at him. The bard grins back then notices that his friend is leaving him behind. Neil grumbles as he catches up with Brion.

"I'm sorry, my friend, but I will have to go with my gut," Brion pats his abs as they walk past the walls. "I would even wager a bet that she is truly Milea Sirus," he continues nodding to the watchful guards when they walk past them.

"Hmmm... well. Alright," Neil agrees. "A wager then. If she is Milea Sirus, I'll cut off my ponytail."

"If she's not, I'll cut mine," Brion agrees. They paused and shook hands. "I'm sure that Vicki has a nice, sharp dagger to help with the haircut."

"She's my sister," Neil boasts and continues to walk. "I'd not expect anything less." Brion kept an easy pace as they made their way toward Dagger Point, following the path close to the sea cliff.

CHAPTER TWO

The Sorceress Revealed

Healthy voices of merchants and customers blast the ears of Milea and Sonja as they pass by Vicki. The woman is observing the sorceress from between two different vendors. She sees her employer purchase supply barrels then, with a wave of her hand, makes them disappear in a rain of golden dust. Stunned and curious, Vicki starts to edge closer but pauses to make way for a pair of shaggy horses. The strong dark animals snort and grunt as they haul a heavy card down the street, their gigantic hooves crushing anything in their path.

Milea is gentle as she pulls her curious child back from the road to allow the animals to pass. A large man sitting on the top of the cart tilts his hat to the lady as a means of thanks.

He emits a loud whistle and shout to his team of horses to head out of the town. Milea did a slight wave in kind then watch as several gypsy children laugh and run after the cart. The creaking and moaning of the wooden behemoth did not deter them as they jump onto the back to hitch a ride. Sonja bounces a little excited until she heard Milea clear her throat. The girl pouts a little, she is not to join the other children, at least not this time.

Vicki smiles when she witnesses the sweet transaction between mother and child and their return to the shopping spree. She centers her attention on the back to the large cart the children rode and let out a curious sound. Several of the larger kids open the crates that are on the cart and hand items to their smaller siblings. After a quick steal, they hop off and hurry back towards their elders. The cart continues its journey, none the wiser of the missing items. Vicki let out a little chuckle at the scene until the cart lumbers past a few scruffy men sitting at an outside bar.

The group appears to be albino, yet despite their white skin, they did not burn or tan in the sunlight. Though they are sitting, Vicki could tell that they are seven feet or greater in size, their muscles bulging every time they lift their arms to down their beverages. Called Devorians, they were once hailed as heroes of a forgotten war, now the entire people are branded as evil and wicked due to the many dark deeds the majority of their kin divulge in to include kidnapping that inevitably leads to slavery. Vicki inches back into the shadows as she observes the men scanning the marketplace. One of them taps his companions on the shoulder as he spots their target. Vicki also turns to see whom their mark is and utters a few profanities under her breath.

"Oh, you guys are a lot more foolish than even my own brother," said Vicki to herself.

Milea and Sonja pause by a weapons smith with the girl admiring the offerings. Vicki stares at Milea knowing the woman will look up from what she is doing to confront the gaze. Eventually, Milea turns her eyes from the weapons to Vicki and meets the woman's stare with curiosity. The l'vane woman tracks her stare from the sorceress over to the devorians. The sorceress follows the motion, a slight scowl gracing her features as she takes note of the issue. The men turn when they witness their prey focusing on them. A few of the men stand and leave the ranks to blend into the waning crowd. Milea follows their movement then once again had her gaze fall on Vicki. The two gesture their heads to each other as Milea turns her attention back to her daughter.

Sonja examines a few of the well-crafted daggers. A silver one with the head of a wolf carved onto the handle caught her attention. Milea watches as her daughter picks up the dagger and practices with it. Her movement is quick, nearly blinding speed. The clerk, a woman, smiles at the young warrior as Sonja performs several jabs and a few blocks. Milea holds out her hand with a gentle smile. Sonja gives the dagger to her mother.

"In combat, there are a few ways to hold this weapon," Milea explains in short. "Hold it this way if you are in a close-quarter fight with an opponent who has the same weapon. Or if it is long as a sword..." She held the dagger in her right hand with the point up. She then switches hands. "Holding it this way will allow you to use your fist as well as the blade of the dagger. Punch first then drag it across to slice through your opponent." She is holding the blade down with the sharpest edge out, demonstrating her short lesson in slow motion so Sonja could understand. "Sharp on both ends means you can come back and finish them off with a second stroke." She points to the two edges of the blade with her free hand.

"Ok," Sonja beams in understanding. She accepted the weapon from her mother and began to practice with it again. Her movements are very slow as she imitates what her mother has shown her. Milea watches her child for a moment then turns and paid the merchant for the dagger.

"I will get Zaria to show you a proper way to throw a dagger," Milea remarks as they continue on their way. "She's also a good source for learning how to defend yourself with it."

"Thanks, Mom," Sonja embraces her mother briefly as they walk. "Where did Cousin Zaria go? She left before we did. Does she know aunt Maya is in trouble?" she asks as she admires her new dagger.

"I doubt it," Milea says while scanning the marketplace. Several of the devorians trails them, surrounding the two with purpose. Milea did not like the situation; the displeasure shows upon her features. "Zaria can be anywhere there are shadows," she continues as she returns her attention to her child. "We will have to wait until she decides she wants to be found." She avoid a mud hole in the street. "Thus is the way of the Shiado."

A small group of young women gush over a strong man as he lifts his best friend, a second large man, over his head effortlessly to their sounds of admirations and applause. Milea and Sonja walk past them with the girl pausing to study the group then continuing her way once her curiosity is satisfied. The small group, along with a vast majority of the customers, began to trickle out of the area, heading towards various venues to find a meal or locate the entertainment of the day. Milea pauses by several merchants and feint interest in their wares, all the while keeping an eye on the devorian group that hunt them. She also notices that Vicki is trailing, keeping to the shadows as she observes what is happening.

Both Vicki and Milea take note of the lead devorian stopping the head of the watch and handing the man a large sack of coins. The head watchman takes the money and gives a small glance in Milea's direction before he orders his men to leave the marketplace. Milea's features go from shock to stoic as she turns herself and child towards the gates to exit the city. Vicki contemplates the situation as the devorians start to make their move, even though Milea is a legendary sorceress, it is wrong to leave her to her devices in this situation. Vicki thought about the situation for a few more seconds before she decides to step forward and assist.

"Milea wait up!" Vicki calls and hurries from the shadows.

"Vicki," Milea greets, "where are Neil and Brion?"

"Knowing my brother, he's either at the docks or already headed toward Dagger's Point. Brion's with him," Vicki answers and arrives at the side of the sorceress. *"You're being surrounded,"* she informs.

"I saw," Milea acknowledges the warning, spying her surroundings.

"What do they want," Sonja asks. The marketplace starts to empty out a little; it is the middle of the day. Several devorians, however, have taken the space over.

"Sonja, ignore them and continue to walk," Milea orders as she starts down the street again. *They will learn a painful lesson today.*"

"*Yes, Màthair,*" Sonja agrees, placing her dagger in her belt, tying the hilt of it to the leather strap.

Vicki takes a deep breath in and out as she rolls her neck and shoulders and follows after the mother-daughter duo. Sonja takes out a couple of well-worn leather straps and wrap her hands with them, tying them down and punching each fist into the palm of the opposite hand as she continues pace with her mother. She scans the threats to note their location and the weakest member of the group.

Milea notices the closing of the shops as merchants, and the last of the guests hurry away from the impending scene, not wanting to witness or get involve with the devorians or their quarry. To the left of them, under a canopy is a man with a whip watching them intensely. To the right is his counterpart with a rope that he tightens then loosen as he appears to judge the strength of the women. Milea speaks to Vicki and Sonja in a whisper about the two. A crooked smile to grace Vicki's features and her focus to go to the man with the whip.

Two of the larger devorians standing on either side of the gates, pretend to have an interest in the junk merchants that squat right at the gates to entice those that enter and exit with their wares. A quick glance behind and Milea note that there are at least twelve more walking and fanning out as if they are herding the three to their destination.

"My such lovely beauties, and look the little one has a silver dagger," the leader of the devorians says with much humor as he and seven more of his companions blocks the exit. "Children shouldn't play with such things. They could hurt themselves,"

"Grown men can hurt themselves, especially if they do not know whom they are toying with," Milea retorts and receives laughter from the entire male group surrounding them.

"Well, at least they are in good humor," Vicki retrieves a leather glove from her belt. "So, what say you, Trapper? Will you allow us to pass?" She pulls the toughen leather glove upon her left hand.

"I recognize you from the stage," the leader of the group laughs. "You still think you're Ra'jil? I'll have you know you look nothing like her. You know, I feel like giving these good folks a show. Tie them up and let's have a little fun with them."

"Now hold still. I don't want to bruise any of your pretty, pretty skin," the largest of the devorians, standing over eight feet tall, chuckles. He tightens his rope between his two hands and stalks to his prey.

Sonja launches forward as Milea quickly stay Vicki's hand, noting the woman is going for her dagger. The girl punches the large man an undetermined number of times then grabs his arm with an angry sound and twist it, snapping it like a branch. The man hit the ground, holding his broken arm and howling in pain. Sonja takes a couple of steps back to stand between her mother and the group of devorians that stare at her to include the leader. She shifts her position to where her feet are equal distance apart and brought up her wraps hands ready for another attack.

Milea removes her hand from Vicki's arm, sensing the woman is in just as much shock as the rest of the witnesses from Sonja's attack. A small bit of pride trickles onto her features from the feat. Vicki whispers a few words of admiration as she rubs her eyes and then once again concentrates on the situation at hand. The leader goes to check on his strong man and sees that the bone is sticking out of the arm, and he is bleeding from the wound created by the girl.

"As you were saying," Milea challenges with a cocky smile.

"I see. You have a little warrior demon for a child," the leader says, his humor gone. "This is my strongest man."

"Strongest babe now," Milea points out. True, the downed man is weeping loudly.

"Why not finish him off? She has a weapon to do so," the leader stands and glower at the trio.

"I did not teach her to kill a downed opponent," Milea smirks at the pompous man. "Maybe in a couple of years."

"Arrogant wench," the man sneers, baring his teeth. "Get them!" he motions for his men to move in.

Several men move forward as the air hiss, catching Vicki's immediate attention. She rapidly turns to her left and hooks the end of the whip with her gloved hand. She spins around, grabs her dagger, and lets it fly in the direction the whip came from. At the same time, she pulls on the whip. The man holding the weapon falls with Vicki's dagger planted right between his eyes.

The whip is now in Vicki's possession as she takes the handle quickly and cracks it twice, causing two more trappers to fall, holding their eyes.

Milea punches the throat of one of her would-be captors and tosses a second one before she causes her staff to appear. She smacks the back of a third who is finished off by Sonja with a quick blow to his head. A fourth is a jab in the ribs, stopping his charge and breaking a few of them as Milea lift him with her staff overhead and throws him into his companions behind them.

Vicki cracks her whip once again, wrapping it around one of the charging men's head and jumping over him as he tries bowling her over as he goes down. She tightens the whip upon his cranium then pulls with all her strength. The head of the devorian twists awkwardly as he hit the ground lifeless. Two more devorians lands on top of the dead body, their legs broken. Milea twirls her staff taking a couple of steps forward away from the wounded men and leans upon it a little as the rest of the attackers hesitate.

Vicki follows her example and coils her whip, placing one hand upon her hip, the other with the whip just dangle to the side for now. Sonja takes a step to stand in front of her mother, ready for action. She is bouncing as if she is made entirely of springs, yet her gaze did not falter.

"Is that all you have," Milea once again challenges with a confident smile.

"I see...." the devorian leader snorts and spits upon the ground next to him. "I guess it is up to me to teach this lesson in manners. I will enjoy every minute of your humiliation."

His eyes begin to glow as he activates his mystical abilities. Milea raises an eyebrow while witnesses retreat.

"Well, I had hoped, he had some sort of intelligence," Milea quips. "Sonja, stay behind me."

"Right," Sonja says and, along with Vicki, moves back two steps.

"Hold still. I won't feel a thing," the man smirks as he holds up his left hand and cast his lightning spell.

The air crackles and sizzles as the light blue bolt race towards the sorceress and her companions. Milea remains calm as her staff disappear and lifts her now free hand as if she is holding something, her eyes flash once. The lightning bolt slows down and starts to condense into a ball, and by the time it reaches Milea, it is now a small abbreviated form of itself. The ball levitates into the hands of the sorceress as the devorian leader takes a surprise step back and gawks at the situation. His battle and anger become lost to him as his mystical gifts unravel from around his body. Milea fixes her attention upon the man as she tosses the ball in the air and catches it a couple of times.

"Who in all Ublivorion are you?" the devorian demands to know.

"Just your run-of-the-mill sorceress," Milea responds with a slight bit of sarcasm to her words. Sonja rolls her eyes. Vicki snickers.

"That is my most powerful spell!" he sputters out.

"Oh? Well, you can have it back then," Milea answers politely.

The leader's companions move out of the way when Milea tosses the ball up one final time and wait until it comes back down before she slaps it, sending the item back to its originator.

The spell explodes back into lightning and slams into the devorian sending him sailing back to one of the junk vendors, a bellow of surprise thrusting from his chest as he flies. The watching merchant swears as he makes a hasty retreat from the booth to avoid the airborne body.

Milea sees the path the man is flying and cast a second spell that erects a wall of air that her opponent hits, harshly. The devorian crumbles onto the ground, unconscious from the spell's blow. Milea then turns her attention to the rest of the devorian team and watches them flee from the area, leaving the wounded and dead in place for the watchmen to take care of. Those with broken legs manage to pull themselves off the road while the large man with the broken arm cowers in a corner, allowing the women to continue to the exit.

"I don't think he'll be preying on any more red-haired sorceresses for a while," Vicki predicts. "That is if he remembers what happens today."

"Sadly, devorians are hard-headed, and it takes more than one lesson to drive it home," Milea explains as she and her companions walk to the gate.

"You're right," Vicki agrees. "I've met a few in my day, none of them ever had a second encounter with me though."

"Perhaps they know better than to mess with Ra'jil's protégé," Milea smirks. "You do have a flare of her about you, Vicki. Perhaps channeling some of her energy."

"You really think so?" Vicki beams. "She's, my idol. As a kid. I often dreamt of sailing the Bri'al seas with her. It's unfortunate that will never happen. Unless I want to sail with ghosts," she chuckles.

"You never know, Vicki," Milea smiles as they exit through the open gate, there is no one to hinder their departure. "Ra'jil is very stubborn. She might still be around."

"I guess that's true," Vicki muses then puff out her chest in pride. "I'll have to believe that Ra'jil may still be sailing the seas somewhere. Bri'al is a pretty big place, a lot of which has yet to be explored. Maybe, just maybe she retired to an island some-where. I'll just have to find it."

"I think that you and Ra'jil will meet when the time comes," Milea grins a little. "We might meet her on the seas as we sail, right now let us get to Dagger's Point."

"Yes, before my brother gets impatient and steals the *Sea Dragon*," Vicki agrees.

The trio increases their pace, heading up a well-worn path to-wards the rendezvous. Small fluffy clouds float in the bright blue skies. The sounds and smells of the ocean waft up the cliff known as Dagger's Point. It is a craggy, triangular edge a mile outside of town. Two of its three sides are sheer cliffs leading down to the ocean. A short grass grows on top of the cliff, the blades waving in the constant winds. Large, round boulders dec-orate the landscape fifty yards from the edge.

Several hundred yards behind the boulders stood a very thick forest with tall trees. A mile and a half to the left and following the cliff is the path to Churn, the port itself is seen if one is brave enough to venture to the point of the dagger and look out. Waves crash on the rocks on one side of the point as if angry for being block by the obstacle. The smooth stone of the wall is indicative of the many centuries the Point had withstood the elements. On the other side is a gentle harbor. Seabirds nest on the walls; many crags and small caves made nice homes for them.

Neil, sitting on top of a giant boulder, tuning his mandolin as he awaits his employer. His mind is spinning with the questions he wants to pose to the woman to include why she lies about her identification and what her true mission is to get to the Boiling Seas. He thought about the situation, then put his mandolin down and picks up his dagger to clean and sharpen it.

He might need to use it if the interrogation goes sour. He'd just have to be faster than her spell to reach his weapon to toss, and for the blow to kill her in an instant. The ocean will take care of the rest. His features show a little concern when it came to the child, not sure what he should do if it came down to killing her mother.

A few of the seabirds take to wings to fish catching Brion's attention from sharpening and cleaning his sword. He is sitting at the base of the rock trying to convince his entire being that it is a good idea to get on the ship. So far in his life, he and the ocean are not on the best of terms, and even the slightest motion causes extreme sickness to overtake his body. Brion shakes his head and goes back to cleaning his sword, not sure why he tries to tell himself that this time will be any different than last time or the time before that.

Voices bring Brion's attention back to the cliff and the path that he and Neil took to get to their destination. He stands up, recognizing Vicki's voice as she talks to someone about sea dragons. Neil hears them too and stands to watch the path. A short time later, he witnesses Vicki walking with his employer and her daughter. He sees that his sister now has a whip in her possession and made a quiet sound of affirmation; if it came down to a fight, they now have the upper hand.

"Well, Sonja, I've never really stopped to talk to an actual Sea Dragon," Vicki admits. "They usually stay in the deep ocean. The ship is named after them because it's supposedly blessed by one."

"Blessed," Sonja asks, confused.

"Sea Dragons are what we know as Elder Breed Dragons," Milea offers an explanation to her daughter. "They along with mountain, ice, and some swamp dragons are among the oldest species and changed very little since their conception many millennia ago. A dragon's blessing usually means that the elder breed has provided some sort of mystical ability to an object or person."

"Ok," Sonja scrunches up at her mother. "Is grandma an elder breed?" the girl tilts her head in curiosity when Milea laughs a little.

"Not sure I want to meet your grandma, Sonja," said Vicki with a warm smile. "She's got to be one tough cookie to have you as a granddaughter not to mention the obvious, Milea as a daughter," she pauses and smiles when she crests the hill and notes her brother and traveling buddy. "Brion, Neil, good to see you made it."

"Ladies," Neil greets to the trio. "I see you have not changed your mind, Lady Milea." He picks up, shouldering his instrument, then hops down from his perch atop the boulder to be level with his employer.

"I know of the dangers that the Boiling Seas may hold for us," Milea folds her arms. "However, I will let you know this. There are far more frightening things in this realm than what the Boiling Seas will ever produce." Milea met Neil's gaze, unflinching.

"Since this is going to be a long journey, I think we need to relax and become a little friendlier," Vicki suggests, seeing her brother's jawline harden. She walks to him, "Neil. *She is truly, Milea.*" The word causes her brother's eyes to widen then relax.

"I see," Neil says solemnly, meeting his sister's eyes. *"You sure? How do you know?"*

"Do you remember the poem about Milea verses the Ajahn?" Vicki quizzes. Her brother appears thoughtful then blinks. "She reenacts it herself, brother."

"No way..." Neil says in slight awe. "I missed that?"

"We both did," Brion says and crosses his arms as he leans against the boulder to observe the group.

"Ajahn is a bit more powerful than the Devorian trappers, Vicki," Milea assures. "I've got a little scar from that encounter," She admits and approaches the two, pausing a few feet away. "However, you are right. For this journey, we will need to get along and trust one another. You have my word that Sonja and I will be on our best behavior." Milea flashes a quick grin at the group.

"As will I," Neil bows. "Milady," he straightens with a confident smile.

"Just Milea," the woman insists. "Unless you want me to call you 'Sir' all the time."

"That would be annoying," Neil ponders and turns toward his silent friend. "Brion, are you alright?"

"Just taking it all in stride," Brion answers and leans on the boulder. "Where is your ship?" he asks, focusing on the sorceress.

"Ah yes," Milea says as if just remembering. "Neil, how long is the journey to the Boiling Seas?" she asks as she walks toward the cliff. Sonja ran to the edge and bounces in excitement at the view.

"From this port, it could take a couple of months at best. That is barring no storms or course changes," Neil answers as he follows the woman. "I check the ports for your ship. It's not there."

"That's because I told it to meet us here," Milea folds her arms and turns her attention down. Stunned, Neil follows her line of sight.

"Whoa..." Vicki whisper when her eyes fell on the view below.

"Well played," Brion expresses with a nod of his head. He folds his arms, smiling cockily.

The wager that Brion has with Neil is all but complete. An ocean hawk cries out in joy from high above as the ship in the once-empty harbor takes Neil completely by surprise. A two-mast vessel, its sails are tied with bright white ropes. The small, gentle. waves rock her to and fro. An anchor holds it in place except for a little swaying from the waves.

The ship's wood is a grey color, unlike any type of wood ever seen upon the years of sea experience between the sibling bards. From the distance, they could see that the white ropes are stronger than usual. The back of the ship elevating a little more than the front is home to the helm. The sleep quarters are just below; a door with the symbol of a large tree marks the entranceway to the quarters. Windows on the cabin allow light inside.

"Are they alive," Sonja asks, waving a hand in front of Neil's eyes. He blinks.

"I think we just brought out the old pirate in them," Milea chuckles. "Remember, they were doing a small play about Ra'jil."

"Yep, yep. I remember," Sonja agrees.

"It's a good-looking ship," Brion admits. "A little familiar though. I think I've seen a painting or read about it somewhere before."

"It should be," Milea says. "It's an exact replica of Ra'jil's ship, the *Dragon Rose*," she turns towards Vicki when the woman takes a deep breath in.

"I think we need to get aboard before at least Vicki faints," Brion chuckles. "How do we get down?"

"Stay close to me," Milea smiles and activates her gifts.

A small red ember swirls about her form then spread to her companions at her mental command. A soft red glow surrounds Milea and her companions. Sonja takes her mother's hand and closes her eyes. Milea reassures her daughter that she is not going to drop anyone. Brion checks to make sure his companions are within the range of the sorceress' spell. He feels himself lift up by a gentle force and decide not to watch them descend but keep his line of sight straight ahead.

The same force acts on Neil and Vicki. Milea closes her eyes, using her mind to push out from the cliff. She levitates her companions and herself down to the deck of the ship. The sorceress and her crew land upon the deck. The boat barely noticing their arrival. The soft glow ceases with Milea opening her eyes. She stretches and centralizes her gaze upon those with her.

Vicki blinks and shakes herself awake and crouches down to touch the wood of the deck. The smooth grain is similar to a finished wood floor. Vicki then stands to examine the ropes in awe that they are made of a fine material, perhaps silk and as tough as any fiber that faces the storms of the Bri'al Seas. She wraps her hand around the thick rope and tug. It continues to hold its form despite her efforts. The l'vane woman's mind begins to race with the possibilities of the various origins of the ship. The wind stirs Neil's hair as he approaches the closest mast. He eyes the close grain of the wood as he reaches out to touch the item. The warmth of the wood did not surprise him as much as the feel. It is as if he touches something living, not a wooden post.

"This is gorgeous," Neil admits with awe. "Forgive my curiosity, but what experience do you have with ships, milady?" Neil turns to Milea with his inquiry.

"I have many experiences from my lifetime within Bri'al. I, however, have never sailed to the Boiling Seas. I do not know the way," Milea admits, leaning on the wall that led to the sleep quarters. "I do know of one other who does, but she is recovering. Thus, I am offering you to be captain of this vessel."

"Hmm...Well the only people I have with me are my sister and unfortunate travel companion, Brion. And he's not good with ships." Neil appears thoughtful at the offer. He scans the woman with care. Although beautiful, there is an aura of enormous powers about her. His instincts tell him not to take her lightly.

"Can't stand them. But I am here. Considering the debt I owe," Brion admits.

"The ship requires a minimum crew," Milea discloses. The wind blew into her hair, playing with it. "It is built from the woods of my home, Selvast Forest. If you steer, it will do the rest." She brushes her long locks back from her face.

"I like it already," Vicki says with a grin. The ocean crashes creating a little bit of spray onto the ship. "So, I guess that Neil is going to do most of the steering." She faces Brion. "Did you want to do lookout duty?"

"Lookout duty," Brion eyes at her with reservation. Vicki only points up. Brion follows her motion and gawks at the crow's nest. "What?! Are you out of your mind?!" He scowls at the woman.

"I can do that," Sonja volunteers.

"I can't make you part of my crew, kiddo," Neil shook his head. "Unless your mom does not mind me borrowing you."

"Hm..." Milea studies her child a little, bending to meet her eye to eye. "Sonja. Crow's nest duties are to be a lookout for obstacles and other ships. You must be vigilant and call down anything you see that could pose as a problem." She straightens, placing a hand upon her hip and continues to focus on her daughter. "You also must use your agility to help tie and untie ropes as told to you by the captain. It should not be a problem with the *Lady of the Night*. This ship will do most of it."

"Got it," Sonja says. She then hurries over to the main mast and climbs up in record speed.

"You know, I could have used that girl on many of my journeys," Neil reflects. He shakes his head and focuses on the present day. "Milea. Thank you for the assistance."

"None more thankful than I," Vicki says as she holds up her hand. "I would have done it, but I would need breaks." She smiles impishly. "The ship moves left and right." She sways a little as if she is a ship. "The top of it looks like it would kiss the ocean at any moment. Even the smallest movement...."

"Stop it," Brion interrupts with a growl. Vicki laughs a little.

"Glad to give her something to do while we sail," Milea admits.

"Fair enough," Neil agrees. "We wait until nightfall," he informs. "Then we follow the blue star. Not as simple as it sounds."

"I believe you, Neil," Milea smiles. "Get familiar with the helm, you will need to be." She walks away. The trio studies her departure, contemplatively.

"She seems a little detached," Neil observes. He walks to the helm and studies the wheel. It is typical of ships, round with spokes centered in a hub. Each spoke had a spindle attaches to it on the outer part of a wooden circle. The center of the hub held a carved tree.

"Think about it," Vicki tests the wheel. It spun at her command. "She is going to the Boiling Seas, something or someone there has her preoccupied."

"Only thing I know in that part of the world is the Temple of Light," Brion recognizes. "But why would she be going to the Temple?" He leers out at the ocean with a look of displeasure. The breeze toys with his mane.

"Who knows?" Neil shrugs. He places his instrument next to the wheel. "The business of mages, sorcerers, and enchantresses is not for me to question. I carry out my mission so that I can receive my payment and move on."

"Worked with a lot of mages, sorcerers and enchantresses have you," Brion asks of his friend.

"No enchantresses. She's the first I've worked with. Like I said earlier, I saw plenty of them even in action," Neil assures. "We will see what happens." He rubs his hand over the wood. It is extremely smooth, no splinters.

"I'm going to check below deck," Vicki volunteers. She starts to walk away but pauses when Brion gently takes hold of her arm. "What's wrong?" she asks with a raised eyebrow.

"Nothing. I just need to borrow one of your daggers," Brion requests, a boyish grin to his features. Neil grumbles as he remembers the bet he haphazardly made earlier in the day.

"Why?" Vicki narrows the opposite eye to the raised eyebrow.

"Neil and I made a wager, and it is time for him to pay up," Brion informs. He holds out his hand. "He gets a nice haircut."

"It's a wager against Lady Milea," Neil clarifies to his curious sister. "I wager she is not the original. Brion went with his gut feeling that she is. He won."

"Oh, good gut," Vicki pats the elf's stomach. She pulls her second dagger and hands it to him, hilt first. "Have fun, boys," she says as she left to explore the ship.

"Give it here," Neil grumbles and takes the weapon from Brion. He reaches up to grab the base of his ponytail. With a quick flick of his wrist, he severs the hair and presents it. "Happy now?"

"I am," Brion nods, walking away. He whistles a happy tune much to Neil's discontent.

With a sigh, the bard walks to the edge to toss the hair overboard. He throws the locks over. They float down to the water as seagulls call out in mock joy. The afternoon sun beams down upon the harbor, the rays reflecting off the water in the distance. Milea exhales and fixates upon the horizon. Her thoughts are on her sister and the Temple of Light. The sun continues to warm the ship, causing Milea to stretch in its light. She decides to occupy herself with a little exercise while she waits for the ship to depart.

Sonja watches from her bird's eye view. Milea is going through slow motions of different battle styles while breathing rhythmically. The girl draws upon her past knowledge and understands that to disturb her mother now is not a good thing to do unless it is necessary. Sonja turns and tilts her head to one side when she sees Vicki exploring the ship.

"Let's see...Brion's a sword master. I see that," Sonja agrees with her thoughts and folds her arms. "But Neil and Vicki only sailors or maybe pirates? Something tells me that there is more to them. I'll go ask." She grabs hold of the edge of the crow's nest and hops out onto a rope. After steadying herself, she makes her way down.

Small seabirds land next to the *Lady of the Night* and fish in its shadow. The ship is a decent size, big enough to hold twelve large men and keep them from tripping over each other. Vicki is exploring about and tests the various ropes and trims the ship host. The front of the ship is home to a figurehead of a woman holding her gown close to her bosom. Vicki leans over to study the object in detail. The woman is either Elf or L'vane, her eyes staring out in front as if she is concentrating on her destination.

"Well, hello there," Vicki addresses the statue. "We are going to spend a lot of time together in the coming week. Just want to let you know, my brother is one of the best captains on the twelve seas. You're in good hands." She straightens and glimpses around. "Now where is that bloody trapdoor?" she asks as she walks away. The figurehead smiles a little.

Vicki places her hands upon her hips. A level change to the deck catches her attention. She walks over to it and bends down. A small handle is carved into one of the boards of the deck. She lets out a triumphant sound when she finally opens the trap door. Vicki is relieved to see a set of stairs provides easy descent into the lower level. She walks down them, keeping as quiet as possible.

A sweet and musty smell greets the woman's senses, at least the ship did not smell too bad. Vicki's eyes adjust to the half-light of the interior. A studious exam around the hull yields that it is new, no signs of use anywhere. It is clean. The wood is a nice pastel, and very clean. Towards the back of the room, Vicki spies two barrels and a door leading to another room on the ship.

"This is a maiden ship," Vicki muses. "Who would give anyone a brand-new ship?" She pauses and touches a wall. "I'd have to say that Milea is either extremely loved or exceedingly wealthy." She thought about it. "Then again, she is legendary so..." she shrugs.

Vicki opens the door and peeps into the room. It is filled with extra ropes and sails for the trip. Charts line the wall of the room, illustrating the known seas of Bri'al and warning of unknown parts of the oceans. Sonja uses a great deal of stealth to descends the stairs as Vicki backs out of the room she finishes exploring. The girl's eyes widen with curiosity, she has never been in this part of the ship.

Sonja watches as Vicki touch the wall again. The l'vane woman studies the wood in detail, noting that the entire ship could have been carved from a single tree. The grain did not change, there are no boards indicating separation. The continent of Bri'mor has plenty of trees large enough for the task. Vicki let out a curious sound. Perhaps the only extra pieces are the masts on the deck. Then again, if the branches of those same trees are large and long enough to be masts on a ship; especially if they are position in the correct location on the living tree.

The barrels catch Vicki's eye for a second time. Sonja sees them but not well enough to make them out at the distance of the stairs. Vicki approaches the barrels, footsteps echoing. The sound causes her to frown and pause. Behind her, Sonja also pauses to make sure all is safe. Vicki scans her surroundings as she resumes her walk, unaware that Sonja follows. Once again, footsteps echo in the large cavernous hull. Vicki knows that she is much quieter than this. She carries on concentrating on her own thoughts while reaching for one of the barrels, perhaps she is out of practice.

"What are you doing," Sonja asks causing Vicki to spin around. "I saw you open a door I never knew exists, so I am curious. Those are the ones Mom bought at the market." She points out the barrels.

"Girl!" Vicki scolds and places the whip back on her hip. "Don't sneak up on me like that. You almost got your head taken off."

"Sorry," Sonja pouts. "I thought you heard me behind you."

"Ah, so you're the one making noise, eh?" Vicki asks with a smile. "Alright. It's forgiven since I ignored it. I thought I made the noise." She turns back to the containers. "These are supplies I hope." She opens the barrels and notes they are filled with potatoes. "Ok, this is bad. No water."

"The ocean is full of water," Sonja remarks, tilting her head in curiosity. "Why do we need to carry any?"

"Ocean water is bad for you," Vicki explains a little. "It causes lots of problems with your body and health if you consume it. A fever that causes madness is most common."

"Ok, that's bad," Sonja knits her brow. "I'll tell mom. She might want to go to the next port to pick some water up."

"That's a good idea. I'll let Neil know," Vicki agrees. She closes the barrel. "I think there is one not too far from here. It's a safe bet that going back to Churn is out of the question."

"Yeah. I don't think they like getting beat up like that," Sonja recollects. She jogs towards the stairs and barely touches them as she ran up, skipping three at a time. Vicki shakes her head and follows the younger l'vane.

The bright light of the day temporarily blinds Sonja as she exits the hull. She shakes her head then hurries over to her mother. Vicki let her own eyes adjust and head over to talk to her brother. Milea exhales and is about to switch her position yet hesitates upon hearing her child approach. She relaxes and turns just in time for Sonja to slide to a stop. The girl scans her mother to make sure she is not disturbing her. Milea smiles reassuringly at her child then listens as Sonja explains about the barrels and lack of water. Milea makes a small sound in understanding; she has forgotten about the supplies. She leans back and recalls a memory; in another life she would have been scolded for such absentmindedness.

"Milea," Neil approaches "It's been brought to my attention that we need supplies." He points towards the north. "Lybrinthia Bay is a half day sail around the coast. I think we should stop there first."

"I'm thinking the same," Milea agrees. "The small skirmish in Churn's marketplace distracts me from collecting them earlier. To return after that action is not a good idea."

"I can imagine," Neil says, rubbing his chin. He made a note to ask his sister for the details of the battle. "How does this ship work?"

"You are the captain. Give it a command," Milea offers. "It is truly that simple." She smiles.

"Hmm..." Neil muses, his body language held volumes of disbelief.

Milea leans back against the rail of the ship and folds her arms. Her eyes, full with humor, met those of the newly installed captain. The snort of a whale-seal catches Sonja's curiosity as she goes to the mast and climbs it again to get a good look at the beasts from above. Vicki and Brion watch the girl go with quiet conversation about her swift movements and speculation of origin as well as that of Milea's. Brion concludes with the simple fact that; whatever her origins are, this sorceress is an extraordinary woman. Vicki acknowledges the fact with a slight nod of approval.

"Alright, Hoist anchor and bring up the sails. We head out to the ocean a bit but follow the coast northeast to Lybrinthia Bay," Neil orders loud enough for a crew to hear. Nothing happens. Milea glance just beyond the disillusioned captain to see the sails starting to rise. Vicki gawks.

"Neil, look," Vicki shouts, causing her brother to whip around.

The gulls holler in surprise as the ship moves. The birds ascend to the sky, afraid of the now animate object. Neil gawk as the sails upon the masts unrolls and ties between the two posts. Ropes slither around, going taut to keep in place. The anchor lifts from the bottom with a clanking sound as it locks in place upon the back side of the ship. Sonja whoops with joy as the ship raises its flag. It is dark blue with the twin moons, one waxing, the other full, and three stars. The flag flutters in the breeze with pride. The wheel turns until the ship faces the ocean.

Vicki and Brion took multiple steps back to watch the item move fluently, clicking every once in a while. A strong breeze from the sea fills the cloth of the sails, pushing the ship into the vast open water. Vicki hurries to the side to see the small wake created by the ship's bow. Brion is just thankful that the push-off is smooth. There is, hardly any movement that could make him ill. After a minute, the ship turns course to Northeast, sails adjusting to catch the most wind. The large white sheets billow out to full capacity propelling the boat to her destination. Neil turns in place, watching the ship work as if several men are handling the entire rig. His face alights with joy and wonder.

"You might want to go to the helm and hold the wheel, Neil. She is very new upon the ocean and will go off course to test you," Milea suggests, the strong breeze blowing against her. It flutters her hair and clothing.

"I... yeah...ok," Neil hurries to the helm. Milea chuckles as she faces the horizon once more. Several dolphins jump out of the water, providing a show for those upon the ship. Sonja cheers the efforts of the distant creatures.

Lybrinthia Bay

The sun barely marches across the sky when the ports of Lybrinthia Bay loom into view. A large multicolor tower greets all who come to the richest port in this part of the planet. The shouts and swears of deep-voiced men upon the breeze reach the ears of those aboard the *Lady of the Night*. Just like Churn, this is a port-city and feeds the large city of Lybrinthia thirty miles inland. The port hosts more piers than the previous and gives the illusion that it is not as busy. Vicki leans on the rail to survey the ocean; they had arrived in record time as it usually takes half a day sail from Churn to Lybrinthia Bay. The rope next to her moves catching her attention as it adjusts itself, slowing the vessel down. The ropes and sails shift efficiently, preparing the ship to dock.

"I think I like this rig. I got to enjoy the views for a change," Vicki affirms to herself. She searches around with a show of discontent. "Alright, where is Mr. Seasickness?" she says with a sigh and goes to search for Brion.

Clouds drift as another ship speeds past the *Lady of the Night* on its way out to the open ocean. The crew aboard the departing vessel hails those on the *Lady*, shouting accolades about the way she looks. Neil hollers back his positive response and adjusts the wheel to maneuver the *Lady of the Night* to the open dock. Sonja slides down the mast to stand next to her mother as they came nearer to the ports.

The closer they got; the more buildings and tents began to come into focus. The streets are filled with merchants moving cargo or setting up shop. Sonja bounces with excitement at the chance to go into yet another marketplace. Milea cautions her child to stay close to her side. Although Lybrinthia Bay is patrolled by the forces of Governor Rex Sa'Jak, it is no secret that people, especially children, are kidnap and taken into slavery. The Governor, like his ally King Darimus, is too busy wrapped up in the war with a mad creature name Sorshana to properly provide adequate security at this time.

"This shouldn't take long," Milea says with confidence. A deep moan catches the attention of mother and daughter.

"Ok, what is that," Sonja asks

The sound of the ports grows louder as the two turn, bit by bit to the noise behind them. Brion groans again, sitting down with his back against the main mast, holding his stomach. His features are slightly green; a good amount of perspiration plastering his clothing to his body. Milea quietly voices her concern as she decides to check on him. Brion raises his head and thought he sees multiple versions of the sorceress. He closes his eyes and groans again, wishing the trip is over. With a sigh, he put his head back, knowing that his troubles have just begun.

"Brion? You look a little green. Will you survive," Milea questions. Brion focuses on the woman's concerned eyes.

"I... or more specifically, my stomach is never happy about traveling by sea," Brion grumbles. "No matter what I try, I usually end up sick." He burps but manages to keep his last meal.

"This will be one hell of a trip for you," Milea says. "I'll tell you what, while we are getting supplies, I will make sure to stock up on dopie ginger," placing a reassuring hand upon his shoulder. "It will help you with your sickness."

"Really?" Brion's features reflect his hopefulness. He then closes his eyes as another wave of nausea engulfs him.

"That is what a good friend of mine gave me when I first got onto a ship. It works well for me," Milea assures, nodding her reassurance to him.

"I'll give it a go then," Brion slides down to the deck. "As soon as the ship stops swaying."

"If the ginger does not work, then I will have to find another trick," Milea offers. She sees Sonja speaking with Vicki near the rail of the ship. "We will be making port soon. Try to relax," she says, walking away to stand with Vicki. "He's not doing well at all."

"I saw," Vicki agrees. "Do you think he'll make it to the docks?" she asks, noting the ports. "That's about another five minutes."

"I hope so," Milea says.

The breeze shifts, playing havoc on everybody's hair and the sails respond to the winds as Neil turn the wheel. The vessel leans into the curve gracefully. All but one sail rolls up, tying in bundles along the posts. The ship's slowdown continues during the approach. Gulls cackle as the *Lady of the Night* bumps up against the outer most piers and let the anchor down with a loud splash.

Vicki takes a rope and hops off the ship. She lands in stealth then walks over to a giant wooden dowel. With quick speed, Vicki ties the ship in place as she's done many other ships for years in her past. The last sail upon the ship folds up neatly, tying into place. Neil places a ramp out onto the port side of the ship. He presses down on it with his foot, assuring that it is in place. A mechanical click indicates that the two pieces are now joining in place.

"Coming through," Milea warns.

The ocean's spray dot Milea and Brion as they take slow strides onto the piers. Milea hesitates to use any mystical means; most are similar to the movement of ships. That is the last thing that Brion needs at this moment. The elf groans a little as he leans against the sorceress for support and balance. Milea takes her time, pausing every once in a while, when she sees her companion gag or heave. Sonja watches her mother, taking in the potential situation. The girl then decides to hop over the edge as Vicki has done.

Sonja almost falls into the water but is safe when Vicki catches her arm. The elder l'vane pats her charge on the shoulder then goes to assist the rest of her companions. Once Brion makes it to the docks, Neil disembarks the ship. He faces the vessel and watches as the sunlight bounces off the wood. The effects cause a shimmering of light up and down the bright wood. Neil chuckle to himself. It is as if the ship figurehead is grinning at him and saying, 'told you so.'

"I think I'm in love," Neil admits. The ship blushes a little, a small reddish tint coming to the wood briefly. Brion groans and sits down upon the pier catching Neil's attention. "Whoa, is he alright?"

"No, he got a very bad case of seasickness," Milea says while crouching down to focus on the elf's eyes. "I would offer you to stay on the ship, Brion. But I think that would not be wise. How did you manage to sail from Cathalian?" she muses. Brion groans a little, unable to truthfully answer the question.

"He must have slept through most of that trip," Vicki hedges a guess as she too bent down to examine the elf. "Here, let me try something," she offers while gently touching Brion's shoulders. She then bends and reaches down to lift up his left hand, touching a spot just above the crease of his wrist. "Relax." She applies a little pressure. "How do you feel?"

"A little better," Brion answers as he stands. "What did you do?" He watches her shrug. The action causes him to glower. "Don't give me that."

"Ah, I saw what you did," Milea took Brion's other arm and studies it. "Interesting. Not many bards know the points of a body such as this." She studies Vicki a little. "How did you become so well versed?"

"Well, let's say I've had my time of seasickness when I was just starting on the ocean," Vicki says with a smile. "It works, sometimes. But not all the time," she admits.

"Sometimes is all I need. I'll stand guard at the ship," Brion offers.

"We should not be long," Milea promises. "Let's go, Sonja." She starts walking towards town. Sonja catches up with her mother and walks next to her. The girl receiving a gentle touch upon her head.

"Are you sure you're alright now?" Neil asks his friend.

"I'm good," Brion insists as he studies his wrist. "I'll have to figure out what you did Vicki."

"Besides lying to a powerful sorceress and hoping that she did not detect it," Vicki admits. "I found it accidentally when I was studying under my father's guidance."

"Oh, one of those tricks. Well, at least you didn't kill him," Neil says. "I'm going to see if I can find a real sword. Mine was lost a little while ago."

"A group of daggers for me and, of course, more supplies," Vicki says. "Anything you want, Brion?"

"Milea mentioned dopie ginger," Brion recalls. "That will do it for me."

"Alright, keep a close eye out for trouble," Neil offers. "The last I remember, this place is ripe with it. More so than the port we departed from."

"Aye captain," Brion acknowledges. "Now get out of here, I have this." He sits upon the piling Vicki tied the ship to.

Neil and Vicki both went on their way towards the interior of Lybrinthia Bay. The merchants grumble as they move their merchandise through the boroughs to the Port Town. The ultimate destination is to get the goods to the city of Lybrinthia. A hand full of dealers decides to try selling their wares at the ports instead of risking the road to the capital. It is rumored to have outlaws and rouges the entire length of it.

Milea stops at the edge of the docks to survey the activity around. Lybrinthia Bay is very different than Churn. The houses are more elegant, despite being in a state of disrepair. The town folk are not interested in the friendly gossip of the day but hurry to their destinations. Merchants of all types, including illegal, hawk items ranging from food to pleasure.

Activity near a shanty building is almost electric, yet that is not what catches Milea's eye. The large three-mast ship swaying in the docks keeps her attention. Sails and the wood of the large vessel are black and ominous. Rumor has it that this ship is burnt on purpose then return to the sea. Sonja follows her mother's gaze over to the ship. Dark and evil vibes resonate towards her causing the girl to shutter and take a cautious step back.

Milea studies her child, curiously. Sonja has not displayed the ability to sense such things until now. Milea places a hand upon Sonja's shoulder and whispers words of reassurance. The girl gives a nervous grin back, takes a deep breath, and relaxes. Milea brushes the girl's hair a little to lend support to her child. The sorceress's attention goes to Vicki and Neil as they approach.

"Neil. Vicki," Milea greets. "How's Brion? Is he still well?"

"He's fine. During this trip, he'll either get his sea legs, or he'll swear off riding on boats for the rest of his life," Neil answers and adjusts his belt.

"With what happened, I would say he'd do the latter," Vicki chuckles. "How about you, Sonja? Are you alright?"

"I'm good," Sonja beams. "Riding in the crow's nest is fun. The views are perfect. I think I saw a sea dragon's head in the distance as we sail." She stretches and places her hands behind her head.

"Really," Milea says thoughtfully while tilting her head to one side. "I wonder if that is Namu. He tends to stick close to Selvast Forest. That's not far from here."

"Why would a sea dragon want to stay close to shore?" Neil asks. He focuses beyond the sorceress, noting the large boat. "That's not good."

"The *Charred Rose*," Vicki scowls. "That ship's been on the seas a long time." She took a step back when she saw pale green lights float around it. "Ok, so that thing is a future ghost ship. It's already got the unsettled spirits."

"Might already be one," Neil says conversationally to his sister. "Her crew operates in one of the most deplorable professions. Slavery. Those that willingly sail upon that ship are Car'laden and Devorians for the most part. I'm sure that lots of people die upon that ship." He shifts his weight a little and studies the vessel. "Besides, it's sister ship is the *Dragodu*. That already haunts the seas until Ra'jil got rid of it."

"Both of you can see ghosts and spirits, Milea asks. "That is a rare gift to have. How long have you the ability to see wondering spirits?"

"Not me," Neil shook his head. "Vicki has that talent. Passes down from mom. The women of our family tend to have that talent. The men are just plain stubborn."

"I know one who has a similar talent to yours, Vicki," Milea smiles at the woman. "It is truly a blessing. I had to learn to sense them. But I cannot see them."

"I try to steer clear of them. I don't want to be possessed by them.," Vicki says while rubbing her left arm a little. "That is one of my qualms against the unrestful dead."

"There is a trick to prevent such," Milea informs. "The same person that shares your talent can teach it to you better than I. Let's get supplies so that we can find her." She starts walking toward the marketplace. "I'm sure that Brion can handle himself if the *Charred Rose* crew decides to become foolish."

"Oh, he's quite capable," Neil agrees. "If they try to go after him, they are in for a surprise."

"A really rude one if they come after us," Vicki concurs.

"Indeed," Milea says and starts her journey. "Sonja, do not stray far from us."

"I won't..." Sonja says, her attention distracts. She witnesses several women distracting another man. At the same time, a child stole the man's coin purse, sword, and belt. "Why do they do that?"

"Some of it is for sport," Vicki answers. She saw the action. "Others do it because they are trying to survive."

"My cousin would be doing it for sport," Milea hints to Sonja. "But she does not need to have her quarry distracted so." She scrutinizes the group of young thieves as they pass. The children quietly retreat to an alleyway.

"I..." Vicki starts then pauses when an interesting sight caught her attention. "What have we here?"

A legion of large soldiers' marches down the street in perfect formation. Those they passed offer a slight bow to them as they carry on their way. More than a few of them decide to belittle or berate a few villagers before they continue. The soldiers scowl at the many different foreigners that dare to cross their path. The seven-foot men are akin to the devorians, yet they did have separate ancestors. They are called Orijetie. Like the Devorians, the Orijetie ancestors were blessed a long time ago, given the strength and longevity of dragons which carry on to their descendants. Their complexion, however, varies from region to region. The orijetie are hailed as peacekeepers for the entire realm of Bri'al.

Just about all the people of the realm request guidance or assistance from them. Their diplomatic skills just as sought after as their well-honed army. Lybrinthia, home of the Orijetie, enjoy many ties to the nations of Bri'al. Very few will count themselves the enemy of these powerful people. A single man stands out from them, dress in Nobel attire. The sunlight bounces off his crown of golden locks as if playing with them. Of all the men in the group, he is the one to garner the most attention, especially from the women as they strut by, and he is well aware of his advantage.

"Ublivorion Gate..." Milea swears and takes a step back. She inspects of her surroundings in haste. They are in the open.

"What's wrong," Neil asks. He watches as Milea cusses again then turn her back to the street.

Animals protest as they are beaten out of the way of the large band of men. Vicki glances at Milea and moves to stand in front of the sorceress. Neil shift to stand next to his sister, further blocking the sorceress from view. He figures he would ask Milea if she is a wanted criminal, then again. It did not matter considering he is still considered a felon from his pirating days in many countries of Bri'al. The soldiers' shadows fell upon the trio of l'vane as they parade past, the ground shakes from the stomping boots.

Sonja scrutinizes the men as they continue their way. She notes the crest of Lybrinthia, a dragon's head with a sword in its maul and a set of double axes cross behind, decorating the breastplate of each man. They are the elite guards of the Lybrinthian army. Vicki silently admits that the orijetie are very easy on the eyes. Their leader pauses when he sees the trio of l'vane and a woman with her back turned. He walks over to them, causing Vicki to indiscreetly place her hand upon the whip she possesses. The man's light green eyes see her reaction to him and grin, humor evident in his features. A half dozen of the men that file with him pause and wait not too far from their leader.

"What do we have here," the man asks with humor in his voice. "Three l'vanes? Did Darimus have more children?"

"King Darimus is not our father," Sonja informs catching the man's attention. Behind her, Milea once again cusses.

"Oh, we have a spunky little one here," the man bent down. His blonde hair shifting with his movements. "My name is Casimir Sa'Jak, girl. It's because of my efforts that you and your cohorts are not aboard a slave ship by now."

"Then why is there a Slaver's ship docked in the port now?" Sonja challenges, meeting the large man's gaze unafraid. "If you are doing what you claim, it would not be there."

"Obviously, you need a good thrashing, child," Casimir warns.

"We'll handle her discipline," Vicki promises to bring attention back to herself. "But the child is not what caught your eye. Is it, milord?" she asks with a hint of mischief in her voice. Casimir decides he likes the sound. Neil rolls his eyes from his sister's actions. He then thinks about it and quietly takes Vicki's dagger from her belt.

"Hmm...my cousin has a l'vane wife," Casimir gently takes hold of Vicki's chin and caresses her cheek with his finger a little. "Which has my curiosity? I wonder what stamina a l'vane woman has over an orijetie. Care to satisfy my curiosity?" he growls those words seductively.

"Not at this time, milord. Perhaps I should talk to my promised love before I partake in such a gift," Vicki answers with a warm smile. Her swinging arm is being held back by her brother.

"If he is a man of Lybrinthia. He will have no choice," Casimir smirks. "I always get what I want."

"Lord Casimir," a soldier calls to his leader. "Your father is awaiting us at the inn."

"Right," Casimir grumbles at the interruption then turns back to his catch of the day. "I will find you later, my beauty. You and I will continue this discussion in a more private location." A feral grin masks his features as he scans Vicki a few times. He then turns to his men. "Let's go, father is anxious to hear how things are going here." He walks towards the inn. His escort fell in step. Once he is gone, Neil let his sister's arm go. Vicki let out an angry sound and punches the air, taking a deep breath in.

"Creep," Vicki snarls at Casimir's back. Lucky for her, neither he nor his men heard the insult.

"I agree," Sonja confirms. "I don't like him very much. This is the first time I've met him."

"He is assigned by his father to protect Lybrinthia Bay from pirates or other unlawful dealings. Yet, he has turned to profit from the crimes that he swore to his father he would protect Lybrinthia Bay from," Milea explains, turning to face her companions. "Are you alright Vicki?"

"I just need something to clean off his slimy fingerprints," Vicki wipes her chin with her hand. "Then I'll be fine."

"Why did you turn away, Milea? Did something happen that I need to know about?" Neil asks.

"No. It is that I do not have the time for confrontations right now," Milea answers as they start walking again. "Casimir has at his beck and call a very powerful Witch. You mentioned her name before, Vicki. It's Ajahn."

"Really?" Vicki did not hide her surprise. "How did he score such a treasure?"

"I have a feeling that Ajahn may be to blame in part for her circumstances," Milea admits. "But I don't want to guess and do not want to linger any longer than we have to. A battle with Ajahn ends up becoming very violent and destructive on both of our parts."

"Yeah, no need to destroy the port before we set sail," Neil agrees. "We need to get in and out before his meeting is over with."

"Especially since he will be searching for Vicki," Milea observes. "He seems to have a curiosity due to his cousin's marriage."

"I tried to castrate him. But my brother held my arm back," Vicki offers. "If he comes after me, he'll end up shaking hands with Oswind."

"He never answers my question, though," Sonja notes.

"I don't think he intends to. Then Vicki distracted him," Neil remarks. "You're not old enough to distract him in a way that Vicki has. Thank the old ones. If he became so bold with you, I'd have to castrate him myself."

The crowd buzzes from the spectacle of the marching guards. Apparently, Casimir is an eligible bachelor. A few well-inform women speculate on his sexual prowess and appetite for the fairer sex. Some of those same women glare at Vicki, unhappy with the attention she receives from the Sa'Jak. Milea resumes her journey to the marketplace with her companions. She is ignoring the crowd until she hears news of Jaide, daughter of Darimus ra Deltoria.

Milea stops and listens to the news of the young woman's marriage to Rex's nephew, Kiyoshi Sa'Jak. The marriage is arranged to make the alliance of Deltor, Lybrinthia, and Chol-bek stronger. There is speculation that the bride is less than pleased with her situation. That causes Milea to touch her cheek in contemplation as she now lags behind her companions as they enter the marketplace.

"So that's why Casimir has such curiosities," Milea muses.

"I'll have to have a talk with my 'little protégé' when I find her."

The sun has slipped through the sky, causing Neil to utter unkind words under his breath. They did arrive late in the day, to begin with. He needs to be on board the *Lady of the Night* before darkness falls, the designated time to follow the star to the Boiling Seas. He also is not in the mood to deal with the slavers that prowl the marketplace. The crew of the *Charred Rose* is boldly prancing about the streets, identifiable by the black rose tattoo upon their cheek or arm.

The quick movement of children catches Vicki's attention. The small band of foragers has been stalking Milea, and her companions since the group enter the marketplace. Milea takes in the surroundings, noting the various dangers in place. She also sees a group of trappers, a separate set of men other than the crew of the *Charred Rose*. They are sitting at an outside bar and watch the group of strangers intensely. A few grunt and turn back once they are discovered.

"I don't like it, but it looks like we have to split up before the market closes. We can meet back at the ship within the hour." Neil suggests.

"We should try and stay within sight of each other, at least," Milea says. She lifts her left hand, causing it to glow a little. "Here, I will pay for what we need since I fail to retrieve it." Two bags of coins appear in front of Neil and Vicki.

"This isn't part of my payment, is it?" Neil knits his brow in concern.

"I will assure you that it is not. We should wait until the arrival at the Temple before we discuss your payment," Milea says.

"Mom. We're being watched," Sonja warns. "They look like gypsies."

"I saw them earlier. They will be handled appropriately," Milea walks towards a clothing dealer as the man sang about his exotic materials. Sonja fell in step with her mother.

"Try to behave and not kill anybody this time, brother," Vicki requests. She scopes out the different booths with her sights landing on a bored weapons dealer. "I see what I need."

"Don't forget to pick up a sword for me. I swear I'll not break any necks this time," Neil promises.

"Good deal," Vicki says, pleased with her brother's promise and walks towards the bored weapons dealers. The woman perks up when she saw a potential customer approaching.

"Ah, he does have fruit," Neil remarks as he heads to a food merchant. The man scowls at him, not liking the fact the women with Neil ignores his stand.

Shoppers walk up and down the large main street of the marketplace. Milea investigates the merchandise of the boisterous vendor with great interest. She sees three of the gypsies' constant vigilance of her every movement out of the corner of her eye. The children are in an alleyway across from Milea's present location. A large animal grunt by, carrying an equally large load upon it's back.

The animals handier use a whip to keep his beast of burden moving. Once the beast is gone, so are the children in the alley. Sonja wonders if the children are going to be foolish enough to try robbing them. Milea decides to carry on with her shopping expedition and worry about the children later. She feels the material as the merchant sings his heart out. Milea gazes at the man and grins as he tries his best to hit some very difficult notes. They did not always turn out the way he wants, but he sings anyway.

"You have such a wonderful gift, kind sir. Your song is very nice, and I thank you for sharing it with my daughter and me," Milea offers to the merchant. Sonja's feature twist into a mixture of awe and surprise at her mother's words. Sonja thinks the merchant's singing is worse than the call of an elk bull during mating season.

"Seriously," Sonja says.

"And you have such beautiful wears. Truly, you are quite a gem in this marketplace," Milea continues and feels the very, expensive material. Sonja mumbles an agreement with her mother on the quality of the fabric.

"My beautiful lady is kind," the merchant smiles with pride.

"My name is Goard. How may I assist you today, Kind Lady?" He wiggles his bushy eyebrows a little. Milea smiles at the man. He is flirting with her.

"I am traveling with three more adult companions and my daughter," Milea describes, placing a hand upon Sonja's shoulder. "I need at least three outfits apiece for myself a woman equal to me in height. A man who is three inches shorter than me and another who is one inch taller. I also need traveling attire for my child. Three outfits.”

“Including shoes,” Goard asks. “I will throw those in for free. For being so kind as to stop by and listen to my ballad.’

“It is very kind of you to share such a beautiful skill,” Milea flashes a warm smile. The merchant puffs up smugly. “How much for such beautiful merchandise?”

“For you milady, I will insist on this instead,” Goard pulls a shimmering jade-colored long sleeve shirt. “It is made from the silk of a Jungle Spider. All the way from Wormag, an Island of Dragonigena in the tropics.”

“Oh, I see. Such fine material is pricy,” Milea touches the silk, noting the truth in the man’s words.

“I will give you all the clothing you need for yourself, your traveling companions and your daughter for one hundred coins,” Goard assures. “I will also toss in matching boots for free. The only other payment I ask for is a kiss on the cheek from such an enchanting lady.” He grins as Milea’s beautiful features become a little mischievous.

“Then it is a deal. Thank you, kind sir,” Milea walks over as the seven-foot merchant bends down and kisses his chubby cheek.

“You are most very welcome,” Goard beams.

The merchant once again breaks out in song again as he gathers the items he promises. Milea winces when he hit a particularly bad note, yet carry on listening and watching. Goard is careful to fold each item and place them in a pile of colorful silk. Sonja beam when she sees the beautiful gold and deep sapphire blue of a few of the articles. Goard uses a silk string to tie around the two piles of clothing, topping the packages with a nice size bow.

Milea smirks as she retrieves the remaining payment of one hundred coins and hands it to Goard. The merchant gives one pile of clothing to Milea, the other he stoops down to give to Sonja. Goard laughs when he sees that his package is bigger than the child that carries it. Sonja assures she is fine, as she is turning and navigating her way to the edge of the tent. The merchant waves cheerfully at the two, still lost in his song.

A procession of carts and horses lumber down the main street to the exit as Milea and Sonja leave the tent. The sorceress stops her child from walking into the path of the parade. The animals grunt as they pull on their load. Legions of arms guards walk alongside the wagons, eyeing those within the marketplace with suspicion. Milea watches the procession with curiosity, many of the armed guards are elves. There are a few humans among them as well. All are wearing the emblem of Jauli, one of the many allies of Lybrinthia.

Milea takes an extremely dim view of the rulers of Jauli. They were very rude the last time she met them. Milea and Sonja press on down the street to meet Vicki at the weapons dealer, careful to avoid stepping into the path of the convoy. A soldier glances over the sorceress appreciatively, especially the nautical way her hips move. His eyes scan up to the red of the hair, causing him to pause in recognition. He stops and pulls a subordinate to the side to give him an order. The soldier salutes then make his way towards the inn.

The noise and commotion of the visiting convoy are ignored at the weapon's dealer tent. Vicki and the female merchant, Cloe, kept on laughing at their various misadventures with daggers. The merchant's husband, Tony, huff as his pride takes an insulting blow and storms into his forge. Vicki takes a deep breath in and tries to apologize but is waved away by the merchant who has yet to stop laughing. The sound of a hammer striking metal fuels more humor. Vicki holds her side, leaning on the counter while Cloe rests against the building wall holding her stomach in laughter. The merchant is pregnant had all the signs that she is ready to pop any minute now, her swollen belly shaking with her good humor.

"Besides..." Cloe wipes a tear from her eye. "Most men do not take kindly to nearly being chopped off, despite it being a mistake." She rubs her belly gently when she feels her unborn kick.

"True," Vicki agrees and made a small sound of content. She chuckles again. "That is a good one. Topped mine hands down. I will be sure to use that in one of my stories to entertain guests. I might even make it a song."

"Oh, so you are a minstrel," Cloe beams.

"That I am," Vicki boasts a little. "I've been singing since I was born according to my mother. She says I would not hush no matter what she did."

"If I may ask, what does a bard need such a fine blade for?" Cloe eyes the beautiful katana blade that Vicki had placed on the counter to purchase along with a fist full of daggers.

"The sword is for my brother," Vicki smiles as she tries not to snicker. "The daggers are for me."

"Oh really," Cloe manages, chuckling. "Well, try not to frighten any unwary men with the daggers. If you aim correctly, cut them off the first time and be done with it."

"I agree. How much for the weapons, my good woman," Vicki asks with a smile, placing a hand upon her hip as she focuses on her new friend.

"You've given me a wonderful story to remember and chuckle to for years to come," Cloe admits. "For payment, how about a song?"

"Hmm..." Vicki took in her surroundings and the variety of weapons. "Alright, I think I know exactly the one you will enjoy. And I'll even throw in a part about daggers just for you."

Cloe laughs, already enjoying the mental image of the song she has yet to hear. Her unborn kicks a little, adding to her good humor. Perhaps it is a boy child. The blacksmith unrelenting hammers out a strong beat at his forge, unaware of the bard that is listening to it. Vicki takes a deep breath in and begins to sing her song to the beat of the forge. Cloe starts to chuckle as the story unfold. The crowd of the marketplace gathers around the weapons dealer, Vicki's voice is like a siren beckoning all those who could hear, bringing in customers to shop around and listen to the music. Milea hears the high-energy melody as she tilts her head curiously.

A vivid picture is painted in the words of the jingle causing the sorceress to chuckle a little. Sonja's head twists left then right to try and figure out the story then requests an explanation from her mother. Milea meets her child's gaze and promises she will learn in time. The sorceress starts to go join Vicki at the weapons dealer then to pause when she hears raised voices from the food vendor. The heat of the argument causes a bit of curiosity and worry as Milea detours to go check on the ship's captain first.

Neil's argument with the food vendor makes him oblivious to his sister singing a short distance away. The vendor, Fred, counters Neil's offer for the fruit sighting that it is rare and hard to retrieve. Neil corrects the man informing him that every island upon the South Seas carries the fruit and he is not in the mood to pay twenty coins per piece. The fruit, in his eyes, is worth only one coin apiece. Sonja agrees with Neil about the price, the vendor is way over his head if he thinks Neil will pay twenty coins for one fig.

Milea takes a deep breath in and mutters a few words as she uses her ability to cause the clothing she and Sonja carry to disappear. Sonja lets out a sigh of relief when the weight is gone. She starts to approach the vendor and Neil but is stopped by her mother. Milea glance down the street then to her child. Sonja takes the hint and hurries to Vicki instead. Milea contemplates a little as she takes in the scene. A quiet word of wisdom exits her along with a breath as she decides to approach the two quarreling men.

"What? Are you out of your damn mind?! That's bloody ridiculous," Neil snaps.

"That is my final offer. If you don't like it then leave else, I will call security on you," Fred snaps back, leaning forward to place his hands upon his table.

"Call them because I think you are robbing your customers," Neil challenges, slamming his fist upon the table. The two men met each other's gaze, each reflecting hostility to the other.

"Neil. Come with me," Milea says gently, touching Neil's shoulder. "Other food vendors in the marketplace will be more reasonable. I did overhear you promise your sister, you would behave." Neil growls then exhale his frustration and walks away. Milea turns to follow her companion.

"Madam," Fred addresses Milea, straightening his stance and popping his vest. "I insist that you keep your slave on a leash,"

"My what?" Milea whips her head to stare at the merchant as if he is insane. "Let me inform you of something. I have friends, allies, family, and traveling companions. I do not have slaves."

She walks until she is an inch from the man. Fred takes a step back, feeling raw heat from the woman. Flames swirl in her eyes, reflecting her displeasure.

"I...I..." Fred starts.

"You will not speak of such things to me again," Milea informs. "Good day to you."

Milea takes a step back and turns and walks away. The merchant trembles as he exhales in relief. Neil notices the ground under the man is now moistens. With a smile of satisfaction, he follows after his employer.

"Milea," Neil catches up with the perturbed sorceress. She turns and faces him. "Thank you."

"You are welcome," Milea says. "I dislike when assumptions are made. Especially when it comes to the servitude of the less fortunate." They start to walk, honing in on the crowd attracts by Vicki's singing.

"It sounds as if you and I have similar views towards that," Neil agrees. "When I was on the seas, some of my best sailors were former slaves. They had a zest for life that is unparalleled."

"I see that in my sister," Milea remarks. "She endured the worst type of servitude to the worst type of creature on all Bri'al." She pauses and closes her eyes, taking a deep breath. "We must finish our shopping and be on our way."

"Agreed," Neil says. "Since Fred is now soiled. I'm sure he is going to inform the guards."

"And I don't feel like dealing with Casimir and his friends," Milea affirms. She turns to the large crowd when Vicki sings another part to the song. "Well, sounds like your sister is having a great time with her song."

"I hear. I hope that's not the one I think it is," Neil glooms.

Applause echoes in the marketplace follow by several accolades. A very large part of the audience calls for an encore. Almost half of the group has yet to finish laughing at the story within the song. Vicki bows to her applauding spectators once she completes her song. Cloe is amused as she claps; once again in tears from chortling at the story, Cloe then places a hand upon her belly, still well humor, as her unborn gives a solid kick.

Vicki straightens when she sees Sonja also clapping among those who gather around. Neil crosses his arms with a confident smile, proud of his sister. Milea's features reflect her good humor and the fact that she is very impressed by those she hired. Perhaps it is true that this trip will be full of surprises and discoveries as they travel to the Boiling Seas. Vicki meets the sorceress' gaze briefly with a smile. The bard then decides to bow to her very enthusiastic young friend, Sonja. The girl cheers as the crowd disburses into various directions.

A few customers stay to shop the merchandise at hand, especially the daggers. Milea and Neil take a few shallow steps into the tent to avoid bumping into the crowd of spectators. Sonja dodges through to get to Vicki's side.

"That is a great song and story, Vicki. I can almost picture it in my mind," Sonja complements, enthusiastically.

"Oh, it is very clear in my mind," Vicki boasts confidently. "A little page from the Dresden history book."

"My gods, tell me that is not a true song. It can't be," Cloe pleads, her voice still holding humor. She manages to calm her laughter a little. Her unborn moves causing her to gasp a little then chuckle quietly.

"Well..." Vicki said as she does a slight shrug of her shoulder.

"What's not true," Neil asks when he arrives. Cloe takes one look at him and burst into a fit of laughter. "Ok, what's going on?"

The merchant is once again holding her belly as her unborn kicks, obviously displeased at its mother's laughter. Cloe continues to laugh anyway.

"Nothing, dear brother. My good woman, I am done with my song. May I take my purchase?" Vicki beams. She ignores her brother's displeased features.

"Yes, yes please," Cloe manages through laughter. She is holding her side. "If you need more, come on back. I will give you whatever you need," she laughs. "For another song."

"Will do, milady," Vicki bows and picks up her purchase.

"Here you go, brother. Just for you." She hands Neil the katana. Cloe manages to calm her laughter to a slight snicker as she watches the transaction.

"This…" Neil holds up the sword and admires the craftsmanship. The handle is delicately shaped into the head of a golden dragon. He pulls the katana out of its sheath and turns it over several times. It is folded precisely, no blemishes or marks upon the blade. "You got this for a song?"

"And a story about daggers," Vicki adds with a very mischievous grin. She waves back at Cloe as they walk away. The merchant returns the wave, still laughing a little.

"We heard you singing when we walked out of the clothing tent," Sonja admits with joy upon her words.

"I've purchased clothing for all of us. Three outfits each. We were on our way to the farmers' marketplace when we saw the crowd," Milea informs as she starts down the street.

"I…" Neil starts. His keen eyes detect a Lybrinthia guard among the street crowd. "Looks like the meeting is over."
"We have to hurry," Milea said, quickening her pace.

CHAPTER FOUR

The Lady's Ruse

A number of large women with giant baskets promenade in the opposite direction that Milea and her group travel. They are gossiping about the latest news of the War. Their baskets fill to the brim with all kinds of fruits, vegetables, and meats. Neil feels at ease; the price must be much lower in the farmer's market. He spies two baskets full of the same fruit he attempted to buy from Fred. Several children rush forward through the crowd with the speed and accuracy of a striking cobra. They home in on their targets and scatters around to take the group on all sides.

One child grab Neil's coin bag. The captain quickly corrals the child and flips him onto his back. The boy loses most of the air in his lungs, gasping for breath. Another tries to take

Sonja's dagger and ends up hitting the ground next to his cohort. A third did manage to nab Vicki's coin pouch only to have a whip snap around his ankle, sending him to the ground. He is drag back to the group as Vicki pulls on her whip slowly. The last boy finds himself levitating into the air, facing the scolding gaze of Milea.

"I had hope that you would not be so foolish. Where is your elder," Milea scolds the child.

The rest of the marketplace ignores the group as Milea's eyes bore into the frightened child. The boy swallows his pride, knowing that he is going to regret his next move. With a shaky breath, he glances over to the alleyway. Milea follows his gaze, turning and folding her arms. A young woman screams out in surprise from the darkness of the alleyway. Milea's eyes flash once as the owner of the voice levitates high into the air.

The young woman yells, unsure what is going on, she shuts her eyes in silent hope that it is not happening to her. The next thing she knows, her body is falling at a fast pace, towards her once intended targets. She stops suddenly, her eyes covered with her hands and still shut. Milea waits a few seconds to study the girl, noting that she may have just turned sixteen. The girl is just about as mixed as they come, sporting the tall lanky body of an orijetie or car'laden. Milea taps her bicep a little before she clears her throat.

The young woman is slow to lower her hands and opens her eyes. She swallows nervously when she recognizes the woman. Still levitating, she turns attention to her left. The boys on the ground in front of Neil are holding their heads. The one that has Vicki's whip tied around his ankle is now rubbing the offended appendage. The young woman's attention falls on the levitating boy in front of Milea. He bows his head slightly to the red-hair sorceress that keeps them both levitating.

"What is your name? Why did you target my companions and I," Milea demands, her words calm for now. The words catch the young woman's attention again.

"Milady, I'm sorry. I did not realize it was you. Ah... my name is Grachel," the young woman blurts out. Her voice is shaking with either nervousness or fear.

"Since I am on a short time schedule, I will let you off this once, Grachel. However, I do want you to provide me a service," Milea said plainly.

"O-ok," Grachel answers as she and her friend return to the ground. They manage to get to their feet.

"The *Charred Rose* is docked at the port. I am sure that there are captives on board. I want you to free them," Milea meets the young woman's gaze. "Do that, and I will not inform A'drianis of what you did or failed to do in this case. Do we have an agreement?"

"Y-yes, Majesty," Grachel bows. Her companions did the same and high tails it back into the alleyway.

"Majesty? You're Queen of Gypsies, Milea," Neil rubs his chin in curiosity.

"Perhaps in a former life. I've many titles throughout Bri'al. Some are fair; a lot of them are deplorable. The situation that I receive them in drives whether or not I claim them," Milea offers an explanation.

"We are running out of time," Vicki notes the closing of many vendors in the farmer's market.

"Right," Neil acknowledges with a small swear. "We need protein, water. Lots of water. And citrus fruit. They keep the longest."

"Sonja," Milea turned to her daughter.

"Got it," Sonja said. She takes off running into the marketplace, scouting.

Men and women shout out deals or greetings those who are in earshot. Sonja ricochets from vendor to vendor at a fast pace. After scouting the place, she leads her mother to the best deals as she bounces in excitement. The prices are more reasonable due to the amount of competition within the marketplace.

Milea and her companions receive rewards of several barrels of drinking water as well as large loaves of bread and cheese. Smoked and salted meats are also among the supplies. Once the purchase is made, Milea causes it to disappear. She assures her companions that it is on the ship, packed into the hull. Some of the farmers became spooked when the items disappear and close once Milea and her friends left the stand. Milea pauses prompting those with her to do the same.

"What's wrong," Neil asks then become keenly aware of a small group of devorians following them among the crowd. The sight is met with a gutter of a few soft cuss words.

"I almost forgot Brion's dopie ginger," Milea answers cupping her forehead. "Go to the ship, I will be there shortly."

"Stay aware," Vicki warns. "Come on Sonja, I'll race you back." She challenges with a bit of smug pride in her feature.

"You might want to think a little bit on that challenge, Vicki. Remember the devorians we faced in Churn," Milea reminds.

Sonja rocks back and forth from heel to toe, an innocent look about her. The girl's hands are behind her back.

"Eh, I'll be fine. Besides, I'm pretty fast myself," Vicki waves the concern away, smiling in confidence.

"I don't know, Vicki. Sonja's got a lot of spunk," Neil rubs his chin.

"I'll be fine," Vicki reiterates and places her hands upon her hip. "What say you, Sonja?" She grins cockily at the girl.

"Ok," Sonja bounces a little then takes off towards the docks.

The people of the marketplace shift and move about, oblivious to the preteen. Sonja is quick to ramp up to full speed as she dodges between the moving obstacles with expert ease. A large trail of dust lifts into the air in her wake. Vicki gawks for a few seconds in amazement; no one has ever run faster than she in recent memory. Vicki's shock turns to determination as she takes to running after the girl. She pushes herself to ramp up to speed in order to catch the girl, her own dust cloud filling the air and falling back to the ground. Neil and Milea chuckle at the sight as Sonja is at least thirty yards in front of Vicki and pulling away, despite the more mature l'vane's efforts to catch up.

"I think Vicki has met her match. As for you, my lady. I am staying until we both go back. The *Charred Rose* is still docked, and I've seen a few of her crew lurking about," Neil motions to his left. The sorceress glimpses over and sees the small group of devorians watching them.

"I see," Milea turns her attention to the right. Several Lybrinthian guards are scouting the area. "I hope Vicki does not run into Casimir."

"He'd have to be able to outrun a l'vane woman. Vicki is not going to slow down because he wants to have a conversation," Neil remarks and adjusts his katana slightly, untying the handle for ease of access.

"True. This should not take long," Milea leads the way to an herbs dealer.

Neil takes in the sights and quietly voices his dislike of several men watching his employer. After a brief count, he follows the woman. The sun continues to march, marking the late afternoon. Seabirds call out as they congregate onto several fishing vessels. The fishermen tie their boats to the docks and unload their cargo. Those who are not wise enough to cover their catch have it pilfer by the waiting animals. Brion mutters words of condolences when he sees the men cuss the crafty animals. His attention turns to the black ship docking a few piers down.

At least a dozen car'ladens grunt as they push large crates onto the vessel. He makes a slight sound of curiosity when he notices a hand sticks out from the bars. Brion attention goes to the ship as he hears the *Lady of the Night* groan a little bit. He studies the vessel; it is sitting lower in the water. He is curious to see what it makes the ship sit so low but knows better than to go onboard. His stomach flips, every once in a while, as if to remind him of his upcoming journey.

"I wonder what's going on. It's been quite some time since they left. I guess I'll look for them," Brion pondered and stands from his seat, stretching to allow the stiff muscles to relax. Brion turns to the shore in time to witness two dust clouds coming his way. "Now what...?" His stomach twists a little. "Not now." He fusses at himself.

One of the clouds of dust out-distances the other and begins to form a familiar shape. Sonja hit the docks first, her rushing feet bouncing the wood creating a constant sound of rattling timber. The girl slows her speed down as she approaches the ship to prevent colliding with Brion or fall off the edge. The girl does a happy jig and a whoop of triumph.

Sonja turns to her unfortunate challenger and wave encouragement. Vicki hit the wood about a minute after Sonja arrives at her destination. The boards once again rattle as they shake from the rapid footsteps. Vicki slows down and stops, her breathing is heavy from the effort of keeping up with Sonja. The woman bends down and places her hands upon her knees as she fights for her breath.

"Are you alright, Vicki," Brion asks.

"Just... trying... to keep... Sonja... from .... *Charred Rose...* Crew," Vicki said between catching her breath. "Ship." She pointed to the black ship.

"I see. I wondered what they took on board in large crates. You are telling me they are slavers," Brion takes a step back to study the black ship

"Yes," Vicki breaths deep then straighten up. "A group of them tried to surround us in the farmer's market. I am not sure if Milea saw them, but Neil and I sure did. He and Milea went to go get dopie ginger for you."

"Then I need to go make sure they are ok," Brion said. Sonja grabs hold of his arm. "What's wrong?"

"Stay here. Mom's not easily captured," Sonja warns.

"That is so true," Vicki agrees. "But I need you to do me a favor, Sonja."

"What's that," Sonja tilts her head to one side.

"If I challenge you to a footrace again, I need a head start of about two minutes," Vicki smiles at the girl. "Do you think you can do that for me?"

"Hm.... I'll think about it," Sonja admits after a moment though.

"You challenged her? Hell, I knew better when I saw Sonja climb that pole," Brion remarks, humor filling his features from the information. His attention became distracted when he noticed three children sneak aboard the *Charred Rose*. "What are they doing?" Vicki and Sonja both turn to witness the gypsy children finish their climb.

"Apparently what Milea told them," Vicki informs. She sees the children split up to search the rig. "And add a little treasure hunt to their adventure. Let me tell you what happened in the farmers market." Vicki leans upon the dowel, recounting the events.

A tiny golden bell rings as the door opens to the herbalist shop calling attention to its proprietors. Milea walks into the shop and pauses when she is hit with the strong scent of a seductive herb. She would have turned around and left because the merchant is obviously busy doing other things but needed to get the item she promised Brion, the dopie ginger.

Neil follows his employer and hesitates after taking two steps into the shop, his senses fully invaded by the thick smoke that fills up the small room. He coughs a few times and clears his throat to stop the effects as a woman whose clothing is barely wrapped around her sauntered into view. Milea sees her and the man that accompanies her slip from behind a wall. His own clothing is disheveled.

"Welcome! Welcome," the man greets with a bright grin. "I did not expect customers at this time of day, how can we help you?"

"I know how this one can help me," the lady herbalist purrs as she slinks to Neil and places a hand on his shoulder.

"My lady is kind, but your offer is not why we are here," Neil assures much to the woman's surprise.

"I am here to purchase a large sack of dopie ginger," Milea requests. The man's grin brightens even more.

"Well, well... you are very seductive my lady. Perhaps you would like to partake in a little of the rebaca root that we are burning. It is free for today as well as lessons on how to use it," the man said and slicks back his messy hair.

"I am well aware of the effects of," Milea pauses when there is a loud thump from the direction of the male herbalist. He also appears to be in a little pain. "Is everything alright?"

"Yes. It will hurt just a little bit," the man manages. "Like my heart."

"I don't think that is your heart," Neil tries not to laugh at the man's predicament. He takes a step back from the woman when her hand goes to his belt. "I'm fine, thank you."

"Yes, you are, very much so," the woman agrees.

"I see that we have come at an inopportune time. However, I am not going to leave without my purchase. Once I am gone, I have to set sail immediately to reach my destination."

Milea folds her arms and stares into the eyes of the male herbal-ist. She then rolls them when he tries sending an enchantment her way.

"You don't seem to be affected by my herb or my charms," the herbalist pouts in disappointment.

"One day you will find the enchantress of your dreams that will fall head over heels for you," Milea said. "Today is not that day, and I will not be that enchantress. Where is the dopie gin-ger?"

The male herbalist pouts even more but calls to his female companion. She makes a long face as she leaves Neil alone and goes to a wardrobe. The woman pulls out a large pile of bright blue ginger-root and places them on the table. Milea and Neil study the herbs and pulls out the best and firmest roots to place in a bag. The merchant tries once again to offer more services not on the list and free of charge but is turned down.

Milea and Neil then left the shop with their prized dopie gin-ger in hand. The door to the shop closes behind them, and they take a few steps away. Neil starts snickering first followed closely by a chuckle from Milea. The remaining farmers in the market stand around to chat with one another while closing down their venues. They pause in the activity when both Milea and Neil journey down the lane laughing in good spirits. The sun is hanging lower in the sky, casting long shadows upon the lands as evening settles in.

"I think he is still swooning over your good looks, milady. The staff totally ignored me," Neil chuckles.

"No, you were not. His assistant nearly took your clothes off. I think they have too much rebaca root burning in their tiny space," Milea said with good humor. She greets a passing woman and child. The babe grins at the pretty red of Milea's hair.

"Herb of seduction. You might be right. But why weren't we affected," Neil asks

"It takes more than rebaca root to set the mood for me. I just think you're stubborn," Milea admits with a shrug.

"Possibly," Neil agrees, "very possible. It's a Dresden man's best talent. We are always strong-willed. It takes a lot to bring us under a spell." He puffs up his chest in pride

"Why do I find it easy to believe that, Neil," Milea laughs. "I..."

A hand grabs Milea from behind. She instinctively takes hold of it, twists it, breaking the wrist before she tosses the man. He bellows in surprise, sailing until he slams into his companions a short distance away. Two dozen devorians surround them now in an ever-tightening circle. Milea prepares for battle as witnesses shout for security. The package the sorceress is carrying disappears in a bright flash, freeing her hands for this next ordeal.

"And here we are in a good mood. Good humor and recollecting very playful memories," Neil scolds.

"I am a little tired of devorians. Now, why are you coming after me," Milea demands

"You'll find out when we sell you to the highest bidder," one of the devorians announces. "Rush her before Casimir gets here."

Three of the men pull their ropes and begin to charge forward. Neil snorts as he also charges with Milea right behind him. Neil pulls his weapon as he nears the three rushing devori-ans. He twists once; swinging the blade around in record speed then puts it back away. Milea stops in her tracks when all three devorians fall to the ground.

One is split in half from the bottom up. The other two are sliced diagonally just under the shoulder. Neil's deadly gaze falls to the leader of the group. Milea blinks in surprise from the damage done by the l'vane man. The rest of the devorian slavers and their hesitant car'laden companions take a multitude of steps back. Unsure of what they have gotten into, the group turns on heels and flees the area.

"Ok, you're not just a bard or a pirate," Milea quietly concludes.

"Milea Sirus, Sorceress of Selvast Forest," Casimir announces loud enough for all to hear. The hair on Milea's neck stands up as she faces him. Casimir grins cockily when she faces him. "I'm surprised you are here. Weren't you avoiding me for a time?"

"And I'm still going to ignore you," Milea agrees. "Neil, *stay close to me.*"

"Right," Neil said and backs until he is close to the sorceress. Casimir grins widely.

"Well, let's just cut to the chase, shall we," Casimir offers. He pulls out a large white pearl, his humor increases as it starts to light up.

"Indeed," Milea agrees.

The winds explode around the area causing the elite guards and their leader to cuss and cover their eyes. A large mystical tornado reached for a clear sky, sucking in dust and debris from all around. Milea's figure could barely be seen as she continues her spell. A smile presses across her features as she fades from complete view. Red lights swirled in the winds then explode out, sending Casimir and his guards to the ground. The Orijetie leader stands up and sneers.

"Damn it. She could be anywhere," Casimir swears in anger.

"Sir," a guard approaches and salutes. "Sources have stated that the Selvast Sorceress bought supplies from various vendors. Perhaps she has a ship in the port."

"Then I guess we go see if that's true," Casimir ground out. He storms in the direction of the docks.

The sun is slowly lowering to kiss the ocean. Many of the sea animals are heading to their roost for the coming night. The docks are no longer lively as ships harbor for the night. The tavern at the end of the docks, however, is more than energetic as music and laughter thump from the thin walls. Sonja sat at the edge of the pier, surveying the ocean as it rolls towards the shore, thinking about the adventure that is at hand. Brion and Vicki both perk up when they hear men shouting from the *Charred Rose*. A glance over shows the captured slaves are escaping and the crew is ill fit to deal with the mass exodus. Some of the former captives toss a few crew members over the side of the ship.

"Well, looks like Grachel has redeemed herself," Vicki concludes as she shifts her weight back a little. "A'drianis would be proud of her."

"Yep. Yep," Sonja agrees. The winds in the area pick up causing the girl to cover her eyes.

"What in Ublivorion," Brion stands up and focuses on the *Lady of the Night.* A large tornado is suspended over the vessel. "What's going on?"

"Mom's back," Sonja cheers. She did a whoop of joy, running up the ramp onto the ship.

"Why did she do that," Brion asks. "That is a teleportation spell, right?"

"I'm not sure. Let's go up and find out," Vicki shrugs and swats his shoulder. She headed up the ramp. Brion scowls then muster up his bravery to follow her.

The village patrol struggles against the flow of former slaves as the people hurry to the exit of the port town to get away. The uniformed men dropped words that could make a sailor blush as they make their way to the black ship. Casimir sees the activity but decides to take a look at the newest ship in the docks. He's never seen the light-colored vessel in the history of his rule. His instincts told him it is enchanted. He sees Vicki's back as she finishes boarding the craft with a grin. Casimir then scowls when he notices Brion follow her up. He is not expecting the woman to be truthful when she said she is promised. Casimir once again glances over at the *Charred Rose* just in time to see Grachel and her friends escape during the madness. Fires start on the black ship adding to the sounds of the crew unclean words as they try to put them out.

"See if you can find out what happened," Casimir orders one of his men.

The soldier bows then heads to the crippled ship. The lead orijetie stalks down the pier to the *Lady of the Night* with the rest of his escort. Unfiltered, adulterated words fill the air as Brion makes his way onto the deck of the ship. Vicki is talking to her brother about the battle in the marketplace. The woman scowls when she hears the news of Casimir. Milea smiles at Brion as he approaches her and holds up her hand. A small light blue root appears clasp between her thumb and finger causing her companion's eyes to light up with excitement. Milea then causes a second object to appear in her hand as she gave the root to Brion.

"Dopie ginger is a powerful herb that has unique needs. Use this to cut off a small piece and chew it," Milea holds up a small golden knife. "Nothing larger than your thumbnail else you run a risk of making yourself sicker. Once every five hours will be fine." She presents the knife to him, hilt first.

"Thank you," Brion accepts the knife. He cut the dopie ginger and starts chewing on the herb. He notices the sweet yet spicy taste of the root and his stomach settle down immediately. "I am in your debt, Lady Milea."

"You are most welcome. I understand about the sea's mischief upon one's stomach," Milea beams a smile. "Nightfall is in about a half hour." She turns to the setting sun. "Neil, your orders?"

"Wait till the sun goes down. Watch the entertainment of the *Charred Rose* and the Guards," Neil waves to the horizon then nods to the antics aboard the black ship.

"Then, I'll go check to make sure the supplies made it in good order," Milea said with a slight bow of her head to Neil. "Captain." She walks to the trap door of the ship. It opens at her mental command allowing her to enter into the hull. The door closes just as quiet.

"Vicki. There's something in the Crow's nest that I wanted to show you. I've never seen it before and wondered if you could tell me what it is," Sonja admits.

"Your first time on a ship, everything should be new to you," Vicki chuckles, placing a hand upon her hip. "Alright, let's go and show me this strange item."

"Ok," Sonja beams and charges up the mast. Vicki takes her time going up the long pole.

"So, Neil, tell me how you steer this rig," Brion asks.

"Feeling better already," Neil laughs. "Alright..." He pauses when he hears several boots on the ramp. "Damn, I forgot to raise that thing."

The call of a seabird mimicked laughter as Casimir boards the ship. Vicki gazes down from her bird's eye view and issues a few insults at what she sees. The woman then ducks down into her new hiding place. Sonja shows a little disapproval but decides to stay put with Vicki. Below deck, Milea hears the heavy boots of the men above her. She makes a quiet yet curious sound as she walks over to a barrel of water. She lifts the lid and waves her hand over the reflective surface.

The image of the deck comes into clear view causing Milea to utter words her mother will not be pleased to hear under her breath when she sees Casimir on the ship. She did not, however, see Ajahn. The elite guards begin to spread out causing both Brion and Neil to give them curious looks. Neil leans upon his wheel and clears his throat catching their attention.

"Welcome aboard," Neil offers. "You do realize that you are trespassing. I do not tolerate that very well. Too many pirates upon the seas." He leaned a little. "I am the helmsman of this vessel. By what reason are there Lybrinthian guards on my ship?"

"You are the one with Milea in the marketplace," Casimir recognizes. "Where is the Selvast Sorceress?"

"Lady Milea had pressing business elsewhere," Neil shrugs. "Brion, can you make sure our supplies are in order."

"Aye Captain," Brion moseys to the hull doors.

"Hold it right there, Elf," Casimir demands.

"Is there something you need, Human," Brion requests with a raised eyebrow. His voice calms at the moment.

"I saw you board this vessel with a l'vane woman," Casimir decided to ignore the elf's comment. "Where is she? Is she yours?"

"She is my friend if that's what you are asking," Brion explains. Casimir's eyes lit up with greed. "As far as where she's at. I'd wager back in the marketplace."

"So, she is a magic user," Casimir concludes.

"Most l'vane women are," Neil exaggerates. "However, it is the l'vane men that you need to worry about. We tend to become very cranky when those we protect are threatened." He motions his head towards the elf. "Brion is raised in the way of the l'vane man. Trust me, he is just as deadly as I am." Brion manages not to scoff at the notion.

"I see," Casimir runs his fingers through his hair and decides to use a canned answer. "Your ship is new to Lybrinthia Port. I need to know who are the members of your crew and what cargo do you possess."

"We are not carrying cargo at the moment. We are docked here to prepare for a long journey to the tropics," Neil said, rubbing his neck with one hand. "As far as crew, well, you should have heard and smelt them in the tavern up the way." He points his chin towards the small building.

"Then since your crew is away, you won't mind if I take a look around," Casimir casually folds his arms and faces the captain.

"Only if you dismiss your escort," Neil counters just as casual. "A big strong Sa'Jak such as you do not need an escort for such a trivial inspection." He watches the orijetie man think about the situation.

"Go back to the inn," Casimir orders, turning to his men. "Tell my father, I'll be there shortly." The men salute, turn, and march in perfect order as they left the ship. "Well, captain."

"Be my guests. Look around as much as you want," Neil offered. He keeps an eye on Casimir as the orijetie enters the sleep cabin. "Hoist anchor. Set course due south towards the tropics, our beckon will be lit very soon."

Brion leans against the mast as the ship once again works her magic. The anchor lifts without making a sound and the sails tie in place. The ship sways a little as Casimir inspected the sleep quarters meticulously. There are six cots on the ship, all of them empty. He bent down and peers under each one just to make sure his quarry is not hiding. Showing displeasure upon his features, he scrutinized the various charts on the walls of the vessel. He grumbles, never bothering to learn to read sea charts. He is not going to be a seafaring man anyway.

Casimir never got the concept of his father sending him to the port town. It is actually a blessing in disguise as now he can do whatever he wants with no consequences. The ship once again sways and leans a little. Casimir gutters more than a few angry and unclean words at the movements as he stares out the window. The docks are drifting away.

"What in Ublivorion," Casimir shouts and hurries out of the sleep cabin to an empty ship. "Captain?!"

He shouts to the increasing winds in an attempt to locate the last living person upon the ship. There is no response to his calls or pleas as the ship coasts to the open ocean. He turns to the helm and sees the wheel moving back and forth as if someone is operating it. However, there is no living creature standing at the helm, unlike a few minutes ago Casimir is taken aback, what happened to the l'vane man he just talked to? What about the elf, surely, he is still aboard the ship. The ropes move and twist on their own as the sails shift to catch the best breeze. The ship increases her speed from the adjustment.

"Lords of Ublivorion, I'm on a haunted ship!" Casimir exclaims.

The *Lady of the Night* lean and adjust her ropes again as Casimir runs over to pull on them. He is trying to lower the sails to stop the ship. The rope snaps at him, slapping his hand as if indignant that he dares to touch her. Casimir yelps a little from the pain then gawks in awe as the entire rig continues to move as if a gaggle of strong men works her. The docks are becoming smaller as her speed increase the ocean now in sight. The laughter of a child causes chills to run down Casimir's spine. He turns then jumps back when he sees Vicki standing in front of the wheel of the ship, above the door to the sleep cabin.

"Welcome aboard the '*Dragon Rose*,'" Vicki announces then leans forward, her left forearm upon her raised knee. "I am her captain, I'm sure you know my name."

"Ra'jil," Casimir barely contains his scream of surprise. "Wait, you're dead." Vicki smiles as he continues to ramble. "Your daughter married my cousin. You were Queen of Deltor when you died. How in Ublivorion are you the captain of this ship?"

"What's your first conclusion? In death, we tend to go towards what we love the most. I loved my husband, true enough, but I defiantly loved my ship as well. Since my husband has moved to another, I figured what the hell." Vicki shrugs. "Did you want to join me? You were oh so eager to find out what stamina I had in the marketplace." She said those words with a slight seductive sound to them.

"I... umm... changed my mind. I want nothing to do with ghosts," Casimir blurts out.

"Suit yourself," Vicki straightens with a shrug. "Toss him off the rig." She calls out to her 'invisible crew'.

The ship leans to the left as Casimir turns around. He sees no one behind him and turns back to the helm. Vicki is now gone. Panic settles in as Casimir hurries to the stern of the ship. The docks are just about out of sight now and he feels that he may have to jump in order to free himself of the curse. Milea fades into view behind the orijetie, his back still to her. She lifts her hand and causes a strong force to raise the orijetie up with such quickness that he gasps for air. Milea then makes a throwing motion.

Casimir feels himself pull back then toss towards the docks. His bellow of fear is cut short when he lands in the water. He manages to right himself out of the sea as he turned back to see the ship turning the corner. He let out a long breath in relief; at least he is free from the cursed ship. Realization settles in causing Casimir to grumble at his predicament. He has to swim back to the shore. Casimir decides that once he arrives, he will get hold of Ajahn to figure out how to send the apparition of Ra'jil back to her grave.

The *Lady of the Night* now on the open ocean increases her speed as the sun slips below the horizon. Vicki laughs as she stands at the stern of the ship just behind the sorceress. Milea dusts her hands with a satisfactory smile upon her features. Neil continues to express his humor as he slides down his rope, he had harbored in the crow's nest as soon as Casimir enter the sleeping cabin. Brion approaches from the bow of the ship since he took shelter in the hull right after Neil gave the command to depart. He has witnessed the events with Milea using her reflective surface thus he too is well humored by the events. Sonja slides down the mast and hugs her mother, congratulating her on the mystical toss.

"Phenomenal performance Vicki," Milea complements.

"Great throwing arm to you, milady," Vicki acknowledges the sorceress. "I'm not sure if he will freak out when he sees me again or not."

"He might think you're still Ra'jil. That could be humorous in certain situations," Milea contemplates. "If the real Ra'jil returned to Lybrinthia. I wonder; what would Casimir attempt?"

"I say we locate Ra'jil and find out," Brion opted. Sonja cheers her agreement. Milea smiles at the mischief.

"I better get to the wheel," Neil chuckles a little. "That's my girl." He pats part of the ship affectionately.

"He loves this ship," Vicki concludes.

"I'm glad. The journey to the Temple of Light would have been very rough if he did not get along with the *Lady of the Night*," Milea says, and watches as the sun's light causes the sails to blush a little.

The night came with a clear sky, the star that Neil has mention blinks as if beckoning them. It is huge and bright blue, immediately swallowing up the light of other stars that surround it. Neil provides an order to follow the brilliant heavenly body. The ship responds to his orders, adjusting her sails. Milea stands at the bow of the ship, surveying the dark, watery, abyss.

The ocean parts freely before the bow of the *Lady of the Night* with a strong current pushing on her, leaning the ship to the left. The sails adjust once again to right the course of travel. Vicki stands up on one of the rails, holding a strong rope to allow the wind to whistle through her hair playfully. Sonja hops from the crow's nest to a rope and shimmies down to stand next to her mother. Brion watches with interest the way Neil steers the ship prompting a quick lesson. After his tutoring, Neil decides to let Brion handle the ship as he goes to stand next to his sister.

"Stars are shining, not a cloud in the sky. A good night to return to the seas," Neil admits with a deep breath in.

"So says the old sea dog," Vicki teases. "Do you want to scare Ublivorion out of a merchant ship?"
"Perhaps a little later. Let's complete Milea's mission first. Then we can see if we can borrow the *Lady of the Night* to scare the merchants. Who knows, their reaction might be more exciting than

Casimir's," Neil promises then grins. Vicki chuckles from the memory.

CHAPTER FIVE

The Storm

The low rumbling of the ocean whispers to those aboard the *Lady of the Night* in a near hypnotic tone Vicki stands at the helm of the ship, watching the bright blue star and making sure that the ship continues to sail towards it. Brion decided to go into the sleep cabin an hour ago, his dopie ginger must have been wearing off. Vicki knows that the elf will have to toughen up. Unless you are a magic user blessed with the gift of teleportation, traveling by sea is the only means to go from one continent to the other.

Then there is the ability of flight and the beings she knows with those abilities have wings that catch the wind. Vicki scowls at the thought, although she has controlled her fear of heights all of life. She never truly rid herself of the panic she feels when she is taken into the air at a rapid pace.

The ropes and sails shift as the winds come from a different direction. Vicki smiles, she likes the ship as well. Unlike her sibling, however, she never captained any vessel. Most ships have men for captains. The one example of a female captain is Ra'jil. Vicki stares into the distance in thought. She recollects a childhood memory of discovering news of Ra'jil's retirement came to the land. The legend's death stunned an entire generation of sailors and pirates. The only happy seamen were, of course, the merchants.

"What's the matter, sis," Neil asks. Vicki glances over at him; her features indicate she is displeased with the surprise. Neil flashes a grin. "Oh, sorry. Glad you're not fully armed."

"Lucky you. I'm thinking about our favorite pirate woman," Vicki leans upon the wheel.

"Ah yes. I think I recall hearing Milea say that the *Lady of the Night* is a replica of the *Dragon Rose*," Neil places his hands behind his head and takes a deep breath of ocean air. "That helped spook Casimir a bit. Not to mention your star performance, of course."

"Thanks," Vicki smiles at her sibling. "Milea and I had a brief discussion about Ra'jil in Churn. She seems to think that our pirate lady is stubborn enough to still be alive."

"Now that legend, I would love to meet. Sadly, unless Ra'jil is raised from the grave. Neither of us will see her," Neil said with a rub of his chin. "Though I guess there is hope for it."

"I'll keep that hope. But like I said before. I think we need to take this opportunity to study the legendary Sorceress of Selvast Forest," Vicki offers.

"With her legend in the making of daughter. That girl is not only quick of feet. But her mind is also fast. Did you see how fast she learned to tie the ropes," Neil said. "It took me several months to learn some of those."

"Years for me. I was a little jealous at first then I thought," Vicki slowly exhales as she reflects on what she saw. "Sonja could make one hell of an assassin, with just a little more training."

"Has to learn a lot of martial arts first and she's a little old to give her a good training lesson. I learned quite a few from my father before I graduated," Neil runs his finger through his windblown hair as he recollects his memory.

"Trust me on this. She's already mastered at least three techniques. I tried to count them when she hit that man, and he went down," Vicki smiles and glances at her brother. "While we were hiking up to Dagger's Point, Sonja admitted she thought she hit him twelve times. Then she broke his arm. All in the time it takes you to blink an eye."

"Twelve? Who would teach her techniques that would bring down a muscle-bound devorian with twelve hits in record time," Neil questions.

"She's standing at the bow," Vicki motions again towards Milea. "Think I'll have to ask her a few questions when we reach our destination. Her mind seems occupied with that."

"She looks like she's by herself. She's very lovely to look at," Neil focuses on Milea with a grin. He realizes that the sorceress is standing alone, her daughter nowhere in sight. "Where's Sonja?"

"Asleep in the crow's nest. She seems to be in love with high places," Vicki nods up with her head.

"I'll have to do an assessment of the rascal's skills later. Right now, let me talk to my legendary client," Neil walks towards Milea.

"Don't do anything crazy, bro. Just remember that something is troubling her and she's had all night to think about it." Vicki chastises a little. She watches her brother wave without turning around. "Alright, I'll just hope she turns you into something unpleasant and not cut your head off when you annoy her."

The ocean breeze blows strong enough to tease Milea's hair. The sorceress habitually moves it out of her line of sight to stare into the horizon. The blue star pulsates as if encouraging them to hurry along. A gentle spray of ocean water wet Milea's face causing her to sigh. Her thoughts engross on what she may find at the Temple of Light. Milea closes her eyes, focuses upon her sister. She did not get a response and the silence causes the worry within to swell a little higher. Milea did not want to fathom losing her twin sister, not after all she has gone through to find her.

Her twin sister, Maya, had been found ten winters ago. The girl, now a woman, had been kidnapped and taken to a horrible place. In that place, she endured a terror most would not have lived through. But Maya did. Their mother saw the pain in Maya's heart and body, so she ordered her to go to the Temple of Light to heal. At the same time, Milea discovered a close friend that also needed to be rescued. This woman is thought to be dead by all, even her family.

Maya helped her sister free her friend, and now she recovers in Dorma, an island located in the tropics, on the equator.

Afterward, Maya was taken to the Temple of Light in the Boiling Seas. Although it is located near the tropics, the Boiling Seas is very hard to find by ship. It is unclear if it is a little north or a little south of the large planet's equator. Milea tilts her head back in thought, closing her eyes.

"Hold on just a little longer, sister. I'm coming," Milea whispers.

The sound of the open sea at night tampers down to near silence as the time and travel hasten along. Every once in a while, a giant whale-seal will crest and snort as it exhales and refills its lungs to plunge into the debts. The ocean current lap against the ship's stern, speeding her journey. Neil is wise to pause at a distance to study the sorceress as he takes a moment to reflect on his quest. Up until now he has not much time to do so between the enchanted ship and the supply run.

Now, his mind reels with the many stories of Milea Sirus of Selvast Forest that he has encountered in his travels. None of those stories prepares him or anyone he thinks to meet the woman face to face. Neil's mind consolidated the different legends and myths of Milea and goes over them in his mind one by one. A particularly popular legend has it that she is raised by a goddess thus blessed with not only immortality but also the wisdom of ages past.

Neil's face seems to twist in a little pain as his brain works overtime and scraps together a group of stories that cast Milea as a warrior queen who could slay a man just as fast as the legendary seductress, she is, could seduce him. Neil held his head when he recalls the final legend that boasts of her defeating a horde of immortals by herself.

Neil grumbles about his head spinning alerting Milea to the known fact that she is not alone anymore. The sorceress turns as Neil brings his eyes up. Milea takes a deep breath in and releases it as their eyes meet. The l'vane man swallows his pride as her enchanting brown eyes bore deep into his auburn orbs.

"I take it that you are curious," Milea observed causing the man to blink.

"Just a little bit," Neil rubs his chin before entering into the moonlight. "I've heard many legends and stories about you. But none live up to the beauty I behold before me. Truly such elegance deserves a song of equal beauty. I've yet to hear one that I would recite to charm such a fine woman." He bowed a little playfully.

"Ah, a bit of a flirt, are we? Let's just say some legends are greatly exaggerated by bards such as yourself, while others remain true," Milea said as humor relaxes her stance.

"Well, Vicki mentioned the battle in Churn and compared it to Ajahn. Are you a forest fae or a goddess," Neil leans on a rail.

Neil's hair flows from back to front as the ship continues her path. He rubs the back of his neck then rests his arm again. Milea studies the bold ship captain, noticing that he is calm and relax. The moonlight brightens a little as she faces him completely and places a hand upon her hip. A slow smile of mischief takes over her beautiful face as she calculates her answers. She is also amazed that he is so bold upon a ship that she provided and not his own. Milea concludes that she will entertain him, if it will lessen the tension of the trip.

"Neither," Milea answers in confidence.

"Alright. Queen or Seductress," Neil asks.

"Umm," Milea places a finger on her chin as she rolled her eyes skyward as if to think about the answer. "Yes," she said and focuses back on Neil. "Why should I be one when I can be both at the same time? I figure that a Queen has to be a bit of a Seductress at some point in her reign."

"Ok," Neil straightens. He sees Milea chuckle a little. "Are you mischievous, milady?"

"Defiantly," Milea confirms. "Most defiantly. But not as much as a forest fae, even if I had been raised among them."

"Ok, one more question then," Neil proposes. Milea nods and waits patiently. "Alright, mortal or immortal?"

"Different from goddess I take it," Milea chuckles. "Hmm.... Actually... I'm not sure. I was born mortal but raised by an immortal. An Eltis to be precise. So can I say simply 'yes' to that one?"

"Works for me," Neil agrees. He then yawned and stretched, pretending to be tired so that he would not push his luck. "I guess it's time to hit the sack. I'll try not to wake Brion and will relieve Vicki in about two hours."

"Relax, Neil. If you oversleep and Vicki is fatigue, I'll take the helm for a little bit. We follow that star, right," Milea turns to the pulsating star.

"That we do. I've a couple of questions about the journey. But I think that it will wait until morning. I'm sure Brion would like to ask some questions as well," Neil requests.

"Of course," Milea said. "Pleasant dreams, Neil."

Milea's voice flows purposefully with a hint of seduction. Neil pauses before shaking his head and grumbling a little as he heads to the sleep cabin. Milea grins mischievously as she watches him take his leave. She notices that Vicki is entertained by her brother's grumbling. Neil orders his sister to 'hush' when she requests if he is fine. That brings a round of boisterous laughter from the lady l'vane. Milea laughs a little and returns her gaze to the pulsating star in the distance. The light shimmies a little, as if it too is humored by the recent events.

The twin moons play peek-a-boo with the ocean as clouds drift pass. The noise of the sea and its residences begin to quiet down. Neil takes a deep breath in and lets it out, collapsing upon his bed. It has been a very tiring day for him, starting out as dancing and singing and ends with a trip to a fowl place with a legend. Neil grumps as he turns onto his back and stares at the ceiling, the journey itself has just begun. On a regular ship, they have at least three months before they reach the tropics then who knows how long for the temple of light.

With the ship being enchanted, he hopes to shave off over half of that time, especially if they are going to a rescue. Neil places his hands behind his head and exhales again, he will get with Brion and they will interrogate Milea of what she knows about their destination. The *Lady of the Night* tilts and sways just a little as Neil mind slows down. The motion starts to rock all of the ship's passengers into slumber. The captain closes eyes drifting off into a deep and satisfying sleep. In a blink of an eye, the gentle motion turns into a violent one, tossing the l'vane man onto the floor of the cabin.

"What the devil," Neil exclaims.

The ship tilts again causing Brion to flip out of his cot as it turns over. The elf shakes his head to clear it before moving out of the way of a large desk. Neil barely gets to his feet to stumble to the exit. He drops well versed unclean words when he lost his footing and tumble to the right wall as the ship once again leans. The sleeping cots scrap the floor as they move back and forth as the lantern battles to stay upon its hook.

The winds howl and moan through the windows, creating a whistling effect that raises hair upon the neck of the listeners. Thunder's muffle roar instigates Neil to repeat his swears, realizing that they have sailed straight into a storm. The *Lady of the Night* rolls the other way. Brion holds onto a large pole as the ship manages to right herself once more. Neil draws upon his great vocabulary of unhealthy words, this time for the ship, as he runs out of the room. The rain hammers his body, lightning streaks across the sky.

Thunder bellow in the sky and echoes in the ears and hearts of those aboard the ship as Neil arrive at Vicki's side. The woman's muscles are bunched as she battles both the ship and the angry sea. Just a few feet from the helm, Milea wrestles with the ropes and jumps back when they snap at her as if angry that she dares to touch them.

"The storm came up all of the sudden. Milea and I were having a conversation when it just hit. Nothing was in the sky. She does not think it's natural." Vicki said through grit teeth.

Thunder crashes as the ship is slammed to the left by a rogue wave. The wheel forces Vicki to jump back away from it. Rain empties from the sky in unexperienced quantities, creating pools of water upon the deck. The wheel spins uncontrollably in both directions as the siblings watch in awe. Neil searches for a pattern the wheel is spinning then moves forward and takes it. The item jerks several times in his hands, the ship groans a little as if in protest to his strength. The wheel itself yanks as Neil growls and holds fast. Another groan echoes upon the winds as the ship yields to the captain's wishes.

"Vicki, secure the sails then secure yourself," Neil instructs. "Give the same order to Milea."

"Aye Captain," Vicki says, then swears as her eyes roll up towards the crow's nest. "Sonja, come down from there." She shouts up. Milea follows Vicki's line of sight as lightning careens across the sky.

"I'm coming!" Sonja yells back down.

Rain pours down in bucket loads creating a thin layer of water between the wood and the feet of those aboard the *Lady of the Night*. The winds whistle and moan as Sonja gets to the edge of crow's nest as it is tilting to the right. She can barely balance until the wind hit the ship, sending it to the left. Sonja gasps at the sudden change in direction, she tries to compensate but ends up slipping.

Milea unleashes a group of unforgiving words when she sees her daughter launched into the air. Whatever spell she cast will not affect the girl due to her natural abilities to resist them. The air rushes by Sonja's ears as well as her cry of fear as she falls to the deck. Her instinct has her reaching out and grabs a rope. It snaps yet she holds on for life and swings down, swirling around the huge mast in the process. Sonja and the rope manage to go around the main mast twice before the girl lands on the deck.

"Sonja, are you alright?" Milea asks with a voice full of worry.

"I... I think so." Sonja admits.

The ship is slam from behind; the stern elevates and all but Neil to stumble towards the bow of the ship. Brion catches hold of a rope and uses the rails to pull himself back to the helm. Vicki slips and falls to the deck yet her fingers manage to find a hold so that she did not continue and fall over the edge. Milea holds onto a rail then her child as they feel near weightlessness from the extreme tilt of the ship. The *Lady of the Night* is then pushed from the front, righting her back to level. Vicki gets to her feet and swears a sailor's oath as she hurries over and yanks on a rope; the ship assists her in hoisting the remaining sails to tie them into place. Neil mutters his relief when he accounts for everyone, no one has fallen into the murky debts yet and he hopes they do not.

"What in the world is going on?" Sonja inquires as she and her mother steady their footing.

"This is a magical storm. I do not know who or what brought it onto us." Milea explains.

"Neil said secure yourselves. Sonja, no more fancy dismounting of the crow's nest." Vicki scolds as she completes her chores.

"Are you ladies alright?" Brion asks at his approach.

The wind whips around as invisible hands untie the ropes. The cloth dangle in the winds and pulled from side to side as the ship turns in response. The groans of the wood are silenced by the roar of the thunder. A strong wind swoops in and around the sails, ripping them to shreds right before the eyes of those on board the ship. Rain knocks the tattered pieces to the deck, pinning them there with the beating of the water. Waves slam into the ship, sending it deeper into the storm with no way out. Vicki gawks at the outcome of the sails, her instinct informing her that this is not going to bode well for anyone if they did not get out of this hurricane.

"Go relieve Neil, he needs to help with the rig. Someone check on the hull door to make sure it's secure. Then secure yourself, this is not going to be a good ride." Vicki gives orders to her passengers.

"I got securing the hull." Sonja hurries over to the trapdoor.

Brion heads to the helm as Milea goes to secure the ropes of the vessel; at least they can keep them intact. The winds spin around like miniature tornadoes as they abuse with the wounded vessel. Brion arrives at the helm to see Neil still fighting even as exhaustion from the battle lines his face. The ocean churns and boils, the storm making it near impossible to distinguish the darkened sky from the angry sea.

The distant horizon nonexistent as both heaven and earth merge into one merciless monsoon. The ocean pushes the ship onto a peak, and seems to pause briefly before letting the *Lady of the Night* slide down a large wave into a valley of the sea. The effects cause all on board to unleash the words of their choice at the sudden change in heights. The towering liquid surrounds the ship for a moment then once again pushes under to lift the vessel up the mountain of water.

Brion finally convinces Neil to release the wheel to him and holds fast as the l'vane hurries off to assist his sister with the rest of the ship. Sonja gasps and holds to the handle of the trap door as the ship tosses left then right. She finishes off tying the latch and announces the hull's secure to the rest of the crew. Neil tosses the girl a rope and orders her to secure herself to the main mast as he battles the elements to reach his employer. Sonja catches the rope and drops it at first; the water makes it slippery to hold. She gathers up the item then move to the mast to complete her task.

"This ship's not sinkable, is it?" Neil inquires when he is standing next to Milea.

"She will be harder than most to bring below the waves," Milea assures. A lightning bolt slams into the back of the ship causing all on board to yell or cuss in surprise. "Perhaps I've spoken too soon."

Waves and wind toss the ship and crew about in an endless cycle. A large wall of water lifts the ship, causing it to stop for a moment then travel backward. Brion cusses and holds the helm with all his might, his grip slip as the nonstop rain hammers all on the ship. Brion witnesses the ship wheel spin around a few times, hesitate for a moment then spin again as if invisible hands guide them into their doom. Brion swears as he grabs the wheel once more and holds fast.

The force upon the wheel tried to once again break free, twisting twice but could not release from the elf's grip. Vicki, with the assistance of Milea, put out the flames started by the lightning strike and flying debris. The ship bucks and sways violently as whitecaps from different directions punch it around relentlessly. Sonja reties her rope, sitting upon the deck of the ship and stays put as instructed by her mother. Neil finishes securing ropes along the perimeter as seawater crest over the sides washing over all of the crew.

"...*mortal.... pest...,*"a female voice whispers upon the winds.

The faint words caused Milea to pause and scan her surroundings and with pure tenacity, the sorceress journeys to the very front of the ship. The ship sways brutally making walking almost impossible. Milea grabs a rope and holds on when her footing slips from an unexpected motion. She exhales some words as her soaked feet squishes under her weight as she regains her balance.

Vicki calls to the sorceress then mutters another oath and follows when she notices that the woman did not hear her over the thunder and typhoon noise. Milea stops at the bow of the ship and listens as Vicki arrives next to her. The view at the front of the ship is a horrific nightmare for any seafaring folk and the stuff of legends. The sky is blocked by several large mountains of angry sea before the ship manages to break through. The women hold on as the water washes over the entire vessel. Vicki glances back to make sure that her brother and companions are still aboard and is relieved when she sees no one is lost, yet.

"Milea what's wrong?" Vicki asks above the howling winds.

"I thought I heard the owner of this storm," Milea answers and glances over the horizon. She blinks and takes several paces back, her features registering shock. "Mother of Light!"

The *Lady of the Night* leans as Vicki once again faces the front and unleashes her own prayers. The image of a large blue dragon glares back at the women from the gloom, its entire body swallowed by the night and undetectable. The head of the dragon, seen with the lightning strikes surrounding it, is at least twelve feet tall. The teeth of the beast are eight feet very noticeable as the dragon yawns, the mouth open, and heads to the ship. The gleam of the enormous ivory reflected the images of those on board through the darkness. Lightning shows that the dragon is either angry or humored right before it suddenly disappears and is replaced by a swelling of the water.

Vicki drops words that would make even the hardest sailor blush as she turns and heads to the middle of the ship. Milea stands her ground and casts a spell using the lightning all around her. The bolt slams into the wave and reflects back at Milea with greater intensity. The sorceress deflected the lightning back into the sky and witnesses it explode in the clouds. Thunder sounds of mock laughter as Milea retreats to the middle of the ship.

"Neil! We have a problem," Vicki shouts.

"What?" Neil slants to her direction and cusses. "Brion, Hard to Port!"

"He forgot to tell me which side is port," Brion growls as he yanks on the wheel.

The ship turns to the face the oncoming tsunami as Milea orders Vicki to tie herself down. The sorceress continues to the helm in order to assist Brion to make sure he is secured to the ship. The ship's bow begins to incline as a moan escapes the wood going up another mountain of the ocean. Neil slips and slides as he heads to the bow to observe the large wave and the ship's reaction to it. A low groan of 'fear' escapes the wooden edifice as it rides up the wave. Neil takes hold of a rope, also noticing that the wind is whirling from all directions. There is no way to know where they are or what time they spent in the hurricane.

Behind him, Milea stumbles to her destination and trips up the landing leading to the helm. She glances back at the wall of water before making her way to Brion. The elf is standing with his feet firmly planted to the floor, concentrating on maintaining the ship's course. He blinks when he feels Milea tie rope around his waist then wrapping it around the base of the helm. Brion expresses his thanks before returning his focus upon the task at hand. Milea goes behind the elf and ties herself to the ship's railing, using one of many knots she has learned from her past. Vicki finishes securing herself then surveyed the ship to see where her brother is at. When she locates him, she cusses and prays at the same time; Neil is standing at the bow of the ship without a rope.

"Oh Ublivorion! Neil what are you doing," Vicki demands. "Neil!"

The rain changes course and blows sideways in the powerful winds. Lightning flashes and thunder roars in response to Vicki's outcry and drowns out any words that she utters. The dark clouds above thicken, stooping lower in the sky and turning it a mind-numbing shade of green. Neil did not hear his sister's words, oblivious to the elevation of the clouds. His jaw slack as he gawks at the sight of the swelling water as it transforms into the shape of a dragon. Neil is keen to see that the *Lady of the Night* is riding up the front of the watery beast.

An evil grin lights up upon the dragon's maul with the lightning as the water swells even higher increasing the incline considerably. Neil spews foul language as he hits the deck and slides until his hands find the rope used by Sonja to tie the hull hatch down. Neil holds on to the knot and grabs a piece rope that tumbles back with his free hand. He hastily ties one end of the rope around his waist then secures the second end to the knot.

"Bravo, Sonja for learning to tie that knot efficiently," Neil showers the girl with accolades as the wave grows even larger.

Gale force winds slam into the back of the ship, forcing it up the large tsunami. The water is rising still higher suspending those tied to the wooden edifice to dangle in the air. The ship stalls when neither wind nor momentum could get it any higher. Sonja glances to the back of the ship and sees they are several hundred feet above the ocean. She closes her eyes and hugs her legs to her chest as those around her discover the same thing and said a prayer or swear.

Milea glares at the front of the ship and the enormous dragon head grinning at them. The dragon opens its mouth in a silent roar and slams onto the ship. Milea erects a barrier at the point of impact. The water crashes into the shield and spreads out across the ship, leaving it unshaved. Milea relaxes when the wave finishes.

A second wave hit right after the first, catching all off guard. Much of the water from it goes over the *Lady of the Night* with the exception of the tail end that wallops the ship, harshly. The cracking of wood causes sickness to swell in the pit of Neil's stomach. The ship moans and groans from the splintering wood. The water finishes going over the ship leaving those aboard the *Lady of the Night* alive. Sonja coughs a little prompting Vicki to make sure the girl's airways are free from liquid by thumping her hand against her back a few times. Brion and Milea did not get hit with the same amount of water but, like the rest of the crew, continues to be soaked by the rainfall.

"Damn, this is a bad night. I've got to get to the helm," Neil said, his words unheard over the winds and thunder

The ship's accent is now turned into a rapid and dangerous decent straight at the ocean that churned many feet below. The ship hits the water but does not sink, bobbing and swaying violently in the winds, all sense of direction lost. Neil untied his hand and stands in determination to take over the ship to get them to safety. Another bolt of lightning crashes right next to the ship but did not touch, electrifying the water around. Milea places her hand on the ship to neutralize the effects to those aboard. The lightning absorbs into the sorceress with minimum effect, she swears a little from the extra shock at the end. The wind starts to tangle up the ropes and anything loose upon the deck. As the ship lurch when a wave pushes into it from the rear.

The violent rocking and throwing nearly toss Neil over the edge of the ship as he made steady yet slow progress to his destination. He regains his footing and grabs hold of a rope when the ship rolls to the left. Vicki calls her brother's name as he is thrown overboard by the movement. The rope goes tight as the ship leans back right. Neil hops back over the rail, still holding the item he is smart enough to grab. He hit the deck, landing upon his hindquarters. Neil drops a few unkind words as he holds his offended rear end and once again struggles to his feet, fully aware of the hazards the rain and seawater made the unstable deck.

"What in all of Ublivorion kind of storm is this? We should have sailed out of it by now," Neil growls angrily at the sky.

Thunder roars as female laughter drifts on the gale winds catching the attention of the sorceress. Milea holds onto the rail and pulls herself back to standing, and listens as the voice once again sounds. The wind whips around her, yanking at her wet clothing and tangled mane as she scans the area. Her eyes focus on the front of the ship as a tingling sensation went down her spine. Milea shutters a little from the sensation, more of a surprise than fear. The sensation intensifies when the voice threatens the ship and crew once more.

Milea frowns as the strong feelings mean one thing, they are dealing with a Tragin. This particular creature has the power to create storms. Lightning careened across the sky as a pair of eyes appears in the clouds, watching the ship and passengers struggle against the elements. A wave whacks the bow of the ship, sending it back into the middle of the storm, despite Brion's efforts to keep it on its path out. Milea scolds herself; she should have known better and paid closer attention. Now, she has to get them out of the maelstrom before the Tragin tires of toying with them and drags them under the waves. She unties her ropes and holds onto the rail, taking steps to get to the wheel.

Neil witnesses the sorceress stand and releases from the safety lines. He turns his attention to the bow of the ship in time to see the clouds dip still lower in the sky as thunder booms. Waves swell and disappear as the ocean churns and gurgles as if a giant cauldron boiling over. The bellows of the winds comes to a sudden stop bringing attention to the bow of the ship from all the passengers. The sky lights up in various green colors as the lower clouds form a tuff of a tail.

The clouds wag as if a scolding feline, then touches down onto the water. Cold winds rushed forward towards the thin line, causing it to grow rapidly. The low rumbling drowns out any hopes of conversation. The winds pull on the ship and those on board ferociously. Milea is just able to hold on as everything that is loose upon the deck soon flies off and heads into the monster cyclone. Neil shakes his head when he sees the new threat and turns to the helm.

"Brion! Face the water spout," Neil shouts at the top of his lungs and points to the front.

"What? Are you crazy? That's not a spout," Brion corrects equally as loud as the captain. True, the twister is at least a mile wide. "We'll be thrown completely off course! If not killed!"

"Already off course. As far as killed," Neil argues. "Trust me on this one."

"Allow me," Milea said causing Brion to glance at her. She untied his ropes. "Secure yourself to the ship. This is the work of a Tragin. I will explain more when we get through this." She replaced him at the wheel.

"What are you about to do," Brion challenge.

"Get us out of this little spin. Sit in front of the wheel and use the rope to tie yourself. This is guaranteed to be a bumpy ride," Milea answered.

Brion stares at her for a few seconds then sits down with his back against the post of the wheel as instructed. He takes the rope and ties himself as securely as possible as Milea places her hands upon the wheel. The winds howl in anger as a small gleam crosses her eyes in her concentration. Milea's focus is broken when the wheel twists in agitation. The sorceress holds onto it and releases a hiss of swears when the wheel twist and turns, trying in desperation to break her grip. The wheel finally breaks free and turns left and right rapidly as the ship attempts to divert course away from the ever strengthening and growing sea tornado. Milea grabs the wheel strongly and plants her feet, keeping it from moving.

The ship groans in protest once but eventually obey the new helms person as Milea turns the vessel back into line with the deadly typhoon. Once she is in control of the ship, Milea glares at the approaching tornado a thin red sheen surrounding her body. The dark clouds spin in place and sucking every bit of water and debris within miles around towards its hungry core. An enormous whale-seal bellows in fear as it is yanked out of the water, into the air and torn apart before it reaches the tornado. Neil gawks at the monster tornado in awe and fear. He has stared down many throats of these sea monsters in his lifetime, yet none as large or as ravenous as this one.

"Oswind's Breath," Neil whispers in fear or awe at the sight.

"Exactly what you will smell if you don't tie yourself down," Vicki scolds causing her brother to jump. He has not realized he is so close to his sister.

"Right," Neil sits down next to his sister. He ties the extra rope around his form. "Any idea what she's doing?"

"Ask her when we get through this," Vicki insists. Another wave washes over the whole deck.

"I will NOT be deterred so easily," Milea snarls to the hidden threat.

The red sheen around Milea exploded into full-on flames around the sorceress. She then cast a very strong arcane shield spell and pushes it out. Sonja feels the rush of wind pass her as the arcane shield stretches out completely. The sky above those on the *Lady of the Night* takes on a reddish tint. The rain stops falling on the ship, hitting the barely visible barrier. Thunder roars as if angered by Milea's words and actions.

The twister then starts to move to them in a slow and purposeful dance, consuming all in its path. The ocean below it began to spin in the opposite direction of the clouds, creating an equally large whirlpool. The ship picks up speed heading straight to the dual devil. The *Lady of the Night* made a strange high pitch groan as it is pulled into the tornado. The shield Milea erected brightens as lightning beat upon it mercilessly.

The sorceress flinches but carries on concentrating and holding the vessel steady. The ship begins to go around the interior wall of the tornado, riding it up to the very top of the cyclone. Sonja glances to the bow and sees they are up quite a distance into the air. Her gasp of surprise prompts Vicki to open her eyes and take a deep breath in. Her eyes widen in shock and fear.

"Close your eyes, Vicki," Neil reassures with as much calm as he could muster. "We'll be fine."

"You do realize that we are so far up that I can almost touch the moons that are peeking through the clouds," Vicki informs. Neil blinks before turning then cussing. "Yeah, I thought so, brother."

The rain stops falling above the ship and the deafening sounds of thunder mixes with the hiss of rain is now below the ship. Brion manages to contain his foul language as he closes his eyes and turns his head. The *Lady of the Night* whips around the tornado spiraling upwards in the grips of the monster. Lightning attacks the shielded vessel, determined to break through to destroy it and those on board. Milea swears bitterly and closes her eyes to better concentrate on the attacks and defense of the ship. She has to get them down, but how?

The feeling of fatigue trickles in every muscle of her body, sleep starts to claw at her mind. The sound of feminine laughter in her mind breaks the siren song of exhaustion as Milea opens her eyes. She glances over her shoulder to the back of the ship; something is chasing after them in the clouds. Lightning brightens the darkness briefly to show the huge bulk of a sea creature with large wings spread wide.

The *Lady of the Night* turns one more time before something slaps the ship from behind, tossing it out of the tornado. A high sound of shock or surprise groans from the ship as it is thrust out into the air. The seconds seem like minutes as gravity takes hold of the vessel and pulls it down into a nosedive towards the ocean below Both Vicki and Sonja hollers at the rapid descent of the ship as Neil tries to back up. Brion did not bother to open his eyes but offers up a prayer to Oswind and the Gods of the underworld. He will be meeting them sooner than he hopes.

Milea shifts her focus from shielding the ship to levitating it. She grits her teeth as she mentally catches the heavy craft. It slows down and straightens up to where its belly is facing the water. The ship splashes down onto the ocean creating a large wave where it landed. A harsh slap to the back of the vessel furthers it along, getting it out of the reach of the unnatural storm. The ship bobs a few times with the water around it until it come to a full-on rest. Milea slowly slides to the deck of the ship, the shield she erected long gone. Her gifts deactivate as she let the levitation spell go as well. Neil unties himself and stands up to turn to the stern of the ship. The storm is now a large distance away from them.

"Mom," Sonja snaps the rope that held her in place. She jumps to her feet and hurries to her mother. "Are you alright?"

"Fine, Sonja," Milea said. "Everyone seems to be in one piece."

"One miraculous piece. My lady, I am truly in your debt," Neil agrees as his sister unties herself. Neil then assists Brion to cut his rope and stand.

"Neil," Milea manages to stand with Sonja's assistance. "We are all on this ship. I am not going to let any of us perish without a good effort to prevent it. Oswind would be very displeased if I did not at least try."

"Last person I want to make angry, is Oswind," Neil vocalizes his opinion.

"We have trouble. Mast is broken, in half," Vicki announces. "Sails are all gone. The ship's in bad shape."

"There's an island before us. We could seek assistance there," Brion scouts.

"That is the kingdom of Cyenzie. Its ruler is known as the Jungle King. There is a misunderstanding between King Orin and me," Neil explains, turning towards the tropical beach.

"So, we are in the tropics," Milea muses then glimpse over her shoulder in a fleeting thought, the ship is in terrible condition. At the current state, it would not make the trip to a friendlier land. "Damn it." She turns back to the island. "I'm sure the King is a wise and understanding man."

"Not when it comes to his wives. Especially his favorite," Neil admits.

"Neil, isn't the Boiling Seas in the tropics? We shouldn't be too far from it," Brion observes.

"This is the beginning of the tropics, the northern parts. It's closer to the southern parts of the tropics," Neil explains. "I have my landmarks; one is an unusual shaped rock."

"Hm. Ok," Brion hesitantly agrees.

"I need to recover after that storm, and I am sure the ship does as well. When we dock, I will see what I can do," Milea scowls. Neil fidgeted, debating his answer.

"We don't have a choice unless we want to swim all the way to the Temple of Light. The *Lady* is taking on water, Neil," Vicki hints. There is a moment of contemplative silence.

"You win, milady. I hope you are right about King Orin," Neil relents.

"So do I," Milea agrees.

CHAPTER SIX

The Jungle King

The red fingers of dawn streaked across the sky as Neil assesses the ship as he shakes his head wearily. The wheel is loose, perhaps from the force needed to keep it in line. The door to the sleep cabin is off the hinges, sea water has ruined all the furniture inside. He turns when he hears a thump to see Vicki and Sonja returning to the deck dry and with large spare sails. Neil enlists the assistance of Brion to go into the hull and retrieve the last few sails they left.

Milea sits on the deck and holds her head. The world is fuzzing up a little in her eyes yet she refuses to go unconscious. She turns her gaze up when she feels a hand upon her shoulder and meets the concerned eyes of Vicki. Milea admits that she is exhausted from the battle but will assist where she can. Vicki hands her a dry set of clothing and offers to assist in standing. Milea accepts and goes into the sleep cabin to change as Neil and Brion emerge from the hull dry and with the last sail.

A short time later, Milea reemerges from the privacy of the sleep cabin to the sight of a makeshift rigging. The spare sail is stretching between the two sides of the ship and tied at the top of the broken mast. Winds fill the cloth and provide enough power to the wounded ship that it groans and limps to the Harbor of Cyenzie Island. Milea and Sonja sit upon the deck in front of the wheel as the Dresden siblings and Brion guide the *Lady of the Night*. The sunlight bounces off something made out of metal or glass a distance into the jungle causing the sorceress's attention. The dense trees make it near impossible to tell what or where the reflection came from. The ship pauses at the beach of the destination, bobbing a little as small waves lap at the hull.

"Mom. Why isn't the ship repairing itself," Sonja asks.

"I think the *Lady of the Night* is in shock from her first storm. This is a maiden enchanted ship," Milea said. She focuses upon the greenery. "I'm sure it will be fine in the morning. Right now, we have to rest."

"This is the back of the island. I remember a large port with several large ships docked," Neil glances at his sister standing next to him. "King Orin has many trade agreements with a lot of countries. I remember seeing ships from as far away as Selcros. Even Sinfil had a ship docked here while I was a castaway."

"Safe to say that Orin does not care about whom he trades with," Vicki said as a sound of disdain barely exits her lips. "I'll go tie the ship."

The wind flutters the sail cloth as Vicki hops on the rail to disembark the ship. The *Lady of the Night* moans as it starts to move again. Vicki unleashes her father's oath as she almost loses her balance and holds to a rope to maintain footing upon the rails of the ship. The ship collides with the sand of the seashore then groans as it pushes onto the beach. Seabirds call out in surprise, taking to the air to avoid the wooden behemoth as it creeps further up the shore. Brion has stepped back from the helm when it once again proves to have a mind of its own.

Milea holds on tight to the raised floor she and her daughter sit to prevent an ungraceful topple onto the lower deck. The scraping of large stones against wood makes the hair on the back of Neil's neck to stand straight up as he battles down the rising words of concern from his gut. The *Lady of the Night* stops and let out a soft groan along with a few sounds of weeping.

The single large sail untied and collapse onto the deck. Many of the ropes go slack and fall into a mass of fibers. Brion touches the wheel then hops back when the item falls off its post. Sonja scrambles down to the shore, using the side of the ship like a ladder. Vicki tosses over a rope so that she can climb down and immediately inspects the vessel. Brion follows her down and goes to the stern in order to make the assessment.

"Lots of scrapes and a few small holes. Can't see the keel but safe to say it's damaged now due to beaching," Vicki says to herself as she walks along the ship's side, ignoring the crabs that decide to escape her footsteps.

"I'm sorry you're in pain. But try and heal up. You'll feel better when you do," Sonja sympathized with someone at the front of the ship.

Vicki makes a sound of curiosity as she walks to the front to stand with the preteen as Sonja pats the ship's front. The girl is focused on the figurehead as she continues to speaks to it. A breeze stirs Vicki's hair as she tilted her head up, her eyes widening in surprise when she sees the features of the female figurehead. The maiden is clutching her wooden cloth tighter to her form; her face shows all the hallmarks of a woman in extreme pain. Her eyes hold unspoken volumes of fear and appear as if she is crying. Trails of water stream from the carved orbs, a small drip collect upon the sands below. The hair is all over her head, the signs of the intensity of the storm. The figurehead's eyes are also focused upon Sonja as the girl is talking. Vicki blinks and touches the wood of the ship. Her sensitive hearing detects a soft groan of pain.

"Vicki, I think we might have a problem," Brion calls from his vantage point.

"I... ok," Vicki takes a step back then goes to the stern. The jungle creatures greeting to the visitors fill the air as Vicki turns and focuses her eyes upon the large hole that has been ripped into the stern. "Well, no wonder she's crying. That lightning bolt did this damage. Neil, Milea you might want to see this. It's not at all good."

"What," Neil hops down immediately and turns the corner He let out a small cry of anguish from the large gaping hole that yawned at him. Water dripped from the saturated wood. "Oh, poor baby!" He rubs the ship and made an 'aw' sound.

"How bad," Milea asks as she makes her way to the rope.

The sounds around Milea left her hearing as she reaches for the rope. Everything within her eyesight fuzzed up, making it hard to distinguish the lines between objects. Her head starts to spin a little, informing her how hard the Tragin's magic struck her during the storm. Milea closes her eyes and shakes her head a little to clear it up. A few moments pass before she opens her eyes to see that everything has returned to normal.

With quiet words of concern for her health, the sorceress descends to the shore. Sonja greets her mother and tells her of the ship's figure head's condition as well as that of the stern. The girl expresses concern as it appears something took a large bite out of the ship.

"Something did indeed bite into her and ripped off a large chunk. So that dragon was not just an illusion of the storm," Milea touches the ship.

A brief image of two eyes enters the sorceress's mind from the simple touch. She withdrew her hand and scowled from the image, who is this antagonist. Brion breaks her train of thought as he reaches up and runs his fingers along the back of the ship. He seems at awe with both the size of the damage and the fact that he is able to reach the jagged edges of the gaping hole. Neil is careful as he caresses the wood as if it is a sick puppy as he speaks words of encouragement and praise to the vessel.

Vicki smiles and rolls her eyes at her brother's obsession with the ship. She touches the wood and mentally estimates the amount of time and materials needed to make the repair. A slight frown comes to her features when she notes that they will possibly be months before they are able to get back on sea let along arrive at the Temple of Light. Milea stares at the wound a little longer as she crosses her arms across her chest. The sorceress then makes her way to the front of the ship to speak directly to the figurehead. Brion watches her go and glances at the sand. A large set of tracks drew his attention immediately.

"That's odd." Brion bends down and studies the tracks.

"What's wrong? I don't see anything," Sonja crouches next to him and stares at the ground.

"Here. This is the paw print of a jungle cat. From the looks of it, it's a very large jungle cat," Brion draws a large paw in the sand. "Much larger than any normal one and I hope we don't run into it."

"Neil, how far are we from Orin's place," Vicki asks.

"Not far. We are in his back yard," Neil follows Milea to the front of the ship. Sonja moves to the head of the group, focus on the jungle.

"We have company," Sonja announces. Milea scowls at the jungle.

The trees move and sway and jungle life sound an alarm from the activity of a legion of large warriors as they exit the greenery. Vicki and Brion both take position next to the girl as Sonja prepares for combat. The warriors are dressed in leather armor with thick cords of silk around the waist. The chests of the men are exposed displaying a rainbow of colorful scales that shimmer in the light.

Milea recognizes the warriors as a race of people called Dragonigena. She has grown up around many of them and all are warriors ripped with muscle coupled with the bad temperament of their dragon ancestors. Those that surround them now are nothing like those she has encountered in her life-time. The seven-foot men are very thin, almost as if they are walking scarecrows with large hands and feet. Their toned muscles are stretch evenly across their skeleton. Their weapons are long spear-like items and crudely made but very efficient in gathering the attention of the intruders.

Brion places his hand upon his sword hilt but is keen not to grab or draw it; the hostile legion outnumbers them at least five to one. Vicki places her hand upon her whip's handle and scans the defenders, searching for the leader. Milea contemplates the outcome of the events should they battle. If her experience and knowledge of dragonigena battle serve her well, she is confident that those that surround them are a small party. The rest of the army is hiding in the jungle, awaiting a signal or a chance to pounce.

Milea decides to take a few steps forward and stand in line with the defenders. Her sight once again fuzzes up causing her to close her eyes and shake her head to clear it again as the men finish surrounding them.

"You there, state your name and your reason for being here," the leader of the group, a woman, demands.

Milea and her companions focus upon the six-and-a-half-foot woman noting that she the healthiest member of the group. She is also built to be strong and sensual. Her dark colored eyes scan the intruders with intense hate, as if she has already decided what to do with them. The wind sifts through her long black hair, despite the leather strip she uses to hold it back. This woman is only female among the men. Small dark green dragon wings spread taunt upon her back as her short tail move showing anger. Milea arches an eyebrow at the emanate attack the dragonigena woman is about to wage. Neil takes his place next to his sister.

"We are castaways. Our ship was hit by an unusual storm. We need to repair it and be on our way," Neil answers.

"I know you. You are Neil Dresden. The one, my father, hates so much," the woman takes a few steps closer, standing a small distance from the captain. "What a kingly reward I will receive once I present to him your head, eh?"

"It would be very unwise to attempt to remove it. We just want to repair our vessel and be on our way," Milea reiterates as the woman approaches her and stops. The tension in the air increases as their eyes meet.

"Your only warning, ship wench, is now. Do not approach or anger me, else you will be punished," the woman warns as she is walking away. "I am Tanwen, daughter of King Orin and his eldest child. You are all my prisoners to be dealt with once the King has judged you. Do you come peacefully?"

"I can say your intentions are not peaceful. What crimes do we have other than being shipwreck upon your shore," Milea demands.

"An innocent question, I'll forgive your outburst this time, ship wench. You do not have much of a choice but to follow me," Tanwen folds her arms and smiles cockily. Her soldiers tighten the circle around the group. "Either you walk, or we will carry your bodies to the palace. The choice is yours."

"Then you leave me no choice," Milea sneers.

The sorceress's vision fuzzes again, this time almost blinding the woman. She closes her eyes to clear them bringing a smile to Tanwen as she sees weakness in the bold woman. Sonja moves until she is at her mother's side, sensing something wrong. Brion shifts his position to where his hand is now above the hilt and preparing to draw the weapon. Vicki fingers her whip, unbuckling the strap that holds it in place as she prepares to use it. Neil takes a quick study of his companions and sees they are ready to either fight to the death or pass out from the storm.

"We will come quietly. Since we are outnumbered and you are persistent," Neil concludes. Vicki frowns at her brother's words as she reattaches the snap on her whip.

"Good choice. Surround them to make sure they do not falter," Tanwen commands. "Take them to the King. I will make sure the ship has no other passengers."

"I assure you, no one else but those you see here is aboard her. The ship requires a very minimum crew," Neil guarantees. Tanwen is slow as she turns to faces him.

"Then your supplies will be taken," Tanwen threatens.

"Good luck in getting to them. The ship will not let you near our supplies willingly," Milea said. Tanwen's anger flashes in her eyes as she faces Milea.

"Oh, you know magic, eh? I can dispel your enchantment, witch," Tanwen boasts, walking towards Milea. "I can deal with you now if you continue to persist." She snarls, standing an inch from the sorceress.

"I do not need magic to give you a lesson on manners. Pay attention, for once I start, I will not repeat myself without retribution," said Milea in a calm and unflinching way. She meets the gaze of the woman, showing no fear.

"What lessons are you able to teach me, ship wench? It does not take much skill to lie on one's back," Tanwen concludes.

Milea backhands the woman almost as soon as the words exit her lips. Tanwen flips around then hit the ground hard, holding her offended cheek. She tries to stand but did not make it to her feet, something holding her down. Milea stalks to the girl as those escorting them watched in awe. Many are stun at the attack and unsure what to do about it. A few of the men lower their weapons to protect Tanwen. Milea pauses a few inches from her previous position and exhales as a red gleam crosses over her.

"Mom," Sonja takes Milea's hand gently. The action causes Milea to rein in her agitation for now.

"We are surrounded by at least fifty dragonigena men. Though we may be able to take this group out, I can assure you that more are waiting in the jungle. This battle is not worth our lives," Neil reasons with the sorceress.

"Neil's right. Let's go along with these warriors to see their King. Then we will be on our way," Brion places a hand upon Milea's shoulder. He knits his brow in concern over the amount of heat emitting from the woman, as if she is on fire.

"Which way to the palace," Milea demands. She focuses upon the guard in front of her.

The man swallowed and takes a step back; his hands are shaking a little as he points his spear to a path in the wood-land. Milea follows the maker to the sandy thru fare and marches toward it. The soldiers encourage the rest of the castaways to follow.

Neil counts the number of men and made a displeased sound as he follows his employer. Vicki is a few steps in front of her brother and Brion takes up the rear as the soldiers march next to them. As soon as Milea disappears into the foliage, Tanwen feels the heavyweight lift. The young woman growls, glaring after the departing sorceress. With another snarl, Tanwen turns her attention to the ship.

Birds sing out in alarm. Their bright color feathers entertain the strangers with displays of warning and protection to their nests. Milea settles into the slow pace through the jungle as she reminisces about a more familiar kingdom of dragonigena, Dorma. She did not know exactly where the friendlier lands are at, however, no matter the distance the *Lady of the Night* is not in any shape to make the trip. Milea allows her thoughts to wonder while lollygagging as she follows the guards. Resting overnight will add to the urgency of the voyage, yet Milea sees little choice.

The sorceress goes over many scenarios in her mind and comes to the conclusion of leaving at first light. This will give all the opportunity to rest and recover, to include the ship, after the violent Tragin attack. Sonja's sudden leap back catches Milea's attention as she follows her child's line of sight.

Above the path, hidden within the shadows, is an octagonal spider's web. The vines appear to grow on it; however, Milea is blessed with the knowledge that the vegetation are not vines but a clever camouflage by very dangerous arachnids. Looking up, she sees the giant spider attempting to conceal itself in the dense jungle sitting in the middle of the webbing. It raises its left hind leg at a slow rate, as if to mask its existence.

A light blue hourglass marking upon the spider's back causes Milea the most concern. She figures that she will notify the King that he needs to get rid of those types of spiders. They are trickier than the black and red and deadlier. The entire group passes under the web except for the very last person. The spider drops down, grabs the man, and then ascends back into the web. Its victim did not make a sound.

"Will your mother be well, Sonja? When I touched her, she had a fever," Brion asks.

"I think once she's had some food and rest, she will be. She's agitated, so you felt her gift activating," Sonja hinges a guess.

"Let's see. Trappers at Churn, Slavers, and Casimir at Lybrinthia Bay," Vicki counts on her fingers. "Mystical storm and disrespectful captor, I'd be a little testy too."

"And we have yet to get to the main event. King Orin himself. He's hard of hearing, to say the least," Neil warns.

"Lovely," Vicki grumbles.

A group of small and colorful birds darts across the path of the perturbed sorceress. A few deer bounce from one side of the path to the other, escaping a hidden predator. Milea stops to allow the pack of dogs to follow their quarry. Sonja takes the opportunity to hold her mother's hand and beam a smile up to her. Milea exhales, calming her anger as she smiles back at her child. The expedition turns a corner and once again views their destination. The palace is carved out of the jungle with long and skinny towers reaching for the sky. A strange shape dome graces the largest part of the structure. Sonja snickers, it reminds her of the rear-end of a spider.

Brion takes in his surroundings to include the giant jungle spiders among the higher branches of the trees. Neil discusses the court of King Orin with Vicki as they are once again prodded along. Milea pauses when she is poked with the butt of a weapon and turns to give the perpetrator a single warning gaze as she takes time to negotiate the slight incline to the palace gates. The short walk to the front of the building is rewarded with up-close details of the entire structure. Made of precious stones and metals, the palace sparkles in the light of the sun.

The jungle itself is barely held at bay, growing right up to the stairs that lead to the front door. The entrance itself is molded from large quantities of solid gold. The pictures relay to all how the palace had been built with many of the main figures shackled in chains. Sonja shifts, uncomfortable with the depiction as Milea studies the details. She crosses her arms over her chest as she contemplates the art and its hint at how the king may treat visitors or even his own countrymen.

The large doors thunder open to allow three men to exit. The very healthy men each are decorated in colorful feathers and clothing and held large, golden, spears. They glare down at the stowaways with a sneer of distaste upon their features then stand at attention as a fourth man struts out of the doors. The way he walks and moves it is not hard to imagine that he pretends he is a peacock, with his very colorful regalia. He takes another step and the escort that held the prisoners all bows to him. Milea's gaze met that of the strutting man causing a slight sneer of dissatisfaction from him.

"What is the meaning of this? What are these trespassers doing at the very steps of our sacred Kingdom? They should have been executed in place," the strutting man said with a strong commanding tone. He walks purposefully, one leg at a time as he approaches the edge of the stairs. His dramatics causes Neil to roll his eyes. Sonja fidgets.

"Sir. Tanwen sends Neil Dresden and his crew to King Orin as a gift," one of the escorts announces.

"What? You dare to return," the man's eyes widen as he took a large step back, his right hand going to his chest. "Where is Tanwen? She must present this find to King Orin at once." He stands straight up with his hands upon his hips.

"Sir, she is still at their ship to make sure no other passengers are aboard and to take the supplies that are onboard," the escort explains.

"I see. Very well. Bring them in," the man sniffs and tossed his head one side then the other. He turns and marches into the doors, the large guards follow his wake.

"Follow me," Neil said dramatically.

The escort stands as Neil turns to the structure and start imitating the pompous man's march up the stairs and into the void of the hall. Sonja plays along with the captain as her mother looks on with a shake of her head. Milea walks up the stairs next then pursued by Brion as he chuckles. Vicki takes up the rear. The group is followed by half of the escort. The other half stands and returns to down the path to the ship.

Soft music greets those that enter the palace and the front doors close to keep it from escaping. The strong smell of spices and herbs fills the area as they are led across the room to a second set of doors. Neil places his thumbs in his belt as the doors open and the aroma got louder. Vicki sneezes as Sonja holds her nose from the smells. Milea takes a deep breath in and out as she focuses on the large male sitting upon a huge stack of pillows and surrounded by several women. Three more women are dancing around in a slow, suggestive rhythm to the music that plays in a chamber down the hall.

The large man emits a loud yawn as he holds up his wine glass. It is immediately filled by one of the women as others massage his broad neck and shoulders. His chest is filled with golden scales yet they are now a tint dark from the amount of liquor in the man's blood. A black beard clings to his chin; a mane of it decorated his crown as his dark eyes scan the dancers hungrily.

Milea rubs her fingers across her eyes and mumbles a silent prayer; the man is dragonigena and a King. She senses a very difficult trial ahead of her. The strutting man saunters over to his leader and bends to whisper in his ear. The king sits up and nods to the man who bows and walks back to the captives. The guards poke at the prisoners to prod them into the room as the king stands up, anger in his features as he focuses on Neil.

"Well, well. Look what the jungle-cat dragged in. Neil Dresden, is it? Tell me why I should not have your head on a spear," Orin grips sarcastically.

"I am not totally to blame, King Orin. Your lovely wife, Celest, shared a glass of wine with me and the next thing I knew, I was waking up," Neil defends himself.

"Which is most unfortunate for you, eh? Celest is my favorite; no one touches her but me," Orin interrupts with a growl. Several of Orin's wives shift either in angry or nervous energy.

"We do not wish to stay long. We wish to repair our ship and be on our way. I have to get to my sister," Milea informs. Her voice catches the King's attention immediately.

"Is your sister as lovely as you? Perhaps that one is your sister? Or the young one," Orin motions to Vicki then Sonja.

"My sister is not among us. We were on our way to retrieve her when we ran into a strong storm," Milea met the King's gaze, her features show displeasure when Orin licks his lips.

"Such fortitude. This sea rat, Neil, I know. But... I do not know you. Perhaps I could know you a lot better," Orin approaches the group.

Milea exhales and places a hand upon her head as the king stalks around her. He is oblivious to the others in the room as he scans the sorceress from head to toe. Vicki watches and fingers her whip, taking in the crowd of the room. She mutters a little when she hears her brother discourage the plan she has. Milea holds her ground, unflinching, as Orin stops in front of her and gazes into her eyes. He exhales with an animalistic sound from the sight. The alcohol from his breath almost causes Milea to close her eye and she does everything she can to keep them from watering from the pungent attack. Sonja takes a step away from her mother in order to find clearer air to breath away from the musty king.

"Perchance we should speak another day when the fortitude of your beverage wears off, Your Majesty. My companions and I must depart upon an urgent mission which the storm has subsequently delayed," Milea said. "We were escorted to see you; however, we will be departing in the morning."

"You want off this island," Orin laughs and goes back to his seat. "For that, you must pay Neil's bail. I've no use of coin or trade. I prefer a more lustful payment." He sits down and holds up his cup, one of his wives fills it up for him.

"Although Neil has become a valuable ally, I do not agree that his bail from your kingdom should consist of satisfying your appetite for the flesh. I think Your Majesty should come up with something different for a form of payment," Milea answers.

"No. I have stated what I want, and I will have it," Orin swirls his wine around and takes a sip. "You look as if you will collapse any moment now anyway. Just fall into my arms, I will take care of the rest. You will not mind at all."

"I'm sure it worked for women in your past, but it does not appeal to me," Milea informs.

"I've had enough. I'm sure there is another way off this rock," Brion said and turns.

The boisterous sound of Brion's agitation makes a few of Orin's wives jump and back away, frightened. The elf is near his destination when the larger guards cross their golden spears to prevent him from exiting. Bit by bit, Brion faces the king once more to see the man is hardly troubled by the agitation of his prisoners. Orin relaxes as Brion once again approaches and stands with his fellows. The king's eyes rest briefly upon the golden hilt of the elf's sword then travels over to Milea and stays as he sips his wine. Milea did not shy away from the man's gaze as he seems very transfixed with her.

A bright grin graces Orin's features at his thoughts as he manages to tear his gaze from Milea to Vicki and scans her, appreciatively. Vicki shakes her head, not liking the sickening look upon the king's features as he turns from her to Sonja. Milea patiently watches as the king finishes off two glasses of wine. Orin lifts his glass once more for a third cup of the strong dark liquor and focuses once more on the sorceresses as her patience continues to erode. He sniffs the drink and takes a sip as she straightens her stance.

"Oh, there is another way off this island. However, the accommodations are not very nice. I can arrange for them easily. My best customers will be arriving anytime now. I'm sure they would be very pleased to accommodate all of you," Orin sips his beverage.

"I've had enough," Milea turns and pauses when those that escorted them blocks her way. The sorceress' features darken. "I suggest that you move."

"Take them to the caves. I will see what they say after a night in the jungle," King Orin orders as he sips his glass again.

"I can tell you what I will say right now," Milea glances over her shoulder. The gleam in her eyes goes unheeded.

"I've a few words to add if that helps," Vicki agrees.

"Mom, you need to rest, remember," Sonja whispers to her mother.

"Vicki, too many soldiers," Neil reminds. He takes hold of her arm. "Come on."

"I could still make it quick," Vicki assures.

"Later," Neil reiterates. "Milady, we should depart so that you can recover."

"Fine," Milea growls in agitation.

The men let her pass under the cross spears, opening the doors that lead to a different chamber. Vicki let out an angry sound as she turns and follows her employer out of the room. The guards eyed her closely due to the whip she has at her hip. Sonja mutters a few words as she jogs to catch up to her mother. Neil glances at Brion and nod to the elf. The gesture is reciprocated as they follow the ladies. The door closes right behind them as the music once again echoes in the palace.

Milea pauses when she notices she is not in the same room she entered the palace, but instead in a room that is full of a handful of large, healthy, muscular dragonigena men glaring at them. Milea crosses her arms and tilts her head up. One of the guards simply motions his head to the hall they need to traverse. The sorceress glances down the hall then to the well-armed men and decides to follow the hall. Her companions join her. The large men trail after them until they are once again in a separate chamber. Once in the new room, the doors close and the castaways are left alone for now.

Neil takes the opportunity to bend down with Vicki and Brion and draw the layout of the palace that he remembers. It is a huge labyrinth but not difficult to navigate as he has memorized it after his first stranding. Milea crouches with the group as does Sonja and both ask several questions about the guards and residence.

Vicki attention goes to the twenty-foot ceiling towering above and sees that it is nothing but windows. This to allow the natural light to flood the gallery. The silhouette of birds gliding past the windows flickers the light and causes shadows to dance upon the nude statues that line the gallery. Each statue is that of a woman in every possible situation that the king could possibly want from any of his lovers.

Vicki shakes her head at the statues then turns to one in the corner when a faint whisper of breath draws her attention. The nude woman statue is posing in one of many sensual dance moves, her hands reaching for the sky. The entire group stands as Vicki approaches the statue and watches it intensely, detecting the slightest movement from the diaphragm of the nude woman.

Vicki takes out a dagger and is about to poke the statue when a fistful of large men fan into the room and surround them. She turns and scowls at the men as she joins her fellow prisoners once again. The largest of the men takes a step closer to the prisoners and sneers at them. The spotted fur cape that graces his perfect form bristles in the light.

"Will you cooperate or will you require ropes to drag you through the jungle," the captain of the guards asked with a gruff voice.

"We will walk, cooperatively. I'm in no mood to have my hands tied," Milea said.

The new guards open a second set of large doors that lead outside of the palace. The calls of birds and other animals filter into the space as Milea and her crew head into the great outdoors. Vicki makes one final glance at the statue then follows her brother when he calls her name. The doors boom close once more bringing silence to the room.

The statue that Vicki concentrated upon starts to move and stretches. She makes a hiss of discontent to the strangers that are in her home. She walks over to the door and waves her hand to make the stones invisible so that she could watch the departing group. She glares at Vicki's back, wondering how it the l'vane senses her presence. Her eyes then concentrate upon Milea's back and her senses did not like the red-haired sorceress.

The woman takes a step back when Milea pauses in her walk and turns to face the palace, her gaze boring into that of the spying woman. The guard reasons with Milea to continue to walk as the former statue solidify her spying mirror. The woman, Celest, then turns to go down a different hall as she ponders her encounters.

CHAPTER SEVEN

The Great Shadow

The sun beams down and blesses those under its gaze with the heat as well as the humidity of the tropics. Birds and beasts call in alarm as the group traverses into the garden of the palace. Dragonigena men and women collect a variety of fruit, ignoring the group when they pass. Many are thin, their bones showing and a select few have distended stomachs from lack of proper nutrition. Children of the gatherers hurry to aide their parents, balancing packages half their body height perfectly upon their heads. Milea takes in the sights of the dragonigena people's condition with an expression of worry.

Never has she seen this in all her years living and growing with dragonigena. These people are starving even in the presence of an abundance of food. The memory of Orin and his pot belly is more than a stark contrast to the garden workers. The king is so worried about wine, women and trade that he cares less if he kills his own people. Milea's mentor and former Queen of Dorma, Avenshire, would never let this happen to those of her rule. Milea reluctantly continues her march to the unknown caves as she ponders her move once she has retrieved her sister. Upon assuring her twin is safe, Milea quietly vows to return to Cyenzie and deal with the ruling party, if not for the sake of the future of the dragonigena as a whole.

A herd of llama trots through the garden, their handlers encouraging them to move at a hurried pace. They are heading in a different direction, perhaps to a port. Neil avoided the mess that the animals left in their wake. The trees sway in a tropical breeze, dropping fruit or nuts upon the ground. Brion utters a few words of displeasure. He could not perceive where the garden ends and the jungle begin. His sharp eye spots the many pathways, natural and unnatural, twisting into the dense foliage. A large animal print causes him to worry; they are from very large predators.

Vicki takes pause when she sees a group of men walk over to a trio of women. The men are not dragonigena, and appear to be car'laden. Vicki scowls, the only car'laden she knows this far in the tropics are those of Sinfil, the slave traders. The rest of her team and escorts pause as the car'laden men point to one of the women and all three cries out in anguish. The youngest of the trio is the loudest as she is taken away by guards.

The remaining two women, the mother and grandmother, plead with the guards to no avail as they are ignored. The scene is repeated throughout the garden as several young people are taken away. Milea feels her unflattering opinion of Orin grow even more so as she and her companions are press by the guards to keep going. Gardeners hurry to the palace, carrying a large load of fruits and vegetables in their arms and upon their heads.

"Mom, can we just go back to the ship? At least we would have lunch and not end up as lunch," Sonja swats a fly that lands on her arm.

"The *Lady of the Night* has to repair itself. As it does that, we would not be comfortable. We can rest in the cave and leave tomorrow," Milea said in gentle tone to her daughter.

"Alright," Sonja pouts a little.

"As far as a meal. I don't think Orin is going to provide one unless Vicki or I agree to his little invitation. I'm not partial to agree to such arrangements," Milea said with a bit of contempt.

"Neither am I," Vicki acknowledges.

The vegetation becomes less tended to as they reach the edge of the garden and start into the jungle. A heavily pregnant woman sits down to observe them walking past. She bears a great weight of bread upon her back that she is transporting to the palace. The castaways rounded a corner as one of the guards goes to speak to the woman. Neil shoos away a large bee as Vicki dodges a large flock of domesticated geese. The large birds honk as if they are dealt a great insult that their formation is interrupted. Neil chuckles at his sister then frowns when he notices that they are approaching a second bridge leading to a darker part of the jungle.

"That does not look inviting," Neil opinionates.

"Sometimes the shadows can be a very friendly place," Milea offers. She hesitates when she senses an irritating presence heading their way. "Now what...?" She focuses on the path.

Monkeys shake the top of trees as they flee the emanate danger. They shriek and hoot to warn those around of the threat as they depart. Birds take to the sky to fly away, calling in alarm to echo those of the monkeys. The escort lifts their weapons then hesitates when Tanwen approaches them from the gloom of the forest. The way she marches to them, it's no stretch to guess that the woman is very angry. Milea is calm as she crosses her arms across her chest and watches as Tanwen came within inches of her. The dragonigena woman emits a low growl and scans the sorceress, walking around her. Milea sees the dragonigena woman's wings stretch and flap, the tail twisting showing fully her agitated state.

As Tanwen circles and scans her, Milea takes in the strengths and weaknesses of her soon to be opponent. The king's daughter is a powerful mage, but not as powerful as the one she is about to face. Milea exhales at an even pace to gather her patience and rein in some of her own agitation, this so she does not kill the girl immediately. Brion takes in the situation and considers what he can gain from it. He turns to his guard and proposes a wager upon the impending battle.

Neil muses on the situation and figures that Brion is right, the odds of them winning are in their favor. The guard accepts the wager from the elf to provide food for them in their prison tonight. Vicki crosses her arms when the guard mentions that if he wins, she is his prize. Sonja analyzes the situation between her mother and the dragonigena woman. The girl concludes that it is best to let her mother deal with the situation and she learns from it.

"A bit agitated, are we? Did you get to the supplies," Milea asks coolly.

"What matter of sorceress are you? You could not have sealed it. That is impossible," Tanwen scans Milea then once again met her gaze. "The seals on the doors are more powerful than you appear to be standing here."

"The seal is far beyond your comprehension. As far as my abilities, they are muted right now due to my exhaustion. Also, due to my exhaustion, my temper is a little shortened," Milea places a hand upon her hip, the other dangles to the side.

"What is your secret? Tell me," Tanwen bares her teeth.

"No," Milea answers calmly.

Tanwen yells in anger and swings out to backhand the sorceress. Milea catches the woman's arm with one hand and kicks out the legs of her opponent, bringing the taller woman down. Tanwen gasps once, then slams into the ground upon her stomach; the air in her lungs left. Milea follows her down and pins the arm she holds against the wings and ultimately the back, restricting Tanwen's movements.

Tanwen's tail grabs hold of Milea's leg prompting the sorceress to punch the lower spine of her opponent. The tail stiffens and goes limp as a sound of pure pain racks from Tanwen. Milea places a knee in the middle of her opponent's back, sending a second round of stars into Tanwen's eyes. Once the young woman stops moving, Neil nods his approval and applauds the sorceress's skills. The guards escorting them gawk in amazement and shock, unsure if they should help the fallen dragonigena woman. Milea bent until she is next to Tanwen's ear.

"Next time you attack me, you will likely die," Milea whispers.

The entire jungle is silent as Milea stands and walks away, crossing the bridge into the darkness of the jungle. Sonja follows her mother, calling for her to wait for the others. Brion dusted his hands and goes across the bridge with his well-humored friends. The guard he made a wager with demands to know how he knew that Tanwen would lose, the woman is the strongest dragonigena warrior upon the island.

Brion attributes it to luck and requests that the meal they won be served within an hour after they reach the caves. If not, then the guards will possibly receive the same wrath that Tanwen just endured. The guard mumbles a few swears as he begrudgingly agrees to the terms. Tanwen is slow to stand and flexes her hands and wings, glaring after those she has taken prisoner mere hours ago. She then turns and takes a quick, angry, look over her shoulder as she centers in on the palace.

An hour of walking later, the trees part then disappear altogether as they arrive at a field of lush green and tall grass. The vegetation sways in the wind, providing a glimpse of large boulders hidden within their mist. The sun's orange rays bounce off the rocks, creating an eerie glow that flickered like flames. An outcrop of a large and ominous boulders pile in the middle of the grassy plain is the destination of the prisoners.

The formation is not created by natural means and at one time, it may have been a nest to a powerful creature. Yawning below a large flat rock is the entrance to the caves. The guards push upon the group to get them walking again. Milea turns on them prompting the guard that dare to touch her to back up and hide beyond one of his companions. The sorceress smirks a little then begins to walk to the formation they spotted on the hill.

Small rodents scatter out of the way for fear of being step upon by the prisoners or their guards. Temperatures upon the grasses are lower than the jungle. The vegetation heights are way over the heads of even the seven-foot dragonigenas. A few of them are nervous as the grass could hide a bountiful variety of large predators that prowl both the plains and the jungle. The expedition arrives in front of the cave without incident much to the relief of all.

The black rocks emit a strong negative energy that Milea feels, not to mention the aura from the darkness within the caves. The rocks may have once harbored a seal of sort, broken many generations ago. It is unclear that whatever the seal held inside is still present or if it is free and gone. The guards press on their captives to get them to start walking again.

"Get inside," one of the guard snarls to the prisoners once they reach the entrance.

"What? No blankets," Neil asks sarcastically. He takes a step back to avoid the man's blow. "Don't be foolish, my lady is not the only one that can body slam a pompous ass."

"Come on, *asai dona*," Vicki coaxes and touches her brother's shoulder.

Neil scowls at the guard for a moment until he decides to follow his sister into the shadows. The darkness of the cave is robust and thickens even more as the group descends into its debts. Neil swipes his sword to make sure it is not a cloth and announces to his friends that it is not. Their voices echo with every word and step they take encouraging Vicki to provide an impromptu concert much to Sonja's delight.

Milea cast an illumination spell to carve through the darkness. The small sphere appears in the palm of her hand, illuminating her face and arm. The ball levitates and bounces a little as it starts brightening a touch. The darkness is hesitant to relent to the small glowing orb illuminating the cave walls and at least four feet in front of the sorceress. The sound of trickling water from deeper into the darkness reaches the ears of the prisoners encouraging them to come down further.

The footsteps of those in the dark tunnel rebounding off the walls and ceiling. Vicki and Sonja soon disappear out of the light. Brion calls to the two as he increases his step to catch up with Vicki. Milea smiles wearily, causing her ball of light to split into two and with a simple motion of her hand; she sends the second ball to float in front of Sonja. The little light bounces in excitement as it brightens, lighting the way up to three feet in front of the advance group. Sonja whoops in delight for the little light ball.

Small sparkles of light bounce off the darkened walls catching Brion's attention. He taps the dark rock and acknowledges at its volcanic roots. The items within the rocks are large and beautiful diamonds. Milea examines the walls as well, besides diamonds, there is lots of jade. The black rock itself is a beautiful gem, obsidian.

"Orin has all this within his kingdom. This could become some very beautiful works of art," Milea rubs her hand against the wall. "So why is he starving his own people?"

The diamonds sparkle and shine in the light as Milea and her crew descend further into the cave, the path lowering a little and turn. Sonja jumps back when she sees her reflection upon the wall. The image is slightly warped, stretching the girl up to twelve feet tall. Her hands and head are gigantic; the rest of her body is long like a string. Sonja chuckles and begins to move a little. Her reflection bent and warped in different ways. Milea grins a little at the effects as she touches her child's head to move her along to their destination. Sonja goes back towards the front with Vicki and Brion. Her little ball of light bounces just as excitedly as she does as it keeps up with her.

A short time later, the castaway prisoners find their destination which happens to be the end of the large cave system. The smooth grounds and gentle slopes of the entire trip have Brion speculating the age of the entire structure. Neil takes a few steps into the space and sees that the dripping water is from a large stalactite above a vivid pool of blue water. Dark shadows around the area start to play tricks on the minds of those present. Sonja whips around when she thinks she sees or feels something brush up against her back. Vicki assures that it is her whip and not to worry about bats or anything living in this cave.

From their travels, she concludes that it is empty. Brion grumbles a little as he sits down and leans against one of the walls, allowing his head to go back just a little more to stare into the darkness of the ceiling so that his eyes could adjust further. Neil finds a boulder he could sit on to contemplate the position that he and his employer are in. Vicki plops down in the center of the pathway, her back to the entrance as she decides to braid her hair as she hums a song. Sonja busies herself exploring the area with her little ball of light, finding lots of interesting rocks and gems. Milea seats herself at the edge of the cave's small pool, pondering the words of the king.

"Milea, can you elaborate on our mission to the Temple of Light," Vicki breaks the silence.

"Ah yes," Milea agrees. "I am going up there to assist my sister. She is there to find solace, but the temple has been attacked. By dragons."

"What," Brion features did not hide his shock.

"A temple of dragons attacked by dragons," Neil scowls at the conundrum. "Why?"

"I do not know that answer, however, let me explain what I know," Milea leans forward a little away from the water.

Milea recounts the conversation she had with her sister over a day ago. From the transmission, Maya indicated that the dragons behaved strangely, as if they were under a spell. There was music playing that annoyed her and a few of the residence as she spoke. Milea did not hear the music from the mirror she uses to communicate with Maya. Communication had been cut short when Maya was attacked. Milea sits back after explaining what she knew of the situation at the Temple of Light. Neil rubs his chin a little, disturbed that the Temple is overtaken in such a manner, just about all the residence there are warriors or powerful mages of one sort or other. Sonja decides to sit down next to her mother for a moment then stretches out to stare into the darkness of the ceiling.

"When I tried to teleport, I ended up in Wild Territory. That is not a place to be in any season yet I happen to land there during the monsoon," Milea explains.

"Monsoon is bad, very bad," Brion confirms. "Since it is on the same continent as Cathalian, I've visited that place more often than I care to remember. There is a ruin there. But I never found it."

"Treasure hunting," Vicki asks. She pulled her knees to her chest and stared into the darkness. She raises an eyebrow when her senses detect a slight breath in the darkness next to the pool.

"More my curiosity than treasure hunting. Like Neil, I have a fascination with legends," Brion admits.

"I've a feeling, that as we travel with our Grand Hostess. We will run into more than a few legends, my friend," Neil assures causing Milea to smile. "Which reminds me," He sits up and draws one knee to lean upon. "Milea, how much are you going to pay us?"

"The determination is contingent on how difficult the voyage and the arrival to the Temple of Light. I suggest that we reach our goal before you divulge a price, Neil. Just in case we run into more than we bargained for," Milea reminds him and unties her hair. It falls like a river of rubies to her shoulders and lower back.

"Like that storm," Neil recollects. "Good point."

Vicki rises to her feet with a few words of surprise or anger as she focuses on the corner next to the pool. Neil also stands his sword in hand from his sister's reaction. He frowns when he sees nothing and inquires to Vicki. Milea directs one of her light balls to the corner as

Vicki approaches it and stares, it is empty. She turns her eyes upwards to see the deep shadows of the ceiling are still unrelenting in revealing its secrets. Brion is slow to put his sword away and concludes that the darkness is still playing tricks upon the mind. He jokes that he thought he saw a large jungle cat sitting in the corner. Milea attributes the illusion of the dark to their exhaustion as well.

"Do you think we might have stumbled into the lair of a Shiado," Vicki asks, sitting back down in her appointed place.

"I only know two. A'drianis and her daughter, Kelsi. I've not seen the Great Shadow in quite some time," Milea stretches upon her back and places her hands behind her head.

"I've seen pictures of her," Brion mentions. "Beautiful woman, but very dangerous. Almost like you, Vicki."

"I am not nearly as dangerous as our Grand Hostess. Or even my brother," Vicki scoffs.

"I'm a pushover," Neil exaggerates. He grins when he hears Milea chuckle at the comment. "Anyway, I'll take first watch." He volunteers and holds his sword upon his lap. "What are we going to do with King Orin?"

"I'm not going to do anything with him at this time. Once we are rested, I feel we should just leave," Milea offers. "I need to focus on the mission at hand first."

"I second the motion," Vicki voices.

"Sound fair. Rest well all," Neil stands and adjusts his sword belt and starts back towards the front of the cave. One of the balls of light bounces and hurries to light his way.

"Neil, I think we might have a meal waiting for us out there. I'll help you bring it in," Brion stands and walks after his companion.

The cave's void sucks up any semblance of time or space yet Milea estimates perhaps an hour has passed since Neil and Brion have left the cave. Vicki assures that they are fine; Neil possibly has gone to check on the ship to make sure no other damage is caused by Tanwen or her cronies. Milea muses that perhaps she should have gone as well to visit the ship and encourage it to heal fast.

The conversation continues with the recent events that place them in the situation at hand, the storm. It is more powerful than anything she has encountered in her life thus far, even going as far as saying that the storm bringer is strong as Keela. The realization did not send comfort to either woman as they discuss the possibilities.

A round of laughter echoes from the dark halls announcing the return of Brion and Neil. Moments later, the darkness lit up as the light ball travels into the space first with the two men following it. Milea watches in curiosity, noting that they both have several large baskets of food with them. Vicki rolls her eyes, she has forgotten about the bet, as she stands to assist her overburden brother with his load.

The twin balls of light combine into one and hover above a spot of the cave as Milea stands to help Brion spread out the bounty. There is one basket full of bread, two of tropical fruits and two of roasted chicken. Milea decides not to inquire of their luck as she goes and gently awakens her daughter then tests out the water in the cave's pool. The liquid is cool and refreshing, and best of all, drinkable.

"Too bad he didn't give us something to use as a drinking vessel," Brion mildly complains as he settles down. Sonja yawns and sits next to him. "Did you enjoy your nap?"

"Yep, even though it's short," Sonja manages and yawns again.

"We don't need cups when we have these," Neil holds up a coconut, proudly. "Observe."

Neil tosses his coconut a few times, turning it ever so slightly as he did. With a flick of his wrist, he tosses the object high into the air. As it falls back down, Neil pulls his blade and slices the fruit in half, then replaces his blade in its sheath. Seconds later, he catches the bottom half of the coconut in his left hand, the top half in the right. Equal amounts of coconut flesh and water graces both halves of the fruit. Neil beams with pride as Sonja stares at him in awe.

"I hope you cleaned that blade before you did that, brother," Vicki scolds at her sibling.

"Of course! I always clean my blades," Neil bows and places his prize down.

"But, how did you cut it in half? Am I still drowsy? I didn't see you draw your sword," Sonja furrows her brow.

"It's a family secret and tradition," Neil chuckles. "Here, I'll try and slow it down a little for you."

Neil proceeds to pick up two more of the coconuts and juggle them a little. Vicki makes a small grumble about her brother showing off. She stands up when he tosses the fruit into the air once more. Neil pulls his sword a little slower, slices the fruit in half then quickly replaces it in its home. The bottoms land in his hands, the tops land in the hands of his sister.

"That is fascinating, Neil. Perhaps when we have better lighting, you can repeat the trick," Milea requests.

"Of course," Neil bows and sits down. "This entire meal is Brion's doing. My thanks," He slaps the elf's shoulder in friendship.

"Eh, it was a simple wager. Milea did all the work," Brion waves the comment away.

"What was the wager over," Milea asks.

"Simple. I wagered with the captain of the guards that Tanwen would be knocked on her hindquarters a minute after you gave her a warning," Brion explains in short.

"It took a minute," Milea glances at the elf; her features reflect a slight shock, she thought it was shorter than that. All shock disappears when she spies a dark oblong shape fruit nesting among the meal. "Ah, darkened dragon fruit. Just what I need." She picks it up.

"What does it do," Vicki asks. She pauses when Milea bites into the fruit. The light balls brighten. Yet, the corners remain untouched. "Wow."

"It's a prime ingredient for recovery, to include mystical recovery. This one is pretty sour, but it will have to do," Milea continues to eat it. Sonja hops up to go to the pool and fill up a few of the coconut shells. Neil decides to help her.

Good humor and light bantering echoes in the chambers during the entire meal. Vicki's senses determine that there is something in the corner, drawing her focus every once in a while. Milea glances in that direction as well, not that she detects something but more out of habit or curiosity. Sonja stretches and sighs as she finishes off her healthy amount of food.

The girl turns to her mother when Milea quietly asks her about her abilities to detect ghosts. Sonja shakes her head; she does not see or hear anything in the cave except those around her. Milea sits back and watches Vicki. Since she is older and more in tune to the gift, she might be detecting something otherworldly.

The meal soon disappears and boredom settles in upon the entire group as the slow and steady dripping of water creates a lulling effect and casts a natural spell of sleep upon them. Milea stretches and settles down when the rest of her companions drifts off to slumberland. The lights that she created flickers then goes out completely as she surrenders to the call of sleep, her mind going deep into it.

Neil opens his eyes momentarily when the light disappears, seeing that it is once again pitch-black in the caves. He hears his sister sound asleep and figures that whatever she detects in the corner is gone now. Neil yawns and stretches as he nods a little, his sleepy senses teasing him with the illusion of the darkness moving about. Neil's eyes close as his breathing pattern deepens, mimicking his companions as he surrenders to slumber.

The water dripping marks a small passage of time as a figure creeps out of the corner Vicki stared at all night. The shadowy person shakes a little and releases a small growl sound, her senses tell her that night has fallen outside of the bleak cave. She glances around in the total darkness although to her it is twilight. She could see the l'vane woman, Vicki, still facing the corner that the shadow emerges from and decides to sleek out of range of the woman's senses. Vicki makes a small sigh causing the shadow to pause then exhales her own breath when the l'vane woman turns over and goes deeper into slumber.

The shadow avoids Vicki and picks up one of three apples left from the meal. She does not step on Brion nor does Neil detect her as she avoids both men by moving left then came face to face with the pathway leading outside. The shadow's senses scream at her causing a shutter to come down her spine as she ganders back at the pool. She blinks when she sees Sonja sleeping soundly upon the floor, how did the girl get there? The shadow mentally grumbles, her total concentration in keeping herself hidden blinded her to the girl's presence. The shadow hesitates in her thought pattern, if the girl is there then so is her mother.

The shadow turns her eyes around the room and finds the sorceress sleeping at the edge of the pool, peacefully. Milea turns upon her side as her mind and body go into an even deeper sleep. The shadow jumps with joy as she quietly makes her way over to the red-haired woman, barely avoiding Brion's leg in the process. Once there, the shadow takes a small breath in and holds it as she slowly reaches to touch the sorceress.

The shadow knows she has to be very careful in awakening the sorceress as it could end up a life-threatening situation in a heartbeat. The figure's hand is within a few inches of Milea's side when the sorceress's eyes snap open. The shadow drops very unkind words as she quickly backs away from Milea who has now gained her feet. A sword flashes as it appears in Milea's hand, her eyes are still slightly glazed over, and she is still partially asleep.

"Oh Ublivorion," the shadow cries out. She dodges to the left, avoiding Sonja. Milea is right behind her. "Bad move, Zaria... bad move," she scolds herself. Milea disappears suddenly. Zaria whips around and lands upon her back, a sword at her throat. "Milea, wake up it's me," the woman yells, rousing Neil, Vicki, and Brion. "It's Zaria. Come on," she remains extremely still until Milea blinks, recognizing her voice.

"A'dri..." Milea shakes her head and pulls her sword back while rubbing the sleep from her eyes with her free hand. "Zaria, what are you doing here?"

"I need to ask you the same thing," Zaria slowly stands.

Milea scoffs as she casts her illumination spell, filling the cavern with light. Zaria nearly falls to her knees as she covers her eyes, blinded by the quick introduction of light. Vicki squeaks a little from the sudden brightness, not ready for it to occur. Brion blinks and stands, nearly hitting his head on the low part of the cave he sleeps under. Neil swore and holds his hands to his eyes, easing them back into functionality. Once clear, he sees the intruder standing in front of Milea and covering her own eyes.

The invader is wearing all black with a head full of black hair reaching her shoulders thus could easily hide in the shadows of the cave. The mane shifts in her movements revealing to Neil that this woman could possibly be an elf, or subspecies of elves. She is thin, much like the starving people of their current location. Milea is patient as she awaits the five-foot woman to lift her gaze and meets it with a smile. The black orbs of her eyes float within a small tint of blue with a golden ring around the pupils signifying her true heritage.

"Blasted! Woman," Zaria scolds.

"I wanted to make sure it is you. There are more than enough shadows to pretend," Milea remarks as she coaxes the light to die down to a more tolerable level.

"Ok, so how did you get into this cave without being detected? That's not an easy thing to do," Neil ties his katana back on his belt. Vicki and Brion also put their weapons away.

"Practice," Zaria grins. One could almost think she is a feline.

"Zaria, how did you get here," Milea reiterates. She watches the woman exhale in defeat.

"Causing havoc on a slave ship. They shipwrecked at sea. I managed to cling to some floating lumber until I landed here about three days ago. It was nightfall, and I found this place to rest," Zaria answers with a shrug. "I must have been sleeping pretty deep not to hear you."

"And I too tired to detect you, properly," Milea rubs her eyes again. Her blade disappears from her hand. Sonja turns over and continues to sleep. "That's a relief." She exhales when she notices her child.

"Noted. When do we leave," Zaria asks as she rocks back and forth from heel to toe.

"I slept for an hour," Milea hints. "I need a little more time to rest before I attempt any spells. Especially after I've battled wits with a Tragin."

"You what," Zaria gawks.

"Besides. We are on our way to the Boiling Seas to find out what is happening to Maya," Milea said, folding her legs under her as she sits down. "Here, let me explain."

Vicki, Brion and Neil all sit down and whisper among themselves as Milea once again recounts what happened between herself and Maya a few days ago. As she explains the situation, Milea checks on her child and is gentle as she removes the leather strap from the girl's forearm. The large patch very fine and smooth silver scales shimmy a little and are unhurt. Sonja rubs the area a little then turns over and continues her deep sleep. Zaria finally sits down as Milea goes over the details of their arrival onto Cyenzie Island. Zaria proves to be a source of intrigue from the trio.

Brion speculates that they are in the presence of yet another legend. Vicki stands and goes to the corner which occupied her since their arrival in the cave since it is now in full illumination. There are no tracks or indication of a nesting animal or being. Vicki takes in the area and finally turns her gaze up and sees a great stalactite hanging precariously above. Vicki's features twist into curiosity as she tries to figure out a puzzle as she returns to her brother's side and sits down. Neil watches the short woman as she stands and paces a little and shakes his head.

"No, Brion. I don't think so," Neil said in hush tones. "I do not see her being the legendary thief, Zaria Shiadokat. Besides, Shiadokat is an Eltis far as I remember."

"I prefer the term treasure hunter as appose to a thief. Keeps me out of trouble," Zaria corrects absentmindedly. "As far as Eltis, why do you think such a thing?" she grins a little.

"Just trying to make sense of something. I did sense something earlier from the corner," Vicki said "But it was gone almost as soon as I detected it."

"Exhaustion plays tricks with the mind," Zaria indicates, touching her left temple. "So does hunger." She holds her stomach when it grumbles at her.

"I'm sure if she is A'drianis, we would have known." Neil said. "Shadow Eltis, she would have used the shadows cause mischief at our expense."

"That is true," Zaria agrees. "But I know better than that now." She mumbles under her breath.

"So, you are not A'drianis," Vicki concludes. Zaria smiles and sits down.

"What happened during the storm, Milea," Zaria asks.

"I heard a woman's laughter," Milea answers. "I sensed a Tragin, I know what it feels like. And... you will eventually have to answer the question."

"In time," Zaria shrugs. "Where's the ship?"

"On the beach," Milea yawns. "I'm going to see if I can get a little more rest before we return to the seas."

Milea stretches out and lays with her back up against that of her daughter's, her mind once again calm enough to rest. Zaria listens to the questions and stories that Vicki and Neil both have about both the Shadow Thief and the Shiadokat. She smiles at them and gives them vague answers as a result of their curiosity. Brion studies her in silence, a big smile upon his features as if he has already figured out the riddle. A short time later the trio is once again lounging upon the cave floor and drifting into slumberland. The light spell that Milea cast to illuminate the space is long gone out as the woman returns to slumber.

Zaria waits until all of those inside the cave have once again drifted into a deep and well deserves sleep then stretches, her shape changing slightly. The symphony of the jungle's night residence penetrates the cave bringing a smile to Zaria's lips as she remembers times of her distant past. The night music suddenly stops prompting her to hop to her feet and check on her companions. To her relief they are still sleeping, to include Milea. A small feline like chuff escapes her as she makes her way out of the cave.

Once there, she notices that there are no guards outside, bringing her to conclude that they are expected to stay put in the cave. Zaria crosses her arms and is about to return to awaken her charges so they could go when a bright white light floats through the jungle just beyond the grasslands. It catches her attention and keeps it as the light grows and glows much brighter, taking on a red illumination with some flickering somewhere in the upper trees. A strong tingle goes down Zaria's spine bringing forth a slew of unkind and unhealthy words from the woman.

The light wavers, as if it heard her resulting in a few extra words from Zaria. The light turns in a different direction and glides to a large building that Zaria assumes is the palace.

Seconds later, there is a bright flash as it disappears. The suddenness of the disappearance makes Zaria frown; there are no powerful ghosts on this island that she is aware of. Then again, she has been asleep since her arrival. She dutifully watches the jungle for a little longer in silence. The trees rustle with the nighttime breeze and many wild animals dodge the edge of the tree line when the winds lift Zaria's scent their way. A feline-like growl escapes Zaria as she turns and goes back into the cave. Dawn is approaching and they will be leaving shortly.

CHAPTER EIGHT

The Ultimatum

The sound of several people sleeping fills the darkness of the cavern, barely covering the thuds of footsteps as they draw ever nearer. Zaria opens her eyes when she detects the noise then squints against the light of many torches when twelve men enter the space. Each man is armed with a spear, and every other one holds a torch. Zaria stands, still wrapped in the shadows of the corner, and is about to take action yet pauses when the strongest of the men kneels down next to Milea and slowly reaches. The shiadokat thinks about it for a few moments then makes her decision.

"I wouldn't do that," Zaria warns from her shadowy hiding place. Her voice echoes causing confusion among the ranks.

The man surveys his surroundings in order to locate the voice since none of the prisoners are awake to speak. With a slight frown, he turns to his companions and gives orders to them.

One by one, the guards pick up the prisoners and wait for the lead to pick up the last of them. The chief guard turns back to Milea and reaches for her once again. His hand is inches away when Milea's eyes snap open. The man scrambles to get back; unfortunately, Milea grabs his outstretched hand, pulls on him, then breaks the arm. He screams waking all the prisoners as Milea gets to her feet.

Sonja frees herself from her captor by punching him in the face. He lands on the ground as the girl lands on her feet preparing for combat. Brion drops an unkind word as he grabs his captor and causes the guard to fall, both land on the ground with the elf regaining his feet first and pulling his sword. The captor manages to get his spear and the two weapons clashes. Neil snaps the neck of the man that is holding him, killing the guard instantly and causing both to fall. Neil lands on his feet as his sister, Vicki, uses a dagger and stabs the man that restrains her upwards, going through the chin and into the skull. She rolls to her feet as his body falls with her still in his grip. Other men move in to try and subdue the prisoners.

Milea grabs the spear from her attacker and brings the butt end around to its previous owner's legs, breaking the one that it smacks. He goes down as Milea turns and inflicts the same end up between the legs of a second attacker. He hits the ground in immense pain, unable to make a sound. Neil pulls his blade and takes the leg then head off his next opponent as Vicki uncoils and cracks her whip. She misses her mark as he jumps out of the way. He then lands on his backside with a dagger in his leg instead. Sonja knocks her opponent unconscious. Brion tosses the one he battles into the pool. More guards run in to assist their fellows prompting Zaria to shake her head, she had enough. Torches go out all of the sudden as the darkness folds into absolute causing all fighting to cease.

"I did warn you," Zaria offers. "Now be good boys and skedaddle."

The darkness lifts slightly allowing all to see each other again. Those guards who could still walk turn and run out of the area. Their footsteps and calls of terror echoing back to those left. The wounded men whimper as Milea takes a deep breath in and slowly releases it, standing tall and leaning upon the confiscated spear. Neil and Brion both sheath their blades and takes full note of the carnage that is left in the caves. Vicki retrieves her dagger causing the victim to scream in pain then pass out from it. Sonja's attackers are moaning, still alive for now unless they suffocate themselves.

Milea turns her attention to the man that attempted to touch her; he is still alive and survives with a broken arm. His eyes are wide with fear and understanding of his situation. Milea's features show that she is perturbed as the guard pulls himself back to his feet, his shoulders against the walls of the cave. The shadows lift completely, removing any hope to hide within from the woman's angry gaze.

"What do you want," Milea demands.

"Please forgive us, we were ordered by King Orin to retrieve you as you slept. He wishes your presence," the guard stutters as he explains.

"I am not in the mood to entertain Orin's wishes," Milea warns. "My companions and I are leaving."

"How can you leave," the guard challenges, "Your ship still has damage, I think more than when I saw it the day that you landed. You have to see King Orin for his assistance as all things, even the wood needed to repair your ship, belong to the Jungle King."

Milea sneers as she turns from the man and takes a few steps to the darkened hall. She pauses to stare down the gloom, collecting her thoughts. The news of the ship's condition did not bode well at all. For it to have more damage means that someone is deliberately causing it. She debates the condition wondering if it is the storm antagonist or someone else. Milea glances over at Vicki and notes that she too is staring into the hall, deep in thought.

Orin has made it clear what his intentions are for them, especially Milea and Vicki when they first met. The sorceress predicts that Orin has not had a change of mind over the short period of a night. His behavior indicates, if anything, he will be more insistent today due to his very nature as a dragonigena male. Milea rubs her eyes with one hand as she recalls the intensity of the dragon born folk in everything they do. She had to castrate a few of the males in the past that refuses to take rejection as an answer. Milea muses that she may have to repeat the process today as she turns to the wounded guard.

"What is the strength of Orin's armada," Milea asks.

"Cyenzie Island does not have an armada," the guard answers. "King Orin relies on his allies of Sinfil and Habvor for protecting his lands."

"We don't want them on our tail as we head for the Temple of Light," Neil offers. "Especially Habvor, they are ruthless."

"I see," Milea digests the information she receives. "Very well," she turns to the guard once more. "Take us to see Orin."

The mid-afternoon sun beams down upon the jungle when a small group of the guards limp back into the palace. Their spears are the only thing keeping them on their feet. Milea saunters into the door, her gait calm yet alert. Sonja yawns and stretches, following her agitated mother. Vicki and Neil discuss their options once they return to the ship and set out to sea. Neil settles on a direct approach in the likelihood that they are pursued by Habvor. Zaria takes a look around as she is following the group, seeing various artifacts that she is not comfortable with to include a menacing looking peacock painted on the walls. Her eyes turn to the two very healthy guards standing in front of a golden door decorated in the same bird.

The tail is spread with several strange symbols about it. The larger guards take in the condition of their lesser companions and sniff in distaste, assuming they are weak when compared to their charges. Brion stands next to Vicki and speaks quietly that he does not see any signs of Tanwen. The news is relayed to Neil bringing a slight concern from the seaman. He did not want to run into the king's daughter when they head to the ship. The two strong guards lower their spears to cross in front of the group as they attempt to enter the king's room. Milea stops and slowly turns her attention to the guard on her left.

"What is the meaning of this? I thought King Orin wanted to see us," Milea challenges.

"The king only wishes to meet with you, Red Lady. In the King's words, to get off the island, he wishes a private meeting with you," the guard answers his voice holding a hint of disdain to it.

"I am not amused. If it were not for the legion of innocent soldiers between us and our ship, we would be gone," Milea warns, her eyes flashing slightly. She closes them and breathes through her anger. "I've little time to entertain this man. Neil, Vicki, Brion. I will be back in a few minutes. Sonja, behave." She turns towards the newest member of the group. "Zaria..."

"I've got your back, cousin," Zaria leans against a wall. "You have five minutes."

"That might be way too long," Neil said.

"Indeed," Milea agrees and focuses on the wounded guards. "Make sure my companions are comfortable. I do not want to hear that they are disturbed in any manner."

"Yes, ma'am," an injured guard bow. "Please follow me."

Two of the escort limps down the hall and open yet another hidden door. Milea frowns, she did not care for all the twists and turns of this palace. It is built to purposefully confuse any visitor or prisoner from escaping. Neil follows the men along with Vicki as they quietly discuss the halls. Neil indicates that the one they are going into is a shortcut to another area they once visited. Brion and Sonja both catch up with their companions to overhear some of the conversation. Zaria focuses on Milea briefly then closes her eyes and slowly fades into shadow. Milea rolls her neck and shoulders, readying herself for the emanate battle she will face as she turns.

"Open the door," the sorceress commands the royal guards. The men appear upset at her words. "You have seven seconds. If you do not open them, I will leave."

The guard on the right opens the door much to the disapproval of his companion. Milea ignores their bickering as she travels into the corridor and listens as the doors behind her close. A second set of doors in front of her opens with a deafening boom. Milea sees Orin perk up as she enters the space by herself. The sorceress surveys the room and finds that there are no other hidden threats and that she and the king are alone. She takes a few steps further in and notices that this room is unlike any that they have ushered she and her companions too so far.

The king's chambers are filled with silks and various types of precious metals and artifacts. Jewels cling to any available edge of cloth and dangle in long ropes around the room. Large, over-stuffed, pillows pile high in the corner of the room. Milea observes that this is where the king is currently sitting and staring at her intensely. From the distance she could see that each and every pillow is well used for one sport or other in the entertainment of the king. Milea edges a little further into the lair and pauses several feet from the seated king. She meets his hungry gaze with defiance as she refuses to acknowledge him with a customary bow. Orin did not seem to care as he stands and stalks to the woman.

Milea holds her ground, placing one hand upon her hip and allowing the other one to dangle free to her side as the king prowls around her. A deep-throated sound of appreciation rumbles from him as he scans her. Milea notices that there is no smell of alcohol from the man, yet, and she assumes he is sober for now. Milea shakes her head as she overhears his words. He speaks praises about her wonderfully curved backside and the color of her hair. It reminds him of rubies or the red-hot flames of passion he imagines contain within her enchanting body.

Milea senses remain on high alert; she did not want him to touch her at all. Milea starts to tap her foot as Orin walks around her once again, his gaze falling to her proud feminine chest. She continues to control her breathing pattern which amuses the king as he grins and lifts his eyes to meet her very impatient gaze.

"You are very beautiful, a beauty that is very enchanting. What is your name," Orin smiles.

"My name is of little concern here," Milea reiterates. She blocks his attempts to touch her cheek. "I am not in the mood, and as I said last night, I am not interested." A trickle of agitation melts within her words.

"I see. Then I guess I will have to execute your friends," Orin fringes sadness as he walks away.

"That would be a grave mistake," Milea hints, eyes flashing from her instant irritation.

"Well, if you want to save them then you have to lay down with me. Let me worship the body I know is under those garments," Orin ignores the tone of her voice as well as the obvious anger she is showing. He picks up a glass of wine and gazes through it, studying Milea. He shakes it a little, causing the sorceress' image to shimmy within the glass.

"You are very insistent with this. Obviously, you are impressed with me. But I am hardly enticed by you," Milea leans back a little. Her hair shifts with her movements.

"Oh, but I can change your mind. Once you feel my hands upon her naked flesh, you will be begging me to relieve you of your arousal," Orin insists.

"It must be some sort of enchantment that you would use. I see nothing that would tempt me otherwise. In fact, you are very boring to me," Milea watches the King place his glass down.

"Ah, you are challenging me," Orin grins evilly. "I am the King of Cyenzie. My nation is powerful with very powerful allies. Not all dragonigena trade with the world, I do and have the riches to prove it. I have eight wives and many more mistresses to satisfy my every need, but even they fail to stunt the strong desire within me." He approaches and stands in front of her once again.

"You have a very large ego and terrible manners," Milea informs. She turns to walk away. "I will assure you this," She faces him again and meets his gaze; "your wives and mistresses are not enjoying your desires. In fact, I would dare say that the majority of them are pretending just to keep you, the king, pleased. This so they can continue to enjoy the amenities that are obviously denied your common folk."

"You dare," Orin's anger reflects as his muscles tighten. "You do not know they are pretending."

"Let's see. Yesterday, I counted at least five of your wives are dragonigena," Milea recollects. "Yes, I will guarantee that at least four of them are satisfying you with bogus enjoyment."

"If you are so sure. Why don't you test for yourself? Then we shall see who is pretending and who is boasting," Orin relaxes his shoulders again as he recaptures his calm. He goes to his bar and once again picks up his glass of wine.

"No," Milea answers flatly.

A quick scuffle outside is followed by the doors to the room being thrown open much to the displeasure of the king. One of the more elite and healthy guards run into the room, his armor is cover with blood, mud and sand. He is wide-eyed and very breathless as he bows to his angry master. Milea sees that the invader also has blood pouring from a very large wound upon his arm and wonders if the kingdom is being invaded?

The sorceress quietly pensions the universe in hopes that it is not the case as the last thing she wants to do is aide this womanizing bastard as she and her friends escape. Orin scowls as he slams his wine glass down and storms to the man. He places his hands upon his hips and glares down at the guard, oblivious to the man's condition and the fact that his eyes are glazing over as death approaches.

"Sire, my apologies. It is an emergency," the man informs as blood trickles from his mouth

"I commanded not to be disturbed," Orin growls at the man. "What is so important that....?"

"Sire, Yabura has attacked the village," the guard blurts out right before he dies. The King's eyes widen with fear.

"It appears that you have your hands full with Yabura. You need to amass your army, King Orin," Milea advises.

"Nothing can defeat that thing. That snake is immortal. It can't be killed," Orin said with a growl.

"I suggest you find a way. We are leaving this land," Milea heads to the door.

"I see. Then why don't you or your friends kill this creature," Orin moves until he blocks the sorceress' departure.

"Terms for our uninterrupted departure," Milea asks coolly. She watches as the king's anger bubbles up. "I assure you that I am trying to do this as nice as possible."

"Really," Orin laughs. "Alright. I'll release all of you and your ship if your friends can kill Yabura."

"Very well," Milea walks around the king to the door. Orin grabs her arm causing her to pause and slowly turn. "I suggest you let me go." Her tone left no room for negotiation.

"You, my red hair beauty will stay with me to make sure that Neil carries out the task. I will inform the sea-rat his mission," Orin said with a smile.

"I am in no mood for these shenanigans, Orin," Milea warns

"You have no choice, my beautiful queen," Orin answers with a definite tone in his words.

"Only one person is allowed to call me that, and he is not you," Milea snatches her arm away from the king.

"Do tell," Orin laughs. "Then I will be gentler with you. I want some assurance that your team kills Yabura thus I will keep you as a hostage as Neil and his band of misfits carry out this mission. If I send all of you, what guarantee do I have that you will fulfill this task before you sail away and break my heart?"

"I see straight through your bullshit, Orin," Milea said.

"But you also see my point." Orin announces with a feral grin.

Milea glares at Orin for several seconds then turns on her heels and walks over to one of two chairs in the room. She sits down and crosses her legs as she adjusts to this new hostage situation. Orin scans the woman and smiles in his victory as he leaves the room via a different set of doors. Servants hurry into the chambers and clean up the dead guard, placing the man's spear against the wall. The small group then mops up the blood and hurry out of the chambers as Milea watches. She notes that they forgot the spear and sits back to contemplate her next move. She will have to be very careful in calculating it or Orin will end up dead. Milea leans to one side and rests her chin upon her hand, her elbow on the arm of the chair.

"Is it such a bad thing if he died," Milea muses to herself.

The room is bright and airy, similar to the one the group occupied yesterday prior to the march through the jungle to the caves. The walls are decorated in landscapes of far-off lands to include Brion's home of Cathalian. The image causes a bit of concern and homesickness to hit the elf when he sees it, noticing that it is of the entrance to the palace. Instead of the queen standing in the door, the artist depicts a strange bird standing there. Neil stands next to Brion and admires the painting until he hears his friend's concern.

Both turn their attention to Vicki as she explains to Sonja the strange depiction that is on the floor in front of them. It is the same derange peacock that shows up in spots around the palace sporting a crown and very menacing eyes. Vicki indicates that if the bird is seen in the future, they should avoid the area. Zaria is leaning against a wall; her breathing pattern and closed eyes suggest that she is sleeping. The door to the room opens breaking the shiadokat's sleep as well as gathering the attention of those with her. Three guards proceed into the room with one making the announcement that the king is arriving. The guards are the only ones to bow as Orin walks into the room much to his dislike.

"Where is my employer, Your Majesty," Neil inquires.

"The redhead? She is fine," Orin said. "Do not worry about her, however. I have a need for your talents."

"My mother best not be harmed," Sonja stands and warns.

"I am sure she told you an answer and should be released," Zaria adds. "Why is she still not among us?"

"Because we have negotiated terms for your release," Orin informs. "There was an attack on a nearby village by an immortal white snake named Yabura. You, Neil, are to destroy this snake and bring me evidence of its destruction. Once you do that, you, your hostess, and your crew are free from Cyenzie."

"What," Neil asks as he turns left then right before he refocuses on the king. "You're joking?"

"You have two choices. Accept and go after the snake or decline and be executed," Orin said. "Your employer as you call her said you can kill this creature."

"I am sure those are not her exact words," Zaria chimes in. "She would not task those she just met with such an undertaking; it is very uncharacteristic of her."

"Believe what you want, woman, however if you continue to speak out of line your head will be the first to roll," Orin threatens. "What is your decision, Neil?"

"Milady has great expectations of me. Why can't she accompany me," Neil requests.

"I want some insurance that you will destroy that thing and not escape into the ocean. She is my hostage. If you do not bring me evidence of its destruction by nightfall, I will have a new wife," Orin answers.

Sonja gawks then let out a sound of anger as she bolts forward. Vicki is quick to grab the girl and pulls her back, preventing the child from making a mistake that will cost them dearly. The guards are now on their feet once they detected a threat to the king and are poised to strike out at it. The woman drops a sailor's oath when she starts to slide forward as Sonja strains against the restraints of her grip.

Vicki redoubles her efforts to hold her back as the girl takes one single step forward. Brion ponders the situation and concludes that a snake, especially a giant one, is not hard to track. The trails they leave are very distinguishable and all he needs is the last known location of the prey. Neil surveys his companions once then takes a deep breath in; relaxing as he figures the king is crazy.

"Very well, I seem to have no choice but to accept your limited offer, Your Majesty," Neil places his thumbs in his belt. "Will you provide a little more information about my quarry?"

"Giant white snake with fire breath," Orin explains in short. "You will know it when you see it and pray to your gods it is not the last sight you see."

"I suppose evidence would be its teeth?" Zaria stands and dusts her arms as she focuses on the king.

"If that is what you can obtain. I doubt if you can destroy it. Like I said, it is immortal," Orin shrugged.

The room quiets down as Sonja stops growling and is released by Vicki. Zaria smirks a little as she turns to leave the building with the girl following after her. Sonja threatens the king much to his confusion before she departs. Neil utters under his breath as his sister swats his shoulder and they head outside followed by Brion. The elf voices his opinion about tracking the snake and the lack of skills that is obvious in the king's men.

The guards did not stop the group as they start their suicide mission. Orin determines that the child will make a challenge for him if she survives in a few years yet the new skinny woman has to go. He will wait until the immortal snake is done with them and have his men discard the bodies as usual. The guards knelt to the floor as Orin heads back to his chambers and to his prey.

The afternoon sun warms the entire room with light causing the jewels to sparkle and gleam. Milea opens her eyes when she hears the doors to the chamber close once again. She ignores the king's smile as she leans on the arm of the chair in thought about the situation and most recently, her child's raging energies. She is not sure if Zaria felt them but Milea sure did in a big way. The girl is coming of age and into her powers sooner than predicted. Milea's attention returns to her current situation when Orin takes his time as he approaches his bar. She watches with half interest as he picks up his old cup and sniffs it.

Making a face of dislike, he tosses it out and pitches the glass to the other side of the room. It shatters upon contact with the wall, leaving a mess of wine and glass. Orin pulls out two new glasses and turns his back to make sure he blocks his guest's line of sight as he fixes her a drink. Milea ignores him as she returns her thoughts to Sonja and the emergence of the girl's gifts, perhaps when this critical mission is over, she will take the girl to the next level in her learning. A glass of wine is held in front of her causing Milea to arch an eyebrow as she stares at it. She then lifts her eyes to glare at the king.

"What is this," Milea asks.

"I do not want you to die of thirst. At least I can offer you a drink while we wait," Orin swirls the dark colored liquor around the glass, temptingly. "It was created several decades ago by my father. The strength of many warriors kept it from several enemies in many wars."

"I'd rather not partake in such fortification," Milea interrupts the man. She sees the gleam in his eyes and guesses his intentions from the slight movement of his free hand. "I would advise you not to even try such a foolish thing. Considering I am capable of bringing forth a very sharp blade and you are in a very dangerous predicament."

"I see. Then for now. We are at an impasse," Orin takes a step back, turns and returns to his bar. "Do you dance beautiful Lady?" He places the glass down and pours himself a drink. "I am curious considering the lovely way your hips sway as you walk."

"Again, none of your concern," Milea answers and leans to one side of the chair. "Do you?" She patiently awaits an answer as he belts forth a deep belly laugh.

"My rhythm is much better when I have you underneath me," Orin hints

"Too bad I will not entertain that idea," Milea counters

"I am King, you should know better than to speak to me as such. In fact, you should be obeying every one of my whims," Orin informs.

"You are not behaving such as a king. You are behaving more like a spoiled Prince whose hormones are a new sensation for him. I am neither a part of your kingdom nor am I a representative of another. My loyalty is to one much higher in virtue than you, Orin," Milea informs. She sizes up the king as he takes a drink from his glass, noticing that his cheeks are already flush. "Tell me, Orin. Why do you starve your common folk?"

"They are none of your concern. Then again, perhaps they are pretending," Orin said sarcastically, purposefully using the words of the sorceress. He laughs when she rolls her eyes and closes them to regain her patience. "My people are fine."

"Really now? Do you understand what it is to be a dragonigena," Milea sits back.

"Do you," Orin counters and sips.

"More so than you it appears," Milea remarks.

"Really? You do not look dragonigena. You look more like an elf or even a human," Orin sips his beverage, smiling at his hostage. "Then I defiantly know how to satisfy you."

"You are very detesting," Milea sneers at the man. Orin laughs at her observation.

CHAPTER NINE

Tragin Hunt

Jungle critters call out in alarm with many of the winged ones taking flight, warning of strangers entering the area. A flash of metal and a few well-placed unkind words alert the villagers of visitors. Brion is first to enter the area, his sword drawn in preparation of an attack. His is closely followed by the remainder of the group with Zaria taking up the rear. The first thing to hit all of them is the smell of decay, soon after that their eyes absorb the disturbing scene of walking skeletons, some complete with sagging skin. Homes made from grass and mud dots a barren field with a large nearly dead tree sitting near the center.

The field itself is a dry lake bed that usually floods when it rains. The land has not been blessed with the liquid in many years now. A wind whips up a large amount of dust, covering those that shuffle through it to go about their daily lives.

Sonja holds her mouth to prevent any upheaval from the sight and smells that are introduced to her. Neil keeps any unkempt words to himself as he trudges deeper into the village. Vicki is not as kind as her brother while following him, noting at least one person collapse in the middle of the road. His body is eagerly taken to a house with a butcher block just outside the door. Brion blocks Sonja's view as the starving people proceed to dismember the dead to quench their hunger. Zaria cups the girl on the shoulder to reassure her then keeps her attention until they pass the gruesome scene.

The first three people Neil tries to talk to stare at him blankly with one running away after a few harsh screams. Vicki watches in disbelief as it is apparent that the villagers did not understand the common language known to nearly all people of Bri'al. This village is a rarity, completely isolated from the rest of the world. Brion tries his luck and only get fleeing villagers, many afraid to come any closer than a few feet. Sonja pauses when she hears the people they tried talking to whisper about the strangers. She watches, listening as the women and men point and speak in a dialect that she actually understands. Sonja turns to see that Neil and the rest of her party have traveled down the street so she decides to walk over to an old man sitting in the shade of a shabby hut.

Although he is sitting, she could tell he is at least seven feet tall. His knees are batting at his ears as he scratches the earth to distract from his growling stomach. Green scales hug his very thin chest and did not hide the ribs. The old man coughs a little, bending to the ground and inadvertently showing off his spine and hipbones as an assessment to his condition. Sonja pauses in front of the old man and meets the gaze of his soft brown eyes, seeing that he is barely clinging to life.

"Hello," Sonja said in the common tongue. The old man stares at her. "Ok. Let's try *Hello*," she switches her language to the one she learned in Dorma.

"*Hello*," the old man answers slowly. Sonja let out a sound of excitement.

"*My name is Sonja. My friends and I are here to help but need information. Can you help us,*" Sonja continues.

"*Wait... how do you know my language,*" the old man asks, his mouth finally moving from the initial shock.

"*My mother has a high position with the dragonigena kingdom of Dorma. I learned from her,*" Sonja smiles, pleased that she is understood.

"*You are not dragonigena,*" the old man squints. "*Not even a young one. And your friends look more like the strangers who took our children away. But somehow different. All of you are too short.*"

"*My friends and I are not here to hurt anyone. I am a l'vane as are two of my friends. The tallest one is an elf, and the shortest one is pretending to be an elf,*" Sonja informs. "*Can you come with me, I want to introduce you and my friends and I have lots of questions about what happened here.*"

"*I...Yes. Help me to stand, child,*" the elder holds out his hand. Sonja is gentle as she pulls him to his feet.

A woman screams in terror as she swats at Neil, determined to keep him at bay. Neil swears by the oath of his fathers as he defends himself and tries not to hurt the old woman. She finally turns and runs away, fleeing as fast as her feet could carry her. Zaria snickers at the sour look that covers Neil's face from the encounter.

Vicki claps her brother's shoulder in an attempt to show support. She snorts as a big grin comes to her features when he faces her then turns away from him to laugh a little. Brion keeps his focus on the small group of terrified adults staring at them from a distance. His attention then goes to his party as he verbally announces Sonja's absence. Zaria whips around then turn back to retrace her steps. She pauses when Neil spots the girl approaching them with an elderly man. Zaria leads the group back to the girl, meeting them in the middle near the tree.

"Neil, this is Hezim," Sonja introduces the elder once the two groups met. "He wants to help."

"You found someone that understands us," Neil asks, excitement in his words until he sees the man stare at him. "I guess not."

Neil's hopefulness fades as the old man turns his attention to Sonja. The girl interprets Neil's words much to the surprise of her traveling companions. Zaria gawks then smile at the girl as she converses with the man. Sonja listens to Hezim's request then introduces the group by pointing to them and providing the names of each one in the dialect that he could understand. The old man asks a couple of questions to which Sonja answers with a little shrug. Hezim then laughs and extends a hand to Neil with a few words to go along with it. The handshake is accepted with a warm grin of friendship.

"He said welcome, Neil. You have two beautiful sisters and a good-looking brother. What happened," Sonja interprets the words.

"What," Neil blinks, taken off guard as the old man laughs from his reaction.

"Of all the elders, you had to find the most mischievous one, eh," Zaria smirks.

"He knows better, right," Neil asks.

"Yep, I told him," Sonja confirms then gazes up at the elder when he said something. "He asks us to come sit on the tree in the shade."

Hezim perks up a little and sings a small song as he leads the way to the old tree with Sonja's assistance. He talks of the significance of the tree, saying that it will bloom once again when the people are no longer cursed and the protectors of heaven come to the lands. Sonja relays the story to her friends as she hops up on one of the twisted branches and settles down. Hezim sits next to the girl, still humming a merry tune much to Vicki's delight. She liked the beat and rhythm of the folk song. Zaria walks to the large twisted trunk of the tree and decides to climb it to the top as Neil, Vicki and Brion sit down across from Hezim. The shade from the tree did not come from the leaves; they are dried up due to the drought. It came from the hulking branches and knots that blot out the sun at this time of the day.

"Alright Sonja, can he tell us about Yabura," Neil requests.

The remaining living villagers use caution as they approach. Sonja turns to the elder and asks the question. Hezim's eyes widen then fill with tears as he explains the happening of the village and the glowing snake. The villagers start to sing softly as Sonja listens then takes a deep breath in and turns to those that travel with her to explain. The palace guards had come that night to detain the royal midwife and her family, news of the baby prince recent demise reaching the village before even the king knows about it.

The men decide that, before breaking the news to the king, they would be proactive and bring the one they deem responsible for the infant's death. The midwife had pleaded with the guards, insisting she is innocent and the child died because he was weak at birth. The villagers were going to her rescue when Yabura appeared from the woods and aglow with rage. The snake centered on the midwife house, the terrible hiss that it makes still haunts Hezim.

The elder continues his tale as Sonja relays it to her companions that the armed men of the palace attacked the snake. They were full on, yet perished for their bravery with only one barely escaping the tail of the beast. That man fled into the jungle never to return. Yabura then turned its attention to the house of the midwife and raised its hood. Horrible words echoed from the snake as it curses the midwife. The woman screams for forgiveness and yells out a name but it is unrecognizable as the snake strikes.

The midwife's death cries were cut short as her body was crushed in the jaws of Yabura. The midwife's body dropped to the ground, landing in a sickening sound as the snake turned and headed back into the jungle. As soon as the snake disappeared, several sharp objects appeared in the sky and rained down on the house, killing everyone inside and out within close vicinity. A large column of flames then exited the jungle and destroyed the home. Hezim closes his eyes and lifts his head as tears flow down his cheek. He said a few, soft, words causing Sonja to take another breath in.

"Hezim said that the midwife was his daughter. Her family, his grandchildren." Sonja announces sadly.

Vicki places her hand to her mouth, a look of anguish masks her features as her brother hung his head, slightly distraught from the news. Neil then offers condolences which are echoed by Brion to Hezim for the lost, losing family is always hard no matter what part of Bri'al they live upon. Hezim wipes the tears from his eyes and stands with Sonja and heads into the village.

Sonja tells her friends they are going to the location of the midwife's home as Neil, Vicki and Brion stand to follow. Zaria jumps out of the tree, landing behind the group and jogs a little to catch up. The villagers trail after the strangers, their voices still in hush tones. It only takes a few short minutes to arrive at the ruins of the home. The wood is still smoldering with a few crackles of flame within the structure. Sonja stares at it and makes a curious face; her instincts tell her that the flames that took this house are mystical. She focuses on Hezim when he speaks a few more words to her.

"Yabura came early in the morning. It is unusual for the snake to be out during the day as it usually comes out at night," Sonja interprets. "He also does not think Yabura is a giant snake, but something else and wishes us luck on our hunt. He will ask the gods that it is prosperous."

"Thank you, Hezim for your assistance," Neil holds out his hand. The elder takes and shakes it confidently. "We will need all the prayers we can get for this hunt,"

Hezim grins as Sonja relays the words from Neil. The elder then takes several steps back and joins his fellows as they continue to sing and gently stomp out a rhythm. Brion goes over to the house and pauses as he studies the ground, finding the large ridges of dirt that pile up from the snake's weight. They are made from Yabura slithering to and from the village and easily followed. The trees that the snake moved through are still tightly woven together which is interesting considering the size of the beast.

Zaria is standing at the edge of the forest inspecting the path; her heightened-sense of smell provides her with enough information to know they are dealing with a Tragin. The odors are potent and very foul, enough to penetrate her taste buds if she lets it. Vicki glances down the path as Zaria turns away and clears her sinuses. Sonja turns her attention from the house and goes over to Brion to learn what he is looking for to track the snake.

"Is everyone ready," Neil asks.

"As ready as I'll ever be," Zaria grumbles.

Hezim and the villagers sang out prayers and blessings to the group as Neil takes his small band back into the jungle on the trail of the Tragin, Yabura. Sonja concentrates on the ground with Brion as they pick up the trail and the pace. The late start, trek through the jungle, and gathering of intelligence took up enough time for evening to start falling to the jungle. The sunrays lighten up the path they travel as it is now directly in front of them.

Sonja pauses at the end of the trail they follow along with Brion. The elf made a curious sound; it seems the snake disappeared as soon as they came to the main path. Brion looks up and down the path, noting there is a lot of foot traffic from all manner of life upon the main road. This might be muddying the trail for Yabura. Neil bent down and studies the path with Vicki and Zaria. The shiadokat snorts a little to free her sinuses then uses them to try and find the snake.

A warm breeze stirs around the group as they meticulously travel down the path a few more feet and pause to once again study the trail. Vicki took to studying the trees, to see if she could make out the path that Yabura cut while slithering through the jungle. Sonja decides to wander ahead a little to see if she could relocate the snake's trail. Neil and Brion discuss the prints they do see especially noting the car'laden and the devorian footprints.

Zaria quietly follows her nose as she beholds her surroundings and stops in front of a vine when her instincts kick in. She studies the flora and marvels at the dark green and browns that blend perfectly in to the jungle surroundings. A deep sinking feeling enters her gut when she makes a closer inspection and sees sticky fluid oozing from the strands and that the vines are multiple ropes of silk. Zaria shakes her head as her feet shuffle back catching Vicki's attention. The woman looks up and swallows the large number of words that nearly burst from her.

A spider, large as a warhorse, is sitting in the middle of her web blending into the surroundings with her camouflage skin. Zaria speaks quietly to Vicki to let her know that the spider is asleep for now to which Vicki attest to not awaken it. Both then cuss when they see Sonja walking, focus on the ground, as she nears one of the vines. The girl ducks under it and continues her way oblivious to the danger. Brion exhales in relief when the spider does not move and appears to still sleep.

Neil and Vicki follow Sonja as the girl continues down the path and out of range of the large arachnid. Brion is next, quickly ducking and increases his pace to join his friends. Zaria takes a breath and starts after her companions. At the same time, the spider drops only to land in shadows. The shadows lift finding Zaria continuing her way and the spider split into many pieces.

"Brion, I think I found something," Sonja informs as she kneels next to a set of large sinusoidal waves.

"Let me see," Brion bends down next to her. "These are fresh tracks," he follows them for a short distance. "They disappear here."

"Hezim said that it is not an ordinary snake, something different," Sonja recollects.

"The way he describes it, sound like a Tragin and they are masters of disguise," Zaria said. "Do you see any unusual tracks?"

"Hmm," Brion follows the snake's tracks. He hesitates when he sees them changed over to a set of smaller human feet. Whoever made them is not wearing shoes. "Here. The footsteps of a woman."

"Really," Neil bent down to study as well. "They move this way then.... Disappear," He follows the prints to the end then face the path of travel. "Well, I'll be."

"The palace. So Yabura is among the women of the palace," Vicki folds her arms as she makes the deduction.

"I think we need to get to Milea. She could be in some serious trouble," Zaria frowns.

Monkeys howl as they swing through the treetops, following those that invade their territory. Sonja knit her brow as she thinks about the possibility of her mother being in danger. The only Tragin she has experienced up close is the one that produced the storm that crippled the ship. Vicki ponders the situation then notes a large saber-tooth jungle lion stalking the group not too far from the main path. Its teeth shining like daggers in the light of the setting sun as it seems to judge the strength of the entire group.

Vicki quietly alerts Brion and Neil to the dangerous beast with all three of them taking in the creature's sure size. It is large enough to take a great deal of effort to fend off should an attack happen. Zaria turns and crosses her arms across her chest as she glares at the creature, making purposeful eye to eye contact with it. The saber-tooth jungle lion trembles as it slinks back with a whimper. With a sound that seems part growl and part yowl, the beast turns and high tails it deeper into the jungle, uncaring as to the noise it made during its hasty retreat. Neil watches the retreating animal in thought, it did not behave in a normal way. The apex predator should have attacked the crew, fearlessly. Sonja turns to Zaria with a puzzled look about her face.

"Looks like something scared it. My guess is that the guys need a change of clothing," Zaria answers the silent question with a shrug then continue down the path.

"Although I will agree, I doubt if it is the lack of fresh clothes that scared that beast," Brion observes. "Something bigger might have done it."

"I think that's the biggest predator on this island," Vicki said as she watches the paths.

"No. it is not," Brion shakes his head. "There is at least one cat twice the size of that one on this island. I'm looking for it, but I don't see it in the shadows of the trees."

"Did you see it before," Zaria asks, in curiosity.

"Only disturbing signs of the existence of the feline." Brion admits. "Tracks only a couple of days old on the beach. A few tracks during our trek in the jungle when we were escorted to see Orin."

"My question is why the lion or even a few of its relatives did not visit us in that cave," Neil muses. "It is dark enough and they would surely have had the advantage."

"Maybe they are afraid of shadows," Sonja said as she jumps onto a fallen tree. "Or the people in the shadows, like ninjas." She did not see Vicki's little grin from her comment.

"We will have a ninja and big cat lesson as soon as we get hold of Milea and get off of this island." Zaria assures.

"Sounds fair," Vicki agrees.

The shadows of the jungle deepen as the sun kisses the horizon, providing just enough light to make it to the palace. As they draw nearer to the door, the sounds of the jungle soon change to that of deep snoring. The closer they got, the louder the sound became and frighten several smaller creatures. Zaria takes the lead and glances over her shoulder to assure her companions stay put as she peeks through the foliage. At first glimpse, she sees that the guards are on high alert, armed to the teeth and standing erect on either side of the double doors. Zaria crept closer as Neil peaks through the foliage and watches. The guards grunt slightly making Zaria drop a few unkind words and dive back into the shadows of the jungle as Neil withdraws back behind the foliage.

Only Neil reconvenes with the rest of the crew, Zaria appears to be missing. Vicki scowls and takes a chance to look past their screen to study the building, perhaps the shadow thief has managed to find an entrance. A warm breeze blows to kiss her face yet her attention goes straight to a vine that has several leaves moving against the wind. She frowns when she sees a dense shadow hovering through the vegetation, silently. Vicki pulls back slowly and announces her findings to her brother. Neil sits back and frowns as he absorbs the information.

The strong smell of rebaca root wafts down from one of the highest rooms in the palace, almost choking those on the ground. The effects of the root are immediate for one occupant of the room as Orin sits back and watches his captive pace. Milea keeps watch out the window to see that the day has marched to evening and grumbles a few words of disdain. The hostage situation she has found herself in is not setting well with her at all. The hungry leers of Orin just add to this discomfort. She keeps him at bay with the threat of her blade so far.

Milea also knows not to stand in one place for very long. She walks to one of many paintings and decorations upon the wall to study it. Once her curiosity is satisfied, she moves on to the next painting or back to the window and peers out into the foliage of the jungle. The sorceress senses her daughter nearby but cannot see her. Milea crosses her arms and stares into the distance as she notices that throughout the day, there is no news of Yabura or if the hunt is even taking place. She hopes that they find the Tragin soon.

"It seems that Neil and your friends have failed," Orin said, gleefully. He holds up a glass and once again shimmies the liquor. The image of his prey moves in the dark color liquid, delighting his booze ridden mind.

"The sun has yet to set, Orin. I have confidence in those sent on this quest," Milea turns her gaze to the ocean a distance away.

"By the time Yabura reveals itself, they will be too late. Yabura is not as easily tracked as you thought. Even my most experienced men have tried to track it. All have died in their attempts. For your companions' sake, I hope that Yabura makes their deaths quick," Orin watches with a big grin as Milea glances over her shoulder at the man.

"What," Milea asks carefully as a single eyebrow arched.

Bit by bit, Milea faces the very drunk king as her body hums with energy. A red glow surrounds the sorceress as the air in the room grows heavy. Orin smiles brightly, liking the sparks of color that flow up and down her body. The door to the room opens catching Milea's attention as a powerful something walks in.

A woman, she defiantly is not a dragonigena but instead is guise as human. Blonde hair bounces as she enters the room and closes the door. Her light green eyes sparkle as she seems to glide to Orin's side. She is about as tall as Milea. Yet she shares the same milky complexion as the devorians that haunt the ports. Milea focuses on the woman and then utters a few unhealthy and foreign words as her senses inform her that Orin's wife is the beast that her companions are searching for.

"My love. I heard Neil is returned. Is he still alive," the woman asks as she settles down next to her husband.

"For now. I sent him after Yabura along with a few of his companions. The jungle will take care of him since he is careless," Orin waves her away as if bored.

"Why did you send him after Yabura," the blonde woman asks. Her pretty face twists in a mask of concern. "Who is this.... strange woman," she glances at Milea with venom in her gaze.

"Celest. That retched Wyrm has been plaguing me for a long time. I sent him after Yabura so that he could kill it. This woman said he could," Orin points towards Milea. "As far as who she is, she's not told me. However, she will soon be a new member of my harem." Celest seems horrified then perturb. She turns to face the stranger in the room.

"You have quite the imagination, Orin. I do not think Yabura is happy to hear that you want to kill her," Milea relaxes her stance as Celest comes closer.

The wife of Orin moves from side to side as she walks like a snake sauntering towards her prey. Milea holds her ground and locks eyes with the woman, noticing the flicker of a green flame within the depths. The energy concentration from Celest increases as she nears the sorceress. Milea looks past the predator and witnesses the king drinking his wine as he watches the action. The apparent rivalry appears to stimulate the man as he groans and scratches his groin.

"If Yabura wills it, you would be dead," Celest let out a hiss at the woman.

"You can try," Milea offers. The silence that fills the room is only interrupted by the gurgling of a distance fountain. The sounds of Orin's anticipation barely break the monotony of the trickling water.

"Celest, come. Dance for me. Perhaps when you do, your new sister will be more willing to romance me," Orin commands the woman, finally. Celest glares at Milea a few moments then sauntered over towards Orin and starts to dance. Milea shakes her head then returns her gaze back out the window.

"This man has lost his damn mind. One hour. That's all the time I'm giving them before I look for them," Milea said to herself.

Milea studies the dance that Celest is performing a little then shakes her head and turns back to the window as she contemplates her next move. The sound of an empty bottle shattering against a wall brings Milea's attention back to the king as she notes that the man has consumed at least one bottle of the pungent wine. She sees Celest do a slow movement of her hips and arms as she sways around the area immediately in front of the king.

Milea muses that she has to somehow get the Tragin to reveal herself in order to properly defeat her. The sorceress gripes a little as she returns her attention back to the window. She has half a mind to leave the Tragin where she is at. Movement below the window along with the slight mew of a kitten catches Milea's ear.

She looks down and straight into a pair of dark blue eyes blinking at her from the deep shadows. The sorceress grins at the sight as Zaria peeps out of the foliage and smiles in return.

"We tracked Yabura to the palace," Zaria whispers.

"I know. She's in the room with Orin and I now," Milea agrees.

"Not good. You're going to have to get her to reveal herself," Zaria said.

"How," Milea challenges.

"Well, past experiences with other Tragin says to make her mad. But be careful. I'm not sure how powerful she is," Zaria cautions.

"Then I do not want her angry at me," Milea remarks.

"Hmm... true...well I'm sure you'll figure it out. I've got to get back down and inform the others," Zaria fades back into the shadows of the greenery.

"I'm sure," Milea grumbles in contempt and turns.

The sights and sounds of Orin grunting and scratching himself has Milea holding her head as she tries to figure out the puzzle. She then turns her concentration to Celest as the woman continues her artful dance. Celest's movements are slow as they are deliberate. Her hips sway back and forth as her arms reach for the ceiling at first then carefully fall back down to her side. Celest shimmies quickly, shaking her upper anatomy to catch Orin's attention and slow it back down as she turns, her back to him. She glimpses over her shoulder at the king with a very seductive gaze in her eyes.

Milea studies the couple a little then grumbles a little as she returns her sights back to the window, noticing that Zaria is long gone. Once again facing the room, Milea ponders how to draw the Tragin out without her becoming angry. The sorceress folds her arms as Celest makes the same motions over again, and Orin's interest has long faded. One corner of Milea's mouth goes down as she figures out a plan that would, hopefully, turn the Tragin's anger. Milea gripes to herself as she shakes her head, not willing to risk the plan yet she sees that she has very little choice. She simply hopes that it goes as she mentally plans it to.

Milea taps her fingers a little against her arms as she stares into the distance, the dance that Celest is performing is very simple. The woman is using an enchantment of some sort that the fortified wine Orin is drinking has created immunity to. Milea didn't want to do it; however, she feels that to end this hostage situation, she will provide Orin the snake that he is looking for. To do so, she will imitate Celest's dance to draw the king's attention and hopefully draw out the Tragin. Milea once again grumbles about it then exhale a little as she raises her arms slightly above her head. Her body tenses a little until she coaxes herself to relax into the slow and seductive dance.

Orin casually gazes past Celest and quickly stands up as he watches Milea's body moving in fluid motion as she dances. She makes a little eye contact with the king as she turns her back on him. Her body swaying to and fro, from top to bottom. Orin practically pushes Celest out of the way causing her to fall to the pillows as he stares at the sorceress's dance. Milea notes the alcohol that Orin consumes as well as his state of arousal are more effective than any enchantment she could cast. She is also keen to notice that her plan is not going as she hope as Celest is now standing at the spot Orin abandoned her, with her fists clutch at her side. A look of pure poison fills her features as the image of a giant snake plays in the smoke of the rebaca root. Milea finishes the silly dance as Celest hurries to Orin's side.

"Orin, my love," Celest calls. "She is using a spell against you."

"Leave me," Orin demands, his eyes still transfix upon Milea. Undaunted Celest takes hold of his hand. Growling, Orin turns and backhands the woman harshly, knocking her to the floor. "I said leave me," he snaps at her.

"Why," Celest sobs as she holds the offended cheek. Tears fill her eyes, showing the extent of her pain.

"I do not have to answer you, woman. Go back to the nursery and take care of my son," Orin dismisses. "I have terms to discuss with my new bride," he turns back to Milea and his features change into rage. She is not dancing anymore. "Why did you stop? I did not command you to stop," he snarls.

"I do not adhere to your wants or desires, Orin. I decided for myself to stop this silly little game. It is time for me to leave," Milea crosses her arms as she notes the king's rage. "If you raise your hand against me, I will take it off."

Undeterred, Orin draws his hand back and swings at Milea to strike her. The sorceress catches the hand and twists his arm, sending Orin to the ground harshly. With a bellow of anger, the king grabs Milea's leg with his free hand and pulls her down. She utters several unkind words as she hit the floor, landing on her back. Orin wastes no time to pounce atop her and pull at her clothing to rip them off. Milea thwarts his attempts and uses a levitation spell to toss the lascivious man off her. He bellows in rage as he sails into the stunned form of Celest. Milea regains her feet as Orin stands with a deep sound of rage and grabs Celest by the hair.

"Why are you still here," Orin challenges as Celest cries out in pain while he drags her. The sound prompts Orin to strike her again. "Silence! I will not tolerate two women disobeying me...." He drags her to the door as Celest's eyes change when complete anger overtakes her features.

"Here we go," Milea whispers when she feels the air in the room grow heavy and the energy level heightens to a dangerous level.

Orin nearly falls to the floor when his grip on Celest is loosens all of the sudden. He draws his hand up and sees that he has a lock of the woman's hair in his hand. He lets out a swear and drops the hair, surprised by the item. A strange rattling sound behind him prompts a turn just in time for his entire being to be blasted by a powerful burst of blue and green flames.

The blow knocks the king backward seven feet, his bare chest smoking from it. He holds the painful burn with his free hand, dropping the hair from the other. White flame light up around Celest. Her body brightens to the color of the flames as they seem to collapse upon her. The snakes tongue flicks out of her mouth, tasting the air with a good deal of steam.

Milea exhales as she witnesses the transformation. She covers her eyes and exclaims a few words of surprise as the flames explode around Celest with a deafening roar. Milea manages to see well enough to avoid the tail of the snake that Celest transform into by taking a few steps to the side. The sorceress notices that Orin is gawking. He is face to face with the very beast he sent Neil and the others to destroy, Yabura. The beast easily reaches the ceiling even though she is coiled up and swaying in her anger. The eight foot head of the snake is surrounded by an impressive hood as a trail of blonde hair trickle from the top of her head to the middle of her back. The glow of her scales drowns out any of the candles still burning in the back of the room. A kaleidoscope of dark color flames flickers from her mouth along with the tongue.

"Celest... you... are Yabura," Orin demands with awe.

"And you are foolish. To think I loved you. Then you started bringing in more women one by one. I tolerated it. But no more," Yabura hisses.

"You had my son," Orin is still awestruck.

"He died yesterday. I should have seen his weakness. You are always filled with alcohol. Yet I took my anger out on the one who helped bring him into the world. A very foolish thing on my part." Yabura's tongue flickers as more flames fill the room. Orin manages to roll out of the way when a blast of blue flame exits the serpent's mouth and slams into the floor. He ends up next to Milea. "Stay out of this, woman, and you will live."

"I've no problem with that," Milea shrugs and walks away from the man, leaving him to his fate. The action is a surprise to both Orin and Yabura.

"I see... very well," Yabura turns her attention back towards Orin and stalks towards him. The man begins to back up.

The room lights up with blue flames, various pictures on the wall melt or explode in flames. Milea walks past the angry Tragin towards the door as the ashes of the paintings hit the ground. She turns to see that Yabura is focused completely on Orin as the man backs away. He is crying out for help, but no one listening. Frantically he tries to remember what happened to his guards. At least two of them should have been outside of the room. Orin finally backs up enough until he is against the wall. His hand finds the spear that is leaning against it, left by the soldier that died.

"You'll not take me without a fight, Yabura," Orin sneers as he stands up, swinging the spear. His balance is barely there, the room itself appears to be swaying back and forth. In truth, it is his body. He mentally curses the amount of alcohol he consumed.

"Careful love. I will only forgive so much," Yabura warns.

"Die demon," Orin roars as he lunges toward the snake. She dodges but not before the spear scraps against her, opening a small wound.

"You leave me no choice, love," Yabura sneers.

Milea watches as Orin once again attacks the giant snake, belting a mighty battle cry. Yabura dodges to one side and swats the man on the back, hard, with her tail. The king hit the ground and skids within inches of Milea. He tries to stand but finds his body not obeying the request. Orin manages to roll his head back and stare at the sorceress, eyes pleading. He tries to speak, but his vocal cords are also frozen. Green ooze replaces saliva as it dribbles from his lips.

Yabura shifts so that the poison barb on her tail once again retracts. She stalks over to the king, her focus on his body. The snake once again returns to the form of a woman and bends down to lock her gaze directly into Orin's eyes. The sound of several women shrieking or cussing causes Celest to stand and face a separate door. She scanned the group of women gathering to witness the noise that they heard. A malevolent grin stretches across the Celest's features as she glances at the paralyzed Orin. She turns Orin to face the oncoming women as a blade appears in her hand. She stalks the group while providing a strong breeze to push all of Orin's harem into the room.

Milea decides that she has seen enough and exits the room by the way she came in. She opens one set of double doors then the other, stunning the guards. She does not say a word but keeps walking down the hall without a backward glance. The guards peek into the room and immediately charge forward to defend the king. Milea pauses briefly when she hears their cries of pain then silence. The sounds of a second battle reach her ears, urging her to move on as more screams echo behind her.

Rounding the corner, Milea comes upon the sight of her companions in full battle with the castle guards and a bounty of bodies skew across the floor. Sonja is using a spear to defend herself against a much taller opponent to the best of her abilities.

The taller warrior locks weapons with the girl and presses down on her. Sonja swears as she feels herself losing the battle of strength against the dragonigena man. Milea's staff appeared in her hand as she goes to assist her daughter. Sonja jumps back and is about to use her weapon when the man falls. Milea smiles at her daughter then whips around and whacks a second attacker. Moments later, the entire group of guards is defeated or has opt for a hasty retreat.

"Did you lure the Tragin out," Zaria asks.

"She revealed herself, yes," Milea said. "I also promised not to interfere and left the two lovebirds to settle their differences."

"So, we abort the hunt and get to the ship," Neil question then grins when Milea nods.

"Sound like a plan to me," Vicki concurs

Neil leads the way to a different exit when the one they decide upon is blocked by a legion of guards ready for combat. Many servants run around; confusion evident in their behavior. The chilling sound of women screaming fills the void. Milea informs her companions to hurry as they finally find an exit to the palace. It happens to be the very same one they entered when they arrived upon Cyenzie Island. The hasty journey is ground to a halt when a fist of elite guards takes up position across the path, blocking the way into the jungle. Milea, undaunted, walks to them and command they move. The guards part ways for the travelers yet they halt once more as Tanwen steps onto the path with her wings spread and her tail twisting in agitation.

"Where do you think you are going," Tanwen demands.

"To our ship and off this island. I gave your only warning earlier, child. Do not test me," Milea answers nonchalantly as she continues to walk along with her companions.

"I will do as I please," Tanwen growls, turning to face the backs of the group.

Milea and her companions do not pay her any heed as they head down the path that led to the beach. The dragonigena men retreat when they see their leader's mystical powers explode to life around her form. Milea takes a few more steps down the path before she instinctively brings up an arcane shield. The flames that are sent her way slam against it as Milea slowly faces Tanwen once again. The dragonigena woman is now floating above the ground with a mossy red glow about her. Tanwen sneers as she starts to cast another spell to attack the sorceress. A gleam cut across Milea's eyes as her gifts shimmer around her body then roars to life in full force.

Tanwen sends a second wave of flames to Milea with a roar fit for a mighty dragon. Milea catches the flames, turns and tosses them right back at Tanwen, adding an additional lightning spell with it. Both hit the woman, sending her backward and to the ground. Milea rolls her neck and shoulders as Tanwen returns to her feet, shaking a little from the effects of the two spells, her skin is charred from the flames. Tanwen then causes a massive number of spears to appear above Milea and yells as they rain down upon the woman. Milea disappears before the borage could strike her allowing the spears to hit the ground she once occupied harmlessly.

The sorceress then reappears and uses a staff to knock Tanwen's legs from under her, breaking the appendages. The dragonigena woman hollers as she falls to her knees. Milea brings the staff down on Tanwen's back, breaking the wings as she is forced to the ground. Tanwen's cries of pain are cut short as Milea delivers the killing blow, snapping her neck to provide instant death. Milea stands and takes a single step back as her staff disappears. Thunder roars and the winds pick up as the sorceress proceeds down the pathway to the ship.

The sound of distant thunder barely covers the noise of the footsteps as the group near the end of their jungle hike. Milea fades into sight walking next to Zaria and is issued a stern warning for such tricks. The sorceress smirks from the scolding she receives. Vicki takes the lead along with Brion as they go under another giant spider's web and head down the straight path, increasing the pace when more gentle thunder is heard. Neil, now walking with Milea, inquiries about Yabura as he wonders which wife the Tragin is posing as. Milea informs him it is Celest causing the man to pause in his hike and stare after his employer. Milea stops and faces Neil as he takes a deep breath in and out.

"That's the wife I got in trouble with. So, when I saw that giant white snake, it wasn't a dream," Neil's features twist into concern.

"She didn't curse you if that's your concern. For some reason, I don't think Celest knows she's a Tragin," Milea assures "Come on, let's keep up else I think Vicki will leave us."

The jungle finally parts finding the group on the beach. The twin moons are half full each-one waxing and the other waning, the light bouncing off the various parts of the ship. Neil stops and gawks at the vessel. The hole in the back of the ship is no longer there. All the scraps and dents along the side are gone. The figurehead seems delighted to see the entire crew once again. Her eyes wide with excitement and her head held high. Instead of clutching the wooden cloth to her form, she allowed it to slip past her shoulders just a little bit.

Vicki stares at the vessel briefly then shrugs and inspects the ship to make sure everything is complete. She nods her approval and goes aboard the ship. Brion grumbles a little under his breath as he follows the woman. The secondary accommodations aboard a slaver's ship did not appeal to him. Sonja quickly boards afterward, catching up with her new mentors. Zaria smiles when she witnesses Neil hugging the front of the ship.

"Welcome aboard the *Lady of the Night*," Milea whispers to her cousin.

"The what," Zaria chuckles. "Oh, this is going to be fun!"

"Milea... how did this happen? I mean. This is not done by ordinary means," Neil steps back to admire the ship as the woman addressed approaches him.

"I told you, that the wood of the ship is from my home. It is enchanted," Milea said and touches his shoulder.

"I... uh oh," Neil focuses pass the sorceress to the forest.

Milea turns in time to see Yabura gliding out of the trees and onto the beach. The open hood is now closed, flames no longer lick at her lips. She flicks her tongue once as the image of the snake fades and is replaced by Celest walking towards the ship. She pauses after taking a few steps.

"Who... are you," Celest requests of the sorceress.

"I am usually your enemy, Yabura. However, not this night," Milea levitates Neil and herself onto the ship. "Farewell."

The ship slides with a slight scraping noise as it pushes back into the water. Once there it bounces a little, turns, and unfurrowing its sails. They billow out and the Lady of the Night once again takes to the open seas. Celest watches until the ship disappears into the night shadows. She turns, glances over her shoulder then heads back to the jungle in order to return to the castle. A warm rain-shower starts to fall upon the jungle.

CHAPTER TEN

The Ghost Ship

The ship sails true to course away from Cyanize Island for at a full day and night. The strong winds carry it to the destination and are aided by cooperative currents covering a distance that Neil estimates take at least a week. The winds whistle a little, carrying the tune of the wooden figurehead as she seems to hum pleasantly during the journey. The positive energy is felt by the current helmsman, Brion, as he guides the vessel under the watchful eye of Neil deeper into the tropics.

The evening is once again upon them and Neil's sharp eyesight finds his mark and points it out to Brion. The ship is adjusted to maintain the path to the Boiling Seas. At their current clip, Neil estimates that they should be at their location within the next few days. Zaria watches as Sonja ties a few well-rehearsed knots that she has learned, to include the one that kept the hatch closed during the mystical storm.

The shiadokat invites the girl to tie the same impressive knot around her wrists and smiles as Sonja obliges. The girl then sits back and grins in triumph when she completes the difficult twist with pride. Zaria studies the rope and complements the girl on the craftsmanship of the knot. Then, with the flick of her wrists, she frees herself and holds the rope, still in knots, up as if studying it.

Sonja gawks at the feat, not sure if she tied the item correctly or not. The girl then starts a barrage of questions as Zaria laughs and answers quite that Sonja will learn in time. Milea sits down with her daughter and is hit with the laundry list of questions from Sonja. The sorceress chuckles a little as she reminds her child that it is the way of the Shiado. Zaria grins in a very feline fashion as she winks at the girl. The banging of a wooden spoon against a cast iron pot captures everybody's attention. Brion mutters a word of prayer when he sees the source of the noise.

"Food's ready," Vicki calls out. "Plenty for all!" She sees the hesitation of the group. "Oh, come on, I'm not as bad as before."

"Neil... should we be so cruel as to feed our hostess this," Brion asks as quiet as possible. He remembers the first time he ate Vicki's cooking. He is still recovering, and it has been about seven weeks.

"We'll have to give Vicki a chance. Maybe she improved," Neil assures.

"Why are you guys hesitating," Zaria asks as she goes over to Vicki.

"Here you go," Vicki hands Zaria a bowl of what appears to be white soup. "Enjoy! Next!"

The soup is steaming with many items floating within a white milky substance. Zaria stirs up the stew and takes a whiff tilting her head when she notices that the food smells spicy. With a shrug, she pulls her spoon out and takes her first bite of the meal. Zaria's eyes widen from the hot spices at first then they watered as the wave of heat spread through-out her body. Even the broth that holds the entire meal together is painfully hot with pepper. Zaria then gags as she tastes the other items within the soup. Is it fish or chicken?

It is very hard to distinguish, perhaps her tongue is burnt to a cinder, and she is now unable to eat again. The vegetables even taste strange to her. Sonja slaps Zaria upon the back to make the woman swallow then get her to breathe. At first, it didn't work until the girl whacks the woman's back, hard. Zaria coughs and takes a deep breath in. The heat of the food travels the entire path and feels like it burst into flames when air is introduced.

"Are you alright," Sonja asks, her head tilting in concern. Neil and Brion both are shocked that the woman is still alive.

"It's... umm... spicy," Zaria rationalizes then coughs. "Among other things." She mumbles under her breath.

"The stew is an old recipe I found in father's book. I followed it to the letter," Vicki beams with pride.

"That would explain why mom did all the cooking," Neil muses.

"Here you go, Sonja," Vicki offers the girl a bowl.

"I'm umm," Sonja jumps to her feet and holds her hands up in rejection. "I'm not hungry right now." She assures and is quick to retreat away from the food.

Milea politely refuses her bowl of stew as she stands and approaches the bow of the ship to peer out at the horizon. The day is almost over with yet there is a spot in the distance that is swallowed by deep and dark clouds. The edifice is towering and gathering as it twists and turns. Milea frowns at the manifestation as it forms into a strange skeletal shape with a red light twinkling within the depths of the strange darkness. A wave of negative energy pushes forth from it like a cold wind washing over Milea causing an involuntary shutter. As the marine vessel solidifies, it resembles the dark ship Charred Rose. The deplorable condition seen even at this distance changes Milea's mind.

"We've got company," Milea announces, her sights still locked on the invader.

Sonja is the first to go to her mother's side and is followed by Neil as he swears and grabs a telescope in passing. Vicki drops her spoon into her stew and pulls off her apron as she goes to the front to take a look out. Brion stays at the wheel, capable of seeing the approaching gloom from his vantage point. He did not like the fact that the ship is sailing straight at it. Zaria hesitates a little and makes sure the focus of the cook is still in front before she tosses the remaining soup over the edge of the ship. Dusting her hands, the shiadokat then joins her companions at the front as Brion watches then chuckles from the actions.

Thunder booms with red lightning flashes across the dark clouds as the unusual storm nears. Neil puts his telescope to his eye and peers into the gloom with a frown. His features soon become a mask of fear when he sees the three-mast ship looming into his view. Its sails are tatter and stringing, a host of spirits spiral around the deck and mast of the ship. It is full of holes and there is no way it should be floating upon the water, yet is doing so effortlessly. Neil cusses up a good streak as he takes his telescope down and charges back to the helm. The ghoulish ship unwraps its clouds which makes Vicki drops a sailor's oath and a prayer as she retreats from the rails. The black wood radiates with evil as strange lights circle it and are swallowed by the ghoulish ship. The black clouds of the storm in its wake blotted out all the stars above yet Zaria did not feel any comfort in the darkness that is created.

Neil yanks on the wheel to turn the ship around and the vessel obeys, completing a near perfect circle as it shifts the sails in order to catch a wind to speed away from the approaching danger. The ghost ship turns and picks up unusual speed as it hones in on the Lady of the Night. The foul winds of the storm that surrounds the haunted vessel fill the enchanted ship's sails, pushing the *Lady of the Night* along putting some distance between the two. Sonja takes a deep breath in and numerous steps back when her senses detect several voices upon the putrid winds. She stares at the ship and sees a pair of hands reaching like chains towards the Lady of the Night. Milea calls to her child and tells her to retreat to the sleeping cabin. Sonja obeys without question as Milea focuses once again on the ship. Even for a ghost ship something is very strange and dare she say, unnatural, about it.

"What is that thing," Milea asks.

"It's the *Dragodu*. A cursed ship. Use to belong to Jackal the Black. He was known to kill without remorse. He ran into a powerful mage one day, raped her repeatedly before killing her. She cursed him to roam the seas forever and inadvertently cursed us as well. He hates the living pirates of today," Vicki explains taking an additional step back. "He constantly wants to add to his crew of trapped souls."

Viki's eyes met those of the ghost captain in the distance. They widen as she tries to take another step back but end up slipping. She falls to the deck of the ship, her legs no longer working for her. Vicki turns away from the pursuing ghost ship as her breathing increases.

"Vicki," Milea goes over towards the woman. Vicki is shaking and sweating.

"He's going to ram us!" Brion announces.

"No! She just got repaired! Damn it, I thought Ra'jil took care of that thing," Neil shouts and runs up to the mast.

Brion utters a few unkind words as he retakes the wheel and tries to maneuver the ship to shake the pursuer. It is in vain as the ghost ship continues to follow the *Lady of the Night*. Neil unrolls a third sail to aide in their escape and feels the ship lurch forward as the speed increases. He swears as he knows they are now way off course, however, escaping the *Dragodu* is the priority now. A growl of determination floats upon the foul winds as the *Dragodu* picks up its speed, closing the gap between the two ships.

Another attack hits Vicki and she cries out in pain as she holds her head, her trembling increases as she battles the ghostly captain from taking control of her. Milea kneels down and hugs

Vicki's shoulders in an attempt to shield her from the attack. The sorceress casts a banishment spell but it is batted away by the evil spirit which has focus upon Vicki. Milea swears a little when she feels Vicki's body temperature going down at a rapid pace.

"Zaria, I need you to keep an eye on Vicki," Milea calls to her companions.

"I'm here," Zaria kneels next to Vicki. "She's trembling, what's wrong with her?"

"She has the ability to see and sense ghosts. Perhaps even channel them. I think she might have one focused on her," Milea explains in short. "See what you can do to help her."

"Got it," Zaria nods.

Zaria holds Vicki close and gently speaks to her in words that the woman does not understand. Milea directs her attention to the stern of the ship uses a short teleportation spell to get there and face the oncoming threat. The air warms up as a different wind surrounds Milea, a thin red glow emits from her form briefly then explodes out into a slow-moving flame upon her body. Milea causes the flames to circle her twice before sending them towards the ghost ship. The fire hit the vessel causing a scream of rage to echo from the ghoul but did not catch as they went out just as soon as they hit.

The waves around the *Dragodu* grab and try to pull it down yet it shakes free and continues forward, this time the sound of laughter came from it. Milea shifts her stance as she tries to recall one of her sister's spells when the *Dragodu* backs off all the sudden and changes course with a growl of disdain. The same pair of eyes that greeted Milea in the storm glares at the sorceress from the clouds, echoing thunder drowns out any words on the wind. Milea stares down the eyes and watches as they disappear along with the ghost ship.

Slowly and a little hesitant, Milea calms her abilities as the sky returns to normal. Stars twinkle as Zaria completes her chant and Milea returns to Vicki's side. The shiadokat stands and scowls as she stares into the distance and sees that the sun has just set. Milea touches

Vicki's shoulder and is relieved when she feels the young woman is warming up as well as her breathing pattern returning to normal. Whatever tried to get her has let her go before the *Dragodu* left the scene. Vicki gets to her feet and leers out past the bow. The last remanence of the sun's rays kisses the horizon. Sonja exits the sleeping cabin when she senses the ghost ship has departed.

"Neil, we can't stay in the open ocean. The *Dragodu* will return for us," Vicki informs.

"I know," Neil admits with a small swear then glances to the left. A large landmass barely peeks over the horizon. "We will go through the strait of Fairge. See if we can make it before it gets too dark." He goes to retake the helm.

"Aye. We will have to harbor next to it so that we can see how to steer the next day," Vicki adds.

"That ship's not gonna get us right," Sonja asks.

"No, the *Dragodu* fears the strait. We will be safe," Neil assures as he set the course.

"Why didn't we go there first?" Zaria arches an eyebrow.

"It's out of our way, difficult to navigate, and... it too is full of restless spirits," Neil answers.

"Lovely," Sonja mumbles.

Night fully arrives as the *Lady of the Night* pulls up to the entrance to the Strait of Fairge and drops anchor. Sonja whistles in admiration as she studies the imposing landmass. It comprises of two large islands that stretch for miles east and west yet is very short down the middle. Jagged rocks and outcrops promise to make the journey perilous yet not impossible to get through.

The high cliff sides are quiet as a graveyard, no birds or marine animal roost upon the shores of the island. Milea focuses upon a darkened land mass, staring down the strait. Starlight did not penetrate the forborne darkness. A cool breeze blows from its surface. Milea's right eyebrow ticks up slightly when she senses a being watching from within the glooms.

Vicki's agitated swearing catches Milea's ear as well as the rest of the crew, it is the most active the woman has been since the Dragodu disappearance hours ago. Milea to turn and observe what has upset the l'vane woman and smiles a little when she discovers it. Someone has rouse Vicki's anger by tossing the soup she fixed overboard during the *Dragodu* appearance. Zaria whistles a little tune as she innocently rocks from heel to toe with her hands behind her back.

Brion, on the other hand, could not help but comment that it is the soup that turned the ship away. Vicki makes the elf eat the first bowl of her new batch of soup for his comments. Sonja decides to take an apple up to the crow's nest and eat it there. She is joined by Zaria with her own fruit to nibble on.

Neil chokes down his soup and immediately picks up a strong liquor to wash it down.

"That's going to give me some powerful heartburn tonight," Neil comments about his sister's soup, "and the liquor is going to give me an equally powerful headache." He plucks the strings of his mandolin to tune it a little.

"Dopie ginger will help settle your stomach," Milea hints as she walks past the man.

"I'll have to get some from Brion," Neil muses and finishes tightening a few of this mandolin's strings. His fingers run across the instrument as he begins to play.

The ocean waves gently rock the *Lady of the Night.* Sonja yawns and stretches settling down for the night in the crow's nest. Zaria smiles at the tired girl then focuses upon the strait when her hearing detects movement. The darkness that masks the waterway is too dense even for her enhance sight.

Zaria makes a sound similar to an annoyed feline before she jumps out of the crow's nest to the deck and walks toward the very front of the boat. She steps out as far as she could to get a close look at the gloom. Still, she could not see into the strait, the veil that hides it did so soundly. Zaria returns to the deck of the ship deep in thought and does not acknowledge Milea as the sorceress settles down to meditate.

The sorceress calms her mind as she closes her eyes, a thin red light surrounds her and starts to pulsate to her quieting breath. Her body lifts off the deck, levitating just at the height of the rails. Her mind is quieting down from her day to prepare for sleep when a sharp pain slams into her. Milea goes on high alert as she focuses on and stops the pain. The same pair of eyes that greet her in the storm sparkle as they appear and slam into her. Milea opens her eyes ready for an attack as she lands upon her feet making a thumping sound upon the deck.

The noise catches Vicki's attention as the l'vane woman finishes tying up one of many loose ropes. The sorceress's instincts alert her to turn to the island as she catches movement out the corner of her eye. A soft glow radiates from the otherwise silent black hills of the strait. It lingers not too far from the waterway, wavering for a few seconds then disappears. Vicki scowls at the apparition remembering that almost all the restless spirits are sailors who drowned while trying to reach the other side.

"What's that?" Milea said as she stares into the darkness. Her abilities deactivating at her mental command.

"It's a dragon lord's daughter, Uzuri," Vicki explains. "Her legend is pretty sad." She paused. "I think Neil's singing it now, actually."

The churn of the ocean is barely noticed by those aboard the *Lady of the Night*. Neil continues to sing a beautiful yet sad song about a woman, beautiful and fair. Her name is Uzuri, and she is the daughter of a Crimson Dragon Lord named Etan, both immortal Eltis from long ago. Tales of Uzuri's beauty reached lands far and wide before she fell in love with a mortal man. After proving himself, the man got permission to marry Uzuri. In doing so, she lost her immortality and became his mortal bride. Uzuri was taken to his home where he changed from a loving husband to a very cruel master. He beat her constantly and did unspeakable horrors to the woman.

Hearing what was going on, the Crimson Dragon Etan flew into a rage. He went to rescue his daughter then punishing the husband and his family before taking her away. On the way back to the Castle, Etan accidentally dropped his daughter over this strait. Uzuri was still mortal and died upon impact. Guilt-ridden and saddened by the event, Etan cast away his own immortality to guard the strait. No one knows if he is still alive, or if he has passed into obscurity. Very few have navigated the strait and lived to tell the tale.

"So... I saw her ghost? She's a powerful spirit, to say the least," Milea said and watches the darkened hills.

"Very," Vicki agreed. "Only a handful of captains have gone through that place and lived. Ra'jil is one. Neil is the other, frequently mind you. All others perished." She finishes her chore and turns to the sleep cabin. "I think I should get some sleep. I can almost guarantee I will have a bad time tomorrow."

"I'd have to agree," Milea said. "Anything else that we should be wary of?"

"This is technically a ship's graveyard. However, I don't see any wreckage, that's one thing. The detail that Neil didn't say in his story is that there is a rumor that the crimson dragon is asleep now, in the strait. He awakens at certain times, and no one knows when those are. Nor do we know what triggers it" Vicki said with a sad shake of the head. The two women started walking as Milea furrows her brow and place a finger upon her chin in thought as they approach the sleep quarters.

"Ladies," Brion greets the women as he opens the door for them. "See you in the morning."

Brion closes the door and walks to one of the mats that he retrieves from below deck and settles down to listen to Neil as he switches to a slower almost lullaby-like song. Zaria leaps from the crow's nest and lands quietly upon the deck to sit down next to the elf. Both listen to the melody in silence for a little while as the captain entertains them. Zaria shakes her head as she thinks about the journey and their goal.

"This is going to add some time to our journey. I hope Milea's sister is as stubborn as she is," Zaria stretches her legs.

"My gut is telling me that she is. Or it could be Vicki's cooking talking to me," Brion pats his belly, pouting a little.

"I would wager the latter," Zaria assures, rubbing her own belly.

The night marches on uneventful as Zaria finds herself the only one still awake upon the mystical vessel, or so she thinks. Milea exits the sleeping cabin and tips to the bow of the ship in order to stare once again into the bleak of the strait. The rays of dawn are just starting to peek over the horizon to illuminate the world. Vicki exits the sleeping cabin next and shakes her head as she closes the door.

Brion stretches as he awakens and watches the I'vane woman make her way to the side of the ship. He rolls to his feet as Sonja lands a few inches from where his head once lay. The girl apologizes then goes to stand at her mother's side. Milea greets her daughter then sends the girl into the hull for her favorite breakfast of granola. Sonja eagerly obliges and does a whoop of joy as she rapidly descends the stairs. Zaria takes a deep breath and exhales as she stretches with the shadows of night yielding to the light of the sun.

The barking of whale-seals delights the crew as they swim by in the distance. The noise of the sea creatures penetrates the walls of the sleeping cabin and awakens Neil. The captain opens his eyes and groans in pain as the admission of light starts his head to pound mercilessly. He sits up and holds it for a few minutes, and then with great effort, Neil places his feet upon the floor and stands to go to the door. His head pounds with every light footstep he takes.

The captain drops a few unkind words as he opens the door and receives a blast of light from the morning sun. He lets out a sound of surprise which only aides to the headache as he covers his eyes at first. He laments a little about the number of spices and liquor he consumed last night as the effects feel like a demon dancing upon his skull. Neil's stumbling onto the deck brings attention from his crew mates with Zaria smiling in an attempt not to laugh at the man's suffering. Brion turns when he hears the cabin door close and shakes his head in sympathy. Neil, complete with disheveled clothing and hair, is slow to makes his way over to the first mast.

"Good morning, Neil," Brion greets, his voice in regular tone.

"Not so loud," Neil grumbles.

"Can you guide us through the strait," Vicki asks.

"Barely," Neil admits, staggering a little. "Brion, you and I are going to keep the ship from hitting the sides by using the bamboo poles I saw below deck."

"I'll go get them," Sonja volunteers and hurries to the trap door that leads below.

"While she is getting those," Neil remarks, "Vicki, you are to make sure we sail under wind power. I think the ship is too new to know what to do."

"Alright. That will work since I'm also going to have a miserable journey into that place," Vicki agrees.

"I'll keep an eye out for things. I can see a little better in darkened places than Sonja," Zaria offers.

"Who's going to steer." Brion asks.

The captain turns to the bow of the ship along with his companions. A strong breeze whips the hair around of all aboard the *Lady of the Night,* though it is gentle. Milea meditates, levitating, at the very bow of the ship in a similar fashion as she did the previous night. She mentally tries to reach out and contact her sister but feels nothing in return, almost as if she is reaching for air. Milea pulls her mind back and focuses on the task ahead of going through the strait. Her ears detect the conversation that Neil is having with those on the ship.

The ship groans a little as Neil's eyes plead with Vicki then watches as she scoffs at him a little and walks away. Winds whistle as Brion walks to the left of the ship and meets with Sonja to retrieve his pole. He checks the length and whispers a few sharp words; the strait is going to be a tight fit. Sonja goes over to hand the second pole to Neil and receives a thanks from the captain. The girl then heads to the crow's nest before Neil could request her assistance with her mother.

Zaria is also out of earshot, going to the same side as Brion. Neil turns to his sister once more to see the woman is now rigging two ropes upon the smaller sail. The large sail is roll up and neatly tied away. Grumbling to himself, Neil staggers a little towards his employer. Upon hearing Neil's footsteps, Milea opens her eyes and lowers herself to stand and face the oncoming man. She smiles a little in sympathy from his haggard condition as he stops and sways a little then shakes his head. Neil's eyes cross a little as he attempts to focus one of the images that he thinks is the real sorceress.

"Milea, do you mind taking the helm," Neil asks as he leans upon the bamboo pole in his possession.

"Not at all," Milea answers and walks with him back towards the helm as she pulls her hair back. "Beautiful performance last night, Neil."

"Thank you," Neil smiles. "Brion, are you alright with this?" He asks as he goes to his side of the ship.

"Fine but a little concern," Brion said. "This pole only reaches out three feet. That is a tight tunnel."

"We won't have three feet of space until we reach the other side. We will barely have one foot on each side, and it gets trickier. You and I must keep the ship from hitting any sharp rocks. Just push on it, and we should be fine," Neil informs.

"Lovely," Brion rolls his eyes.

"Sonja's in the crow's nest. Zaria's out front," Milea says as she notes the location of her companions. "Vicki has the sails," she reaches her destination, "we go as quiet as possible."

"And hope Etan's not awake," Zaria whispers.

The wind fills the small sail, clicking from behind indicates that the anchor is lifted. Vicki walks backward until the rope is taut against her lower back and moves to the left, pulling the sails with her. The ship hesitates to obey the request but ultimately yields to it and turns from the adjustment. Brion readies his pole, standing firmly upon the deck as Neil did the same on the other side. The warm light of the sun is replaced by the cold shadows of the strait.

Zaria holds her breath as the ship tips past the first set of jagged rocks. They appear to be the teeth or very strong tail spikes of an unimaginably large animal. Brion decides to return to the front of the ship and use his pole to gently push the ship away from the large rock. Neil does the same at his post pushing extra hard against a strange-shaped boulder. The rock moves a little under the pressure of the pole but remains in place as the ship glides by. Both then walk down the ship to the stern to make sure it did not hit the sharp points. The two return to the bow and repeats the exercise.

Milea keeps a tight grip upon the wheel. She adjusts the projection of the ship it every once in a while. Zaria calls out an exceptionally large boulder that neither Neil nor Brion are in a position to push past. Vicki shifts the sails as the light breezes are detected from two main directions, behind and over the shorter of the two large landmasses. A light and whispers of voices catch her attention yet are ignored. Vicki scolds herself to keep focus upon the sails and not gander into the darkness.

Sonja keeps quiet and low in the crow's nest. Her senses scream danger as soon as they enter the darkness of the strait. Peeking over the edge of her hiding spot, she sees hollow outlines of men and beasts engage in a battle that waged centuries before her birth. Multi-headed monsters are taken down by a large beast with a single horn. Shaking herself,

Sonja decides to duck back down once again in order not to draw any attention to herself. She is not sure what the restless spirits are capable of.

Shadows deepen as the water slosh from the passage of the ship. Zaria scowls at the darkness, wondering if there is another Shadow Eltis responsible for the deep gloom that she herself cannot lift. The prospects are slim but not impossible as one of her kin could have perished upon the rocks of the strait long ago. Zaria studies the cliff face a little to locate the source of the shade. The sight that greets her are skeletons lining both sides either dangling from above or lodge into the cliff faces them-selves. The bones are from all folks that reside on Bri'al. it looks like a massive force drove them into the cliffs then glued them there as trophies. Zaria shutters at the thought then returns her attention back to the front of the ship to continue her lookout.

Ghost float about concentrating on Vicki to gain her attention some to the point of touching her. She ignores them however; her breath does quicken a little. Vicki pulls herself together mentally and concentrates on the far, unseen end of the strait in a renewal of determination to get out of it. A woman appears out of the gloom on one of the bigger rocks that Neil is about to push the ship away from. The l'vane man swears and Zaria echoed his words as she nearly falls on her backside. The ship comes to a sudden halt as a variety of spirits howl and float about, spiraling into the air and around the main mast.

Vicki falls to her knees and holds her ears to blot out the noises. In the crow's nest, Sonja shut her eyes and covers them with her arm, the silver scales upon the left arm are tingling to an almost painful level. The ship shakes and bucks a little with

Milea keeping a tight grip on the wheel until the enchanted vessel calms down. The sorceress then focuses upon the intruder with a stern gaze of disapproval. Neil repeats his swears as he stares at the woman on the rock. She is a specter, that is clear as her body is transparent and off color from the living.

A strange, unnatural, shade of blue graces her skin that is showcased in a torn and tattered dress. The gruesome details of her demise, large sword like rocks, protrude out of her back and pulsate with angry energy. Brion mumbles unfiltered words under his breath as he recalls Neil's song from the previous night. They are gazing upon the daughter of the dragon lord, Etan. Milea takes in the situation and comes to the same conclusion as her companions.

"You cannot go this way. Why do you disturb my peace," the woman said in a haunting tone.

"Lady, Uzuri. We ask for passage through your strait. We seek to go to the Temple of Light in the Boiling Seas," Milea hops down from her vantage point and touches Vicki's head in passing. The I'vane woman shakes herself a little and glances after Milea before she jumps up and goes up to take the wheel.

"Why," Uzuri asks.

"I go to the aide of my sister. The temple she is visiting has been attacked during her stay. This is the only means of travel to the temple of light as mystical means have been futile," Milea answers in a gentle way.

"And those with you," Uzuri questions.

"They accompany me. Two are guides, one is their traveling companion. One is a cousin that was stranded on an island but rescued and lastly, my daughter," Milea responds.

"I see," Uzuri focuses on Milea. "No names? I would like to learn who you are as I sense at least two aboard this ship that have powers familiar to me and I do not have kind memories of these powers."

"Oswind's Lamppost," Zaria whispers her oath. "Don't make her mad, Milea." she warns.

"We did not mean to disturb you. We seek safe passage. In passing, names need not be exchanged," Milea remarks calmly as she folds her arms.

"Foolish mortal..." Uzuri snarls, her eyes flashing in anger.

A purple bolt of lightning careens across the sky and aims for the ship. Milea draws the bolt in and redirects it beyond the rear of the ship. It slams into a bolder wall twenty feet behind the stern, blasting out a few large rocks. Uzuri watches the bolt in surprise at its projection then sneers as she returns her attention back to the ship and those on board.

The winds pick up to near howling, rocking the ship back and forth as it groans in an effort to stay in one place. Zaria digs her fingers in the wood in an effort to hold onto the ship as a force tries to pick her up and toss her overboard. She hears Neil's practiced oath and assumes that he is in the same situation. Brion grips the rail as Vicki strangles the wood of the wheel in an effort to stay aboard.

Milea rolls her shoulders a little then mentally calms down the winds much to the ghost's surprise. Neil exhales in relief, the motion and sounds are echoed by Brion. Zaria lets a low rumble of discontent escape her throat as she keeps an eye on both Uzuri and the shadows around her. Vicki relaxes her grip on the ship's wheel once the winds calm down. Sonja peeps from the crow's nest and sees that whatever creatures that accompanied Uzuri have departed. Milea meets the gaze of the specter unflinching at the very apparent anger in Uzuri's features. She sees the anger morph to curiosity then admiration as Uzuri takes a step closer.

"You are no ordinary mortal," Uzuri observes. "Not all are powerful enough to face me without ill effect."

"I did not claim to be ordinary, milady," Milea said. "My mission is critical. I cannot tally any longer to entertain your curiosity." She watches the ghost grow a little perturbed by the words. "I ask you this, if you are given the choice, would you save one dear to you? Such as a sister? As it is my case." A strong silence fills the strait.

"So be it... I feel the presence of the *Dragodu* on the path from which you came," Uzuri spies each member of the ship. "For that reason alone, I let you go on your way. But do not ask for my aide should you disturb my father, you will be on your own," the ghost fades from sight.

"Thank you, milady," Milea bows her head a little as she returns to the helm. Vicki stepped out of the way, returning to her post. "Keep a sharp eye out. I am not sure what to expect out of her."

"I think you might have upset her." Zaria points out.

"It would not be the first time she becomes upset," Milea assures. "I will guarantee, it will not be the last."

"Let's get while she's in a decent mood," Neil concurs

The winds pick up to fill the sails once again, and the ship starts to glide down the still dark path to the far-off exit. Neil and Brion once again take up their positions on the ship keenly aware that they may encounter other unexpected hosts as they travel. Zaria calls forth whatever obstacle they are headed towards and informs them that the strait appears to be opening in the distance after the very narrow channel they approach. She can see further down the waterway, a stark contrast from when they first entered. Sonja peeks over the edge of the crow's nest, she sees that the skeletons also disappeared once Uzuri left the scene. A disturbing thought came to the girl when she concludes that the skeletons may have just stood up and walk away.

CHAPTER ELEVEN

Crimson Dragon

The strait grows even narrower as they continue the way through the strait. The shore on either side of the ship towers inches from the vessel. A ghost groans as it reaches for the ship. It is thwarted by a mystical force. Milea shifts her shoulders as she continues to concentrate on the road ahead. The darkness began to lighten as daylight returns. Streams of light struck the wood as it moves by a few more stones. Neil wipes his brow as he leans on his pole, the strait is now wide open with just one or two more rocks to push past.

Sonja takes a deep breath in and out when the sunlight returns, lying on her back to admire the clear sky a distance in the air. The shape of the hole she is studying reminds her of a giant dragon in flight with the tail stretching towards the direction they just came from and the head in the direction they are going. The wings are wide and spread out as if the beast is gliding.

The girl blinks then sit up and looks left and right, noting the huge area they are in now is a mirror of what she sees above. She almost unleashes unkind words at the realization and glances down at the ocean and sees a long row of rocks leading back towards the interior of the strait. They are lined in a nice row and could pass as the defensive scales upon the back of a giant earth dragon.

Curious, she goes to the rear of the nest and notices that the sharp boulders reach for miles behind. They are, in fact, the rocks that Brion and Neil push upon to steer the ship around. The girl concentrates and peers down into the water. There is a large and dangerous shadow submerged just under the ship. A strange sinking feeling grows in the pit of Sonja's stomach when she realizes that she is actually looking at a submerged enormous dragon.

"Mom," Sonja calls from her vantage point.

"In a minute, Sonja," Milea responds back. She is concentrating on maneuvering the ship into another corridor. The route to the open sea.

"Ok," Sonja climbs down the ropes. "Zaria, something is not right."

"What do you mean?" Zaria concentrates on the girl.

Sonja points up which Zaria follows with a studious look about her at first. Upon seeing the shape and realization of what it is, she swore and turns her focus down into the water with Sonja to see they are gliding on a thin sheet of water above a giant creature's head. The warm breeze beacons and Brion sees the open ocean just beyond the rock that is in the way. With a firm nod, he pushes on the last rock. It gives way a little then, much to his surprise, pushes back.

Brion let his pole go and watches as it rockets towards the other side. It shatters against the cliff face. Neil turns and uses his arm to shield his face from the debris. He faces Brion as the elf returns his gaze back to the rock. The stone lights up, becoming dark red in color. The waters churn violently, pushing the *Lady of the Night* away from the strait. Brion and Neil both focus upon the back of the boat when they hear Sonja gasp of surprise. Zaria turns and drops a few words of her own, causing Milea and Vicki a minor curiosity.

"Oh..." Brion starts.

The water explodes behind the ship, forcing the *Lady of the Night* further into the open ocean. Vicki stumbles then turn around and a slew of unkind words drop from her lips. Milea is forced into the wheel briefly then props herself up and whips around when she hears the dragon's bellow of rage. The cliffs are dwarfed by the size of the dragon, his deep red scales seem to glow all around. His large eyes focus upon the small ship, their golden color light up with a red flame to reflect his fury. His red scales shimmers in the sunlight as they move from his inhalation. Zaria takes several steps back when she sees flames lighting up upon the dragon's maul. The shiadokat cusses, there is way too much sunlight for her to fold the ship into the shade. Etan digs his claws into the cliff as he to props himself up and draws his head back and up. His wings lift up, blotting out the sunlight and replacing it with an ominous red glow.

"What did you do," Neil demands of the elf, an edge in his voice.

"I only pushed on a rock," Brion snaps back.

A very audible whoosh echoes around as Etan inhales, expanding his chest. Flames dance around his maul as he opens his mouth to display the terrible fire within. Milea frowns at the dragon and steps away from the wheel to face the dragon. The sorceress plants her feet and centers her attention upon the bright flames as the dragon exhales with a bellow loud as thunder.

The force of which causes waves of water to press against the ship's stern, pushing it away rapidly. A bright gleam crosses Milea's eyes as the flames approach, causing the element to falter a little in flight. The flames reach only a foot away from the ship then double back, aiming straight for Etan's nose. The fire smacks the giant dragon harshly, bringing a sound of surprise from the beast. Etan rears his head back and roars into the air as if he is lamenting. More waves slam into the ship, pushing up the speed considerably and enough to avoid the large claw that Etan reach with, whacking just the tip of the ship.

"Hell! Hoist all sails. Catch the fastest wind possible," Neil shouts out. The sails roll out into place and shift to find a strong wind. Neil swears when he notes there is nothing more than a light breeze at the moment. "Not good."

Milea raises a shield as Etan uses his long tail to smack the ship, causing a sound of pain to escape the wooden edifice as well as send it way off course. Milea flinches as the tail strikes again, shaking her head to rid of the sting as she focuses back on the dragon. Etan roars once again as flames belch from his maul in an extra wide column.

The fire hit the shield knocking Milea down to the deck onto her back. The sorceress rolls over and gets back to her feet as her features reflect her displeasure of the dragon and the lack of the wind. She concludes that if the wind will not come willingly, she will force it to do so. The *Lady of the Night* stops in its motions forward and starts to retreat back to the dragon as Etan draws breath, shifting the direction of the ocean surrounding him.

"Zaria, take the helm," Milea calls out.

"What going on and what are you going to do," Zaria asks obeying the request

"Etan is many times stronger than his child. I'd wager he strong as Keela. Thus, I am going to get us the hell out of here," Milea sits down just above the cabin door.

Milea quickly takes in the direction of travel, south, and closes her eyes to pull in the wind from the north to fill the sails. The breeze is small and gentle at first causing Milea to frown and concentrate, her body pulsates with energy as she pulls harder on the stubborn element. The cool north breeze warms up and surrounds the ship, licking at the sails lazily. Sonja cries out in alarm as Etan takes to the sky, his roar filling the sky as his powerful wing beats deafen those aboard the ship. Milea ignores the calls and oaths of her fellows as she completely captures the element she mentally chases and sends it forth. The winds explode to a gale force, filling the sails in a matter of seconds and jolting the ship forward.

The *Lady of the Night* moans as ropes pull full extent and all sails spread to capture the mystical winds. Those at the front of the ship reach well beyond the bow. Vicki cusses violently as the ropes pull her to the front of the ship and gets out of them before they go taut. The ship lifts up barely keeping in the water as the speeds continue to accelerate it to an unknown destination. Dragon fire just misses the stern of the *Lady of the Night.* Milea pushes a second then third wave of wind into the sails, pulling in the east and west directions as well to increase the speed of the ship threefold.

The winds toy and fight each other, twisting in a frightening tornado every so often then dissipate and become part of the acceleration. Zaria lets out a strong sound of effort as she holds the wheel in order to keep it in as straight of a line as possible. Sonja holds fast to a rope to keep from falling over. Brion follows her example and swears when the rope bites into his hand.

Neil starts to the helm in order to assist as the ship jumps a little, skipping above the water and nearly taking to the sky. He drops unkind words and grabs hold of the wheel itself to prevent from running over the back of the ship. Neil figures that his arrival to the helm is a record. Zaria's eyes widen a little when she feels Neil stand behind her and wrap his hands around the same pegs upon the wheel as hers. Both she and Neil cuss as the ship jerks in protest to the speed, tweaking the wheel in the process. The moans of the wood are drowned out by the winds rushing in the ears of all.

Etan bellows as he twists around in his rapid pursuit of the fleeing ship, angry that it is getting away. The dragon unleashes another column of flames at the ship. He misses it as the flames dive into the ocean just behind the stern. Etan snorts and increases his flying speed to catch up with the fleeing vessel. His enormous shadow hides a second pursuer below the waves. A gleam of hate reflects in Etan's eyes as he closes in on the ship.

Sonja calls out in fear when she sees how close the crimson dragon has come. Vicki and Brion both swear and duck as another bolt of flames fly over the ship, landing in front of the vessel and off to the right as Milea steers the ship using the winds and sail. Neil and Zaria both grit their teeth and grunt a little as the ship skips over a wave and continues the course.

"How long is she going to sustain this speed," Neil asks well aware that his muscles are fatiguing just by holding the wheel.

"As long as Etan is chasing us," Zaria answers. "Etan is something she does not want to face in a mystical battle. In the grand scheme of things, this is easier for her."

All but Milea cries out in surprise as a large burst of flames slam into the ship, shaking it and pushing it down enough for the hull to once again touch the water. The sorceress draws the flame to her and wraps them around her before sending them forward as red light into the sails to boost the power for the winds. Vicki looks down and around, noticing that the ship as well as those aboard are still in one piece and not burnt to a cinder. Etan roars in anger, bringing attention back to the gigantic dragon and the ever-shrinking gap between the dragon and the ship.

The dragon increases his speed, ignoring the snort below as he becomes determined to catch the ship. Etan locks his wings and takes a long and quick breath in then bellows as he exhales another flame, nearly hitting the side of the ship. The *Lady of the Night* made a high pitch noise as it veers off to the left. Neil and Zaria work together to bring the vessel back to what the hope is the right course.

The bouncing of the ship causes Brion to cuss as he loses his grip on one of the ropes to slide backward. He hollers a little then grunts as he bumps into the wall leading to the sleeping cabins. The rope that Sonja holds breaks, causing the girl to slide and flips over, grabbing the deck of the ship to keep on board. Her grip slips and she ends up sliding until she too is against the wall of the cabin.

Vicki's feet left the deck from the speed, causing a gasp to escape her as she loses grip on the rope as well. She grabs a second rope with both hands as she soars by it. The cord bites into her palms, initializing a sharp sound as she flinches from the pain. Regardless, she did not let go and ends up coiling her legs around the rope to make sure she stays on the swaying and speeding vessel. Milea continues to concentrate. In her mind, however, the sorceress is weaving, pushing, and pulling upon the elements to press the winds into the sails as well as block and use the flames of the dragon to recharge her mystical energy and use it to continue her spells. The hours of the day wear on as red energy swirls around and smack into the sail as part of the winds.

"Persistent old bastard isn't he," Zaria asks as the morning turns to evening.

"Unfortunately, we do not have anything to discourage him with," Neil said.

Vicki watches as various landmarks whiz by, visible for a few seconds before the next one, usually days away is looming into view. The enchanted ship, with Milea's wind magic, is covering a distance that takes several days or weeks in the span of a few hours. The roar of Etan, as well as the rain of dragon fire upon the surrounding ocean, reminds all that the Crimson Dragon is still a factor for their speed. A few balls of the fire slams into the deck momentarily catching fire. The element is waft out by strong winds or drawn onto the sorceress herself.

Bellows of rage fill the air, masking the splash of the water as a second dragon jumps once and splashes back under the waves as it follows the ship. The whistling of the winds is a testament of the high acceleration of the ship. Sonja closes her eyes and prays a little to keep her last meal. Brion holds his own stomach, not liking the speed or the swaying of the ship. He reaches in his pocket for the dopie ginger but finds it missing.

Vicki hears the elf curse his luck and glances behind to see her companions and their current positions. She also scowls at the persistent dragon wondering if she could sing him a lullaby to put him back to sleep. Etan's deep snarl indicates otherwise as he pauses in mid-air, spread his wings high and inhales greatly, once again drawing the air all around into his great lungs. The ship barely slows down as now Milea is using her gifts to be the winds to push the ship.

The great crimson dragon opens his mouth; a bright white slight erupts in the depths of the maul as the beast concentrates. The water below Etan starts to bubble a little then explodes upward as the crimson dragon exhales his flame. The fire is put out, and a sound of surprise escapes Etan as he sees a sea dragon, larger than himself, jump high above him. The large aquamarine color creature grins at the Crimson Dragon as he locks eyes with him. The invader then whips around and does a belly flop down upon Etan's back. The Crimson Dragon bellows in surprise and pain as he splashes down into the ocean from the weight of the sea dragon.

A tidal wave results from the collision of the two behemoths into the water and careens towards the Lady of the Night. Vicki gawks at first from witnessing the attack of the massive dragon then drops a few unkind words when she sees the resulting tidal wave heading for them. The giant sea dragon makes a second appearance right in front of the wave and allows it to break upon his back then sinks below the ocean, unharmed. Vicki manages to bring her mind back from its stupor and turns to the front of the ship to see that they are still going a breakneck speed and rapidly approach an island. She cuts her sailor's oath short as she turns back to the helm.

"Etan's gone! He was attacked by a sea dragon. There is an island in the distance that we are coming up on very fast," Vicki calls. Neil looks behind as Zaria focuses on the landmass in front.

"Ok, Milea You can stop now," Zaria announces.

The winds die down as Milea opens her eyes and releases her hold upon the elements. She thanks them as she stands and stretches, her gaze falling out over the ocean. The sails relax back to normal forms with many of the ropes retying to take up the slack. The rapid pace of the ship starts to break as the enchanted vessel slows itself down. Brion moans and holds his stomach. He not sure he wants to journey at such speeds ever again. Sonja grumbles as she slides down onto her back and hugs her belly, the speed made both she and the elf ill.

Vicki releases her grip on the rope and goes to check on the two obviously unwell passengers. Neil steps to one side to allow Zaria to leave and check on the two. The captain turns to the stern of the ship to look out beyond, amazed that the sky shows that it is now evening.

The water near the horizon bubbles and churns then explodes as Etan once again launches into the air. His wings are flapping a little odd as he makes a strangled roar and turns to fly back to the strait. Milea turns when she hears the roar and Neil's unethical words. She witnesses another dragon head peeping out of the water then goes back in, fast, when found out. Milea makes a sound of curiosity as she places one hand upon her hip, where they pursued by two dragons?

"Where, are we," Zaria asks.

Neil frowns as he shares Zaria's sour look and takes to studying his surroundings. It is still daytime. The sun is hanging lower than noon in the sky indicating early evening. He turns his sights to the bow of the ship and focuses on the island that they are sailing to. From the distance, he notices that the dirt or sand is light in color, almost white and there is an odd-shaped rock towering above the beach towards the middle of the island.

Zaria looks up when she feels a very uneasy feeling brewing within the pits of her stomach and eyes the island with more suspicion. True, they got away from Etan, but where did they end up? The shiadokat feels that she has seen this land before, and the memories of it are not favorable. An hour later, the ship is much closer to the island and is enveloped within a dainty light green fog that wafts around the island. The pungent smell causes more than a few gasps or unkind words from all but Neil. The captain nods his head as it means one thing in this vast ocean.

"My lady, you have brought us to the very edge of the Boiling Seas," Neil announces. "How do you feel?"

"Exhausted. But I really did not want to end up a cinder," Milea assures with a yawn and stretch.

"I'm with you there," Neil agrees. "How is everybody else doing?"

"I'm alright," Zaria walks towards the sorceress. "Milea, I'm a little apprehensive about that island."

"What's wrong," Milea asks.

"Neil, let's get closer to the island. Sonja and Brion are sick," Vicki calls and straightens.

"Give me a few, and I'll guide her into the deep part of this harbor," Neil agrees as he turns the wheel.

"We'll talk later," Milea promises the shiadokat. She walks over to check on Sonja.

The Shadow Revealed

The noxious smells of the Boiling Seas permeate the senses every once in a while as Neil guides the ship to what appears to be deep water. As he is docking the ship, he explains that the gas from decaying ocean vegetation and various dying sea animals is what makes the seas boil in that part of Bri'al. He also cautions of creatures made from the vegetation but does not predict they will run into them. Water laps at the sand of the island as the ship drops anchor a few feet from it.

Sonja is the first to get off the boat, eager to calm her rising seasickness as she climbs down the side. She lands in ankle deep water and manages to trudge to the dry beach. Her legs started shaking a little, forcing her to her knees as she recounts the journey. It has taken a toll on all her senses so far, especially the chase from the Crimson Dragon. The sound of the landing board being deployed rips through the silence of the island and is followed by heavy steps upon it.

Vicki uses extreme caution as she takes up the role of assisting Brion down the board and onto the beach. Once on land, Brion falls to his knees and lose his stomach contents. Vicki cusses and jumps back, thankfully missed by the sudden projectile. Brion mumbles an apology and receives a sympathetic pat on the back. Milea and Neil climb off the vessel next to check on various companions.

The sorceress stumbles a little and is caught by Neil before she falls. She assures the man that she is fine and he lets her go so she could check on Sonja. The girl turns and watches as her mother sits down next to her and sighs. It has been an exhausting experience so far into the journey, and it is near an end. Milea props herself upon her hands as she leans back and surveys the sky, hoping to get some rest and substance before they enter the temple. There is no telling what they will run into, and she feels she needs to be ready for anything.

Zaria hops down and takes the time to survey the area, her senses are on high alert as the scent of the island reaches her senses, not liking the way it smells. It is as if they are sitting in the middle of Tragin territory, yet she admits that she could not be sure as the odor of the Boiling Seas is mixing with the rest of the scents.

Taking in the sights of the island, the shiadokat could see that it has very little vegetation on it, the shrubs that are there are dead. Small weeds that grow in the cracks of the rocks did not look appealing. A very small crab raises its pinchers in protest when it is almost stepped on by one of the landing parties. Zaria lets out a small chuff sound, instinct is telling her to get everyone away from this island as fast as she possibly can. She glances up at the sky and makes another sound of resentment when she sees that that, although it is afternoon, there is still plenty of daylight left before night would cover the land. The shiadokat decides to approach the ship captain with a plea.

"Maybe we need to rest a little bit here and set sail at night," Zaria suggests, "This place does not make me very comfortable."

"Sailing at night in the boiling seas is hazardous. Many geysers and large creatures exist in the seas. We can rest here for the rest of today and night then leave first thing in the morning," Neil informs. "We all could use rest, especially Lady Milea."

"I don't think it's a good idea to stay here. I can help us through the seas. Just trust me ok," Zaria implores.

"You are going to have to trust me when I say the seas are dangerous at night." Neil counters. "As captain of the Lady of the Night, I am responsible for all of our lives. My decision is based on experience. I will not budge."

Zaria watches in amazement as Neil walks away to go tend to his ill friend and talk with his sister about the journey. The shiadokat snorts then goes over to his employer, Milea to try and convince her to leave the island sighting the same reasons she gave the captain. Milea listens, and although she has stressed the urgency of getting to the Temple of Light within the Boiling Seas, she is in no condition to face any new threats that they may encounter.

Milea needs to replenish her energies either through substance or rest so that she has the strength to battle should the need arise. The sorceress scans the beach as Zaria shifts tactics to inform what she smells and senses with her eyes resting on a set of bleached bones reaching for the ocean. Zaria makes a strange feline sound of defeat then proceeds to gather driftwood for a fire. Vicki stands up and dusts off her backside as a hand full of nearby crabs raise both pinchers and walk away from the rising woman.

"I'm going to see what I can find something to augment our rations," Vicki volunteers. "These feisty crabs are not going to do."

"They're a strange color and might not be palatable." Neil agrees. "Alright, while you are at it, I can look at the charts to see if we are close to a friendly port? Once we are done at the Temple, we will head there to complete the contract."

"Aye captain," Vicki teases her brother then turns as Brion struggles to his feet. "What do you think you are doing, Mr. Seasickness?"

"I'm going with you for two reasons," Brion said. "One, exploring strange islands alone is never a good idea, despite your abilities and unique hobby. Secondly, I want to figure out how far we are from Cathalian. That might be our closest friendly port."

"He's got a point, sis." Neil offers. "I can go with you if you like."

"No, I think you need to stay here with our grand employer," Vicki hints, "and see if the nearest friendly port will satisfy the open contract, we have with her. I will let Mr. Persistent accompany me."

"Glad to be of service," Brion bows playfully and starts to a path he spies among the bushes. "See if we can find something other than snakes."

"If they are as big as Yabura, I will side with Zaria and vouch to get off the island and fast," Vicki said. The two disappear down the path as Neil relocates to sit with Milea and Sonja.

The crashing of ocean waves fills the eerie quiet of the uncharted island. They have been exploring the barren rock for an hour and a half with nothing to show but a few scrubs and small crabs. Brion pauses as he bends and examines the ground around, frowning as it offers up nothing. There are no birds, insects, or even lizards wondering which causes to Brion to believe that this land really is dead.

Brion grumbles a little under his breath at the lack of tracks and scans ahead while still in a crouch. Vicki walks past him and heads to the edge of the plateau that they ascended while following the very old path. Brion scans the woman's lines as he stands and follows her to the destination. Vicki glances at him then returns her focus to the south as she studies the strange yellow cloud covering part of the ocean. A breeze carries the smell of the offensive gasses to the two prompting a frown of disdain from the elf.

"Does the Boiling Seas always smell so terrible," Brion asks.

"No. It's actually much worse when we get into them," Vicki answers.

"Joy," Brion grumbles then takes a stroll towards the left. "I think there might be something not too far from this island." He shields his eyes from the sun. "The waves are not acting as if this is in the middle of the ocean."

"Very observant," Vicki smiles and folds as she looks out upon the waves. "We'll make a pirate out of you yet."

"No thanks," Brion shakes his head and placing a hand upon his sword's hilt. "Boats and I typically do not agree. My thanks to Milea for clueing me in about the dopie ginger."

"Not to mention all the things we've gone through so far. I hope Neil is negotiating a kingly reward for our journey," Vicki bent down and examines one of the broadleaf plants that dot the landscape.

"To me, traveling with our legendary employer is half the payment," Brion said as he too bends to examine the plant. He makes a sound of dislike. "This is no good. It's poisonous."

"I noticed," Vicki agrees and places her elbows upon her thighs as she takes in details of the plant. "I am trying to figure out what the effects are if ingested."

"Ah yes, your other profession," Brion teases as he picks the leaf and examines it. It is yellow with a variety of green and red veins. A bright orange liquid oozes from the stem. "Well, I'd say that it would kill instantly or paralyze then kill." He drops the plant onto the ground and stands up. "I'll not take a chance with that." He notes the ooze of the liquid from the plant itself. It is heavy, like an open wound. "That's odd."

"No, kidding," Vicki agrees and stands. "Let's see what else we find." She walks to the other side of the hill. After a moment, Brion follows.

The same landscape greets them as they explore further across the island consisting of dust and poisonous plants. Brion and Vicki arrive at the other side of the island a few minutes after they left the top of the hill. The ocean view is a welcome break to the monotony of the barren landscape. Vicki notices the different shades of blue and green as the ocean climbs up to the beach. The varying colors highlight the different depths of the water. She concludes that it is possible there is a coral reef near the beach.

Brion examines the skeletons of beached whales that lay upon the shore and sees that they are clean. He runs his finger along a rib taking in the small nicks that are in the surface. Something either ate all the flesh from the animal or used a knife to carve it off. Vicki approaches the edge of the beach and shades her eyes as she squints them to scan into the distance. She just able to make out the bow of a sunken ship a short distance away and figure they got caught on the reef. She turns to the beach and utters words of curiosity when she sees that the only skeletons are those of the whales. A shipwreck usually yields casualties that typically wash upon the shore.

"Brion, do you see any tracks for anything other than the whales," Vicki inquires.

"Actually," Brion stands and studies the beach, "I do not see any tracks for the whales. Nothing. Wait." He hones in on an outcrop of rocks. "These are strange."

"What is it," Vicki heads over to the location and scrutinizes the ground. "I'm not seeing anything right now."

"They are a few days old," Brion uses his finger to trace the shape. "This is what the track looked like before water eroded them. It appears to be a fin and a human foot combined." He follows them, pausing in front of a cave. "Hmm..., should we explore?"

"After you," Vicki offers, pulling one of her daggers.

"Stay close" Brion draws his sword before walking into the cave.

The floor of the cave is sandy, dry and at least ten degrees cooler than the outside. The light of day filters in from vertical caves above and does little to light the way. Vicki pauses when her senses alert her of eyes on them. She touches Brion's shoulder, causing him to pause as well, and both scan their surroundings. The two remain quiet as they continue their way and rounds a corner then stop as the cave ends abruptly with a thick wall of sandstone. Brion shifts his sword to one side and pushes on the wall with a grunt. Vicki assists him, and both take a step back, noting that the item will not budge.

Brion frowns, the tracks that he follows appear to cut off at the wall, so he concludes that this wall is false, he just has to find the trigger. He takes a step back, scans the entire area seeking a clue to the door. Vicki runs her hands over the wall and knocks against it listening to the differences in sound finding none.

Scowling, Brion turns around to return to the beach with Vicki hesitantly follows him. The elf takes another look around the beach to see if he can find a back door. His exploration comes to a halt when Vicki calls to him so they can return to base camp.

The sun is starting to set, and she wants to get back before nightfall. The two head back upon the path they forge as the sun sinks below the waves. Once they are gone, the back of the cave scrapes as a thick sandstone door slowly slides open.

The sun's journey is over for another day allowing night to fall as Brion and Vicki return to base camp. Thick smoke from the fire adds to the light green fog, creating a thicker cloud around the camp. Brion laughs at Vicki's comments as they defend into the thick fog and head straight to the fire. Milea acknowledges the return of the duo with a simple nod as she then refocuses upon the flames. Brion sits down and informs his companions about the unpalatable and poisonous plants upon the island. Vicki simply grins when her brother mentions samples to grow when they leave the island. She did not collect any, as Brion sights that it would possibly kill those aboard the boat by contaminating items aboard.

Vicki then mentions to the group about the other side of the island. Zaria sits down at the fire when she hears this news and listens as the two scouts inform of the litter of whale bones and a very strange cave. The shiadokat frowns from the news, it is something she did not want to hear. Neil rubs his chin and recounts the fact that there is nothing to augment their rations. He eyes the small crabs that continue to feast upon the sands around them.

"Well, I guess we have no choice but to have a few dozen of these guys for dinner," Neil announces.

The small crabs all flee towards their hidden barrows or the ocean waves. Their short legs move at a swift pace until they are safe. In the matter of a few quick seconds, the beach is clear of crabs.

"I don't think they would have been edible anyway," Brion said with a shake of his head. "They are feeding off the stuff from this island. They might be just as poisonous."

"That's true, but you can't deny it was entertaining to watch them flee. My brother knows how to clear a beach." Vicki admits.

"A talent that we are all grateful for, Sir Neil," Milea says with great humor.

"At your service," Neil bows. "I'll go into the hull and see what I can scrounge up from our supplies. Might even try my hand at spearfishing using the poles."

"That should prove entertaining," Milea muses as Neil departs. Sonja follows him.

"Entertaining or fruitful," Vicki agrees. "Anyone has any good campfire stories while we wait?"

"Na, I'm good," Zaria stands and paces into the shadows.

"Is she going to be alright," Brion inquires. "She seems a bit nervous or tense."

"Ever since we set foot upon the island," Vicki agrees.

"This island is overwhelming her senses," Milea says and stands. "I will go see if I can talk to her to gain more insight."

The low rumble of the ocean disguises the feline sounds of discontent coming from Zaria as Milea approaches the pacing woman. The sorceress walks with the shiadokat for several rows in silence until they both stop. Milea listens as Zaria once again besieges her to leave the island. The sorceress responds by assuring they will go as soon as all have rested.

Milea then informs the shiadokat of her odd behavior and the observations from the rest of the crew. Zaria frowns and apologizes as she follows the sorceress back to the fire's edge and sits down. She fidgeted despite her efforts not to as she listens to the conversations around the flames. The topic of Tragins comes up, and a cold chill goes down Zaria's spine at the mentioning of them.

"I know that Tragins are immortal creatures," Vicki says. "But I also hear legends and lore about them being killed or dying. So how does one kill a Tragin?"

"Usually an Eltis, Tragin or another immortal of sorts would be able to kill a Tragin," Milea explains.

"Really?" Brion frowns.

"There are, however, at least two mortals that have killed both Eltis and Tragin before," Milea continues with a soft smile.

"One is Justin of Lortis," Zaria points out. "That legend and story are circulated throughout all Bri'al."

"That's just a myth, right," Vicki asks. "As the legend goes, he is the strongest Dres Ledren of all time, but he could not possibly be strong enough to kill an immortal."

"Justin has done feats that even I cannot comprehend," Milea admits. "Yet he does not slay creatures just for the satisfaction of doing so. Usually, if it is something as powerful as a Tragin or Eltis, he is protecting someone he cares deeply for."

"Ah, the greatest Dres Ledren of all times is a softy, eh," Brion says bringing a smile to his companions. "Who is the second one? You mentioned two mortals."

"The second?" Milea leans forward to the fire. The light of it reflects from her in a particularly threatening way. "I have killed at least three immoral creatures in recent memory. Most pertinent was the one that harbored inside of Maya. There is a reason we draw Tragins out to kill them. I didn't in that particular instance, and the deed nearly cost my sister her life."

The sorceress stands and walks away deep in her troubled thoughts. She pauses to observe the lapping waters as they gently lick at her feet. She stares off into the darkening distance in the direction of the Boiling Seas, silently hoping she has made the right decision. The dangers of the seas are too great for her to face after the bout with the crimson dragon. Neil drops a few unkind words when he misses his intended prey and spears a much smaller fish. Milea turns to the shore in time to see Sonja snap her fingers.

A few short hours later, total darkness envelopes the land finding Zaria still awake. She is unable to rest as her senses continue to work overtime, danger felt in every direction. The shiadokat chuffs a little and seats herself among her companions. Zaria stretches in the shadows of the night as the fire goes out. As the ambers become ashes, her mind reels with questions about her discomfort and the island itself.

Feeling antsy, Zaria stands up again and once again paces back and forth, glancing up at the large rock that decorated the island every once in a while. She also takes note that the crabs, the only animal on the island, have not returned since Neil's announcement. Zaria thinks the behavior is not normal, no matter if she is there or not crabs should return to the beach at least out of reach of the predator. She pauses and stares out at the ocean, trying to relax to allow her memories to kick in. Zaria's eyes widen in shock when it did kick in. This island was not always such but once was a mountain that homed a very powerful family of Tragin. Her mouth drops open as she whips around and takes in the entire landscape.

"By my Mother's Soul, this is where it all started. The Thousand Year War. This is the Mountain that Gaunt and his family lived. The rest of the continent was sunk during the battle. Boy, we need to get off this thing," Zaria shakes her head. "Why in Ublivorion did I let Milea talk me into staying here? Because she is tired, damn it!" She cusses at her own gullibility.

Soft footsteps do not catch Zaria's full attention. The movement in the dark draws her from her thoughts. She looks up and sees strange creatures creeping just beyond the camp. Zaria faces them and folds just a little shade around her form to keep them from detecting her as she studies them. The intruders move like and appear to be large potbellied humans, yet they have the head of a large fish nested upon their shoulders.

Zaria takes note that the creatures are using the moonlight to guide them to their quarry. Shaking her head, she takes a deep breath in and stretches. Her body becomes taller and much healthier, stretching to a height like Milea. Black hair rains down to the middle of her back as she finishes growing. She takes a deep inhale before opening her eyes, displaying a nice shade of blue that replaces the whites of her eyes. Zaria, now A'drianis, scans the beach and sees that there are a lot more of the creatures than she first anticipated.

"Let's see," A'drianis counts the people coming towards her. "Eighteen of you, one of me. No, wait," she turns to the shore where the *Lady of the Night* is docked. "Over a hundred. I hope you're not thinking of sinking the ship."

Several of the fish-men charges forward, a few of them toss harpoons towards the invaders. A'drianis lifts her hand and causes the weapons to fall to the ground. The attacking creatures increase their pace, causing her to raise an eyebrow as she smiles cockily. The shadows then darken considerably, folding in over the invaders. Once they lift, the landing party is no longer on the beach. Spooked, the creatures retreat the way they have come.

On the ship, in the sleep quarters, A'drianis makes sure to tuck her charges as she places them on separate cots so they can continue to sleep in peace. She carefully maneuvers Milea's sheet onto her body. The sorceress let out a soft breath and turns over, prompting A'drianis to take three steps back then exhale quietly when the woman didn't wake up. Nodding to herself, A'drianis disappears again in shadow and reappears on the deck in time to see the creatures are studying the craft as if discussing the best way to take it apart. A'drianis whistles catching their attention.

"You guys may want to leave," A'drianis instructs. A group of the creatures charges her and run into complete darkness. Inside of it, many collided with each other. "Well, I gave you a chance." Her voice echoes in the shadows.

The sounds of the ocean are replaced by the haunting, eerie screams of an unknown creature Milea jumps to awareness when she hears the sound. It is a cross between a high pitch whistle and a low moan of a tree when the wind whips through the woods. The sound increases, prompting Milea to jump out of her cot and her companions to awaken. The sorceress hesitates, how did she get on the ship? More screaming and female laughter brings Vicki and Neil to their feet. Sonja goes to try the door and gets toss back by it. The girl shakes her head when she realizes she is on her backside. The door will not budge.

"What in Ublivorion is going on," Neil demands. "How did we get on the ship?"

"Where's Zaria," Vicki asks.

"I'm not sure," Milea answers all questions with her one statement.

The ship moans once, leaning hard to the left. Milea gasps and holds onto a pole. The ship rocks slow at first then thrashes back and forth violently catching everybody off guard. Neil swears and hit the floor, sliding towards one wall then the other as the ship continues to move. He manages to grab hold of a solid pole to prevent his sliding. Vicki grips the wall that she is tossed into, her fingers digging into the wood. Brion grabs the door, doing his best to stay on his feet. The sound of several bodies splashing into the ocean reaches their ears along with more than a few blood curdling sounds from the unknown. The screams and laughter stop and are replaced by a strong, uncanny silence causing the group a little concern. Brion releases the door and steps back as it opens by itself with a small squeak.

"Ok, what was that," Neil challenges as he pulls his weapon. "It's quiet."

"Too quiet," Vicki agrees and retrieves her whip.

"I'll go first." Brion volunteers, pulling his sword as he creeps out onto the deck.

The clear sky of the tropics greets the elf with a few small green clouds hovering just above the ocean to the south. The twin moons cast their beams down upon the shimmering waves as if nothing ever happens. Brion advances out the door followed closely by Neil. The ropes are all tied in place, the sails still roll up for now. Light from the moons and stars glistens upon the wood of the ship showing little to no damage at least to the mast and rails. Milea and Vicki exit the cabin next with Sonja taking of the rear.

The decks are clear of any type of debris, small scrapes along the wood, however, did hint to something large being aboard the ship. Milea walks to the side of the ship and studies the water. She is able to see a purple tint upon the waves. Sonja scans around then go and kneel next to Brion as he bends to examine the marks upon the deck. His complexion twists with curiosity when he sees that the marks are made from a very large jungle cat and it seems that the creature is using the ship as a scratching post.

"What beast has boarded the ship and done this to it," Neil kneels next to his friends and examine the markings.

Sonja scans around and stands when she sees what she feels is the answer and points it out to her companions. Milea turns to the direction indicated noting the outline of a taller elf-woman. The sorceress places her hand upon her hip and shakes her head, with a knowing smile upon her lips. Neil and Vicki also follow the line of sight to the direction and sees the well-humored woman at the front of the ship, her back to them as she continues to laugh.

"Ok, that has to be one other person," Vicki places her whip back on her hip. "That's Zaria?"

"It is," Milea agrees.

"Are my eyes playing tricks on me or does she look taller," Neil asks. "Zaria?" He calls to the woman causing her to jump a little.

"Uh-oh," A'drianis mumbles as she turns around. "Ok, think fast woman." She whispers to herself. With a smile, she jumps off the deck and fades from sight. Vicki and Neil both arrive at the bow then scowls when they are met with empty space.

"Up Here!" Zaria calls and smiles when she gathers the attention. "You guys are pretty sound sleepers when you eat peppered fish," She picks up a rope and swings down to the deck with a whoop of joy, landing without making a noise. "Crabs started coming out again, so I took the liberty to drag everybody onto the ship." She grins. "Since everybody's awake, I guess we start out a little early."

"Shiadokat," Milea folds her arms across her chest. "Truthfully, how did you bring us aboard the ship, and why?" She watches the short woman shift uncomfortably under the gaze.

"You do have your mother's tendencies," Zaria admits. "We were attached by fish-men."

"What," Neil and Brion both ask.

"The cave," Vicki recollects.

"They tracked us back to the camp. Here I thought that I imagined the prints," Brion concludes.

"I think we offended them by trespassing or something," Zaria continues. "I managed to get everybody on board before they attacked."

"What about the violent swaying of the ship," Brion cross examines. "The claw marks on the deck," he taps the evidence with his foot. "Did I miss something on the island?"

"Eh, I wouldn't worry about that," Zaria dismisses the question.

"Alright," Milea takes a deep breath in. "So, what happened to the fish-men?"

"They all ran," Zaria shrugs. "Ok, I'm going to steer the ship." She quickly left to take the helm. The wheel feels warm to Zaria's touch. "Yep, I'm humored too. But our little secret, eh," she whispers to the ship. "Neil, let's get this show on the road."

"I'll guide the ship if you do the lookout," Neil relents and walks to the wheel. "We have good lighting right now. But the clouds in the Boiling Seas will remedy that in a matter of minutes."

"Right," Zaria said and skips merrily to get to the bow of the ship, whistling a little. "No rocks, no obstacles, and no big, bold bad red dragon to block the way. We are clear." She announces.

"Lift the sails, and bring up the anchor," Neil commands. "We go into the Boiling Seas as smoothly as possible. Zaria, keep an eye out for anything. Sonja, Brion, Milea, and Vicki, go and get some rest. This is going to be a very unpleasant smelling journey." He turns the wheel. The sails shift until they find a strong breeze. The *Lady of the Night* tiptoes out of the harbor and set course for the Boiling Seas.

CHAPTER THIRTEEN

Temple of Light

Thin clouds whiff by, blocking the sky while the ship adjusts to make the trip as smooth as possible. Brion decides to sit on the deck and clean his sword. His mind wondering over the tracks he has seen on both islands. He ponders if the jungle cat followed them and if so, how did it get on the ship undetected? He studies Zaria when she calls out an object. The logical thought in Brion's mind is that somehow Zaria is the jungle cat, but she did not exhibit any shapeshifting abilities that he is aware of. The elf concludes that he would have to keep a closer eye on the woman to determine his theory.

Neil adjusts the ship, and they avoid the many obstacles that Zaria alerts him to. He is amazed at her ability to see into the void of the night. Vicki sits down next to Brion unable to sleep as she remembers the events of her past when she and her brother journeyed to the boiling seas. Sonja stands behind the captain, deciding to study Neil as he steers the ship. The l'vane man would adjust his footing every once in a while, the wheel clicks when turned to the left or right. Milea takes up the post on the port side of the ship, looking out in an attempt to spot the temple or the warriors that greet them as they entered the temple's territory. This will give her new hope and calm some of her anxiety.

"So, why do they call it the Boiling Seas," Brion asks. The sound of rumbling, along with a very offensive odor, answers his question.

"Oh Dang," Zaria covers her nose when she smells the gasses. Her eyes are watering. "The water is green! It's bubbling and making a lot of noises."

"Keep an eye out for the haggos," Neil warns. He unties a scarf he has around his waist and ties it around his nose and mouth.

"My eyes are watering," Zaria admits. "Can't stay here long. Milea, can't you do anything?"

"Not this time. You may want to try the crow's nest," Milea offers. She ties a scarf around her nose and mouth much like Neil. "Not sure how it is up there, though."

"From experience, I can tell you it's much more horrible," Vicki assures. She is speaking through her cloth. "The clouds are thickening, and it's still dark. Should we drop anchor?"

"What? Are you kidding," Zaria nearly snaps. "No way, I'll get us through this."

"It gets worse before it gets better," Vicki assures. "Usually, lets up near the temple."

"Great," Brion grumbles under his scarf.

Sonja decides to retreat to the sleep cabin in an attempt to get away from the boiling seas main defenses, itself. The *Lady of the Night* groans as it continues deeper into the boiling seas. Thick clouds of green gasses replace the sky and surround the ship making it just about impossible to see let along breath. As luck will have it, a strong wind prevails, assisting the ship through the thick mist pushing them closer to the destination. Milea decides to retreat to the cabin and join her daughter with Vicki and Brion in tow, leaving Neil and Zaria to suffer the wrath of the seas.

Zaria coughs a little then shakes her head clear it so that she could concentrate. She sees a large lump of vegetation bob up and down a little in the distance. Her watering eyes blink several times to bring it into focus; once she does, she nearly cusses. It is a large mound of grass with giant disks for eyes that glow as green as the mist. A large open mouth exhales much of the gasses that created the fog within the seas as the water bubbles around them. More obnoxious gasses rose up from the bubbles that surround the strange beings to add to both the mist as well as the smell of the boiling seas. Zaria scans the area and sees several of them surrounding the ship but not near it.

"Neil, see if you can shift the ship left a little then bring it back to the right," Zaria calls out.

"What's the matter," Neil asks.

"Just follow the instructions," Zaria offers. "After that go to the right a little way then back on course. We should be out the field by then."

"Ok," Neil is hesitant as he obeys the requests.

The ship tips past the large haggos, barely brushing against it. The ship rocks a little as it goes through the field of bubble rumbling up from under the strange swamp creature. The closeness of the haggos allows Zaria to see that they shaggy beasts are asleep and it is their gasses that causes the water to boil. Shaking her head, she focuses back on the front then cusses under her breath when she sees the large haggos that emerged from the water right in front of the ship.

Zaria swears again, there is no way that Neil could turn the ship fast enough to go around the goliath creature. With another slew of unkind words, she causes the shadows to cover the entire vessel. Neil blinks when total darkness envelops him, this is new for the seas. He stares in the direction of his hands and could not see them nor the wheel. His senses kick in, sensing danger from somewhere yet the fumes and clouds disorientates him enough that he could not determine where. Neil scowls, what happened?

"Zaria," Neil calls out.

"Shhh! Not so loud," A'drianis scolds. "You don't want to wake the haggos." She touches his shoulder a little. "Easy. Don't slice me up. Let me take over a minute. Take two steps to the side and three steps back."

"Ok," Neil slowly did as request.

The ship moans again as A'drianis takes the wheel and turns it to one side. Neil decides to stand where he is in silence, unsure if he should reach out to feel his way down to the sleeping cabins or even the bow. The ship pushes through the thickening water slowing down to a crawl. The side of the ship brushes up against the large haggos that A'drianis is trying to avoid prompting the woman to cuss.

The haggos shrills an alarm that sent a chill down Neil's spine. He turns to the direction of the sound and is met with darkness. The haggos screams unrelentingly, awakening his companions. All of them wail as they retreat away from the moving shadow. A'drianis whispers words of relief when she sees the creatures retreat and the waterway become passable once again. The cabin door opens.

"What in Ublivorion," Vicki demands when she sees nothing but darkness.

"Relax, we're almost through the haggos field," A'drianis answers. "Milea, any chances on setting this place on fire?"

"The whole boiling seas would go up then," Milea answers. "As well as everyone in it. Including us."

"Damn the luck," A'drianis scowls. "Well, at least the air is clearer since those smelly things retreated. I'm going back to the bow."

A'drianis releases the wheel and tips back to the front of the boat, her footsteps muffle in the darkness. The shadows lighten up, giving way to the sky above and moonlight that trickles down to play with the water. Thin clouds whisps around and weave between the stars creating a delightful celestial show. Enough light from above is cast down to reveal Zaria at the bow of the ship, Neil standing just beyond the wheel of the ship and Vicki right in front of the cabin door. The Dresden siblings both appear to have the same puzzled look upon their faces.

"When this is all over with, I am going to sit back and try to comprehend what in all Ublivorion just happened," Neil vows, taking the helm.

The *Lady of the Night* reaches the very center of the Boiling Seas as dawn creeps into the sky. Thick, dark smoke rises like a hand and wraps around the glowing sphere as if to choke the life out of the day. Milea stands on the deck and waits as the veils pull back, expecting to see large towers reaching for the sky on either side of a long, strong building. The statues of Eltis, past, and present, will be lining the rooftop in various poses. A posse of sapphire blue dragons will fly out to inspect the ship before it is allowed to come any closer to the temple. None of that activity, however, happens and the reality of the situation finally settles in on all who are aboard the vessel.

The roof of the temple is collapsed in many locations with the towers toppled into the sea. All of the statues that line the building are beheaded or destroyed by the attackers. Fires crackle from within the depths of the ruined building, adding the smoke and rising ashes to mix with the gasses that float into the area from the boiling seas. The entire building is in ruin with only a small portion still standing in defiance even though it looks as if it will collapse at any moment. All the land surrounding the temple is scorched by dragon's fire. Sonja takes hold of her mother's hand and turns her eyes up at her, worry and sadness filling her features. Milea stares straight ahead for several more minute then turns to her daughter.

"Keep hope, Sonja," Milea said. "Maya could still be in there, alive. We shall see."

"There is a cave that appears to go under the Temple," Neil directs the attention of his client. "We should dock in there."

"I hope it does not smell as bad as this water," Brion said. He steers the ship towards the destination. The sails shift to obey the request.

The heavy smell of charred bodies fills the air as the ship coasts to the large cavern. Twin statues of a beautiful woman standing next to a winged horse grace the two sides of the entrance and watches as the *Lady of the Night* tips into the opening. A strong tide pulls on the ship, assisting the vessel with coasting into the large cave.

The top of the ship is just short enough to fit, scraping the ceiling every once in a while, and causing Neil to hold his breath with each rise and fall of the water. Sonja gawks when they enter the giant cavern, enormous columns line the walls of the grotto, purposefully holding up the temple above. The tops of the columns could not be seen by the girl as it is quite deep in shadow above; however, she did see the craggy feet of an ancient creature at the base.

Sonja cranes her neck to look up, her senses whispers danger in the shadows above. Zaria peers up when the girl asks her a question and sees the tops of the columns appears to be an alligator creature holding the ceiling of the cave with their heads. Within the structure itself, are dozens of skeletal remains of dragons clinging to the rough stone that lined the bottom of the temple. Zaria describes what she sees to the rest of the crew as she studies the shadows causing Milea to turn to the wall, contemplating if the temple itself is built on a battlefield.

Large natural limestone shelves hug the walls of the entire cavern with one large enough to serve as a dock for smaller ships. Neil goes to the helm and takes over the steering from Brion to guide the *Lady of the Night* into position without damaging the ship. Vicki joins Milea at the bow of the ship to watch the approach, both focus on the large darken doorway just off the docks.

The ship bumps into place, and Vicki hops down with rope in hand, her landing-though soft-echoes in the grotto. She shakes off her nervous energy and ties the ship to one of three small dowels sticking out of the floor. Vicki turns to examine the rest of the space as her companions disembark the ship. The flooring changes from limestone to marble as it approaches the doorway they spied upon the ship. Three large marble steps provide access to the entry, which is blast wide open by a powerful force.

Brion is careful as he approaches the doorway, taking time to climb the three steps and stand off to the side as he peers into the structure. Sonja follows his example and peeks in from the other side along with Neil. Zaria approaches and peeks in just under Brion and groans in exasperation when she notices stairs as far up as the eye could see. Milea and Vicki spy the obstacle on the same side as Sonja, and both mumble their own variations of colorful words. Milea surveys up and about noting that each set of stairs create a flat landing as it spirals against the wall offering a break for those that traverse them in between assenting.

"Well, this will be a workout if nothing else," Neil tries to sound enthusiastic as he spies the stairs just past the door. "I don't like the quiet though. It is gravely, so."

"I agree," Brion said. "Something feels unreal here."

"Keep alert," Milea said. "We will be in and out before whatever did this knows we are here." She starts to the stairs with
Sonja jogging a little ahead.

"Can't we levitate up," Zaria groans.

"Sure, as soon as you cast the levitation spell," Milea offers.
"Keep in mind that our enemy may be able to sense any magic
that we may use. To assure our presence stays undetected, I
think we should limit the use of our gifts." The sorceress finishes
her explanation. Zaria grumbles her discontent and starts walking up the stairs after the sorceress.

"No jogging up these things," Neil advises. "I want to keep
myself ready for what's to come." He starts walking

"That door down there is blasted off the hinges and incinerated," Brion reminds, walking with his companions. "What
could do such a thing?"

"Or who," Vicki agrees. She studies the walls as she keeps up
with the leaders.

Small glowing orbs light keeps the staircase leading up to the
temple in twilight as the group traverses the path. Petite pictures of maidens, heroes, and various Eltis line the entire wall
side of the staircase retelling various legends of old. Milea is ear-
liest to reach the first landing and turns to see a longer path
going up into darkness above. Neil scowls when he arrives, being right behind the sorceress, mentally scolding himself for not
estimating the height of the cliffs while they were outside. If he
did, he would have known approximately how many levels they
will be climbing to reach the top temple itself.

Brion did not pause as he reaches the landing but instead continues to climb with Sonja hurrying after him. Milea decides to

follow her daughter up as Vicki takes her place next to Neil. They study the walls a little then follows their hostess leaving Zaria at the first landing, grumbling as she glowers up at the edifice and the disappearing group. If it is not for the danger that they may land in, she would have used the shadows to get them to their destination faster. With a deep breath and a healthy number of unkind words for the builders of the temple, Zaria quickens her step after her companions.

They reach the next landing sooner than expected, which is a delight for those in the lead. Vicki pauses when she sees a depiction of a woman standing next to a unicorn. The creature behind the two is what catches her eye being a dragon, perhaps as big as Etan, black overall and with a single horn spiraling from the center of its massive forehead. Vicki decides to study the woman a little more and sees that she appears to be car'laden with long black hair that cascade down her back and grey eyes. The whites of her eyes are sapphire blue that would sparkle if the light hit them. She wears a green toga to hide her nudity from the world yet there is a long split on one side that did show her leg.

"Hello, what have we here," Vicki muses as Milea approach her from behind. "This is Keela, right?"

"Indeed," Milea acknowledges. "She is now the Guardian of Selvast Forest. I do not know all of her past roles, but I do know that she was once an Eltis of Wisdom. The Temple of Light is a place where Eltis resides -in spirit at least. Their teachings passed from generation to generation."

Milea continues up the stairs to catch up with Brion and Sonja at the next level. Neil studies the picture a little as Vicki follows the woman up the stairs and into the gloom above. He pauses in his pursuit of his friends when he hears Zaria breathing a little hard as she comes up to the landing and leans against the wall a little. Shaking his head, Neil decides to continue following his other companions as Zaria catches her breath and contemplate. She thinks about changing forms to go up the stairs then growls a little when she smells something that may prevent her from doing so easily. There is something similar to a Tragin in the temple above, and she did not want to take chances. Taking a deep breath, she focuses and, with dampened determination, walks up to the next set of stairs.

At the third landing, all the group is pausing to catch their breath and ease the pain of the long climb. Brion sits down on the next set of steps and stretches his legs, nodding a greeting to Zaria when she finally makes the climb. Sonja is studying the wall this time, fascinated with the handsome and familiar man sitting on what appeared to be a cloud with staff in hand. He is muscular wearing a black vest and long black pants, black hair is cut at his neck with an equally black beard well shaped to his handsomely sculpt face. Next to him is a depiction of a child with black hair and either dark brown or black eyes with the whites similar to Keela's picture below. Behind him is a long and skinny dragon with large antlers and flowing mane and beard. It twists upon itself as if turning in mid-flight.

"Mom, who is this," Sonja asks of the picture. Milea stands and approaches her child to see what she is studying.

"Ah. That is Oswind," Milea answers. "He is the one that escorts the dead to the other side. In this temple, his teachings are of the more deadly arts of battle as well as the magic your aunt mastered."

"Oh wow," Sonja backs up in haste. The carving appears to be humored by the girl's actions.

"So, each Eltis has a special ability," Brion observes. "I know A'drianis is a shadow."

"Yep. That it is," Zaria agrees proudly. "Oh, come on..." She whines when her companions start up the stairs again.

The glowing starts to dim a little as Milea explains the different abilities of the Eltis they see on the walls. She says that Keela's magic is stronger to green magic, the magic of the forest while Oswind's magic is as she said before, similar to Maya's. That means he is master of the dark and black magics of the realm.

Oswind can also kill with a single touch, and it did not matter he touches the person, or they touch him. It is a bad idea either way. Milea listened as Sonja inquiries about the Eltis that is not here, Frey. The sorceress explains that the Eltis of Healing is too young to be among her family. The temple is older and built long before her birth. The group comes to the last few steps and pauses.

"I don't hear anything," Vicki said, unhooking her whip.

"No chanting, talking, mock fighting...or any sort of life," Brion agrees as he pulls his weapon. "We proceed with caution."

"What does Maya look like," Neil asks, causing Milea to grin a little.

"Me, with black hair," Milea answers.

The large stones of the oversized archway glower at the group as they approach. The large grey masses are darkened with soot, dirt, and blood that dried as it trickles down the sides of the arch. Neil and Brion take to either side of the archway and glance inside to see several shafts of daylight raining down into the gloom of the room. A shadow causes the light to flicker alerting Vicki that they are not alone.

Sonja shifts a little, apprehensive at going into the temple as it feels like someone is telling her to flee. Milea places a hand upon her child's shoulder and spoke encouragement to her right before taking a step into the room. It is one of many main halls of the temple, the ceiling has several large holes in it, letting the sunlight stream through and would usually be warm. Yet the light is anything but the usual warm caress and feels cold and forborne.

Milea eases a few more steps in the room to allow her companions to enter her eyes, absorbs the massive number of skeletons that line the entire floor. The bones are scattered about, skulls shattered from a strong and destructive force. Dried blood forms a carpet in the entire room as the smell of burnt flesh assaults the senses of the visitors. Milea notices the clear spot on the floor is the path from the door they exited to the statue that greets them.

The statue is larger than life and depicts a nicely built but tall woman. The long flowing hair, as well as the entire statue, is carved out of a single block of marble. The arms of the statue are spread out as if she is singing a greeting to those who came into the room. Milea takes a few steps deeper into the room and glances left or right as she scans the skeletons. Most are warriors of Kaidar, some are the fighters of Tadious, and a few seem to have known the teachings of Keela or Oswind in their lifetime. The rest of the skeletons are from the lesser warriors of the Eltis such as Ilandere.

Vicki jumps when she sees a specter moving about and trying to get Milea's attention. Sonja takes Vicki's hand as she watches the specter move then disappears as if something sucked it up. Milea shakes her head, then completes her path to the statue. It is darkened with blood and soot as if something threw a large amount of blood at it then burnt it to adhere to the statue. Milea reaches out slowly and touches the statue, closing her eyes to see the strong image of her sister raising her arms to defend against a powerful blast of light. The image disappeared as Milea retrieves her hand and opens her eyes. She turns and notices all her companions are now in the temple.

"Looks like we docked below the Hall of Ilandere, an Eltis of Song," Brion pays homage to the statue.

"Too bad she can't tell us what in Ublivorion happened here. I'm going to take a guess that all the residence of the Temple are in front us," Neil sheathes his katana as he goes over to examine a dragon's skeleton. "How long has it been since you contacted Maya?"

"Not all that long ago," Milea whispers. "I sense that Maya was attacked here. She defended herself, but... She didn't do all of this. No. this is not done by anything ordinary. Something extraordinary did this. Maya is not among the dead."

"Are you sure," Zaria asks. She holds her ground from the anger felt from the woman. "Ok, calm down, woman. We don't need you getting angry in here."

Brion ignores the interaction as he studies the carnage. He tilts his head curiously when he sees a trend. Although there is an insurmountable number of skeletons, not all of them appear to have perished from the direction he and his companions are facing. Some of the unfortunates were coming out of two additional halls, one on either end of the room they occupied. Those that came from the left are piled up as if the bodies are stack on top of each other afterward, the flesh incinerated from their forms. The carnage from the right is scattered and seems to have been used as projectiles to destroy several of the members that tried to flee to the large set of doors in front of the group. The doors themselves are still closed.

"What or who has the ability to destroy an entire legion of warriors in one blast," Brion queries his companions.

"Many ancient weapons, a few powerful magic users. None that should have an interest in this type of devastation," Milea searches her memory in a slight pause. "Perhaps, Tandon, but why would they do this?"

The light in the room flickers catching the group's attention as they search for the source. Neil looks up, wondering if there are dragons flying outside or even birds. Aside from the temple dragons, he has seen neither inside the boiling seas unless there are now swamp creatures that flew. He shakes his head to release the thought of a flying haggos. Vicki takes several steps back when a hand full of small glowing orbs fade into sight then disappear.

Sonja did a little jump when she sees them; her attention goes to the skeleton just a few feet away as a warrior ghost appears. She got into a defensive stance, surprising her mother when the ghost pulls a weapon to charge forward. The ghost then falls backward when a force hit him and lands on the skeleton he appeared above. Sonja jumps again when she is touched by her mother then turns as her ears detect Vicki's quick breathing. Vicki has a tight grip upon her whip, ready for it to fly as she stares into the room. Her hands and body seem to be trembling from the sights.

"Vicki," Neil touches his sister, causing her to turn and look at him. "Easy now, are you going to be alright in here?"

"I'll be fine as soon as we find Maya and get the hell out of here," Vicki assures. "We should not stay here long, the spirits of the fallen are still attached to this realm."

"Then we have to split up to find Maya," Zaria said. "Be careful and silent. Whatever is in here hasn't left. I feel it in my bones. Brion, you and I should go that way." She points to the left of the statue. "See if we can find Milea's lookalike and bring her back to the ship."

"Vicki and I will go through that hall over there," Neil thumbs to a darken corridor across from the statue.
"Sonja and I are going through the double doors then," Milea focuses across from them. "Take care and use caution. We meet in an hour."

CHAPTER FOURTEEN

Maya

Heavy smoke creates the illusion of fog in the hall of the temple with the nonexistent ceiling lighting the way in the otherwise dark path. The crackling of flames echoes and assault the senses of the two explorers. Neil coughs a little to clear his lungs of the smoke and putrid odors filling the main hall they travel. Looking down a few of the smaller corridors, he sees that they are blocked off and filled with the bodies of those that defended their home. Vicki peers over her brother's shoulder and sees the carnage but no spirits to go with it. Her instinct tells her that the building, though in ruin, is still occupied and not just by Maya.

The main corridor is cut off with two different directions to choose from. Vicki and Neil glance left then right before deciding to go right since it has light from the sky filtering the darkness. Tapestries eaten away by the flames cling to the top of the walls, the marble material blacken with the flames and splatter. The red stains on the floor, walls, and stones that came from the ceiling hints to a full-on massacre. Deep grooves in the wall are made from both dragon claw and a very strong blade, the latter being the deepest of the cuts. The smoke leaves they continue forward and the ceiling returns with just a few holes in it, letting the sunlight in.

Even though the smoke is gone, the air feels very heavy as if they are still wading through the boiling seas at its thickest point. Neil is the first to see the door and come to a stop as he examines it. The door is made from a single piece of light stone, perhaps sandstone, and is closed tightly as well as darken with flame or mystical means. The handle of the edifice has dry blood upon it with several deep cuts marking the walls around it.

"I'm no magic user. But from what I've witnessed in my lifetime, I've seen nothing like this," Vicki remarks, nodding to the walls. "No dragon's fire does this type of damage."

"I know. This right here is a sharp and strong blade," Neil places two fingers on a long, deep, gorge in the stone of the wall. "This took off the head of a tall creature with little effort. The warrior that ripped through this temple is one hell of a weapon."

"There are a lot of unsettled spirits here," Vicki admits "Although they don't appear to be evil or vile, most are avoiding us." She reaches and grabs the handle to turn it.

An electric current goes from Vicki's hand all the way down her spine to the floor causing a great deal of bad language to exit her core as she tries to pull away yet her hand and body refuse to obey the command as if she is stuck in place. Vicki loses her voice as the winds around both she and her brother increase to a gale force.

Neil jumps when audible moans are heard in the winds as it whips every loose item upon his body around, tugging and pulling at them. The feeling of claws is very real, causing another slew of unkind words from Neil as he tries to pull his sister off the door. A strong force slaps him back with an angry, disembodied voice scolding him in a language different from any that he knows. Neil calls his sister's name as Vicki starts to convulse and falls to her knees, her hand still holding the doorknob.

Vicki closes her eyes, and the image of a violent battle comes into her mind. Several of the warriors are up against one single man and loses badly. The two large dragon guards stand in front of the door to protect what is inside only to be cut down in a single stroke by the man they face. All of his features are unseen except for his brown colored hair. The doorknob became covered in blood from the guards as their strangled death cries echoed in Vicki's mind, as did the man's deep voice. Several more men round the corner and are also taken out with little effort by the man. Once he is done, he turns and opens the door. Back in the current temple, Neil takes in the sights of his surroundings in a panic. The hallway glows as a multitude of vivid lights seems to bounce off of his sibling.

"What in Ublivorion is going on?! Vicki!" Neil calls to his sister.

The clicking of the door catches Neil's attention as he turns and watches his sister turn the handle and open the door. The room is empty except for a half of the book lying in the middle of the room. It is open, face down upon the floor with a pool of blood congealed just beyond the book. Several burn marks surround the item as did the remanence of a tattered robe. Light from above shows the travels of the sun and that their time is almost up. Another strong wind whips down into the room from the sky and slams into Neil, sending him back a little. He manages to stay on is feet and struggle once again to get to his sister when he sees her trembling even more.

In her mind, Vicki is watching the battle that had been waged in the room between the high priestess and the unknown foe. The priestess blocks a blow and in the next moment is slammed by a strong spell which brings her to her knees. She gathers that energy and sends it back to the man that hit her with it. His laughter fills the hall as he did not seem affected by it. The high priestess regains her feet just in time for the man to drive a long object through her chest. The high priestess falls to her knees then to the ground, her body engulfed in flames soon after that. In the ruins, Vicki herself crumbles to the floor, her hand now free from the doorknob is resting in the area that the high priestess's head had laid to rest. Vicki continues to have her vision, watching as the room lit up with a bright light and everything explodes around her

"He... killed her," Vicki whispers.

"The high priestess," Neil blinks his surprise.

The winds center on Vicki at one time as restless spirits try to claim the woman's body. A figure appears standing over Vicki, blocking the efforts of the attacking souls to possess the young woman. She grabs and tosses one spirit while using a blade to sever a second. Both seem to come back for more or combine with others to present a stronger front against the defender. The woman's robes flutter around as if they are wings as she continues to fort their efforts with strength, grace, and speed.

Lots of speed it seems as she is sometimes a blur when multiple attacks happen at one time. Neil gawks until his instincts tell him to dodge to the left then right. He moves to obey them and just misses getting hurt by an unseen force. Neil pulls his blade and blocks another invisible attack causing sparks to erupt from the encounter. He swings his sword where he thought the head would be but connected with nothing. Faint laughter came from his invisible opponents as they move in and attack him again.

"Damn it," Neil blocks again but feels the cold edge of an invisible knife grace his left bicep.

A strong force knocks him on his rear end and holds him down. The ghost defending Vicki glances behind at Neil then disappears. Vicki's body shutters a little, jerking to her feet. The woman's eyes open and flash once. Her arms extend out as a mystical circle jumps to life behind her. It spins around twice with all symbols lit up. Vicki moves her hands together, lifting them above her head. The wind increases around her body as ghosts howl towards the open ceiling. Vicki's body pulsates with a light blue glow. Neil feels something fly past him and up the glowing winds. A loud thump resounds in the hall as the mystic circle shatters. Vicki falls to her knees, her breathing quick, the glow about her is gone.

"Vicki," Neil hurries to his sister's side. "Say something. How in all Ublivorion did you learn magic in such a short time?"

"Wasn't me," Vicki assures her breath still quick. "That was the High Priestess, Nadine. She said I had to let her possess me to save you." She focuses on her brother. "That's not a good feeling."

"The one you seek had that feeling for many Decyars," A female voice whispered prompting the siblings to look up. The high priestess' ghost floats just in front of them. "Maya Sirus is still alive in this temple. She headed towards the sanctuary of Keela when I last saw her. It is past the library."

"The library," Neil's eyes shift several times as he tried to think. "Where is that?"

"The large double doors past the statue of Illandere," Nadine explains. "If you came up the stairs from the docks below the temple."

"That's the only way in from what we saw. This place is hanging on by a thread," Vicki remarks.

"Safe to say that Milea will be finding her sister," Neil relaxes as he regains his feet and put his blade away.

"Yes, it is," Nadine agrees. "Vicki, take the book that is on the floor. It is but one clue as to what the future will bring."

The sunlight brightens a little as Vicki stands and manages to steady herself by holding onto a wall. Shaking her head to clear it a little, she walks into the room and bends down to pick up the book. She hesitates a little and then let her fingertips touch it first. Vicki focuses on the priestess and sees the woman nod and smile with confidence before turning back to the object and lifting it off the floor. Neil requests information from Nadine as to who is the responsible party that devastated the temple of light. The answer he got caused

Vicki to pause as she exits the room, Tandon is the one to attack this mighty fortress. Nadine also informed them of the very unusual alliance she saw to include Slone, the Son of Roathis.

"Is he still here," Vicki asks.

"Yes, Slone is still here as well as his mage. Beware the mage," Nadine answers and closes her eyes. She fades from sight, leaving the siblings in the hall.

Neil studies his sister and rubs his chin, noting that Vicki seem less distressed yet she is still alert to her surroundings. Vicki flips through the book and observes that all the intact pages are blank. She provides the object to her brother when he asks, and he too sees they are blank. They begin walking back down the hall then pause when they hear it rumble. Turning, they see that the hall is starting to collapse. Vicki is the first to swear, turn, and run back down the hall, followed by her brother. She sees the ghost of a giant dragon tearing through the stone walls to get to them. Her speed increases as she describes what she sees to her brother.

Neil kicks in his own speed as they turn and haul ass back down the main hall that they entered. The main hall looms into view as they near the end of the corridor, the statue of Illandere seems to encourage them to hurry. Vicki and Neil both dive out the corridor at the same time, a split second later it collapsed on them blocking any way back to Nadine's room. The high priestess's spirit appears holding a shield against the wall to assure the dragon ghost did not come through. She then disappears, taking the beast with her. The dragon howls in protest as it fades from the realm.

"You alright, Vicki," Neil requests.

"I will be even better once we leave this place," Vicki assures.

"I agree," Neil said then hugs his sister much to her surprise. "Do not touch anything else in here, do you understand? Not until we have a magic user around anyway."

"Alright! Alright! I promise," Vicki said loudly. "Let me go, will you?!" She exhales when her request is fulfilled. "We are in the main hall, should we go into the library after Milea?"

"No, I think we will wait here until the allotted time is passed," Neil suggests. "That's in about twenty minutes. Do you think you will be ok, then?"

"I think so," Vicki responds. "If not, I will go down to the ship and wait there."

The silence of the temple is interrupted by Neil's contemplative sound as he rubs his chin. The notion of waiting on the ship left him when he realizes that if Milea or Brion need assistance, they will not be in earshot as they are now. Vicki places her hand on her brother's shoulder and assures him she is kidding about waiting on the ship. Neil starts to protest but quieted as he hears footsteps coming from behind. He and Vicki both are quick to jump to the top of Illandere's statue and hide within the many folds of her carved hair and clothing.

The owner of the footsteps exits the door, they entered the temple and pauses as he scans the room. He may have been mistaken as a giant elf, standing seven feet and five inches in height and build of a powerful warrior. His light brown hair flows with every movement as he turned and looks, studies all directions. He shakes his head and makes a 'tsk' sound as he then starts to walk to the double doors. The man hesitates, something or someone has caught his attention.

Neil crouches down lower as the man comes to the statue then walks past it into the hall that Zaria and Brion entered earlier. Neil peeks from his hiding spot but is stopped by his sister from going after the man. Apparently, he is the one that Nadine warned them about and will not be easy to take down even by their combined talent. Neil releases a few unkempt words under his breath as he exhales. They will have to wait for Milea and hope that Brion and Zaria are savvy enough to avoid the terror that marches towards them.

Dust and hints of smoke clung to the air and dance in the streams of sunlight that flood the library. An extreme volume of shelves is knocked down and toss to the wall, splintered to nothing more than sawdust, the books they held are half burnt or ashes upon the ground. Several of the books are shred to pieces in a powerful explosion from someone or thing that invade the library. Milea and Sonja separate for a short time in order to explore the various smaller rooms off the library and find no one inside of them.

The two meet up on the middle of the floor and continue to trek to the back of the library and a set of doors they have yet to explore. As they travel, the floor begins to turn colors from the pristine brown of the hardwood to blood-soak flooring that warp and bend in different directions. Skeletons then start showing up with a few against the wall, many with weapons sticking out their sides or ribcage.

Sonja takes hold of her mother's hand when she sees strange and unnerving images on the dead of the room. The girl sees a dark wrap around the bones that made them appear to move ever so slightly. Milea looked down and turns to her child when she feels the nervous energy and flashes a reassuring smile at her. She listens to her daughter as Sonja describe what she sees and hesitate momentarily to scan the skeletons. Milea then kneels down gazing at her daughter, locking onto her eyes and gently stroking her hair.

"Do you see and hear ghosts, Sonja," Milea requests with a gentle tone.

"I'm not sure," Sonja shifts nervously. "I see balls of light for the most part. I usually sense powerful energies, especially opposing forces."

"And what do you sense now," Milea asks.

"I," Sonja starts then turns towards the entrance of the library.

Milea also turns, sensing something powerful coming towards them. The entity pauses right outside the door then departs in a different direction. Milea watches the entrance for a moment. She then decides to evaluate her child later. The sorceress stands and turns back to their destination in the short distance. Whatever they will face leaving this temple will have to be dealt with at that time.

The floor soon becomes so warped that it is barely holding together, the wood is blacked with a flame. The two once again stop and gawk at the new obstacle they have to overcome. There is a gigantic crater in the middle of the floor, keeping them away from the doors on the other side of the room. Milea peers up to see rafters above the hole are burnt with the flame from whatever create it, to begin with.

The sorceress approaches the side of the crater and bends to touch the floor, she draws back when she senses the enormous amount of magic used to create it. Milea stands as she ponders the situation, the temple was filled with warriors and mages, many of them powerful. Maya herself is a force to be reckoned with when threatened. Something more powerful than Maya must have thwarted her from using her full gifts against her assailants.

Sonja turns to take in the entire scene, the library is massive many of the shelves on the wall are still intact, but only just, and hung on by either a nail or the powerful glue that put them there, to begin with. Sonja's eyes then fall on a small skeleton sitting not too far from the crater, the back of the person is broken marking the untimely death. Sonja inspects the wall and blinks at the script that she sees, it is in a language she does not understand.

"Mom, look. There is writing there," Sonja points to the wall.

"*Rabhadh, droch shùil,*" Milea read the words. "Warning, evil eye? Looks like our unfortunate friend saw what did this." She places her focus back to the crater. "Evil eye."

Milea feels a strong energy field coming from the other side of the large granite doors just beyond the crater. She turns to them and studies the symbols. There is a tree with several branches spreading out and reaching the height of the door. An equal number of roots digs down into the floor. On one side of the tree is a rampart unicorn, the front hooves touching the trunk of the tree, the other held a large dragon with its front talons holding onto the tree. Within the twisted nobs of the trunk itself is the image of a woman holding her hands up in welcome.

Milea concludes that they are standing at the doors to the hall of Keela. Sonja suggests the bookcases that held to the wall as a means of getting across, causing Milea to appear thoughtful.

"Hm... alright. Show me," Milea playfully challenges her daughter.

Sonja smiles as she runs over to the bookcase closest to the crater. She jumps, landing halfway up the twelve-foot structure before climbing all the way to the top. Sonja then spies a long bookcase that is a little shorter than the one she stands upon lining the walls. She concludes that the books must have fallen into the crater. Sonja eases to the wall before climbing down onto the second, shorter, bookcase and using it to move over and pass the crater. As she reaches the middle, the wall unit cracks, but she did not notice it. Once on the other side, she hops, landing in front of the door. She then does a happy jig before turning and waving to her mother.

"Clever girl," Milea said and waves back.

Milea walks over to the bookcase and jumps, grabbing the top of the item as she pulls herself up with a little grunt of effort. Milea then proceeds to follow her daughter's route, maneuvering to each bookcase and watching her footing. Once she reaches the center, however, the wall gives way, and the bookcase falls into the crater. Milea cusses as she lets go and cast a levitation spell upon herself. The room pulsates briefly as a set of female eyes glare at the sorceress from the ceiling then disappears. Milea takes note of them and knows that the eyes are unlike the ones that came with the storm. The walls pulsate again as she lifts herself up and out of the crater, landing next to her daughter. Sonja gives her mother a bear hug, happy she is safe, breaking Milea's thoughts from the altercation. The sorceress pats her daughter's back, smiling at the girl's strength and her own relief. She starts to walk, causing the girl to let go and follow her mother.

An abundance of caution is practiced by the mother-daughter duo as they approach the room. There is a very strong dark energy radiating from the depth, felt even clearer after they cross the crater. Milea cracks open the door and peeks into the room to examine it from the relative safety of the library.

The walls are darkened with fire, whatever bodies are in the halls are now charred ashes upon the floor, the smell of the burning flesh is thick upon the air. Milea notes that the ceiling is still intact as well as the statue of Keela, standing proudly in the back of the room. Milea places a hand on her daughter's head as a non-verbal command to stay in the library and keep an eye out for their stalkers. Sonja nods, understanding the danger they are in as she turns to watch the room. The girl focuses on the door at the far end of the great hall; out of sight due to the great distance and whatever shelving is still intact.

The sorceress enters the room and pauses a little bit as her eyes adjust to the darkness. Once they did, she could see deep purple and red symbols lining the walls. The maroon glow from them cast an eerie illumination about the entire room and providing light in the space. All windows and outside doors are blocked by the collapsed tower that once stood above the hall; making the doors to the library the only exit and entrance to this sacred space. Milea pauses when she senses the overbearing presence of a dark magic spell centering from the statue of Keela.

Standing proud and strong, the image of the Eltis is an imposing sight. The statue's legs are spread shoulder length apart, one hand is on her waist, the other holding a staff. The statue's eyes focus upon the door as if daring the intruders to disturb the one she protects.

Milea takes her time towards the statue, just in case the spell cast turns the monolith being into a living golem. She is not in the mood to deal with the statue of the guardian of her home. The groaning of wood and slight screeching of metal caused Milea to hesitate and listen, it is not coming from the statue but the ceiling, the weight of the collapsed tower is taxing on the structure, and it will not be holding much longer. The sound of short, frighten breathing brings her attention back to the statue. Milea grows even nearer and sees the teeth of a few dozen dragons scatter throughout the room with the majority of them close to the statue. Milea pauses when she hears the slight whimpering of a living being behind the statue.

"Whoever you are, I am a friend," Milea announces. "I've come to help. Please lower your ward."

"W-who are you," A woman's voice whispers. Milea blinks at the sound.

"Maya," Milea asks. There is a small silence.

"Milea," The woman retorts.

"Yes, it's me, sister," Milea relaxes. "I've come to get you out of here. I'm sorry it took so long. Teleportation did not work for me. I ended up in Wild Territory. I had to use a boat." She exhales in relief when the dark spell is canceled.

"I could not teleport out either," Maya peeps around the leg of the statue. Her black hair shifting with her movements as she leans a little further from her hiding spot. She narrows her dark brown eyes before widening them. "It is you!" She hops down and hurries over to her twin. "Can I tell you what happened later? I want out."

"Sure," Milea hugs her sister. Maya relaxes and returns the hug. "We have to find our guides and shiadokat first. Then we go." She turns to leave the room. "Sonja is here too. She is waiting for us outside the room."

"Ok, well we need to find them as fast as possible," Maya said with urgency. "Jasmine Underak is here."

"Who," Milea's features reflect her confusion, she did not know this person.

"She's in cahoots with Roathis. In fact, she, Roathis' favorite son and a man from Tandon all showed up, and then all Ublivorion broke loose," Maya explains in short.

"I see. We need to hurry," Milea concludes as they exit the room. Sonja hugs her mother immediately. "Yes, we're back."

"Aunt Maya," Sonja gives the woman a crushing hug. "You're alive!"

"I am very glad to see you too, Sonja," Maya manages and pats the girl's back a little as she is released.
The room pulsates again as a loud rumbling fills the room. The trio turns back to see that the hall of Keela gives way to the pressures of the collapsed tower and caves in on itself. The room trembles as the bookshelves disintegrate from an unseen force entering into the entire space. Milea and Maya both drop unkind words as they use their levitation skills to get over the crater

and into the library. Sonja lands with her mother as Maya follows suit not too far behind. All three run at full speed into the
library to get to the door, and the main hall before the room collapses.

CHAPTER FIFTEEN

Flight from the Temple

The squeal of frightened rats penetrates the mind-numbing darkness of the hall. Skeletons of dragons and other creatures line the corridor, the hiss of a distant fire reaches the ears of the travelers every once in a while. Zaria pauses and listens when her senses tell her that they are being followed. She turns to peer down the hall and sees nothing which is very unusual for her. She holds her hand up to touch Brion's chest, causing him to pause as well, taking the hint and listening to the silence of the dark hall.

Several minutes will pass before Zaria decides to continue down the corridor until they came to a door. The shadows are light enough for Brion to look up and take in the symbols of the door and the words above it. The door is decorated with a dead tree whose branches reach for the top of the archway while wilted roots snaking along the bottom of the door. A long skinny dragon wraps around the tree and glares at those that approach. The image of a man standing on top of the dragon's head in the middle of the tree trunk completed the décor. Above the door are words written in a language that Brion now regrets that he did not learn.

"This is the hall of Oswind," Brion reads the writing on the wall. "Not sure I want to visit there."

"I hear ya, but Milea said that Maya's gifts are similar to what he taught," Zaria reiterates. "We are here to find her, so we have no choice. I'll go first to make sure everything is OK."

She takes a deep breath as she inches into the dark doorway. Her whole body is swallowed by the deep shadows. The shadows of the halls deepen as Zaria exhales and moves closer to the doorway. She places her hand on it to find out if it is locked then perks up when it opens at her simple touch. Brion ignores the uneasy feeling that settles over him as the door yawn into the more darkness. Zaria glances back at the elf then disappears into the dark hall; her body is swallowed by the deep shadow. Brion mentally counts until his ears detect movement behind him. He turns and searches the darkness for several minutes and thinks he sees the outline of a man then it fades once he blinks. Scowling, Brion decides to follow Zaria into Oswind's hall just in case he is being stalked by ghosts.

The darkness envelopes him and makes it almost impossible for him to see, similar to the cave on Cyenzie Island. Brion concludes that this, like the darkness there, is not ordinary but enhance by something. In this case, however, that something is not as friendly as the cave, danger is everywhere in this particular gloom. Brion pauses when his senses tell him that he is about to collide into someone or something. In the darkness, A'drianis has stopped and thinks it is good that Brion has followed her into the gloom. Her senses inform her that she is being stalked by someone. With her powerful sight, A'drianis sees several more dragon skeletons and very liquid pools of blood; several of the skulls had strange and dangerous symbols written on them in the blood.

Movement catches A'drianis attention and leads her deeper into the room, followed by Brion. Both pause again once they are close enough for A'drianis to see who is in the room with them, and she drops a few unkind words under her breath. The woman is standing next to the statue of Oswind and seems to be a priestess of some sort. She is a little taller than Brion and bears resemblances to an elf yet certain features such as the dulled point of her ears echoes a different folk of Bri'al. She is a car'laden and is dealing with powers both dark and dangerous according to the markings on her almost nude body. She is defiantly a priestess of death magic, something Oswind himself did not condone for mortal or immortal.

A'drianis notes the woman searching the room; apparently, she heard footsteps presuming from Brion. Her light brown hair shifts with her movements as she continues to focus on various parts of the room. She places a hand upon her hip as she weighs a large, well-used, dagger in the opposite hand. Her green eyes scan just as much as her hearing as she seems to realize that the darkness has fold deeper than she has created. A'drianis concludes, with some pride, that the woman could not see in this deep dark.

"What's going on," Brion demands causing A'drianis to swear as the woman's focus came to their direction.

"It appears I have guests," the woman said with glee. "One who I least expected, what a treat."

"Oswind's Beard," A'drianis takes a step back, bumping into Brion.

A light blue light caresses the woman's hand as it lights up and forms into a ball that she throws in the direction she heard the voice from. A'drianis, grabs and tosses Brion to one side while she dives to the other. The Eltis lands on her fingertips and toes, facing the direction of the death mage as Brion lands on his backside and slides back a few additional feet. The spot they occupied explodes, creating a large hole in the floor.

Brion drops an array of profanities and returns to his feet to face whatever opponent is in the room. A'drianis also stands and yells in surprise when the woman at the statue cast a light spell. The entire room illuminates causing A'drianis to fall to her knees and revert to Zaria. Brion rubs his eyes to clear them then scowls at the person in front of him. Zaria growls as she returns to her feet and glares at the offender. The woman at the statue grins at the two.

"I suppose my hearing is not so bad after all," The woman smiles. "Hello Brion, it's nice to see you again." She stands coyly and scans the male elf appreciatively.

"Niceties on your part, Jasmine. I for one am not at all happy to see you," Brion said with spite.

"Who is your friend? You know I am a jealous woman," Jasmine said sarcastically.

"Friends," Zaria asks of Brion.

"Hell, no. I would say she's more an enemy," Brion snaps his answer. He focuses on a humored Jasmine. "Are you the one to attack this temple?"

"Glorious isn't it," Jasmine smiles as she motions to the skeletons.

Zaria squints when the room brightens then gawk at the carnage the light reveals. Even she did not see all the defeated dragons, humans and other beings scatter about the room, a few of them were killed by the dagger in Jasmine's hand as sacrifices for one cause or other. Brion takes in his surroundings and sees that a few of the skeletons did still have flesh or skin attach to them, and the entire room is covered in the blood of the slain. He looks up when he hears Zaria swear to see looks up that the statue of Oswind is missing its head and hands, taken by a powerful blow or long and sharp blade.

"These warriors were not easily defeated, and I know you are not a warrior, Jasmine," Brion observes. "What happened here?"

"They battled well; unfortunately, Slone was just too much for many of them. Oh, and Tandon showed us a new toy, I am so thrilled. You may have seen it work if you entered in the hall of Illandere," Jasmine smiles. "An Eye of Gaunt."

"Oh, no way," Zaria takes a step back in surprise at that announcement.

"But even with this new toy, we still have to give thanks to our third ally and his lovely harp," Jasmine gloats. "Many in the temple turned on their own, those whose minds were not strong enough to resist the Harp of Hestor."

"Double Ublivorion," Zaria reinforces her swears.

The sound of footsteps behind causes Jasmine to look up towards the door in surprise. Zaria turns as a sinking feeling fills the very pit of her stomach. She jumps, barely holding back her usual spill of profane words as a lone man enters the room. Brion did a quick glance over his shoulder when Zaria did let one of her foul words slip from her lips to see the new threat. He takes in the full features of the cocky man. The intruder looks similar to the ghost he thought he saw in the hall.

Brion faces the intruder, forgiving himself for his mistake in the darkness as the seven-foot car'laden stalker draws nearer. The new threat's powerful shoulders play host to the locks of light brown hair that spread over them. His light grey eyes flashed with humor and an unbridled power within. The clothing he wears is stained with blood from a few of his victims, but it did not seem to bother him. A large, well-used, sword hangs by his side and shifts as he folds his strong arms across his powerful chest. His eyes pulsate with humor as he scans the two he stalked.

"We have guests I see," the swordsman said with humor upon his deep baritone voice.

"Lord Slone, I thought you departed from here by now," Jasmine bows to the man. "Let me introduce you to Brion, the exiled King of Solis. The woman I do not know, but she is a minor annoyance."

"Oh, I know who she is," Slone smirks. "Isn't that right... cousin?"

"Don't call me that," Zaria scolds. "Sick bastard." She folds her arms, clearly insulted. Brion arches an eyebrow.

"Cousin," Brion quizzes.

"King," Zaria counters and glances his way. She turns back to the threat when Slone laughs.

"I guess I should take off your head then," Slone announces as he charges. He pulls his blade and swings it only to meet the metal of another. "What the...?"

Slone takes a step back with a look of pure shock gracing his features as he watches the animated sword float in place, ready to attack or defend against him. Zaria reaches out and touches the sword sensing that it is not enchanted yet it did have a lower hum and slight glow about it, the vibrations are coming from the force that holds it. Zaria jumps, and Slone stares as the unmanned sword flips twice then fly towards Brion. He catches the hilt of this sword then shifts his stance to challenge the car'laden.

"Are you crazy," Zaria demands of her companion.

"Perhaps a little. But I can blame it on influence from Neil," Brion said with a cocky grin.

"If you wanted to die, all you had to do is say so. I would have accommodated you sooner," Slone said.

Zaria dives out of the way as Slone attacks Brion with a powerful swing. The shiadokat turns her attention to the room, noting that the shadows are now in the corners and Jasmine is leaning against the statue. The car'laden woman's features indicate that she is enjoying the battle between the two lords. Sparks fill the air as the blades clash with Brion blocking a blow meant to take his head. He blocks another blow and grunts as he slides back a few feet from it. Brion manages to stay on his feet, causing a growl of disdain to emit from Slone as his body lights up. Zaria squints and swears when lightning caresses Slone's body, she is too far from both the shadow and Brion to assist in any manner. She is even unable to deal with Jasmine as the woman is right behind Brion with Slone and his brilliant light in between.

Slone gathers the energy around his form into the palm of his hand and tosses it in his opponent's direction Brion relaxes as his eyes flash once, activating his invisible gifts, and holds his sword at ready as the red lightning nears. Zaria is about to react then gawks as the lightning turns to the left of Brion and goes around him. Slone straightens in surprise when his spell is now streaming right back at him. He tries to block it but is struck and tossed back to the wall. Zaria jumps and rolls out of the way to let him pass. Slone slams into the wall then the ground, his sword clatters to the ground, unattended. Jasmine gawks at the smoking body of her lord then hurries to his side as Zaria runs over to Brion.

The air in the room goes heavy as Zaria grabs hold of Brion and almost drags him towards the entrance. Jasmine looks up and sneers before she uses her abilities to cause the doors to slam shut. The two unwitting guests slide to a halt, nearly colliding with the object, both releasing a few healthy unkind words. Zaria turns when she hears Slone grab his sword and get to his feet, her gasp of surprise causes Brion to turn and scowl taking a step forward. The room vibrates with Slone's agitation, and the lights lower a little, casting a darker shadow in the corner just left of Brion.

"Damn it, now what," Zaria grumbles.

"Find a way to open the doors or find another way," Brion suggests, readying for combat.

"You are going to pay for this, Cur," Slone growls as he takes a step forward. The room quakes from each step.

"Make it quick," Brion calls to Zaria.

A deep whoosh resounds as Slone lights up with anger. Jasmine takes a few steps back and covers her eyes from the intensity of the light. Zaria ignores Slone and focuses on the shadows in the corner, making them darker and fighting against the bright illumination that Slone is producing. Slone wraps the light around and lifts it above his head to form a large and powerful ball of energy. He whips it around then sends it screaming towards the two that agitate him. Brion shifts his sword to hold the hilt with the left and the flat of the blade against his right palm with the tip of the sword point up.

The light hit the sword and stays a few seconds. Brion grits his teeth as his muscles bunch up, his feet slide back a little before he manages to push the light back towards Slone at the speed which he received it. Slone catches the ball with both hands and bellows in rage as he sends it right back to his intended victims. Brion is about the repeat the exercise but is tackled into the shadows by Zaria. His yell of surprise is mask by the sound of the annulation of the doors as Slone's spell connects to them. The light dies down, allowing Jasmine to lower her arm from shielding her eyes yet the heat is still very intense. Slone, steaming from his rage, growls and goes to the corner. The shadows are unyielding until he cast a light spell. His rage deepens when he sees the corner is empty, no trace of Zaria or Brion there. Slone lets out a sound of pure rage.

"Destroy the elf," Slone demands, "and bring me A'drianis' head!"

"As you wish," Jasmine bows before turning to the room.

"Arise my pets! Arise and hear my command!" She sneers when the skeletons start to come together in the room. "Kill those who dare enter this sacred hall of the dead! Kill them all!"

The voice of the death mage echoes throughout the entire temple. In the library, Milea and Maya pause when they hear it, a look of confusion is on one twin while the other has a look of recognition. Sonja points to a few skeletons that start to glow and move. The action propels the three into an all-out run to the entrance to the massive library. Skeletons in the deeper parts of the temple moan or groan as they rise to obey their mistress commands. Vicki and Neil hear the unnerving sounds then crouch low on their perches as the entire structure shakes and rattles. The siblings both jump from the hiding spots as the statue of Illandere topples over, and the library doors fly open.

Milea leads the way out with Maya then Sonja on her heels. They stop and meet up with Neil and Vicki near the staircase that leads down to the ship. A strong energy wave rolls over the area and just about knocks the twins down. Neil sees the strange reaction but did not have time to ask as he looks up. Something stirs in the shadows of the ceiling prompting unhinge words to drop from Neil, and he moves out of the way as first Brion then Zaria fall from the dark ceiling. Brion lands on his feet, straightening to catch Zaria. The shiadokat then hops out of Brion's arms. She nearly screams out when she realizes they are in a room full of skeletons. When they didn't move, she realizes that she is fine for a few brief moments.

"Zaria," Milea calls, causing the woman to jump and turn.

"Oh, you found Maya, good," Zaria smiles her relief. "Glad to see you're safe, we need a counter spell."

"Counter spell," Maya asks, "for what?"

"Dead things," Zaria answers

"What?!" Maya blinks in surprise.

The sound of bone scraping against stone causes all in the room to slowly turn to the pile of dead. The skeletons in the room start to move and shutter as they piece themselves together. The bones take on an eerie yellow glow and stand up, weapons previously discarded in death clutch in boney fingers. Red lights illuminate the center of the skulls, replacing the eyes of the dead. Sonja shrinks back from the skeletons, unable to fathom how they move on their own. Her left forearm tingle as different lights pulsate about the room. Sonja shakes her head to concentrate as several skeletons line up and stalk towards the living. Neil pulls his weapon, scanning his surroundings. Although he is a seasoned warrior, this is his first time fighting the dead.

Vicki unhooks her whip and squints when her head starts hurting. She shakes it off and holds it a little before concentrating on the threat that faces them, determined to get out of the temple alive at least. Maya turns and faces the undead, taking a step forward. Her staff appearing in her hands. It is at least three feet taller than she, the wood black. The head of a black snake graced the top. Milea notes the stairway is still free of skeletons, for now. Brion also takes notice the stairs and back towards it, weapon raised.

"Maya, not this time," Milea takes hold of her sister's arm. "This way." She pulls her twin.

"But," Maya protests as her staff disappears.

"Jasmine is going to raise the entire temple," Brion informs. "Let's go!"

The skeletons charge at the group is interrupted when they are thrown back by a strong force. Maya assures her sister it is not her as they all turn to go into the staircase. Maya hesitates a little when she sees the ghost of Nadine standing between the living and the undead. The high priestess turns and encourages the woman to go and is quickly obeyed. The sound of bones scraping against stone echo in the ears of the living as they make their way back down the stairs to the *Lady of the Night*.

Walls explode as skeletons burst forth from their graves. Milea defends against them then decapitates the head of the large dragon that blocks the way. Maya dodges the snapping jaws and follows her sister. Brion jumps over the skull, landing several steps down. He almost loses his footing as the hand of a skeleton grab his ankle. He cusses and breaks free to follow his companions. Neil blocks and tosses what use to be a human martial arts master into the mass of bones that are assembling and stumbling after them.

Vicki holds her ears to blot out the screams of the damned, increasing her pace to the point where her feet are barely touching the stairs in her haste. Sonja keeps up with her friend to assure she makes it through, ignoring the strong negative energy that is cascading in waves all around them. The deafening sound of stone cracking against itself echo catching the retreating group's attention. The wall in front of the group starts to close. Milea realizes it is a door, and it is closing at an increased rate.

"Hurry up," Milea shouts and increase her step, following Vicki and Sonja at the same breakneck speed they are running.

"Go," Zaria instructs and turn to face the oncoming army.

"Don't argue," Maya grabs Brion's arm, seeing the elf about to protest. She yanks on him to pull him along. "You too," she pushes Neil towards the door.

"But," Neil protests then swears a little. "Fine," he quickens his pace.

The light in the staircase starts to dim as the large stone continues to lower onto the stairs. Milea makes it under the item as it is halfway down, keeping Vicki and Sonja in sight. Maya is next and had to duck to get under it while Neil and Brion both slide under the door as it is very close to the floor. The deep boom of the stone as it connects with the floor resounds in the staircase as Zaria rolls her neck and faces the coming threat of several skeletons, their glow as not as bright as other light allowing her to change her form.

A'drianis is about to crouch to change once again when the skeletons stop moving. They then slide to one side to allow their master through. She swears when she sees Slone step into the half-light of the hall with the undead. Jasmine is nowhere near him, causing A'drianis to frown, is there another way to the ship?

"Well, cousin, it looks like you are abandoned," Slone smiles

"Looks are deceiving, Son of Sliminess," A'drianis assures then takes a step back when she sees a small glow in his hand. "Oh no you don't."

The darkness in the hall goes absolute, catching Slone off guard. He swears and blocks to one side then the other as a large black claw swings at him from the shadows. The skeletons all fall, taken apart by the hidden shiadokat. Slone yells as he cast a light spell that fills up almost all the corridor prompting swears to come from A'drianis as she reverts back to Zaria.

Undaunted, the shiadokat is quick to go for the shadow still clinging to the wall. Slone purposefully cast a spell of light towards the shadow, causing it to disappear. Undaunted, Zaria growls as she lands on that wall then jump to the second wall across the hall before leaping high into the ceiling. Slone looks up with mouth agape, forgetting about the height of the ceiling where the light never touches. He is also surprised at how high the woman could jump. His surprise became anger as he sneers at the black tail of a feline as it twitches back and forth, scolding. It then disappears along with the rest of his prey before he could drag her back out.

"No!! Open the doors. I want her head," Slone bellows.

The entire structure hums and shakes as waves of energy pulsate upon all the walls to include the caves. The sound of the stone against stone echoes again as the doors are reopens from somewhere above. Vicki and Sonja exit the staircase heading straight to the ship. Both climb aboard the vessel even as Zaria encourage those behind them to get on the boat as fast as they can. Milea slides to a stop and turns to make sure all her companions and her twin are safe. She exhales in relief when Maya exits and stops next to her.

Neil and Brion exit the doors and the entire staircase collapse from a power surge. All four then head to the ship, ascending onto it at great speed. Brion cutting the rope on his way up. The ship did not move prompting a curious sound from Neil as he glances over the side. An oath that his mother would disapprove of exits his mouth as he brings his head back before a rusty blade takes it away from him. He moves back with several as the skeleton boards the ship.

"Any ideas from anyone would help," Neil announces. He pulls his blade and defends the skeleton.

"Jasmine is controlling them. She calls herself the Mistress of Death," Brion grunts as he too blocks his opponent.

"Mistress of...," Zaria cusses as she dodges her opponent. "Is she an Underak?"

"That's her last name," Brion answers as he takes the head of the skeleton he battles. It shutters as the head floats back to the neck. "Damn it!" Brion blocks the sword of his returned opponent.

"That's not good," Zaria remarks.

"Fighting dead people is not good." Sonja points out.

The boat rocks and pulls in an attempt to be free of the undead as Sonja dodges and knocks the head off of her opponent with a mighty blow. The skull flies over the side of the ship yet the skeleton continues to battle. Sonja once again moves to allow the headless undead to attack his own then defends against as a second one came after her. A whip cleaves the arm that holds the weapon in half as Vicki lend some assist before she has to deal with her own opponent. Milea calls her daughter to her prompting Sonja to jump and dodge around a few more undead to reach her. The girl then protects her mother as Milea's mystical abilities light up upon her person.

Maya uses a staff to whack her opponent before she yells and causes a black flame to belch to life, surrounding the living and consuming the skeletons on board. Milea blinks, her spell lost to her as sees the flames and sense the dark abilities behind her. She turns to see her twin sister is glowing purple, the light radiating from her eyes as she concentrates. Maya then sits down upon the deck and closes her eyes to concentrate on her spell.

The floor of the ship lights up in different purple symbols and words. The flames turn into a cascade of different yet dark colors. The undead moans and releases the ship, splashing back into the water. The *Lady of the Night* groans as it finally frees itself and began to move towards the exit of the cave at a slow rate. Brion pushes his opponent into the flame and watches as it is consumed before looking forward. He cusses, catching the attention of Neil and Vicki.

"What are they... hello!" Neil jumps when he notes larger skeletons, dragons, pushing on the columns that hold the cave up. "Ladies, we need to speed up the boat."

"I..." Milea starts then takes a step back when she sees the skeletons. Several columns are ready to collapse any minute now. "Oh, hell..."

The large skeletons continue to move down the wall as if they are giant spiders and pull at the columns, taking out chunks of stone and tossing them at the ship. Milea stands with one foot in front of the other and does a push-pull motion, concentrating on the water behind the ship. Her body is swaying with the motion as the water starts to imitate her movements, slamming into the back of the cave at first then ramming into the back of the ship.

The cave itself starts to rumble as it collapses around the group. Large stones just miss the *Lady of the Night*. Zaria yells in surprise when one almost hit the ship. The boulder barely scratches the side. Milea stops her wave spell and lights up, casting a lightning spell at one of several large columns behind the ship. The stone goliath crumbles down, taking the dragon skeletons clinging to it with it, crashing into the water and creating very large waves.

Several gigantic stones fall from above as the column's twin on the opposite side collapse. The resulting splash down creating another large wave. The mountain of water slams into the ship. Brion cusses and holds onto a rope. Neil manages to get to the helm and grab the wheel. Vicki grasps onto Brion's arm. The force powers the *Lady of the Night* forward, coming up on the entrance rapidly as it starts to collapse.

"Mom, the entrance is shrinking," Sonja calls out.

Milea once again switches her focus and cause a large bolt of lightning to slam into the top of the entrance, widening it. The ship is spat out of the cave's mouth still traveling at a fast rate. Maya concentrates on shielding the ship as large stones rain down. The huge boulders push the vessel further along as the entire cavern collapse, sealing the cave. Those skeletons that are still clinging to the side of the ship fall off indicating that the lifeforce that animate them has disappeared.

The ship maintains a quick escape as Vicki let out a sigh and turns to look back at the ruin. Instead of being relieved, she takes in a long breath and let out a terror-filled scream. Neil stares at his sister, not use to the sound from her as the rest of those aboard the ship turn in the direction Vicki is looking. A variety of sound from the crew prompts Neil to also turn and look at the object and let out a slew of unkind words drop from his lips at what he sees.

A hollow sound exits the gigantic skeleton as it lumbers to climb on top of the ruins of the temple. Made out of the skeletons the fallen, it is humanoid in appearance with large and dangerous horns on either side of its composite skull. Red eyes glow as they focus upon the departing ship, a yellow glow above catches the attention of the group. Jasmine mentally focuses her creation as she glares at the ship. The *Lady of the Night* bobs and slows down as Maya takes a step to the back of the boat along with her twin. Both center on the skeleton until another object presents itself.

Slone yells profanities at the ship surprising Zaria at his appearance. The car'laden lord then starts glowing as he leaps from the island and heads to the ship. Milea and Maya both unleash individual swears as they turn, in unison, to cast a quick mage-winds spell right at the sails. The sturdy cloth fills up quickly being smack by purple and red winds causing the ship to leap forward at quick speed just in time as Slone misses his mark and lands in the water. He bellows at the boat in anger as it sails out of sight and he is retrieved by the hand of Jasmine's creation. Once the temple is out of sight, Maya deactivates her gifts, causing a small sparkle of light to flash as she once again sits down upon the deck of the ship. She exhales her relief and wipes her brow Milea sits with her back against Maya and did the same. Sonja goes to her mother and aunt to watch them, noting that both are extremely tired.

"Mom, Aunt Maya. Are you two alright," Sonja asks.

"Fine Sonja," Milea assures and smiles when she receives a hug from the child.

"Nothing a good week of rest would not help. That along with a good meal and a strong ale. Yes, that's what I need right now," Maya agrees. A chuckle escapes her when she receives a hug from Sonja as well.

"Milady is right about her twin," Neil said as he approaches, catching the women's attention. They both turn to face him but did not bother to get up. "I would dare say you are identical."

"There are some differences. Most notably, the hair," Milea combs her long red locks back with one hand in an effort to tame it.

"A key factor in identifying who's who that is ignored by just about everybody," Maya points out, "even the man that brought that giant eye to the temple."

"Giant eye," Milea shoots a strange look at her twin. Her mind begins racing. The words at the Temple once again came to it as well as the image of a handsome man with a giant orb floating beside him. Milea stands up. "Brandon?"

"That's him," Maya said. "He kept calling me 'love.' You're not involved with that creep, are you?" She gives her twin a curious look.

"No, thankfully," Milea said bluntly. "His little joke that I do not find it funny."

"No kidding, especially when he uses that thing on me," Maya scowls. "If I were conscious after I got hit by that thing. I would have sent him straight to the deepest pit of Ublivorion."

"Oookkkaaayyy. You survived a blast from an Eye of Gaunt," Zaria stares at the twins in awe.

"That's what it's called," The twins ask at the same time.

"Legend has it that no one supposed to survive that thing once it is fired," Vicki explains in short. "That's what the spirit of the priestess told me. She also said that Slone, Son of Roathis, is the one that killed her. Nadine also said that there had been a strange song that drove over half of the temple crazy."

"Let's talk more when we get out of this place. If you do not mind," Brion suggests. The sounds and smells of the Boiling Seas are not helping his seasickness.

"Where's your dopie ginger? That should help some. Remember, we are not in the worst part of this ocean swamp," Milea approaches the elf.

"I know," Brion acknowledges. "The piece I had flew overboard when we were chased by the Crimson Dragon." He sits down when his stomach twist and the ship's movement play on his senses. "Ok, this is bad." He holds his stomach.

"All the skeletons leave, and you get sick," Vicki chuckles. "Neil, let's get him out of here. I don't want to clean the deck."

"I'll help you get him into the cabin. I don't know about you, but I am not going to see if Jasmine will send more skeletons just to keep your illness away," Zaria volunteers to assist

Brion. She helps the elf to his feet. Vicki catches him before he goes back down.

"No fighting right now," Brion shakes his head slowly.

"I'll get the door. Then I'll go get the dopie ginger," Sonja jogs until she is at the cabin.

"We have to move," Neil returns to the helm. "Raise the sails; let's get out of this place." He holds the wheel.

"I hope he doesn't expect us to," Maya frowns.

She jumps to her feet when the ropes of the ship begin moving. She turns to see the sails raising and tying in place. They shift until they find a strong wind. The ship moans a little as it coasts to the exit of the Boiling Seas. Milea clears her throat to garner her twin's attention.

"Enchantment," Milea answers the silent question. "Try to get along with our new friends. We are going to need them to get home. Unless you've enough to teleport, I do not have enough in me to even try that spell."

"I am barely standing up," Maya said. "Teleportation is not in the works right now." She waves the suggestion away. "Don't worry. These guys helped save my life. I am not going to turn anyone into un-pleasantries when I just met them... unless they are a jerk."

"Relax sister," Milea chuckles. "You don't know how glad I am to see that you're still with us." She once again gives her twin a brief hug. "I was very worried about you."

"I did not give up hope. I knew you were on your way," Maya smiles wearily at her twin. "Thank you, sister, for coming for me. I'm not sure what would have happened." She stumbles a little when the ship tilts slightly to the side.

"Come.   Let's sit down before you tumble overboard," Milea smiles and escorts her twin towards a large coil of rope.

The Brewing Tempest

The green fog of the boiling seas surrounds the ship, folding it into obscurity and hiding it from any prying eyes from above or around. Neil turns the wheel and steadies the craft, noting that the smell is not as bad as when the haggos are around. Zaria informs her companions that the strange beasts are miles away and back asleep, they are heading out the boiling seas via a slightly different route than what they came in. Two hours of unpleasant sounds and smells pass before the *Lady of the Night* break through the dense fog and back into the regular ocean; the winds swirl around clearing the rest of the air upon the ship.

The sun assists in the cleansing by beating the green clouds down and raising the spirits of those on board. Milea takes a deep breath in and out when they exit the Boiling Seas. Her motion is echo by all those upon the ship and includes the vessel itself. Sonja rejoices a little as she climbs back up and into the crow's nest without being hindered by the boiling seas. She makes quick work of the climb and looks about, spotting the island where the fish people attacked them prior to rescuing Maya. Zaria turns and focuses on the island, taking note that the giant boulder at the top of the island now resembles a fish's head.

In her memory, she knows that it was once homage to the Tragin Gaunt and was in the shape of a giant eye. Her mind turns to the present day when she recalls that both Maya and Milea survive the blast from the Eye of Gaunt. Two other sorceresses did the same in the ancient past, neither one of them survived long after the one-thousand-year war ended. Vicki returns to the deck from below and informs her brother that most of the supplies they picked up are ruined from the storm they encountered prior to Cyenzie Island, several barrels of water are broken open and spilled upon the floor destroying the persevered dry meat that mingles with it. The mess is almost as smelly as the Boiling Seas and will need to be clean up. Neil scowls at the report and looks over to the fish head island.

"We already know that there's nothing palatable there," Neil recollects. "Supplies are low, we need to find something soon."

"Brion and I noticed the current on the other side of this island. It looked as if there may be another landmass close by," Vicki offers while looking out upon the open seas. "Maybe we should try there."

"Right. I need to reassess our route anyway. Safe to say that the Strait of Fairge is out," Neil steadies the wheel.

"Unless we want to go pass Etan again. I'm sure he's still suffering from that sea dragon landing on his back though," Vicki rubs her neck.

"I'll not take that chance," Neil turns the wheel of the ship.

The *Lady of the Night* eagerly obeys his commands. The winds and waves tangle in a playful wrestling match and shift the ship a little. The sails turn to catch the winds righting the vessel and speeding it on course. The sleep cabin door opens as Maya exit the room in a complete change of clothing thanks to her sister. She spots the woman at the bow of the ship and decides to join her to look out among the waves. The illusive island looms into view catching the lookout's attention.

Sonja calls out what she sees as Neil hands the wheel to Vicki and picks up a telescope to survey it from a distance. The land is odd in a way, with a small beach leading to a cliff that is accessible via a very steep yet short sandy hill. Two palm trees dot the beach, the cliff house an entire forest at the top and Neil deduces them to be oak trees. A calm harbor beckons the ship with the promise of shelter and uneventful night. Neil takes his instrument down and stares at the landmass as he recalls his charts and maps. The captain makes a noise of curiosity when he does not remember any island or continents near the Boiling Seas.

Seagulls call as the ship enter the harbor, guided steadily by Vicki. It bumps a little when the water is too shallow to sail. Maya takes note of the small beach and steep climb on the sand with a curious look. She estimates that the ship is taller than the hill at this point. There is enough room to swing, if done correctly, up the hill and land on top. Thoughtful, she leaves her sister's side to find a suitable rope. Milea smiles at her twin as she watches Maya proceed to climb the ship's mast.

The ship pulls up close enough for Neil to hop down and wade through the shallow water to shore with a tether rope. He trudges to the closest palm tree as Brion follows his lead and tie the rope secure enough to stay for the night. Zaria jumps off the ship, clearing the water before landing near the hill. Her hand sinks into the sand at the bottom of the obstacle causing her to pull back and swear a little at it. The sand is as liquid as water.

The ship sways a little as Vicki stands on the rail and invites Sonja up for her first 'ninja' lesson. They are about to proceed when Maya swings past them on a rope with a whoop of joy. The ship leans to the ocean to assist with the swing up the short hill. Maya reaches the top of her swing and the hill before she let go. She lands near the edge of the only path up. The sand sucks on her foot, but she manages to free herself and get on solid ground.

"Wait. I thought that your aunt is a sorceress," Vicki asks Sonja, a very confused look on her face. "Why did she do that instead of levitating?" She watches the girl shrug.

"My sister has a zest for life," Milea said. Her daughter and friend turn to face her. "And that hill will be an interesting climb. I think it's mostly sand." She holds out two ropes. "Care to join me?" Sonja did a whoop of joy before hurrying over to grab a rope.

"Oh, hell why not," Vicki beams. "This is, after all, a replica of the *Dragon Rose*." She accepts her rope. "We're going to need some height to get all the way up that hill." She walks over and starts climbing the mast. Milea and Sonja follow.

The groan of the ship sounds more like a chuckle emitting from the wood as Neil gawks at Maya waving from the top of the hill. The hardy cry of a lady pirate turns his attention back to the ship then up in time to see Vicki and Sonja swinging out in similar fashion as Maya. The girl is cheering in joy as she let go and lands near the top of the hill. Sonja slides back a few inches but manages to scramble to the top.

Vicki lands right behind Sonja and also scramble to get out of the sand as she sinks to near thigh deep in it. Maya reaches out and assists her rescuer to the top of the loose mound and pat her shoulder. Milea swings out, her rope is a little longer than her companions. As the rope nears its peak, she lets go and continue up and out. Maya and those with her watches as Milea sail over their head and land on the top of the sandy hill. The woman slides a little to stop but remains standing.

"Showing off are we," Maya teases her sister.

"You started it," Milea counters, her voice also teasing.

"Hey," Neil calls from below, "Milea! Maya! Is that all? I can do better than that!" The twins look at each other before both turn their gaze downhill simultaneously.

"Prove it," Milea calls out her challenge back down. Neil waves and goes onto the ship along with those that are on the beach with him.

Vicki watches from her vantage point as her brother climbs to the crow's nest with Brion and Zaria. The shiadokat takes up the rope that Sonja had used earlier and swings out first, reaching the highest point and seem to bounce off the air to gain more height before she lands at the very top of the hill. The sand slides backward, taking her foot with it and causing her to slip.

Zaria swears a little as she balances herself and with assistance from Sonja gets up the hill onto solid ground. Brion picks up Vicki's rope swings out, landing at a point a little lower than Vicki has done so earlier. He immediately starts to sink down causing high alert from him as he struggles to the top. He is almost waist deep before he is able to get to the top and get help hauling himself out with assistance from the previous landing party. Turning, Brion sees that his landing and his trek to the top are gone as if it has not been disturbed. He bends down to study it as Milea and Maya focusses their attention on Neil.

"I hope he knows what he's doing," Vicki scolds her distant brother under her breath.

The wind tangles with Neil's hair as he stands and takes a deep breath in and out, looking at the object he must overcome. His backpack adds a little extra weight but is filled with the charts and scrolls needed to chart the rest of the journey. He is determined to get them to the closest friendly port so that the quest can finally come to an end. With Maya in their mist, the task he is hired for is all but complete. Neil shifts his backpack a little, taking great care to keep the half book that he and Vicki found tuck in the folds. He figures the book itself will hold clues to Maya's survival in an otherwise brutal bloodbath. Neil picks up the rope Milea use to swing out and smiles a little cockily when he notices that he is the center of attention from those on the hill.

He climbs out of the crow's nest onto the long timber that holds the sails then dos a short run to the edge of his path and leaps into empty space. The ship leans towards the beach a little. The rope snaps and begins to swing up as the *Lady of the Night* leans towards the ocean as her captain swings up the hill. Milea and Maya both watch as he goes above their heads quite a bit. Neil let his rope go at the very peak of his swing and did a series of three flips before landing on the top of the hill a foot from where Milea landed, the sand stirs just a little bit from his landing. Milea and Maya glance at each other before directing their attention to Neil. Maya is the first to clap, applauding the captain's effort. Milea joins her sister with a nod and a smile.

"Thank you," Neil bows to his audience. "I'll admit that is a great deal more fun than jumping off the ship the usual way." He straightens and smiles. "Surprise I didn't think of it first."

"My pleasure for showing the way," Maya smiles.

"This looks more like a forest than a jungle," Brion notes, scanning the large trees that guard the top of the hill.

The sounds of the sea fill the silence as Brion bends down to check out the beach, scanning it for any signs of life and finding very little of it. The white sands of the shoreline have given way to a richer tone brown at the top where they landed and houses extra-large crabs that mosey the sand to scavenge for food. The speckles of grass that dot the landing site gives way to long grasses as well as the tall trees marking the entrance to the deep woodland.

Brion stands and takes in the tree line, not seeing any obvious pathway into the woods as if the animals avoid this area. The trees that line the outskirts of the forest have their bark separating from them in large chunks revealing the creamy white interior of the trunk. Neil mumbles a few choice words as he surveys the area. Unless they want seafood again, they have to explore to see if they can find anything to go with them upon their voyage tomorrow morning

"I brought the charts so we can see where we are at tonight," Neil offers and place his backpack on the ground. "I'm going scouting and hunting. If I'm not back in an hour, I found something too good to leave." He grins as he picks up his sword placing it in a sash around his waist.

"I'll go with you," Brion volunteers. "At least we won't run into giant jungle cats here." Zaria grins a little at the comment.

"Well, if we find something huge in there. We might need it," Neil opts.

Birds call out as Brion and Neil slice through the tall grass in order to gain entry into the forest. They swear a little when they nearly trip down a hill to get into the deeper part of the forest, their sounds soon become distant to those left on the landing site. Maya turns to Zaria and inquire about the giant jungle cat. She gets a small grin from the shiadokat in response. Zaria then dismisses the notion and focuses her thoughts upon what she saw at the temple of light. The fact that both Milea and Maya survive a blast from an Eye of Gaunt also disturbed the shiadokat in many ways, the most important is that the Eye is not supposed to exist.

"I think we really should get to Selvast Forest. Not only because of the Eye and Slone but Brion mentioned that Jasmine is an Underak. That family was wiped out by an apex slayer long ago," Zaria assures.

"Did the assassins miss one," Vicki asks.

"Not that I am aware of," Zaria scowls at her thoughts and memories. Did she miss one?

"She's a powerful bugger," Maya rubs the back of her neck. "Temperamental and a sense of humor I don't care for."

"The Eye takes time to recover, you'll feel limited in your abilities for at least a month. I know, I was hit by it twice," Milea pats her sister on the shoulder.

"You what," Zaria blinks then cover her ears. "No, no. I'm not hearing this."

The forest is alive with all kinds of life ranging from deer to monkeys swinging in the trees. Brion bends down to study a recent set of tracks made by a wild boar and decides to follow them. Neil watches the different birds; smaller than the ones he has seen in the northern tropics on Cyenzie Island. The tiny monkeys sound as if they are chirping as they warn others of the strangers stalking in the forest. Brion pauses and ducks behind a bush prompting Neil to do the same.

Peeking through the foliage, they see the *Charred Rose* turn out from a small port and head out to sea once more. Their crew yells hardily on the ship as they disappear on the horizon. Neil takes a good look at the direction the vessel is pointing so that he could chart out where the dark ship may be going when he returns to camp. The insight could assist him with his decision of the next and perhaps final destination of the *Lady of the Night*.

"That was close," Brion said. "I wonder why they are here."

"Secluded land, not too far from that fish island. Why not set up a hideout," Neil offers.

"This could shortcut our search for supplies," Brion suggests. "Should we go back to camp and get Zaria?"

"No, I don't think I need to enlist her help," Neil said right before he hears rustling a few feet away from him.

Brushes shake violently with the movement of a hidden creature. Snorting follows by loud squeals alerts both Brion and Neil that their prey is closer than they thought. Neil looks up, noting the branches then crouches and jumps straight up with a slight grunt. He lands among the foliage, frightening a few monkeys as he waits for the arrival of the wild pig. Brion is slow as he draws his blade, focusing upon the bush. He listens to the grunting as the prey got closer to his location.

The hidden creature let out a mighty squeal, hopping out to face his hunter. It is a baby pig a few feet tall and long and still wearing its stripes. Although small, it will feed the entire landing party at least twice. Brion scowls at it causing the animal to back up and run away from him. Neil cusses, pulls his blade and tosses it at the fleeing creature. The katana flips through the air before skewering the piglet, pinning him to the ground. The creature let out a few more squeals of pain before dying.

"Well, it's not enormous," Neil hops down and retrieves his blade. He wipes it clean before putting it away. "But its dinner." He picks up the small piglet.

"That is way smaller than the one I was tracking," Brion scowls. "I set sights on one is at least as tall as you are."

"Eh, this one is fine. That big one would take days to fully cook," Neil reiterates with a shrug.

"Then we better hurry back to the camp. Before the big one finds us," Brion cautions. They pause when they hear a deep grunt.

"I think it might be a little too late for that," Neil turns to look behind. Brion turns and cusses, taking a step back.

The large animal glares into Neil's eyes from the short distance between where the piglet emerge and the spot of its demise. The beast's large shoulders host a bristling mane of deep brown and very stiff hair. It is lean and muscular from head to tail, a boney ridge of small horns line it from the nose to the back of the head. Brion's attention is on the tusks on the extremely angry beast. They are long and as sharp as any spear or sword that he has mastered. Sticky fluids secrets from its open maul as it bellows in anger.

The beady eyes of the wild boar turn blood red. Neil swears before he turns and runs with his catch reaching his full speed in a few short seconds. The boar roars again as it steams after him, shortening the gap to his quarry just as fast as Neil is running. Brion leaps out of the way of the enraged animal. The beast ignores him, focused completely upon the I'vane man.

"Damn it, Neil. Drop the damn thing," Brion growls, hurrying after the boar.

Monkeys howl and call out as if encouraging the action below their roosts. Neil quickens his pace, still carrying his prize. The animal behind him belts various bellows of anger as it thrashes all vegetation that is between it and the fleeing I'vane. Neil grabs a small sapling and uses his momentum to turn to the pirate camp. His chaser is right behind him, destroying the small tree in the process. Brion arrives at the springing debris and scowls hesitating at the top of a hill. The boar is creating a very wide path down the hill, undeterred by the steep incline as it closes the gap between itself and the man that holds the dead piglet.

Neil finished navigating down the steep slope and goes directly into the camp without slowing to catch his breath, his legs seem used to such drastic changes in incline. He scolds himself to think as he tucks his prize and dodges left then right to avoid a few of the surprised residents of the camp. The boar, however, ran right through, killing the group of four immediately. Neil once again switches directions, dodging a group of barrels. The boar rams right through the barrels, destroying all supplies that are left in the pirate camp. The animal turns, corrects course and continues after its prey. Neil scampers down a narrow alleyway and is surprised to hear the boar pursue him.

The sight in front Neil has him cussing up a storm as he slides to a stop. It is the side of a mountain. Looking up, Neil deciphers that it is way too high for him to jump. The noise behind him tells him that the boar is still charging. The tusks of the beast slices through the thin wooden walls of the buildings on both sides. Neil is quick to calculate his chances then charges towards the animal.

The wild boar's mouth is foaming by this time, steam emitting from its nostrils, eyes red as lit coal. Neil increases his step then jumps and flip over the charging animal. He lands and continues to escape out of the alleyway. The wild boar made a grunt of surprise as it tries to stop. It rams into the cliff face head-on, effectively stopping the charge. The animal's body goes limp and collapses to the ground.

"So much for that," Neil pants a little. He holds up the dead piglet he carries. "You better be worth all this trouble." He reprimands his prey then takes a small scan of his surroundings. "So much for the supplies. Damn it." He scolds himself. His ears detect the voices of more devorians. With a scowl, Neil makes haste to depart the pirate camp.

Neil meets up with Brion in the forest and they head back to the beach following the sounds of the seagulls. They purposefully rattled the vegetation as they approach to alert the women of their return. Neil is the first to break through then grin sheepishly when he sees his sister glaring at the woodland with her arms cross. She holds the whip she confiscated with one hand and a dagger with the other. Behind her is Zaria watching the trees then snorts and walks away when she sees that the hunting party has returned. Brion eases past Neil then nods respectfully to the sentry, Vicki, as he approaches the hill of shifting sands to study it.

Neil goes to one side closer to the trees and digs a pit in order to roast the piglet he captured. Sonja crouches next to Brion to study the hill as well. She tosses a stone and both watch as it sinks into the sand and the spot it lands become invisible. Brion sits back and stares at the hill with a frown as Milea walks up behind him and looks down at the obstacle. She shakes her head and leaves the two to figure out the puzzle on how they are going to return to the ship, settling on a spot that has an unobstructed view of the ocean. Maya joins her sister to take in the beautiful sights as well as the smell of freedom.

Milea closes her eyes and relaxes as she focuses on contacting Keela or Frey, the guardian and guide of Selvest Forest. She feels her mind being blocked by a strong force, almost as if she is hitting an invisible brick wall. Milea opens her eyes and frowns, staring into the distance as she contemplates who or what is blocking her from communicating. Maya focuses her attention on the horizon as she senses something dark in the distance. She tears her eyes away when she hears her twin quietly swearing.

"No luck with Mom either," Maya says the obvious source of her twin's frustration. "Did you want to try and contact Oswind?"

"Do you really want to contact Oswind," Milea counters and faces her twin with a questioning look gracing her features. "Disturb the one that could make it snow in the tropics?"

"Desperate times, desperate measures," Maya answers with a shrug. "We can both try, to minimize the trouble. I really don't like trouble."

"Alright," Milea relents. The twins close their eyes to concentrate. A few seconds pass before they open them. "I got nothing."

"Me neither," Maya responds.

"We can find a pool or reflective surface somewhere and try later," Milea turns to focus on the forest. "I'm sure there is something in there to that effect."

"Or we can try the ocean later on tonight," Maya suggests. "It looks like a clear one. The waters should be calm."

Milea and Maya approach the secondary fire started by Vicki and sit down with the woman and have an interesting conversation as the blue hues of the day turn lavender as evening comes. Sunlight bounces off the ship as it sways in the harbor breeze. The winds curl up the hill, creating a few small dust wisps before ruffling Sonja's hair. Brion stands up when the wind reaches him and stares at the hill, it looks like nothing disturbs it yet moves fluidly.

The elf catches Sonja's attention and they both go to sit by the fire Vicki started. Zaria paces a few feet away from the group until Milea calls her over. The shiadokat grumbles a little and goes to sit next to the sorceress and stare into the flames in her thoughts. Vicki excuses herself and goes to check on the meal as well as her brother. Neil acknowledges his sister several times as she speaks. His head snaps up when she mentions a missed assassination attempt from the past.

"Who missed and who was the victim," Neil quizzes his sibling.

"I don't know the assassin, might have to ask Zaria. But the intended victims were the entire family with the surname of Underak," Vicki explains what she knows.

"Underak? The necromancers from ancient times," Neil stares at his sister when Vicki nods.

"Apparently, she and Brion ran into one in the temple, and that's not supposed to happen," Vicki informs. "Zaria thinks she is a decedent but looked disturbed about the incident and did not elaborate."

"I see," Neil puts his finishing knife down. "Yeah, I'm ready to listen now." The rush of waves echoes as Neil and Vicki return to the group fire and take places next to Brion. Neil focuses on Milea and figures he should just ask the question directly. "Milady, it appears that you've more going on than our contract allows," Neil remarks.

"I have thought about that, Neil," Milea agrees. "You, Vicki and Brion have placed your lives on the line ever since I've met you it seems."

"That it does," Neil concurs. "But I am more interested in the troubles that took out the Temple of Light. My understanding is that it should not have been such an easy task."

"You are right," Milea agrees. "Maya?"

"Right, I will tell you what I saw," Maya focuses on the fire.

Maya brings her eyes up from the fire and focuses on the forest in front of her as she brings her thoughts together. Maya recalls that it started as a typical day. She awoke to the droning of the Warriors of Kaidar, her room was next door to that part of the Temple. She just walked out of her room when a student hurried over towards her. Apparently, the Head Priestess, Nadine, had requested her presence. Something urgent had happened.

Maya stares at the fire as she continued. When she arrived at the main entrance, there was a man standing there. He was a dark mage; various symbols decorated his skin and skull. Bald and skinny, he did not look a threat at first. He called himself Nul and demanded to see the scrolls of the Dark Dragons. Zaria scowled at the news. Nadine refused to give them to him, but that did not deter him. Nul stated that the Temple had until dark to hand over the scrolls, else they will be destroyed. With that, he left.

"Who is Nul," Brion asks, interrupting Maya's recollection. "I don't recall hearing his name."

"Nul is the dark mage that teamed up with Sorshana," Milea answers. "That's all I know about him."

"From what I saw on the back of his head, he is a Dark Mage of Sentical. One of their more active members," Maya informs and draws her knees closer to her chin. "Oh, don't worry. It gets stranger than that."

Large crabs mosey around the group, keeping an eye on them while they feed. Maya once again focuses on the fire as she remembers where she left off and continues her recollection of events. Maya says that an hour after Nul left, Jasmine Underak paid the Temple a visit. She had two men with her, Brandon from the wizard province of Tandon and Slone, who claimed to be the son of Roathis. Needless to say, Nadine was not impressed by the trio. Slone demanded that the Temple of Light surrender to him or be terminated. Maya recollects her conclusion that several people wanted to threaten to destroy the temple that day. She relays that Nadine asked the trio to leave. They would have argued if Brandon did not notice Maya. With a smirk, the man had persuaded his companions to leave, at least for now.

"Ugh...my head," Neil rubs his temples a little. "Slone, Roathis, Jasmine, and Brandon of Tandon... what in all Ublivorion is going on?"

"What happened after they left," Vicki asks.

"Nadine and I had dinner to discuss the events," Maya said. "After that, All Ublivorion broke loose with some extra punch."

Maya recalls passing through the Hall of Ilandere when she heard harp music. Neil and Vicki perk up when she starts to explain the events that happen with the sound. Maya said that the sound was terrible to her sensitive ears yet it kept playing and vibrating the entire temple with the strange and unkind melody. Not only was it giving her a headache, but it was casting a very powerful spell. Maya traced the music towards the lower docks just under the Hall of Ilandere. She had paused, her senses telling her something was very wrong. She turned to see several of the temple members approaching her and appeared entranced. A few pulled weapons out when she spoke to them. A group charged towards her in an attack. Maya informs her audience that she used a strong spell to send the attackers backward into their fellows. Maya shutters as she remembers that the group shifted into dragon form causing her to panic, turn, and hightail it into the hall to find the High Priestess.

Maya trembles a little as she holds her head. Milea places an arm around her twin and quietly calm her anxiety down. Maya takes a deep breath as she turns her mind back to the events at the temple. She relays that the fire began to envelop the entire temple as those who were not in a trance battled their friends. More dragons came from the ceiling as it was ripped off by a power stronger than any Maya has ever sensed before. The temple rocked with explosions that threw everybody to the floor. Maya remembers sliding around the corner towards the High Priestess' room and seeing Slone cut down some of the most elite warriors of the temple as if they were nothing but toys. She was about to go assist but found herself facing a multitude of dragons instead. Maya once again managed to get away and made it to the library where she came face to face with Brandon.

"What does Brandon look like? I don't think I've seen him before," Sonja tilts her head.

"He's actually rather handsome," Milea informs. "But...."

"He has an evil aura that neither of us wants to be a part of," Maya concludes. "There is something about him that seems, well, icky." Her features twist slightly when she thinks about the man.

"That feeling, sister, may be because he calls Dee, Mother," Milea said calmly. Maya gives her sister the strangest look. "Yes, and he's her son by blood."

"I.... exchanged a few words with Brandon," Maya decides to continue rather than engage in the frightening conversation her sister is gearing for. Milea smiles at her twin. Maya focuses back on the flames. "He held up his hand with a wicked grin and some false words."

Maya closes her eyes as she relives the images of the temple's last day. She says that the ceiling of the Temple of Light exploded before a giant eye lowered itself into view. Maya describes the eye in great detail indicated it is quite literally an eye. It has no lid but did have whites, and the color of the center is dark at first but lights up like fire when Brandon is commanding it. Maya goes back to her explanation as she informs that many of the surviving members of the temple that were not under a spell ran

into the library. She remembered the words some of the warriors said and did not repeat them. Brandon commanded the
Eye of Gaunt to fire at Maya. At the time, she was standing in
the middle of the library.

"Before he fired, he said something like 'goodbye love' and
let loose," Maya shakes her head and opens her eyes. "I really
hate that guy."

"So do I," Milea agrees.

"You said earlier that you faced Jasmine," Brion leans forward. "What happened there?"

"It's after the Eye," Maya said.

"How did you survive the blast from the Eye of Gaunt," Zaria also asks.

"I blocked it with the most powerful shield I could conjure.
Three seconds after impact, I knew I was in trouble," Maya
answers. "The entire room lit up, my hearing left me temporarily as a resounding boom filled the room. I remembered
seeing debris lift up around me."

Maya takes a deep breath and assures her twin she is fine
as she recalls the last of the very violent end of the temple. The
entire building shook viciously from the impact, knocking
many books down the crevice. Those in the room with Maya
were not as lucky as she. Some died instantly, others died not
too long after the blast. Maya remembered pushing books off
of her body then being face to face with Jasmine.

Brandon, apparently, left the scene before she returned to
consciousness. She also noted that Nul had been in the library and found what he searched for. Jasmine attacked
when Maya set her sights on Nul. The battle with the woman

did not go well for her. In a desperate attempt, Maya tried to teleport out of the library. At the same moment, Jasmine threw a strange light ball at her. The explosion knocked the rest of the books off the shelves. Maya reappeared in the rafters above the crater much to her own surprise. Jasmine, upset at not seeing a body, decided to burn all the books in the library.

"While she threw her temper tantrum, I made my way to Keela's part of the temple," Maya said. "I reached it and relaxed behind the statue of Keela. Several dragons came into the Hall of Keela and homed in on me. I.... killed them to save myself. They were not going to listen." She shakes her head.

"What did their eyes look like, sister," Milea asks gently.

"They were in a trance. A yellowish glow was in their eyes," Maya answers and shutter. "After that, I put up a ward to keep anybody else out. I was tired and scared. The temple continued to shake, and its people scream their deaths for about three hours after my battles. When it stopped, the silence was deafening."

"How did they put an entire temple of warriors in a trance," Neil asks.

"Jasmine mentioned the Harp of Hestor. That would be the reason," Zaria answers then note both Vicki and Neil stand up.

"What," Both Dresden siblings exclaim at the same time.

"I thought that thing was destroyed," Vicki adds, very upset at the news of the harp.

"It was destroyed," Zaria insists. "Ilandere destroyed it near the end of the ten-thousand-year war when she yelled at it."

"Ok. Brandon is from Tandon and controls the Eye of Gaunt," Neil rubs his temples. "Jasmine Underak, someone who should not be born, is controlling Slone the bastard Son of Roathis. Who's controlling that blasted Harp of Hestor?"

"I want to know who is cooking," Vicki counters. Neil perks up. The smell of smoke and scorched meat greets his nose. He cusses, hopping to his feet in haste to save the meal. "I guess we should wait until he comes back."

"Neil is fine, he already knows the answer," Milea said and leans upon her leg. "The harp is controlled by Sorshana. Nul brought it to the Temple of Light."

"Could it be that Tandon, Slone, and Sorshana are all allies," Brion reasons.

"It would be an uneasy alliance. However, not an impossible one. Especially if they have someone to hold them together," Milea explains.

"I know what I saw," Maya growls, a little agitated. "They did not attack each other. Instead, it was a coordinated attack against the temple. They teamed up. Nul brought that blasted Harp and Brandon that bloody Eye. Who knows, maybe Slone was testing them."

Maya rubs her arms and stares into the fire as she focuses on closing the last few days out of her mind. Milea places a hand upon her sibling's shoulder and offers to go for a walk to calm her down. The twins stand up and Milea speaks politely to those that she hired as she and Maya take their leave and walk to the forest closer to the coastline.

Sonja jumps to her feet and follows after her mother and aunt, curious to the woman's well-being. Neil grumbles a little from the information as he goes over to the cooking pit to continue his task with the meal he and Brion hunted. Vicki digs out the charts so that she, Brion and Zaria could go over in order to navigate a path that did not involve the strait or *Dragodu*.

"Maya seems very upset with what she saw at the temple," Brion said the obvious. "I hope she will be ok."

"I think Milea is taking her for a walk in order to evaluate that," Zaria hypothesizes. "Last thing we want on board a ship is a stressed-out dark sorceress."

"The fastest means to Selvast is teleportation, why are neither Milea or Maya doing that?" Vicki inquires.

"I'm sure if that's going to happen, we would be sitting in Selvast by now." Brion offers. "Although I think Neil's plan is to get to the closest friendly port. There, we can collect payment to fulfill this contract. I see Tenze over here, that's a neutral port last I heard." Brion taps the map. "Oice is here, but not sure what their status is."

"Hm…" Vicki studies one port then the next. She centers on the large swath of land known as Selvast near the top of the map. "Why can't we simply take them all the way home?"

"That would be up to Neil," Brion reminds. "He is the captain."

"I think the open contract can be amended," Vicki said. "Let me go talk to him." She stands up and approaches her brother.

"I hope she can persuade him to take us all the way," Zaria wishes.

"If anyone in this group can do it, Vicki can," Brion notes. "She knows her brother better than he knows himself." He follows Vicki over to the cooking fire.

The crackle of the flames roasting the piglet keeps Neil's attention until his sister taps him on the shoulder. He listens to his sister as his eyes focus upon the path the twins ventured a moment ago. He makes a grunting noise as Vicki talks about the two ports they discovered while studying the charts. Neil argues that the closer ports will be more ideal so they can leave before they become too deeply involved. He very much wants to avoid the coming tide that Maya fore-warns of in her recounts of her encounters at the Temple of Light. Neil repeats a few things from Maya and the fact that they saw Slone himself at the temple. Vicki kindly reminds him that there is also the Harp of Hestor. The item had been defeated with assistance from their ancestors. Least they could do is destroy it completely so that the family can rest in peace.

"And how do we do that," Neil challenges as he turns the food once more. "In the past, they used something called the Dragon Song." He recalls. "I know plenty of songs about dragons, but I doubt if it is the same as that legendary Hymn."

"We could ask Keela," Vicki reminds.

"Good idea. I need to learn more about the Eye of Gaunt and Slone anyway. Perhaps with the information, I can assist with some of the threat," Brion voices his opinion.

"Oh, come on Brion, not you too," Neil gripes his frustration. "Have you both gone mad?"

"Not yet," Vicki folds her arms. "The twins are out of the Boiling Seas now, I'm sure they would prefer magical travel, but the boat's the next best thing. Besides, I think we are rubbing off on her. At least to Selvast and then we will go our separate ways from there." Neil contemplates as he continues to roast the boar. With a heavy sigh, he stands and faces his smiling sister.

"Selvast and that's it," Neil assures.

The rushing sound of the ocean calls to the landing party like a sirens' song as Neil goes to his pile of charts. Zaria snickers as Neil grumbles and he sort through the items. After a few moments, he returns to the cooking fire and unrolls the items to mull over the chart to the next place. He studies at the sky, the stars are not out yet, but he has a general idea as to where they are. He looks down at his map and scowls, the land they are on is called Habvor.

Neil swears and informs his companions causing Brion to frown and Vicki to echo her brother's words. They will have to leave at first light to avoid trouble and hope Milea and Maya do not run into any. Neil then starts charting a course as Vicki leaves the cooking fire and go sit with Zaria. She asks the shi-adokat lots of questions in regard to the botched assassination of the Underacks.

Bird calls echo announcing Milea and Maya while they continue their slow walk through the dense forest. Sonja has run off ahead and found a grove of fig trees, returning to tell her mother of her discovery. The trio pause at the grove to pick a little of the fruit to eat as they walk. Milea makes a plan to stop back by to stock up the ship for the journey.

Maya requests and listens to her sister as she describes the various adventures and misadventures during the journey to the temple. Sonja gets very excited as she explains how they met Neil, Vicki, and Brion. Maya chuckles at the introduction then frowns in concern when she hears about the devorians. The mystical storm and King Orin brings a deeply rooted look of disapproval to Maya's features. The Crimson Dragon, Etan, and the trip into the Boiling Seas conclude Milea's quick review of her trip. Maya admits that she would have panicked at the sight of the giant crimson dragon.

"No seriously, I would have died because my heart stopped," Maya expresses.

"I know. I know," Milea chuckles, shaking her head in humor. She pauses and exhales a little to regain her thoughts. "I think I will provide Neil his reward and send them on their way."

"Something very nice, I hope. They went through a lot it seems to get to me," Maya requests.

The sisters stop at the edge of the cliff that marks the end of the forest they travel in. Sonja takes a deep breath in and out as she looks out over the ocean with her mother and aunt. The evening sky greets them as they watch the sunset in silence. Thunder from dark clouds in the distance indicates a brewing storm. Milea's attention goes straight to it when she sees red lightning and senses something dangerously familiar about the storm.

Maya whispers a couple of inappropriate words as she notes the negative force coming from the haze as she stares at the dark clouds. The shape of a dragon in the distant clouds almost causes her to panic. Instead, she calms her nerves and describes what she sees to her sister. Milea crosses her arms upon her chest as she contemplates her strength and that of her sisters. Currently they are not ready to face the antagonist, no matter who or what it is.

Milea turns and starts walking back into the woods to avoid contact with the entity. Maya takes one last glance at the approaching clouds then follows her sister, calling to Sonja to join them. The girl jogs a little to catch up with the quick steps of her mother. The trio journey deeper into the woods as the winds tangle around them.

"Milea, whatever happened to Ra'jil after we got her to Dorma," Maya asks as they pause by the fig orchard

"As far as I know of, she's still asleep. I am going to go to Dorma after I rest a little to see if I can awaken her," Milea answers and pick some of the fruit. "I fear only she will be able to take Sorshana down."

"From what you tell me of her past. I think you are right. Too bad she did not awaken for this adventure. I'm sure she would have enjoyed the ship," Maya agrees to accept a few dozen figs from her sister. She holds them close in her arms.

"We would not have met Neil, Vicki, and Brion either," Milea said. "Ra'jil would have mastered the ship, and she does know the way to the Temple of Light." She watches her daughter climb up a tree.

"Mom, do you think Lady Ra'jil and Vicki would get along," Sonja inquires as she hangs upside down from one of the fig tree branches.

"I think they would get along nicely," Milea says with confidence. "Ra'jil and Neil, however, would take time. Especially when a ship is involved."

"I think Ra'jil would win any argument that they might have," Maya shifts the weight of the figs a little. "That's what my instincts are telling me."

"She is very strong-willed," Milea agrees as she takes in her surroundings. "I see the trees are healthier a little further in, perhaps there is a water source near. Let's see if we can contact someone there." She continued. Maya followed her sister. Sonja hopped down and jogged to catch up with her mother.

Milea heads to the spot she spies with Maya closely behind her. The two are careful to pile the figs they hold on the ground once they reach the entrance to the deep woods. Sonja hops down and catches up with them. The girl acknowledges her mother's orders and sits down to guard the figs as Milea and Maya fold into the trees. Colorful birds and smaller primates hop from tree to tree to keep an eye on the intruders. Milea ducks a low hanging branch, detecting the slight trickle of water not too far away. Maya pushes the branch to one side. The branches twist around each other, creating a protective thicket.

The wood's warm tones, however, kept the sisters at ease. Milea pauses when she sees what she searched for. A small stream snaking through the thickets providing the appropriate nurturance for those who live within the woodlands. The edges are rocky, creating small rapids towards the sides of the stream. There are, however, a few pockets of still water. Milea heads to the closest one to her. Maya hesitates when a dragonfly buzzes past her. The insect pauses, backs up, and then darts a few times around Maya before disappearing in the thickets.

"This place is deep woods," Maya observes. "Perhaps we can get Mom to teleport us home from here."

"We have to contact her first," Milea agrees. "Then bring our friends in. I don't want to leave them without rewarding them."

Milea sits down upon a large stone next to a pool of still water. Maya rests next to her sister and settles her senses down. Milea waves her hand over the water and whispers a few soft words. The pool wiggles gently for a few seconds then allows the image of the twins to slowly fade as the pool lights up brilliantly. Milea smiles until the light changes colors forcing a few unkind words to exit her as she stands up and pulls Maya back with her. A pair of light blue eyes replace their reflection in the pool. Milea motions for her twin to remain silent and still for now.

"Where are you pest," The image growls angrily. Milea and Maya continue to remain silent for several seconds. The image let out a sound of angry frustration. *"You cannot hide for long. I will find you."*

The light explodes out, creating a large hole in the thicket above it and destroying whatever birds are trying to escape. Maya and Milea both turn away to keep her eyes shielded from the brilliant light and heat that erupts from the water. The light and energy fade down enough to allow Milea to lower her arms and her shield. They wait a few seconds more before going back to the pool and are greeted by their own reflections.

"That is not mom," Maya observes. "Who is she? She's apparently not happy with you, sister."

"I believe that's the storm antagonist," Milea admits. "We must get back to camp. We have no choice. Neil needs the stars to navigate us back to Selvast. We should rest but be vigilant tonight."

"That's not going to come easy for me. I'm going to be busy trying to figure out who in Ublivorion she is and why she's after you," Maya rubs her arms a little, worried. "I'm not sure I like what I sensed from that brief encounter."

"Relax sister," Milea coax. "We will be fine, at least at night. Remember, we have A'drianis with us."

"That's a relief," Maya smiles nervously.

The twin moons begin their ascent into the sky as Milea and Maya return to the camp. Sonja is now carryings a large pile of figs, towering above her head. Brion stands to assist the girl a little with her load with a healthy laugh. Milea and Maya place the fruit they carry upon the ground, piling it neatly for now. Neil flips the piglet again before assisting the women with the figs. He confiscates a few and tosses them onto the flame to add flavor to the pork.

Milea and Maya both dodge the resulting smoke yet Neil is not as nimble as the two. The l'vane man coughs a few times and steps out of the thick cloud. Vicki glances up from the small flame that is away from the meal. Since the conversation with Zaria ended, she has been studying the blank book retrieved from Nadine's room. Vicki greets to the twins as they sat down with her.

"What is that," Milea asks.

"A book or half of one anyway," Vicki said. "Nadine provided it. I'm not sure but it may hold clues of some sort. Neil and I both looked at the book, all the pages are blank. Perhaps it is magical?"

"Hmmmm," Milea takes the book and flips through it. "Maya, do you know anything about this book?"

"Let me see," Maya accepts the book half. "Well, luckily it is torn in half, or else you would be cursed." She turns it over. "Ever Sleep? That does not make sense. My guess is to understand this book, we have to find the other half."

"At the temple," Vicki scowls.

"Maybe. But let's get to Selvast first before we return to a grave," Maya hands the book back to Vicki. "I'm not up to fighting Jasmine or those who are too stubborn to leave."

"I hear you," Vicki acknowledges. "I don't tolerate ghosts very well."

"Me neither," Sonja agrees with her friend.

"I see," Maya studies both of the l'vanes. "Remind me to give you something to help ward off the ghosts. I have to be at Selvast to do so though."

The evening is yielding to the stars as Neil calls all to come to dinner above the roar of the flames. The announcement makes Sonja jump up to her feet and jog to the cooking area. Vicki chuckles at the preteen's enthusiasm as she and Zaria approach the fire pit. Brion is already there and assists with cutting up the main course. Milea and Maya arrive at the banquet as Zaria is starting to eat her meal, looking up when Neil and Vicki speak about the night sky. After dinner, Brion decides to balance his sword on the tip of his finger to entertain Sonja. The girl tilts her head in curiosity then jump in surprise when the elf removes his hand completely, and the sword remains in place.

Milea smiles at the bantering going on within the group as Zaria finally starts to laugh again, especially at the 'bug' on Neil's shoulder that Vicki has to hit extra hard following the comment on her cooking. Milea stands as the camp settles down for the night and takes a small walk to the edge of the strange hill to stare out at the *Lady of the Night* as it sways peacefully in the harbor. Maya joins her sister, and they quietly enjoy each other company for a few minutes.

"Maya, something tells me that we are about to embark upon a very urgent quest," Milea said to her sister.

"You got that sinking feeling too, eh," Maya agrees, turning to her sister. "What do you think we have to do?"

"We'll have to wait until we talk to Mother. I am very sure we will find out what it is we have to do, especially with Slone and Sorshana alliance with Tandon," Milea faces her twin.

"What about them?" Maya nods to the group, her sister turns with her.

"They have placed their lives in so much danger already, I want to minimize that as much as possible on this return trip," Milea contemplates. "This return trip is over and above the contract that I had with him." She watches the interactions of the group a little. "I will talk to them in the morning about it," she relents as she heads back to the fire. Maya trails after her and smiles at the laughter.

CHAPTER SEVENTEEN

Twin Challenge

Night soon gives way to day once again as Zaria stretches, allowing the shadows to yield to the light. Brion wakes up first and goes to stand at the top of the hill facing the ship, his eyes focus upon the horizon as the sun rose. He takes a deep breath in and out, pleased to see another day then bends to study the sand a little more as his companions stir for the day. Sonja stands and stretches before she did a few acrobatic flips to warm up for the day. Neil completes his task of carving up the piglet and wrapping it in fig leaves. He placed the cutlets in his backpack and walks towards the hill noting that, although it is not very steep it is very treacherous.

Milea and Maya study the hill as well, standing on either side of Brion. Milea bends down and tosses a large rock onto the surface of the hill. It starts rolling down then is swallowed halfway to the bottom. The sand moves a little, but it is gone. She stands up still focus upon the mound of sand, is it quicksand? Neil, Vicki, and Sonja are now standing with them.

Zaria places a hand on the loose sand and once again she watches it go down before she pulls it out. She scowls; it is not her imagination nor a trick from exhaustion that fool her yesterday when she first land near it. Maya stares at the sand a few seconds more; then announced that the sand is not enchanted; it is in its natural state. The declaration causes a frown from Neil, what could cause sand to become nearly liquid and impossible to negotiate?

"Let me see," Brion picks up a stone. He pulls back and grunts a little as he flicks the stone. It skips over the sand, reaching the bottom of the hill in a short period of time. "There is the clue on how we can get down."

"We get changed into rocks and tossed down," Sonja asks. The words cause Brion to chuckle.

"No... When I was a kid, my sister and I climbed Mount Decorn in Solis. Unfortunately, there is a large wingless dragon that guarded the mountain. We had to get down a steep and slippery slope in a hurry. If we didn't, we would have been dragon dinner," Brion goes to the trees and pick up a large piece of discarded bark. He examines at the front and back with an approving nod.

"How did you get down," Zaria asks. She watches as Brion shifts his sword to his back.

"Well, we had two shields and a lot of snow. Observe," Brion tucks the bark under his arm and runs towards the hilltop.

Sonja moves out of the way as Brion nears the top edge of the hill. He leaps into the air tucking the large flat bark under his feet, then lands on it. The tree bark glides on top of the sand as Brion shift his weight left then right to keep himself moving. Neil watches as the elf continues down the hill, leaving a long trail in the sand. It is cover up almost immediately as if the beach is made of water.

Brion makes it down to the shore and leans back, turning the board to stop. He picks up his tree bark and wave at his companions up the hill. Sonja does a whoop of joy and a small jig when she sees her friend make it to the bottom. Maya has a large grin from ear to ear along with Neil. Zaria stands and stares with an open mouth, her features are of shock or joy. Vicki and Milea go to the tree line to retrieve more tree bark.

"I'm not sure which one is more fun," Vicki admits. "Swinging on the rope or sledding down a slope."

"Let's get to the ship and compare then, eh," Milea suggests with excitement in her words

"We can go down two at a time," Zaria said.

The tree shakes a little as Zaria grabs a large piece of bark and hurries back to the hill, her example followed by Sonja. Milea selects thick and large bark with a few curves in it to sled down the hill. Vicki chose something similar to Milea, and they head to the slope. Neil searches for a suitable piece for his sledding and looks up when he hears Maya has found one and return to stand with her companions.

Neil grumbles at all the good bark being taken by his companions and picks up a little smaller sled when his ears detect rustling in the forest and notice that the forest animals are silent. He focusses and swears under his breath when he sees the members of the *Charred Rose* heading in their direction as stealthy as possible. With another set of unkind words, Neil whips around and runs.

"We don't have time for two by two," Neil announces.

Zaria and Sonja are both jumping in the air when an arrow whizz past the girl's ear. Sonja glances back to see the attacking devorians then turns and focus on getting down the hill as quick as possible. Maya turns briefly, drop unkind words, then jump and land on her board on the sand, leaning into her side. Her speed increase rapidly and soon she is just a few feet from the first two. Vicki and Neil follow Maya's lead coming up to speed within a few seconds.

Milea jumps in the air and dodges a few of the arrows as she lands on her board. She flips around and faces backward, her bow and arrow appearing in her hand with a flash. A single woman stands at the edge of the hilltop. Milea scowls recognizing the new adversary as a Sand Witch. The witch raises her hand causing the sand hill to swell slightly. At the bottom, Brion cusses and board the ship to avoid the rapid incoming of his companions. Sonja hit the large bump first and goes airborne. The girl crouches low upon her board as she sails back down and lands near the bottom of the hill. She turns the board to the side and leans back, digging into the much courser sands to slide to a halt. Zaria cusses when she goes airborne as it is not as graceful as the preteen. Her board leaves from under moments before she lands on the sand and is immediately swallowed up.

"Zaria," Maya calls out as she slides past the part the shiadokat went under.

The wind whistles as Milea takes aim with her bow and releases an arrow. The woman at the top of the hill cries out in pain when her arm is hit, breaking her concentration. The sand goes back down as she retreats to safety behind the men with her. Milea smiles in satisfaction until she sees several archers line up on the hill and take aim at her. Very unlady like words exit Milea's lips as she turns around and speeds up her decent.

The archers at the top of the hill aim and release their weapons sending a rain of arrows to their mark only to miss her as Milea continues to move down the hill. Neil and Vicki reach the bottom of the hill but did not break but keep going, leaping from their boards as they near the ship and landing on the deck. The bark slams into the side of the ship causing it to groan in protest. Sonja urges the remaining sliders on as the devorian archers once again load their weapons and take aim. Maya swears when she is nearly hit, her sled breaks apart causing her to jump and use her levitation magic to get onto the deck of the ship. Milea leaps from her breaking sled and flips before landing on the deck. She looks around and sees that one member of their group is missing.

"Zaria has been swallowed by the sand," Maya informs her sister.

"What," Milea exclaims and turns to the beach.

The archers are about to release another round when a figure explodes from the sand. The men either cry out in surprise or release their arrows errantly from the sight. Sand flies high into the air as the figure lands on the shore. Zaria cusses and holds her back as she stands up slowly, taking in her surroundings. She grumbles and boards the ship, slicing through the tether rope along the way. The *Lady of the Night* bobs a little bit as it turns and heads out to sea. The archers on top of the hill retreat to their camp causing Neil to scowl as he knows that they are heading towards their ship.

"Zaria. Are you alright? I saw you get swallowed by the sand," Maya asks causing the addressee to jump and turn.

"Giant crab. That's what kept the sand moving. It's a trap that is used to feed the beasty. I'm not palatable, so it spat me out," Zaria dusts herself off.

"We have to get a good breeze before they bring the *Charred Rose* around. Raise the sails and head out into the open ocean," Neil orders and gets himself to the helm. The ship obeys his requests. "I looked over the maps and charts last night. With the knowledge of this ship's speed, we are a couple of weeks from Selvast Forest."

"You are going to take us there," Maya asks, surprise and joy in her words.

"All the way," Neil agrees.

"That's good to hear," Zaria assures and sits down with the girl on a large coil of rope.

"The whites of your eyes are blue," Milea whispers to the shiadokat. Zaria blinks in surprise then closes her eyes and relaxes backwards, laying in the coil of ropes to meditate.

"Brion and I made a determination that we are near two ports to replenish our supplies for the trip to Selvast. The Port of Oice and the Port of Tenze," Vicki informs.

"Tenze," Milea insists. "I have a slight misunderstanding with the Lady Mayor of Oice."

"Nothing like mine with Orin I hope," Neil frowns.

"No, nothing like that. It is a long story. One that involves a lot of plots," Milea said. Brion goes to assist Vicki with a few of the ropes.

"Milea... what is the misunderstanding," Maya asks. Her sister just shrugs. Maya folds her arms and raises an eyebrow. "Milea..." She speaks the name slowly and methodically as she meets her sibling's gaze. Sonja fidgets a little, sensing the tension between the sisters.

"I'm proud of you, sister. You are becoming a little bolder," Milea smiles. The tension eases much to the relief of her daughter. Milea faces her sister. "The mayor of Oice is also a ritual priestess. Apparently, she is one of very great importance. She had many lovers one of which had been worshiped as a God. That's the one I accidentally killed."

"You what," Maya asks

"I accidentally killed someone that they worshiped as a God," Milea repeats with a shrug. "An honest mistake, I did not know he was supposed to be a powerful being."

"Ok..., Tenze it is," Neil said. "I'll set a course. We should be there by dawn." He holds the wheel as the twins walk away.

"Accident? Somehow, I don't think it's a total accident," Maya laughs quietly. They continue to the bow of the ship. "Was Ra'jil with you? That is her home country, right?"

"Yes, and she thought it, humorous. Then she lost her non-existent temper, and the building was destroyed," Milea defends herself. "She has an awesome power that needs to be controlled. However, she is afraid of it."

"Well, I just hope she does not wake up and destroy Dorma. Amadahy would have a fit if that happened," Maya leans upon the rail, staring out into the ocean.

"Luckily, she does not wake up such as you or me when we are being awakened from a deep sleep. She usually growls then has a sour attitude, but that's about it," Milea said.

"Lucky us," Maya grins.

The day marches by with a few tense moments of cat and mouse as the *Charred Rose* appears on the horizon every once in a while. The *Lady of the Night* is quick enough to avoid the hulking ship. The winds pick up a little, filling the sails and speeding the ship towards her destination. Many uneventful hours later, Vicki steers the ship as Neil fix dinner using the leftovers from the landing. She smiles when she sees her brother yawning as he tosses multiple handfuls of pepper upon the pork, thankful that she is not going to eat that to-night. She is going to have a few of the figs they brought with them.

Brion studiously studies his meal then takes a bite only to yelp in pain from the hot peppers and down a large amount of drinking water in an attempt to quench the flame. Zaria laughs at the misfortune of her traveling companion, her joy stemming from the fact that she is not the first one to take a bite this time. Neil waves as he yawns again and goes to retire for the night, closing the sleep cabin door. Sonja watches the man go to bed then turn back to her plate with a puckered look as she tries to figure out how to eat the meal. She picks up two slices of fig and places a small amount of the pork between them then eats it.

"This isn't bad actually," Maya admits. She takes another bite. "A bit spicy but nothing I can't handle."

"It is flavorful. Though I think we both need a bit more than that to teleport," Milea agrees, polishing off her dinner.

"Seven courses, I think. Not to mention a full day's rest. The sand was anything but comfortable yesterday night," Maya sets her dishes to the side.

"Alright, wait. Neither of you feels the intense flame of the meal? You can even see how spicy it is," Brion picks up a slice of pork to show off the thick coat of pepper.

"Well, for me. Fire is one of my most powerful elemental spells. I'm nearly immune to it," Milea admits.

"Same for me. Except mine is Dark Fire," Maya shrugs. Her senses cause her to look up and stand up. "What the...?" She walks to the stern of the ship.

The sun rays sink below the horizon and are replaced by a dark fog swirling a short distance behind the *Lady of the Night.* A ghostly image takes form out of the mist causing Maya to cuss and step back. Her actions bring the attention of her fellows from their meals. Zaria takes the liberty to go stand next to Maya and focus on the darkness. She sees the darkened hull of the ship as well as the tatter sails and swirling lights in the distance. Her mouth drops open momentarily before she announces the return of the *Dragodu.*

Sonja drops her meal and goes up the mast to the crow's nest to scout an escape route. Brion wraps his sword belt upon his waist as he goes to the bow and also seeks out a way to avoid the ship. Milea goes to her sister's side and peers out at the ship, a displeased look upon her features. Vicki glances behind and drops a sailor's oath before issuing a command to the ship for full sail. The cloth on the main mast lowers and tie into place causing the *Lady of the Night* to jump as it picks up speed.

"Vicki there is an island up ahead, see if we can get there before the *Dragodu* captures us," Brion calls from the bow.

The image of a dragon slams into Maya's mind causing her to cry out and fall to her knees, her body quaking from the encounter. At the same time, the ghost captain once again tries to grab at Vicki. However, the woman manages to ignore him as she focuses on getting the ship to the destination that Brion found. Maya shakes her head and pushes back at the dragon, turning him away from her and the ship causing the *Dragodu* to laugh and press forward. The winds from the ship's accompanying storm pound the *Lady of the Night* as a hand made from the clouds reaches out to grab the enchanted vessel.

"That ship has a dragon on it. A very powerful one... I'm too tired to fight it right now. I can't free them," Maya trembles.

"Can you help me divert it," Milea requests. She watches her sister nod and slowly stand.

The sky illuminates up with purple and red light as the two sorceresses activate their gifts. The twins extend their arms out, one up the other to the side. Milea moves her left arm up as Maya does the same with her right and both move the opposite arm to face in front with energy gathering in front. The twin sorceresses bring their upper hand down and also extends it toward the *Dragodu* unleashing a strong red and purple flames. The dual fire columns twist around each other and slam into the ghost ship. The *Dragodu* bucks and is turned away for a few seconds giving the *Lady of the Night* time to widen the gap between them.

Undaunted, the ghost ship roars, righting its course and once again pursue the living ship. The *Dragodu* picks up speed and seems to growl in anger as it bears down upon the *Lady of the Night.* The wind it creates pushes upon the sails of its quarry, inching her towards her goal. The *Lady of the Night* goes through what appears to be a shield of some sort causing the *Dragodu* to roar in anger and turn. It slams into the same shield as it could not stop in time to avoid it. The ghost ship slaps it twice more as if making sure. The haunted vessel then turns and sail back into the open sea.

"Let me guess, you didn't raise the shield, did you Milea," Brion asks, watching the ghost disappear into the dark horizon.

"Neither of us. This place feels strange," Milea said.

"I'm not so sure I like this place. However, the alternative is much worse," Maya said, approaching the port side of the ship.

Like many of the islands they visit in the subtropics, it is sandy at the beach and a rocky interior. A few palm trees dot the beach with a lush jungle of bamboo growing a distance away. Milea scowls as the ship drops anchor just off the shore. She feels the presence of a powerful being living in the woods. She takes a look back at the shield still shimmering in place then once again focuses on the woods. The entity that brought it up is still concentrating on it to keep it in place. Maya scans the area with an expression of worry upon her features, feeling that she has visited this land before. Vicki hops off the ship and splashes until she is on shore. Sonja follows the l'vane woman down and surveys the beach. Neil exits the sleep quarters and pause, why are they docked.

"Brion, what's going on," Neil asks.

"You are one hard sleeper," Brion comments. "*Dragodu* attacked. A shield or something blocked it coming from this island. Apparently, we have a friend here."

"I hope a friend," Zaria mumbles.

The dense foliage in the middle of the island captures Zaria's full attention. She focuses upon it and sees movement within the stalks of bamboo. A small and deep growl trickles from her body as she continues to concentrate in an attempt to force the shadows to free the secrets locked within the unique foliage. The shade of the bamboo, however, did not yield to her prompting her to snort in distaste. Zaria vouches to wait until the full of night to venture into the bamboo grove itself. Especially after she makes sure the landing party has safely gone to sleep.

"I sense that ghost ship just beyond the light behind us. I think it is safe to say we camp until dawn," Maya hops down and land on top of the water, making her way to the dry beach with Vicki and Sonja. Milea follows after her twin, a level of concern upon her features.

"I know there is a ghost ship out there, but why do I feel I would rather face that than whatever is on that island," Brion said.

"Neil's cooking giving you a case of indigestion," Zaria remarks then jump off the boat, landing on the beach

"My cooking is not as bad as my sister's," Neil defends himself. He and Brion disembark.

The moons peak out from behind clouds to shine upon the beach, providing enough light to see a few of the crustaceans come out of hiding. The sounds of the night residence of the bamboo jungle reach the ears of the landing party above the soft crashing of the waves. Large crabs scavenge the beach then raise pinchers as the landing party spread out to find a suitable camp site for the night. Neil pauses as he sees the amount of wreck ships that scatter upon the land. He imagines that there are more unfortunate vessels on the other side of the island. The skeletal remains of their hulls reach for the sky.

Vicki scans the sun bleach wood and detects no spirts among the wood, perhaps they are awaiting nightfall to awaken. Maya stands next to Vicki and announces that the ship and island itself is not haunted by those that were claim by the sea. Maya leaves her companion's side with the ominous note that the island is still occupied by an otherworldly being. Vicki grumbles a little as the dark sorceress then goes to assist her twin in clearing a spot for camp. Neil calls to his sister and requests her assistance in collecting driftwood for a fire to light up the night. Vicki agrees after getting her brother to swear an oath not to tell ghost stories tonight.

"Oh, you don't have to worry about that," Neil said. "This is one of the islands I was told to avoid. Many of these ships were lured here either by the *Dragodu* or whatever is occupies this space."

"I'm very uneasy about this place and it's not because of the ships," Vicki counters.

The siblings pick up a few more pieces of wood and heads back to the rest of the group. Neil piles the wood into a shallow pit, arranges it so that it will burn all night long. Milea offers to light the pile, turning up her right hand and allowing a small flame of red and urge to dance in the middle of her palm. Neil stands up stepping back and out of the way as he watches Milea bends down and blows upon the small flame encouraging it to leap from her hand landing on the woodpile. The fire, small at first, starts to go grow as it consumes the dry material. The beach illuminates, beating back the shadows of the night as well as warming a small zone for the crew to sit and warm up. Zaria grumbles a little at the light yet relents to the fire being one to take advantage of the warmth.

The light washes over the area highlighting the tracks made by a woman that catches Brion's eyes as he sits down by the flames. He sees they lead straight to the bamboo forest and makes a curious sound. He addresses Sonja when the preteen sits next to him and asks questions about the tracks. They are recent, as if the woman is invisible among them. The two seem more perplex when they notice Vicki and Neil both sit down by the fire to warm their hands, perhaps the intruder is no longer among them.

Maya shutters a little and looks to the sky, it is clear now indicating that the shield is now gone. She exhales a little as she stares at the fire, contemplating the island. Sonja lets in a sharp breath when her scales start to tingle a little. The sensation is annoying enough for her to rub her forearm a little and frown. Milea notes her daughter's discomfort and is about to sit down but turns and glare into the darkness instead.

"Who are you? Show yourself or you will be shown," Milea demands.

Maya looks up in surprise from her sister's demands as Zaria frowns, she scans the darkness and does not see anything or anyone. The shiadokat kicks in her other senses and defiantly smells someone other than the group present. She stands when she also hears the sound of a strange heartbeat, as if two hearts are beating together. Brion inches to his feet followed by Sonja. Milea exhales then arch an eyebrow when she hears a little snickering directly in front of her.

"Oh, a tough one, eh," A female voice said from the darkness. "Well, I guess there is no reason not to show myself." A slight chuckle escapes from the invisible guest.

The flames roar, reaching for the sky in a column causing both Neil and Vicki to swear as they gain their feet. The intensity of the flames has them shield their eyes and back away from the swirling element. Brion takes several steps back and away from the flames to draw his sword as he is unsure what to expect. Maya drops some unkind words and moves several steps back to study the flames. A familiar power is causing them to act this way yet the person responsible is not Milea.

Maya decides to go stand a little behind her sister to get a glance at who would be bold enough to enter their camp in such a way. Sonja postures herself so that she is able to strike said intruder as soon the person becomes visible. Zaria places a hand upon the preteen's shoulder and shakes her head, whatever is there has the ability to severely harm the child. The shiadokat edges al little closer to Milea and Maya as the light from the flames stretches all the way to the bamboo forest.

Milea holds ground as the intruder fades into sight, the image solidifying into a five foot nine inch tall human with black hair. The hair is not as long as Milea's mane and is pulled back into a manageable ponytail, tied with a light blue ribbon. Milea keens in on the woman's almond-shaped eyes, noting that they shift from green to grey. Milea did not flinch but swears under her breath when she sees the whites of the woman's eyes are sky blue, indicating she is an Eltis.

The red light of the flames reflects off the stranger's blue green robe. The rich silk holds tight to the lean and tone body of the intruder. Other than this robe, she seems to be completely nude. A beautiful katana hangs at her side, the handle of which indicates that it is used very well in many battles. Milea also notes that the intruder is standing a few feet from her, a distance that could spell instant death should she use the katana. The stranger seems to be a little surprised as she scans Milea then once again met the sorceress's eyes. It is evident that neither is impress with the other.

"You don't recognize me, eh," The woman asks. She does a ticking of her tongue. "For shame."

"Should I," Milea arches an eyebrow, "I would deem that impossible since I've never met you before. If I had, I would guarantee that we would not be standing here in such a manner." She folds her arms and the intruder appears to be humored by the stance.

"I... unfortunately, recognize you. You are Reis, a Warrior Eltis. You are from the House of the Daonna," Maya addresses causing the intruder to focus upon her.

The angry flames crackle, drowning out Neil swear as Vicki takes a deep breath in surprise. The siblings know about the Eltis and her sister, hearing about their deeds throughout the thousand-year war. Brion hears his friends whispering and makes his way over to join the Dresden siblings. At their advice he puts his sword away and listens to the transactions as Sonja inches to stand next to Zaria. Reis scans the entire group and then returns her focus on Milea then Maya with a grin upon her lips.

"Ah, I see. Twins," Reis says with enthusiasm. "I would never think there are two of you. This is far more entertaining."

"How is this possible," Zaria asks. "You and your sister are dead, you both died during the war."

"You are sort of right Kitty Cat," Reis said and watches with humor as Zaria's expression changes twice. "True, my sister and I battled to the last breath, then we did something that guaranteed we would not end up in Oswind's realm. My sister and I are two separate beings, but we are sharing one complete body."

"Two Eltis, one body," Maya rubbed her temples as she mulls over it. "That means that you and your sister are way more bonded than Milea and I."

"Bonded," Sonja inquires.

"That means that she and her sister were able to feel each other's pain, pleasures and fears." Milea focuses on the intruder.

"Just about all aspects of life," Reis interrupts and seems amused by the group's reactions. "Claries and I bonded the last few years of the Great War."

"Are you the one to shield us from the *Dragodu*," Milea asks, keeping calm.

"The ghost ship? Yes, I did that." Reis rubs her neck a little.

"You have my gratitude," Milea nods.

"But now you have a slight dilemma, Red." Reis announces her voice full of joy. The corner of Milea's right eye ticks from the word. "In order to leave, you have to defeat us. Of course, I am an Eltis, and you are a mortal, so I will go a little easy on you. Or, my sister will. It looks like you're more of a mage than a warrior. The way you start the fire is quite delightful."

"Looks are sorely deceiving. To assume based on such short sight will get you killed," Milea warns, a slight seen flash emitted from her eyes.

"Oh, how I know that," Reis agrees as she yawns of boredom. Neil and Brion glance at each other before facing Reis.

"Really," Neil speaks up and folds with his head tilt back. "Brion, would you be so kind as to ask the obvious question?"

"Indeed," Brion said and gazes at Reis. "What is the challenge?" He requests in a calm tone. His sea blue eyes boring into those of the Eltis.

"Well, that is quite a pleasant surprise," Reis straightens when she hears the elf's voice.

Maya and Vicki both swear as a ghost version of Reis appears in the lesser light of the flames just behind the Eltis. The ghost woman is wearing a priestess robe and seems otherwise alive. The transparent woman postures as she scans Brion with a nod of appreciation, intrigued by the elf. Maya shakes her head and takes a deep breath in and releases it as Sonja focuses on the ghost woman. A bright grin plasters Reis features as she too focuses on the elf. She and her sister quietly communicate.

"Looks like you surprised my sister as well." Reis said. "Don't worry, handsome. Nothing to the death. I just want a little exercise, and then I'll let you go."

"What type of exercise," Brion continues. He is still calm as he asks his questions in a clear and gentle voice.

"Hmmm...," Reis contemplates her answer with a wide smile. The hilt of her sword starts glowing catching Neil's attention. He watches it intensely even as Reis closes her eyes and made a small sound of disagreement. "My sister is such a spoilsport. The exercise is combat. I'm a swordswoman, my sister is a sorceress. Every once in a while, we want to test our skills against castaways. Once we are done, we let them go on their way."

"And the wrecked ships," Vicki asks, motioning to the sea.

"We didn't do those. They wrecked through their own negligence," Reis answers.

"Very well," Milea rolls her neck and shoulders a little. "Exercise it is then." She starts forward, her hands illuminating.

"Not tonight. I think you need to rest before you accept the challenge," Reis relents. "We will begin at dawn."

The laughter of the Reis echoes as she fades from sight, leaving the tower of flames in her absence. Milea sneers a little as she glares into the darkness, visible annoyance very evident of the Eltis and her insane challenge. Heat rises of her as the inferno continues to light up the night. Maya places a hand upon her sister's shoulder to garner attention to the flames licking the sky. Milea takes a deep breath in and turns to the fire to bring it back down to a normal camp fire.

"She's annoying," Milea grumbles, sitting down to face the fire.

"I don't think she knows who she is dealing with," Vicki tosses a board on the fire to keep feeding it. "I saw an image of a woman next to her."

"That would be Claries," Maya said. "You're not going to face that woman alone, sister. There are two of her in that one body. I, unfortunately, battled her magically a while back when I was under control. Next to you, that was the worst pain I've felt after a battle. No offense."

"No. I am not offended, sister," Milea says as she stares into the flames, contemplating. "What information do we have about Reis and her sister?"

"Father made Vicki and I study the ways of Reis and the warriors of her family," Neil sits down on the other side of Milea. "I had no idea she was an Eltis. According to my reading, she is a hell of a fighter."

"Reis and Claries are part of the Daonna clan. They are powerful in both magic and physical combat." Vicki shakes her head and holds it a little.

"That entire family had been defeated and killed during the Thousand Year War. That war ended tens of thousands of years ago. They are Eltis, so even that long of a time is like a drop in the bucket compared to the age of some more legendary Eltis," Zaria shakes her head. "My question is, how in ublivion is she still alive, everything I know tells me she should be dead."

"We can reserve that question for Keela or even Reis herself after this trial," Milea said. She turns her gaze up to the sky and notes that one moon is full while the other is waning. "This is going to be a hard battle." she muses.

"Don't worry, mom. You can do it," Sonja beams.

"Thank you, Sonja," Milea smiles at her daughter.

"Alright, I will have to do this," Neil gave in to his conscious. "Milea, I insist that you let me help you with this threat." Milea, Maya, and Zaria study the l'vane man.

"I don't know," Zaria muses.

"I've seen some of his skills in the marketplace of Lybrinthia Bay," Milea admits. "Vicki's in Churn. However, slavers and trappers are hardly any comparison with what we face now."

"Let's see... Magical storm," Vicki starts. Neil nod and makes an agreement sound. "Overly zealous king, army of dead folks, annoying devorians, persistent dragon and a very determined ghost ship. Even if I were one of Bri'al's most powerful sorceresses, that list would leave me very exhausted by now."

"Don't forget Casimir and the less than respectful captor, Tanwen," Brion adds. "Though I think Tanwen might have been more a nuance."

"Made me tired just hearing that list," Maya scowls. "And me with my own experiences." She holds her sister's hand and meets her gaze. "I'll be helping you, sister."

"Me too," Sonja volunteers.

"And if Sonja helps, then so do I," Neil insists, getting to his feet. "We are on this island as well, milady." He places a reassuring hand on Milea's shoulder. "We will help get us on our way to Tenze. Then to Selvast as fast as the waves will carry us."

"She still does not seem convinced," Vicki notes. She grins and hops to her feet. "Avast scurvy knave. Unhand the fair lady; else you will be facing my wrath." She notes that Milea arches an eyebrow and turns to Vicki's direction at the same time Neil faces his sister.

"You don't have a sword," Neil observes. He then cusses and jumps back when the tip of the whip smacks the area he once stood. "Oh, that's more deadly in your hands than a sword."

The air hisses and crackles as the whip once again sings through it. Neil moves back to escape the weapon. His sword is at the fire which makes him scowl. Vicki continues to advance towards her brother and watches as he does a backflip. Neil's hands find a long pole in the sand. He pulls it out as he landed upon his feet, ready for combat. Vicki shakes her head and places a hand upon her hip. Neil has a curious look upon his features then glances at his weapon.

It is three feet long and made of rotting wood, barely holding up as he grips it in his hands. The whip hisses again catching Neil's attention back to his situation and forgetting the condition of the weapon. He cusses and holds his rotting staff up to defend against the incoming threat. The whip slices the rotting wood in half right where his nose would have been. Neil flips again, finding a second staff in the sand.

He stands up and holds it at ready feeling that the item is much sturdier than his previous choice. Instead of rotting, the staff is white and pristine wood, one end of it has branches in the shape of an egg. A beautiful diamond is in the middle of the carving. Neil glances over at Milea and watches as the sorceress nods to him. Vicki sees it as well and smirks.

"My thanks, milady," Neil positions the staff vertically in front of him as the whip once again sounds. The whip wraps around Neil's weapon before Vicki yanks it away. "Hey! That's my weapon!"

"Well let's see," Vicki catches the staff and studies it. "Fancy for a whooping stick."

"That's what she uses it for," Maya calls. Milea elbows her twin in a gentle way. "Well, you do."

The crashing waves barely cover the sound of rushing feet as Neil charge forward. Vicki looks up then cusses, jumping up and over her charging brother. She lands and places the whip back on her hip. Vicki twirls the staff twice and holds it behind her as Neil retrieves his sword. Vicki brings up one hand and encourages her brother to come forward.

Neil places his sword on his belt before holding the sheath with one hand on the handle with the other. He charges towards his sister with quick speed, kicking up a large amount of sand as he did. Brion stretches as he relaxes, mentally connecting with his weapon on his side. His sword lifts out of its scabbard and flies to Vicki. The woman takes one step back as her brother nears and pulls his weapon. Instead of meeting with wood, Neil is met with the harsh ringing of metal against metal, jarring himself a little.

"What the...," Neil jumps back. The sword flips once then present the handle to Vicki. "Brion, what are you doing?"

"Protecting the ladies. Since Vicki does not have a sword, I figured she could borrow mine," Brion answers from the fire. He tosses a board on the flame.

"Why thank you, Brion," Vicki smiles as she takes the handle of the sword. "It's a bit heavier than my liking. But it will do."

"This is Mutiny," Neil accuses. Applause behind him caused his attention. Vicki turns to her audience and bows prompting her brother to turn. Neil shrugs and bows as well as Sonja cheers.

"That was entertaining," Milea said while the two return to the fire. "And I see there is more to you than what I saw in our brief time together. I will relent to your assistance with Reis and Claries."

"And we didn't even get to the good part," Vicki grins. "Your staff, madam." She presents the weapon to Milea with a bow. The sorceress says her thanks and accepts the staff. It disappears as soon as she touches it.

"I'll keep watch for tonight. Though she is eager, I doubt if Reis will disturb us until dawn. Bards, ha!" Zaria stands up and dusts the sand off her bottom. She walks into the shadows, shaking her head.

"She's one to talk," Vicki returns the scoff as her gaze follows Zaria into the shadows. The woman disappears almost as soon she left the ring of light produced by the fire.

"Are you ready for this one, Sonja," Maya asks. "This will be unlike anything you faced so far."

"Worse than the skeletons," Sonja quizzes and sees her aunt nod. "Great, this should be fun." She grumbles a little sarcastically.

The stars twinkle as they march through the night. Reis watches from her hiding spot as the group of warriors start to doze off. She focuses on the twin sorceresses sleeping a few feet from each other. Milea is sleeping on her left side while Maya is on her right. Their backs are facing each other. Reis sensitive eyes and hearing could also detect the twins are breathing opposite of each other. When Milea inhales, Maya exhales. Reis rubs her chin, wondering if they did so consciously or is it an unconscious action.

Reis jumps when A'drianis sits down just in the shadows of the group and stares in her general direction. Curious, Reis walks to the left and note A'drianis follow her pattern. The Shiado Eltis grins before fading from sight. The last things to do so are her light blue eyes and feline grin. Reis makes a sound of disdain at the tricky nature of the Shiado Eltis. A'drianis seems to be friends with the mortal twins.

Shaking her head, Reis looks over towards Milea then Maya again and scowls as she focuses. Both are much stronger in magic than any mortal that has come to this island before. Perhaps there is a reason they are here. She also sensed something familiar about them both. Reis once again turns her eyes to Maya and notes that, unlike the last time she was here, the woman is timid or shy. "I wonder what happened. It's almost as if she's hollow," Reis mumbles.

"Milea freed her sister from a Tragin," A'drianis answers causing Reis to jump and pull her sword. "You are truly the last of your family."

"Woman! What are you trying to do, kill me," Reis snaps.

"That would be a feat, eh? Survive the Great War and then die from being scared by a mere shadow." A'drianis muses with a snicker. "I wonder, does Keela know you are alive."

"It is possible that Keela does not know I'm alive. I prefer it that way. I do not owe Keela my allegiance anyway," Reis puts her sword away. "Why are you traveling with them, Kitty Cat?"

"Stop calling me that. I have my reasons," A'drianis warns with a growl. Her eyes holding a small light blue glow to them indicating her agitation.

"Do they know you are an Eltis? I guess they do not," Reis arches an eyebrow when A'drianis laughs. "Ok, you're mad."

"I would say at least three of them know I am. The other three have their suspicions, but I will neither confirm nor deny the fact that I am an Eltis," A'drianis says in a riddle. She folds her arms and scans Reis. "You are always eager to test your skills. Have you tested them against Kaidar I wonder?"

"Oswind's oldest child, no. I have not. Figured I would be too much for him," Reis shrugs. She notes A'drianis laughter again. "Ok, you are crazy."

"Not I," A'drianis shakes her head. "I'll let you find out which one of us is touched in the head tomorrow." She fades from sight.

CHAPTER EIGHTEEN

Twins vs Twins

A thick fog haunts from the bamboo forest as A'drianis sits back down near her charges. She yawns and stretches as the fog seems to surround her then decide to lay down and rest. The silence of the night is interrupted by the barking and snorting of whale-seals as they take their migratory route past the island. The sky turns amber as the sun rises and A'drianis turn back to Zaria once the light touches her. Milea wakes up from her rest and takes her time getting to her feet along. Maya stretches a few moments later and joins her sister at the water's edge. Both take in the warmth of the morning sun.

The rest of the crew awakens with the exception of Zaria as she continues to stay in a deep sleep. Sonja shadowboxes under the watchful eye of Vicki and listens as she corrects a few of her moves every once and a while. Milea stretches and relaxes, warming up her muscles as she awaits Reis. Maya follows her sister's example, taking on some of the moves that Milea made to really stretch the larger muscle groups. Brion walks back into camp from the ship in a fresh set of clothing and sits down to watch the twins exercise. Neil plops down next to his friend, entertained by the movements of the twins and the shadowboxing of the girl. Zaria turns over to her back and seem to attempt to wake up but falls right back into slumber.

"Fascinating, almost as if we are watching a dance," Neil said of the twins.

"I'm wondering if we are. See how Milea would bend, her arms slowly go down to her side. Then Maya would copy the same move," Brion explains, focusing on one sorceress then the other.

"Hm," Neil watches the twins. The movements are subtle, but he defiantly sees a beautiful yet sensual dance within the exercise. "Do you think I could get them to dance if I play a lively tune on my mandolin?"

"Should be entertaining to watch you try," Brion said.

The air rushes as Reis appear right in front of Milea catching Brion and Neil off guard. The two stands as Reis swings her katana at Milea with no luck as the woman jumps back. Reis retracts the blade and swings up just as fast as her first attack, meeting with air at first. Milea causes her sword to appear and brings it up to block Reis' katana producing a solid ring. Reis pull back then advances again and the two cross swords once more before they separate by a few feet. Milea keeps her sword at ready as Reis studies her opponent.

"No warning," Milea observes. "That's not very honorable." "Well, you do have a sword, interesting," Reis counters.

"Figured you'd be ready at dawn," she holds her sword at ready, "the hour of the dragon."

"I am just stretching and waiting for a confirmation as to what style you wish to partake in today," Milea said as her sword disappears.

"Since there are two of you, I volunteer to help my sister," Maya stands next to her twin. The two then cross their arms over their chest wait for a response.

"Hm," Reis glances from one to the other. "Well, since we are not fighting to the death. Free for all is a good style. The first person to toss their opponent into the water wins. I hope you can swim, girls." She grins.

"Can you," Milea and Maya ask at the same time, both arching an eyebrow.

"Cocky? I like it," Reis laughs charging forward to attack.

"Here we go," Neil grunts as he ran towards the battle.

The winds pick up as Brion calculate his position. Vicki and Sonja both swear as they start to the battle in the opposite direction Neil approaches at a rapid rate. Milea sees the l'vane man approaching out of the corner of her eye as she and Maya jump back to avoid Reis. Maya releases the sandstorm she is holding, blinding their opponent, for a few moments. Undaunted by the sand, Reis swings and strikes metal as the winds die down. She is surprised that she is facing Neil instead of Milea.

Neil shifts his position to attack, taking advantage of catching his opponent off guard. Reis defends herself from the fast-moving man, their blades clash several times creating a melody of metal. Milea and Maya reappear a short distance away to watch the battle, searching for clues to how they can toss Reis into the ocean. Vicki and Sonja stop when they are next to the twins and observe the activity.

Sand is kicked up as the they duel near the ocean to the cries and cheers of the wildlife. Neil tries to take Reis' head but fail to do so when he is blocked by the Eltis then he has to duck to avoid the same fate. The two cross swords twice more before Reis lets out a sound of frustration and disappears just as Neil is swinging at her mid-section. Milea and Maya both perk up when the woman reappear yet she seems just a little bit different.

The woman is similar to Reis, but with a gray streak of hair going down one side, her eyes a shade lighter than her twin. She wears a skirt that slit up on both sides and a half top. Part of her hair is pinned back in a ponytail. She smiles at Neil as the winds stir around her. Maya's mouth drops open at the sight of the woman then utters words her mother defiantly would not be proud of catching her sister's attention.

"Claries," Milea asks.

"Yes," Maya answers in short.

"Tricky, tricky," Claries scolds.

The lights dim a little as Claries pull energy from her surroundings and gathers it onto her form. Zaria stirs a little, still attempting to wake up but still could not break the fog that surrounds her mind. The light upon Claries focuses upon her hand as she raises it and points toward Neil causing the man to take several steps back. Brion positions himself just behind his friend and focuses on the incoming spell. Claries yells as she releases her spell, the force of which rustles her clothing and hair as well as scoots her back a few inches.

"Oswind's Teeth," Neil exclaims as he takes three steps back before leaping high into the air. The spell passes right under him. Neil lands and sees Brion in the path of the spell. "Don't become a cinder, crazy elf."

Brion pulls his blade and holds it vertically in a similar way that he did facing Slone. The light of the approaching spell reflects in his eyes before it takes a sudden left turn and whip around him. Claries gawks and takes a step back when she sees the action as well as the fact that her spell is now heading right back at her. Neil hits the ground as the spell passes over him this time, the heat of it almost scalding his exposed skin.

Claries cusses and crosses her arms right before the spell impacts her resulting in an explosion that tosses sand several feet into the air, a few specks of it falls on the sleeping shiadokat causing her to groan a little. Atop of the towering sand is a figure as it flashes once before heading back down to the ground at breakneck speed. Brion watches his foe closely as he moves back and holds his blade to block the incoming attack. Reis's katana rings out with anger when the two metals strike then appears stunned that she could not pull back immediately. Brion has turned his sword to hold her blade and look deep within her eyes, noting that the whites of them are a dark and dangerous blue.

"You have some nice eyes and a very distracting voice, but I insist that you and your friends stay out if this," Reis finally is able to push back and swing again. Brion blocks easily.

"Can't really do that, Reis," Brion said as the corner of his mouth ticking up slightly. "You did mention Free for All. And besides, I thought you were challenging all of us. Not just the Lady."

"I could listen to that all day," Reis admires. "Too bad you won't keep your head."

Reis does a quick turn and brings her blade around to take Brion's head. She misses her mark as he moves back a couple of steps. She growls and continues to press forward, bringing her blade around again, this time it slams into a stronger blade, the sudden stop jars Reis' body slightly before she sees that she is now facing a new opponent. Milea wastes no time in grabbing Reis by the shirt, surprising the Eltis. To Reis' further astonishment, the sorceress then turns and tosses the Eltis towards the water. Reis swear as she flips in the air and land just a few inches from the waves. Milea cusses when she sees the Eltis is still on the beach and dry.

"That was a close one. Any more oomph and you may have done it, Red," Reis smirks. She twirls her blade, studying the four combatants that she faced so far. "Well, a bit more diffi-cult than I bargain for I suppose. I guess it's time for me to be a little tricky as well." Her eyes flash once.

Seabirds cried out, encouraging the combatants on the land below their sounds and shadows barely distract the com-batants as Milea charges forward, her blade appearing in her hand. Neil decides to also charge forward, his own sword ready for an attack. The sound of a roar catches the attention both charging swordsperson and shakes the entire beach, bringing attention to the bamboo forest. Zaria moves a little, her left eye open yet it closes once again as she continues to snooze.

Reis see the distracted opponent Rent and goes straight at her with full fury. Milea whips around and blocks with a few unkind words when Reis came too close. Milea then disappears and reappear to gain some space from the warrior Eltis. Unfortunately, Reis to reappear with her. Maya watches her sister, timing to the battle so that she could intervene as the ground shakes again. She releases her vocabulary of dirty words turning to the bamboo.

Maya takes a breath in surprise when she sees a creature emerging from the foliage. Vicki and Sonja turn to see what has capture Maya's attention. The two to gasp or cuss when they see the strange beast. The emerging monster has the head of a large crocodile with the body is of a limber mountain goat. Thick balls of wool cover its shoulders and rump. The rest of the creature's body is bare and infested with sores. Green puss oozes out of it, creating pools upon the sand. Vicki takes a step back, noting the beast is at least twice as big as the ship and has poison dripping from its mouth.

All three of them swore in one form or other when they see that Zaria is still asleep and in the path of the beast. Vicki drops another set of bad words before she runs towards the sleeping shiadokat. Neil sees his sister move and turns to the place she is going with a cuss of his own before he calls to Brion. The elf turns, drop his own unkind words before he tosses his sword and uses his ability to speed it forward.

The beast reaches Zaria and is about to snap her up when the sword slams into its maw. It lifts its head to howl in pain as Vicki reaches Zaria, jump and grab her before flipping them both out of the way of the beast. Brion's sword yanks out of the beast and flies straight back to the elf as blood and drool from the monster hit the sand causing the spot to bubble then turn into glass. The creature turns to Brion and charges towards him as Vicki tries to awaken Zaria with little success. The shiadokat open an eye, she tries to mouth something then falls back to sleep, her body tensing and relaxing as she did.

"What in Ublivorion is that thing," Brion demands.

The beast picks up its foot and tries to stomp on the owner of the sword that hurt it then snarl when Brion jumps back and out the way. The elf almost lost his balance when the ground shakes from the stomping of the monster. He then dodges the teeth and swings his sword. It grazes against the nose of the beast ringing out as if it scraped against a slate board. The monster yowls in pain then howl at the sky allowing Brion to escape to get closer to Neil.

"This is what we get when we agree to free for all, she has friends too," Neil said as he moves to the side to avoid the tail. "Can you take out the legs?"

"On it," Brion said.

The sound of battle rings out as Brion retreats a few more feet from the beast before releasing his blade. It levitates in front of him for a few seconds then flip twice as Brion point to the attacking beast. The sword screams towards the creature with intent to cut off at least one leg. The blade scrapes against the beast to open another deep wound on the side closest to the leg. Green ooze pours from the new sore like a river. However, the leg remains intact. Brion cusses, recall his sword and sends it back. This time it whirls around and slices through the leg, sending the beast to the ground. It yowls as another limb grows out from the spot of the severed leg. The beast stands back up much to the dismay of the combatants.

"This is going to be difficult," Neil gripes. He did not note the discarded leg wiggle.

The sound of metal against metal echo in the morning breeze along with a healthy amount of trash talking on both sides as Milea and Reis engage in battle. Sonja wisely runs over to check on Zaria, avoiding the battle between the beast and the men to arrive at Vicki's side. She tries to shake the shiadokat to wake her up to no avail, the woman keeps sleeping as if a spell has placed her there. Milea once again disappears from the water's edge, reappearing a few feet from her daughter and is followed closely by Reis.

The Eltis continues her advance, please with the sudden change as she is now facing the ones she wants to battle. Reis grab Milea by her vest and toss her with all her might straight at the ocean. Milea swears as she sails out over the water then disappear before she hit the waves. Reis yells her swears in anger when she sees the woman reappear next to Maya, the ocean now closest to the Eltis.

The sky thunder Reis changes into Claries, her powers exploding to life. The staff in her hand glows ever bright as she swings it up then down, facing the two opponents. A large lightning bolt exit the top of the staff, hissing, and crackling as it nears its destination. Maya takes a step forward and grabs hold of the lightning bolt. She turns and sends it right back to Claries. Angry, the Eltis bats the spell back, returning it towards the two she intends it for.

Maya causes her own staff to appear in an eruption of black flame. She then uses it to knock the lightning back to its originator once more. This time, she adds a second spell to it. Claries once again tries to send it back, the spell to explode when she impacts it. She yells in surprise and pain, flying back towards the ocean. Before she falls, however, she disappears, reappearing on the beach as Reis.

"This is turning into quite a circus," Milea said through grit teeth.

"And we are the entertainment," Maya reminds.

Reis runs her fingers through her hair, studying the twins then glances over at Vicki and Sonja as the two try to awaken Zaria. The Eltis smirk, knowing that the shiadokat will not be awakened easily. However, Claries' spell will not last long, and as soon as Zaria awakens, Reis will have a hell of a battle, especially if the shiadokat awakens near dusk. Reis glances at the creature she summons, noting it is attacking Brion with great furry, upset at losing the leg. Neil battles the creature as well, his sword, however, could not penetrate the thick hide of the beast. The sound of a groan caused Reis to turn her attention once again back towards the group of three and take a step back. Zaria's body tenses and starts to move. Reis is not ready to face A'drianis, unsure as to what abilities the shiadokat retain over the years.

"Looks like we are going to have to elevate our game," Reis remarks, cockily.

A strong wind slams into Milea, pushing her into Maya and causing them to tumble away from the rest of their companions. Milea cusses and causes the winds to calm down as she and her twin stand up. A bright light erupts several feet away from Milea and Maya alerting them before the entire beach they stand on starts to rise. Sonja gawks momentarily as she stands then takes off running to the rising sand, the speed which she is going cause a large amount of sand to kick up behind her.

Vicki is right behind the girl, her own cloud of sand filling the air as Sonja jumps and grab hold of the top of the rising beach. The girl pulls herself up then turns to see how fast they are rising. Vicki reaches a certain point then leaps high into the air and seems relieved when Sonja catches her hand and pull her up onto the rising landmass. Reis cackle in humor, oblivious of the two intruders as she stalks toward the twins she wants to battle. Milea, unafraid, pull her blade and take a few steps forward, focus on defeating the twin Eltis.

On the main beach, the sounds of battle finally break through to the mind of the sleeper. Zaria turns over and opens her eyes and sees the floating landmass. The sight causes her to gawk as she sits up. She shakes her head when something tries to make her go to sleep again, standing up in an attempt to fight it. Her instinct scream at her prompting her to jump to the left to avoid the leg of the creature that is attacking Neil and Brion. Zaria shakes off the sleep and takes in her surroundings. There is a giant hole in the sand, and apparently, it is now up in the sky. The shaking beach and noises from an unknown beast demand Zaria's attention.

The monster has Neil and Brion scrambling to think of ways to destroy it. Grumbling and growling about Reis and her cheating ways, Zaria pulls out her dagger and head towards the battle to assist Brion and Neil. She barely passes the discarded leg when it springs to life, growing a smaller version of the battling giant. Zaria cusses as she dodges the creature as it tries to snap her legs off. She jumps and lands beside Brion with the new beast hot on her heels.

"Finally awake," Brion observes. He blocks the tail of the creature and is push back along with Zaria. "What kept you?"

"Don't know. Feel like a fog hit me," Zaria is quick to digests the information and comes to a conclusion. "Claries."

"Look out," Brion shouts. The two dodge the teeth of the large creature until they are standing with Neil "Milea and the girls are taken up to that platform."

"I saw," Zaria said. "Sun's up to high. Shadows are limited...." She cusses. The beasts regroup and attack in unison, separating the trio. "Any ideas?!"

"Fresh out," Neil admits.

The ship sways back and forth in the harbor as it seems to shrink to the eyes of those on the platform. Vicki drops a pirate swear or two and turns from the sight, focusing on the battle at hand. Milea grunts as she slides back, oblivious to the sky that whistles by as she concentrates on keeping her own against Reis. Vicki motions to Sonja to go a certain direction. The preteen nods in understanding and moves, with speed and care, to her destination. All but Reis stumbles when the ground rises a little higher and now hovers above the clouds The island they land upon last night is nothing more than a speck below. They look up as the sky lights up with a purple haze.

"Time to get a little nasty," Maya sneers.

Purple flames snake up Maya's body as she focuses on her spell then yells as she cast the strong incantation right towards the Eltis. Milea moves back, but Reis is not as swift to react as the spell slams into her, pushing her further away from her opponent. Vicki manages to dodge the woman making a little sound of fright as Reis changes into Claries.

The Eltis snarls as she gathers the light that Maya sent into her then tosses it back at the twin opponents. Milea expresses her displeasure as she rolls one way. Maya echoes the words of her twin and jumps to a different direction; the lightning explodes in the air missing them. Milea and Maya are now breathing heavily, the battle is taking more out of them than they first expect. Maya then stands up and rolls her neck, calming her breath to a more normal pattern. Milea got to her feet and draws her sword, ready for another onslaught.

"Impressive," Claries scans Maya then Milea, a smile across her features.

"How are you holding up," Maya calls to her twin.

"Same as you," Milea answers then gasps "Look out!"

Maya turns then causes her staff to appear in time to block the one that Claries is using to try and knock her down. Maya digs in her heels despite being push back by her stronger opponent. Her eyes flash as determination crosses her face causing Claries to smile then nod in admiration when the mortal stops sliding back. Claries disappear again, the sudden departure caused Maya to stumble but maintain her balance as she utters a few unhinged words to express her weariness of the 'exercise.' She is about to go check on her twin when Claries reappear.

The Eltis motions with her hands in a clock like way, the air crackle as her ability light up around her. Maya faces the Eltis and causes a strong purple circle to explode from around herself, the various symbols line up as she decides what spell to cast. Claries grins, pointing her staff directly at her opponent and sending a strong flame in her direction. Sonja blinks in surprise then charges forward quickly to stand between her aunt and the oncoming flames. She crosses her arms to block resulting in a powerful explosion to occur on contact. Maya covers her eyes then lowers her arm to see Sonja standing in front of her, the sight of which shocks her. The preteen shakes her head then growls and charge towards the Eltis, ramping up to speed.

"Sonja, no," Maya calls catching her sister's attention.

"Foolish child," Claries laughs. Blue flames jump from her fingertips.

Milea gets to her feet when she sees her child and swears when she figures it is too late to stop her, Sonja is at a full charge and going straight for the Eltis. The spells hit Sonja and seem to dissipate, causing surprise to mask Claries' features. Fire caresses up and down Sonja's legs before she slams her fist into her stunned opponent. The explosion of energy sends Claries backward for several feet then into the ground, creating a groove in the sand and causing her body to smoke from the power and the punch. Her staff slides in the opposite direction of her body, landing near the edge of the makeshift arena. Claries turned over to her stomach and glares at Sonja. The staff shifts to a sword as Reis growls and stands up, holding her stomach for a few moments then limbering up as she glares at the interfering girl.

Sonja, undaunted, charges forward once more focus upon her target. Reis dodges to the side and grabs hold of the girl's shirt, flinging her to the edge of the platform. Sonja manages to flip and land with her hands, and the balls of her feet digging into the sand as she stops herself from going over. The sand then explodes as the girl once again charges. Reis block three of Sonja's blows then gets hit by the fourth, fifth and sixth. The last blow connects to Reis' jawline. The Eltis hit the ground and grabs her opponent's leg to bring her down as well. The girl falls to the ground then is quick to roll back to her feet and back up from her adversary.

"What in Ublivorion are you," Reis grounds out, rising to her feet. The slight sound of thunder echoes in the distance.

"I should ask the same question of you," Sonja counters.

The wind whistles in anger as the temperature starts to lower with the darkening disposition of the Eltis. The sounds of the battling trio below reach the ears of those on the platform. Milea takes care as she looks over the edge of the floating island and note that she could not see what is happening on the island below yet the roar of the beast is very distinguishable. She hopes that Zaria has awakened to assist the men as she turns from the sight and notices Vicki's approach. Maya is leaning on her staff, to keep on her feet as the ordeal from the temple along with this trial is starting to catch up with her. Reis glares at Sonja for a few minutes then looks up and past the girl to see Vicki standing and talking with Milea and Maya.

"Are you two alright," Vicki asks. "And what's the plan?"

"Getting very tired," Maya answers.

"And the plan is to toss either Reis or Claries into the ocean," Milea finishes. "The task is more difficult than we imagined."

"Difficult explains a small part of it," Maya retorts.

"Hmm...," Vicki appears thoughtful. She then has a spark of inspiration. "Do you remember the tale of the battle between Ra'jil and Lanacane?"

"I was there. Oh, I see. Very well," Milea recalls the memory. "Let's end this."

"Perfect," Vicki said smiling in response.

"I'll ask later," Maya assures.

"How did you and your friend get up here," Reis demands of her smaller challenger. "I knew for sure I had the twins by themselves."

"We climbed," Sonja answers. "I think we had enough of your weird game. Time to stop and let us go."

"Oh, but I'm just getting started," Reis chuckles and wipes her mouth, removing moisture. "Alright, let's see what we can do here." She charges.

Sonja gets up to speed to meet the charging Eltis then swings out but goes through the image of Reis. The girl slides and almost topples over the edge of the platform only stopping by putting her backside down and digging her hands into the sand. Her feet dangle over the edge briefly as she then scrambles backward to regain solid ground and stand up. Milea whispers graciously in relief that her daughter was still on the floating arena when her instinct told her to jump backward. She obeys as Reis reappears and swings her fist at her opponent.

The hiss of a whip cut through the air as it wraps around Reis' arm in mid-swing. Vicki then pulls on her weapon with all her strength, yanking the Eltis hard enough to pull her to the ground. Reis yells in anger as she turns over to glare at the l'vane with murder intent as she stands. Vicki pulls her weapon back and once again let the whip fly. This time Reis catches the whip's end and snatches it out of the owner's hands.

The Eltis continues to glare at Vicki as she then tosses the whip over the edge of the platform into the unknown. Reis then attacks the perpetrator, leaping into the air. Vicki leaps back then backflips to land a distance away. Reis come into contact on the spot the mortal once occupy. The Eltis slowly stands as she pulls her hand from the ground. The spot that Vicki vacated is now a large hole. Vicki takes another step back then glances behind the threat to see Milea preparing to face the Eltis once again.

"You should have stayed out of this, wench," Reis snarls, blue steam emitting from her lips. Her eyes are glowing a rich royal blue light.

"That comment is going to cost you," Vicki retorts.

A loud clap of thunder disguises Reis' hiss of anger as she attacks the woman. Vicki jumps once then flips twice with breakneck speed to avoid colliding with the Eltis. She scowls when she realizes she left her daggers on the beach below. Vicki did a cartwheel then leaps high into the air and did an arcing backflip away from Reis. Vicki gracefully lands quite a distance from the Eltis as Reis watches her with distaste. The Eltis then snorts and disappears, reappearing right where she saw Vicki last and lashes out with anger.

Vicki seems to disappear and is replaced by Milea who captures the swinging arm and twists. Reis yelps in surprise then cusses when her legs are kicked out from under her, and her arm being relentlessly twisted until it is behind her back. Reis cry out in surprise when she hit the ground, landing on her stomach. The air blasted from her lungs from the blow as well as the one of Milea using her elbow to strike the middle of the Eltis' back. Reis lets out an angry sound then disappear once more causing Milea to grumble in disdain.

Dark clouds accompany angry thunder as they circle in the heavens heralding the appearance of Claries in a brilliant flash, her features full of wrath as she glares at the group. She lets out an angry sound as she causes the cloud to swirl into dark lightning and stream towards Milea. The intended victim rolls her neck as she is about to retaliate. Her twin steps in instead and smack it back at the originator. Claries catches the spell, condensing it down, the force of the action causes her to slide back a few feet as the lightning became a dark ball. The Eltis then jumps into the air and let go of the spell, allowing it to fly off into the ocean and explode.

"Get ready," Milea calls.

"On it," Vicki acknowledges, studying the scene in order to adjust her position.

The air crackles as Claries changes into Reis once more. The Eltis stops her assent then dives down towards Milea. Maya moves to one side, pulling her niece with her. Sonja didn't argue with her aunt, this time. Milea stands her ground as her opponent nears her. Vicki positions herself behind Milea close to the edge of the platform, making it a point not to look down. Reis aims for her original opponent, pure rage filling her features and permeating in the air. Milea catches Reis, rolls then tosses the woman towards the edge of the floating beach. The Eltis lands and roll to her feet with a growl. Though this starts out as a game of skills, it is now time to end it, permanently.

Reis call her sword to her hand. It jumps to obey her request as the woman's features turn deadly. Milea causes her own blade to appear in a flash, keeping the focus of the Eltis off Vicki as the woman quietly approaches from behind. Reis take a step forward then is grabbed by the back of her shirt and her belt. She yells when she is tossed once more, this time off the plane. Vicki dusts her hands before ducking the spell that Claries sends her way.

"So much for being clever," Vicki said to herself.

"Oh no you don't," Milea activates her gifts and causes a strong wind to slam into Claries sending her further out and over the ocean.

The sky lights up purple around Claries while she tries to recover from the blow she receives. Various symbols line the area causing her immediate attention. The Eltis cusses before Maya cast a spell of black flames to slam into Claries from above. The spell and the Eltis both scream as they plummet to the ocean below. Claries impact the ocean causing a large amount of water to splash up into the air. Maya exhales and sits down, lowering her left hand. She uses her right to wipe her brow. Milea places a hand upon her sister's shoulder and also wipes her own brow.

"Remind me not to battle any more Eltis for a while. Suggest a game of chess or something," Maya offers.

"I will keep that suggestion very close to my heart," Milea agrees. "Vicki, good reminder and great assistance." She smiles at the woman. "Thank You."

"It was just a long shot but," Vicki said, a little modest. Her ears detect the faint sound of a few very strong oaths. "That's my brother."

The news of Reis's defeat has yet to reach the trio that battle upon the main beach. Brion dodges and block the smaller, quicker, beast with his sword and once again tries to take off its head. The sword bounces off the beast's thick hide as it turns and slaps the elf with the long muzzle for trying to take it down. Brion hits the ground then is quick to roll back to his feet to face one of now three beasts that are on the field, thanks in part to his ability to cut off a second limb from the giant. Zaria jumps to one side to dodge the teeth of her opponent then jump onto its head. The creature shakes wildly to get her off. Zaria hangs on long enough to drive her dagger through the beast's skull. It howls in anger prompting one of its own to bite at it. Zaria jumps off as the second creature crushes the skull of its friend. The beast falls, dead.

"Good job, now see if you can get the other one to do the same," Neil compliments.

Zaria scoff at him as the creature once again attacks. Neil moves out of the way through various acrobatic motions just to dodge the tail of the giant. He then slides under the smaller one as Zaria leaps over the same creature both avoiding the teeth. Neil scolds Brion for cutting off the limbs then grumbles when he is reminded that the cutting off the limb is his idea. Zaria yells at both to stop arguing and try and figure a way to kill the big one.

The clouds float peacefully beneath the platform as Sonja eases to the edge and peeks out over it to see what is going on. The battle below is very small, almost invisible from the great height that the Eltis has brought them. Milea kneels next to her daughter to look down at the battle as well, noting that it is just about impossible to make out anything but the giant beast that those they left behind is battling. The ocean that Claries lands in is silent, moving as if nothing has ever happened to it.

The ship rocks back and forth with the gentle waves, usually a beautiful sight if it is not for the great height of the makeshift arena. Vicki is about to ask how they are going to get down when the floating land they stand upon bucks. Sonja almost topples over the edge when it happens and back from it as quick as she can. Milea watches as Claries' staff disappear and notes her twin's profanities when it did, the power that holds the floating island has let it go. The landmass quake violently as it starts a rapid descent.

"Sonja, take my hand," Milea instructs.

"I've got Vicki," Maya assures, taking hold of the woman's hand. "Close your eyes and hold tight, this is might be a bumpy ride."

The sky and wind whistles by during the rapid descent. Both lessen up a quarter of the way down as both Milea and Maya cast their levitation spells. Vicki took takes a deep breath in and out, thankful to feel the levitation instead of the alternative. She still refuses to open her eyes until they are on solid ground. Zaria sees the island falling and quickly runs between the largest beast's legs. It immediately follows her, standing in the large pit created when Reis took the twins to the sky.

The shiadokat stands in place keeping the beast under the trap. It snarls then opens its mouth and let out a mighty roar. The teeth gleam in the sunlight. Zaria almost loses her dinner upon inhaling the foul odors wafting from the beast's open maw. The shadow of the falling plain is not noticed by the roaring beast until it looks up. Its roar turns to a sound of pure shock seconds before it is crushed by the sand returning to the beach. When nothing moved, the trio expresses various words of relief, until the smaller version screams. Milea and Maya, together with their passengers, land just as the beast turns and hightail it into the bamboo forest.

"Well, I guess that's that," Neil placed his sword away. "How did it go?"

"We would still be battling if it were not for Vicki's quick plan. I don't know about Maya, but I am fit to be tied, tired of Reis and her sister," Milea said.

"I'm there with you. Though in the end, I think Reis and Claries both seemed tired of us," Maya agreed.

"I could tell," Milea said. Bubbling water near the ship catches her attention.

"Now what?" Maya turns and places a hand upon her temple, shaking her head as Reis stalks out of the water. Milea faces the very upset Eltis with the rest of her crew.

"We met your challenge, and we defeated you, Reis," Milea said, taking a step to her opponent.

"I did not expect you to let your friends interfere," Reis complains. She is now standing a few feet from Milea.

"You said," Neil stands next to his employer, "that in order to get off the island, we needed to grant you your exercise."

"I think she used the term 'defeating her'," Brion offers. He is on the other side of Milea. Vicki and Maya flank either left or right of him.

"So now you have to live up to your end of the bargain," Zaria reminds. She is in front of Milea causing the Eltis to take a step or more back. "Unless you have become as dishonorable as your sworn enemy." Reis stares at Zaria a few minutes. She then scans at the group and exhales strongly.

"Alright, a deal is a deal. I got my exercise," Reis grumbles and put her sword away. "Tell me, what is your name? And why did you use your friends to assist you? I sense you are more than capable of battling me without them." She addresses Milea.

"Very well. You know Maya. She has changed since you last saw her," Milea introduces to her twin. "I am Milea and with me are Neil, Vicki, Brion and my daughter, Sonja." She motions to the different people of her party.

"Ah, the wonder girl with the very strong right hook," Reis rubs her jaw. "Claries was stunned you ran through that spell. How?"

"I've a special talent for magic," Sonja answers.

"Very much so, it seems," Reis agrees. "Alright, Milea. What about my second question?" She addresses the red-haired sorceress. "Maya and I are a little worn from the past few weeks," Milea explains and rub her shoulder a little. "For me, it is the voyage to rescue her."

"Me, I faced a giant eye that I recently found out is the Eye of Gaunt," Maya said with a raised hand.

"What," Reis interrupts, her eyes are wide with shock. "Ok. That's not good. Who in all Ublivorion has an Eye of Gaunt besides the obvious?" Her features are of anger and curiosity at the same time.

"Eye of Gaunt, Harp of Hester, the Underak," Maya counts on her fingers. "All of them visited the temple of light and destroyed it. Even Slone." The entire group prepares for combat when Reis growls, a flash of light erupting from her being.

"Ok... I need to know what's happening," Reis requests. "What about Slone's wacky half-sister? Did she show up?"

"If Wyonna was there, she didn't show herself," Zaria admits. "We were hell-bent on getting out of the place when the Underak raised the dead."

"I hate Underaks," Reis grumbles.

"We are on our way back to Selvast Forest via ship. Unfortunately, we need to get to Tenze for supplies first," Milea said. "Unless you have supplies for us."

"I see. I do not have the supplies that you seek else I would provide them so you can go straight to the forest. I think Keela needs to know what's going on," Reis said. "I will have to talk to Claries about this. If Slone is involved then possibly that lunatic Wyonna will also be involved. Although, I cannot see them working together. There is always the possibility. If she's there, I will be more than happy to assist you."

"We will let you know if that's happens," Milea said. "Neil," she turns to the man, "ready when you are."

"Right, let's get out of here before daylight gets away," Neil said. "With the present time, we will make it to Tenze by sunset." He walks away. Vicki follows after her brother.

"I will see you later, Milea," Reis predicts as she fades from sight. "The shield is down, and you are free to go on your way."

"Wyonna huh," Zaria shakes her head as she follows the twins to the ship. Brion trails behind. "Reis, like Wyonna, is not very trustworthy. I guess that's a good reason to not like each other." Sonja jogs ahead to catch up with Neil.

The ocean waves crash into the shore, rocking the ship gently. Neil grunts a little when he pulls himself up onto the deck. Vicki hauls herself up and helps the next person. Sonja climbs the side of the ship and goes to the crow's nest. Milea is last to board the ship. The sails lift, ropes tying in place. The anchor clicks into place as the *Lady of the Night* turn out towards the open ocean. Reis watches from the bamboo thicket as the sails billow in the winds, speeding them to their destination. The Eltis has a feeling that she will one day see the entire crew again. She crosses her arms and allows her body to relax as a feeling of loneliness return when the ship sails over the horizon. Perhaps she should have gone with them.

"No," Reis said more to herself than her sister, "the last thing that group needs are three Eltis causing mischief on the ship." She turns and walks deeper into the bamboo forest.

CHAPTER NINETEEN

Trouble in Tenze

The sun's life-giving light bounces from the metal tips of the temples like the sparkle of tall and wondrous stars shining for all to behold. A flock of pigeon flies between the spirals causing the light to flicker from the passing. Late afternoon approaches as the *Lady of the Night*, and her passengers arrive at Ports of Tenze. Sonja announces land from her bird's eye view in the crow's nest. Neil scans the ports and notes that the first few buildings did not change from the last time he visited the town. The shabby houses near the coastline give way to more permanent structures a block inland.

The large spirals of Temple Avenue beckon pilgrims from around Bri'al. The town itself did expand, reaching for the mountains beyond the horizon. Although the tips of the grand behemoths are seen by all who visit Tenze, the mountains themselves are still several leagues away. Tall and silent, the tops of the mountains are always covered with snow. Neil ponders his memories, leaning forward a little as his remanence about the mountains.

"Recollecting, Brother," Vicki stands next to her solemn sibling.

"A little bit," Neil pats the wheel then takes a few steps away to stand in front of it and look out. "Good memories though. Very good ones."

"I think this would be the fifth time I've come here," Vicki admits, automatically taking over the wheel to guide the ship into the dock. "First time aboard an enchanted ship though." She watches the sails once again adjust to dock.

"Tenze is a merchant town. You got honest ones and lots of dishonest ones," Neil places his hands behind his back. "We should get supplies as well as a good set of weapons for you. I see you lost your whip."

"Reis didn't appreciate me yanking her arm with it. In good truth, I'd rather lose the whip than get hit by the Eltis," Vicki shrugs.

"Yes, blocking some of those sword blows was bone jarring," Neil agrees. He scowls when he spies the empty deck. "Have the twins awaken yet; I need to discuss a few things with Milea."

"Not yet," Brion answers and approaches his friends. He climbs the stairs. "I just peeked in on them. Zaria warned me not to go in."

"Not unless you are really curious about Milea's sword skills," Zaria said, walking with the elf. "Not sure about Maya. My guess is that she would just place a curse on you. Or send you to Ublivorion."

"Neither sounds like a good thing," Neil said.

"Just think of it like this," Zaria sits upon one of the side rails. "If she did send you to Ublivorion. She'd be in more trouble than you when Oswind finds you."

Vicki guides the ship with expert ease, past those ships that decide to get an early start on their journey. Occasionally, she feels the wheel jerk a little but figures it is some sort of sea animal hitting the keel. Neil walks down the sides of the ship and wave at a few fellow seamen as he checks the ropes. Thin silk slides up and down, preparing the rig for the ports. Brion studies the city as they approach finding it like all port cities around Bri'al. A large tavern marks the spot where the docks end and the city begin.

Across from the tavern is a brothel with women of all shapes and sizes hawk to the passing sailors. Most times they would receive the patronage of the sailors both drunk and sober. Zaria sees the businesses of the port and figures it is similar to all others she's visited. There are few exceptions. The shouts of the men of the ports are heard once the *Lady of the Night* reaches an empty docking space. The ship bumps up against the port and drops the anchor.

From her vantage point, Sonja bounces a little with joy when she sees the marketplace. She's never been to this one before, and it seems to go on for miles. Many bargains and interesting products will defiantly be abundant in such a place. A chill goes down the preteen's spine causing her to turn and gasp. The dark wood ship sways in the breeze, patiently awaiting the return of its crew.

"Neil, look," Sonja calls as she shimmies down the mast, "it's that ship from Lybrinthia Bay." She hurries to him and points across the docks.

"What," Neil focuses his attention across the docks. The sunlight caresses the many vessels that line the ports. On one of the ships, however, the light shunts away. Three piers away is the *Charred Rose*. "I see. We better be careful here. See if we can get supplies and leave before they cause any trouble."

"Depends on how long they've been here," Brion scowls when he sees the ship. "They might have already caused trouble."

"Hmm," Zaria stares at the ship, her mind swirling with thoughts. She cusses under her breath at her conclusion. "You guys go ahead; I'll stay behind just in case someone's bold enough to come aboard. Sonja, if you go. Behave."

"Always," Sonja beams a bright smile. "I've never been to Tenze before, but I saw a huge marketplace from the crow's nest. What else is here?"

"The highlight is the marketplace where you will find just about anything that Bri'al has to offer," Neil recalls, rubbing his chin. Sonja's eyes light up with joy from the announcement. "Then there is Temple Avenue."

"The marketplace and its wares might be why the *Charred Rose* is here. They are offloading," Brion ponders. "Never heard of a Temple Avenue, would they have something to do with it?"

"It's similar to a Temple of Light except it's been broken out into several separate temples. Each discipline has its own space," Vicki describes. "Even A'drianis has a temple here."

"I see," Zaria shakes her head, "a city of Fanatics. Well, I guess it is better than going across to Oice." She folded her arms. "There is an entire mortal family that's worshiped as Gods there."

"The Gods of Oice," Neil said. "I know the story, want to hear it?"

"I'm going to tie the ship," Vicki announces. She makes a quick step towards the port side of the ship before jumping onto the rails then off the ship. Sonja does a jig then follows the woman.

"I'm going to guess that's a 'no'," Brion chuckles and jumps after Vicki.

"Hey now," Neil scowls. "It's not all that bad. It involves Ra'jil and everything. I even have a new one from Milea, come on." He jumps down last.

Merchants call out to those that passing their tents, offering different discounts on wares of all price points. Sonja covers her nose and jogs by a man that is selling cow manure. Neil stops by to ask about it and informs his companions that the merchant is selling sacred cow manure. Brion rolls his eyes, figuring that the merchant is the one full of fertilizer, not his cart. Vicki scans the area for the crewmembers of the *Charred Rose* or evidence of their 'merchandise.' She didn't see either and figure they are either still at the docks or somewhere in Temple Avenue. The marketplace's boundaries are somewhere along the lines of the beginning of the famous avenue.

Sonja scans the marketplace with a large grin upon her face as she takes in each vendor, but remembers to keep within arm's reach of at least one of her friends, despite her excitement. Vicki focuses on all the food vendors and notices that they are empty or close for the day. When she pauses by to ask about it, the man states a huge armada of men from several of Lybrinthia's allies stop by and bought up everything. They just miss them as the men set sail an hour ago.

Neil scowls when he hears the news, this war with Sorshana is heating up. Perhaps the King of Deltor has finally amassed an army that can take out the crazed creature. But at what cost? They continue down the street, fascinated by the various weapons and vendors of souvenirs as well all vying for their attention among the throngs of people that flow up and down the streets of Tenze. The ringing of a hammer is barely heard above the hustle and bustle of the marketplace. Brion pauses with Sonja in as they both listen to locate the hidden metalsmith. The crowd swallows up Neil and Vicki as they walk down the street, oblivious to the pause of their companions.

"Blacksmith," Brion questions.

"Sounds like he's not a very good one," Sonja said. "It's like he's trying to be a smith, but he's really not."

"Hm," Brion places a hand upon his chin, debating. "My sword needs a little sharpening. I hope he can at least do that." He starts towards the ringing. Sonja trails behind the elf, her own curiosity peek.

Women gossip, pausing when Brion and Sonja past them. The residences scan the handsome stranger and little girl with great interest. Brion speaks a universal greeting to the women before continuing his way, heading towards a shabby looking stall that holds a furnace. Once they are gone, the women begin to chat with excitement about the elf as the ringing of the hammer once again fill the air. The merchants on this street did not call out like their counterparts on the main, eying the strangers with suspicion as they wonder why they are in the neighborhood. Usually, travelers would stick to the main row to visit Temple Avenue as it is the main tourist attraction; this is out of the norm.

Sonja takes in her surroundings, feeling nervous energy all around. Her ears once again detect the ring of the hammer this time very close to them. Several residences wonder up, and down the street, a few of them did give way as Brion and Sonja arrive in front of their location. Brion's features take on a slight concern or disappointed look as he notices the blacksmith's home. It is shabby, the furnace is not on good working order, and many of the metal works are scattered throughout his shop. Several of his blades appear to be hap-hazard or hurried as he made them. That simple fact is the reason the weapons remain on the shelf.

The blacksmith turns over the work then continue to strike the hot metal as if he is very angry with it. Sonja covers her ears from the shrieks that came from the metal as the smith hammers, they sounded as if the object is in pain. The smith didn't seem to care as he tosses the blade back into the fire and makes the flames rise still hotter than they are, the fur-nace chokes to obey the man's request. Brion and Sonja step up to the fence as the man brings the metal back out and slams his hammer into it several times.

The two visitors look at each other then back to the bald, tattooed blacksmith as he assaults his work. Sonja shakes her head as if warning her friend to which Brion nods in silent understanding. The blacksmith hammers his metal a few more times before slamming it into a vat of cold water. The steam rises in a strong whoosh, the sound of metal cracking is almost drowned out by the steam. The smith pulls out the metal and cusses the warped blade. He snarls and bangs it back into the flames.

"I don't think that's how you are supposed to form a blade," Sonja observes. She is speaking to Brion but the blacksmith overhears.

"What did you say," the blacksmith growls and slam his hammer down. He stomps over to the two causing Sonja to back up and get into a defensive stance. "What, little girl, do you know about smiting?" A group of merchants watches the scene unfold.

"I am taught that you are supposed to coax the metal into the shape you want, not force it," Sonja informs with care to her words. "To force it means you have a weakens blade."

"Words of wisdom," Brion complements. The blacksmith turns to glare at him. "Mind you, I am not intimidated. You need to mind your manners around the young one. She is just observing you."

"Are you buying anything, elf," the blacksmith grinds. It is obvious that he did not have like the visitors.

"With your current attitude and the quality of your work, no I am not," Brion answers, folding his arms and meeting the man's gaze. "Human." He watches as the smith's nostrils flare and flames seem to erupt in his cold black eyes.

"What did you say," the man's eyes gleam with anger. "I am no human, boy. I am an Orijetie."

"An ill-mannered oversized human then," Brion corrects. "Hey kiddo, let's go find our bard friends before they become worried about us." He places a hand upon Sonja's shoulder.

"Right," Sonja said and turns with her friend. "Are all Orijetie blacksmiths like that?"

"No, some are well mannered and friendly," Brion explains to his small comrade. "We just happen to run into the bad egg of the bunch." They both walk back down the path of travel.

"Makes sense... almost," Sonja stretches her arms high above her head. The silver scales of her left forearm glimmer in the light of the sun while she places her hands behind her head. "Mom says nobody is perfect. Not even her."

"I can imagine," Brion said.

"What in Ublivorion," the blacksmith demands and stomps after the two. "Hold on, you two," he blocks the stranger's retreat, "a silver dragon?" He grabs Sonja's arm much to her surprise and pain.

"What the hell are you doing here, silver dragon?" He tightens his grip with his anger.

"Let me go," Sonja growls.

Several of the back street merchants perk and watches the scene unfold as Sonja tries to pull away from the man but finds that he is much stronger than herself. The girl feels her arm being crush by the man as he increased his grip and pulls her off the ground by the arm he has captured. The pain from the limb shot through Sonja's body when she tries to punch or kick the man, rendering her helpless as she glares at the blacksmith. She notes the deadly look in the orijetie man's eye. Brion pulls his sword and places the tip of it under the blacksmith's throat, pointing up towards his skull. The blade seems to hum in anticipation as the smithy blinks in surprise then widen his eyes when he feels the very tip of the sharp blade and realizing his predicament.

"You have till the count of three to release her," Brion warns. "One... Two..." he pauses when the blacksmith let the child's arm go. "Good man. Now go back to your weapons so that we can be on our way."

A small crowd gathers behind the blacksmith as Brion puts his sword away and start walking. He takes quick strides to exit the backstreet market Sonja rubs her arm, it is still paining her, yet she keeps pace with her friend. The girl even jogs a little to make sure she would not stray behind. The blacksmith brow furrows into a deep scowl as he turns. He pushes his way back to his forge and scans his weapons. He picks up a heavy double blade ax as Brion and Sonja makes their way into the light of the main marketplace and turn towards Temple Avenue. The blacksmith trudge after strangers with a sneer about his lips.

"Leon, what's going on," one of the merchants hails the blacksmith as he walks past them causing him to pause.

"The little girl is a silver dragon," Leon, the blacksmith, answers. "We have to find her before she drives this entire city mad. We don't need her infecting those of Temple Avenue." Several merchants speak among themselves as they gather their arms to follow the blacksmith.

A set of strong oxen groan as they pull a large cart full of shaggy and musty carpets towards the marketplace. Neil hops onto the creaking cart and searches it quickly before hopping back off with a very concern look upon his features. The cart wobbles down the street as several children decide to do the imitate the man and hop on for a free ride. Vicki watches the shenanigans as she recalls the day. She and Neil have search just about everywhere for Brion and Sonja, even the most unusual places. She mumbles a little in contemplation as they start towards Temple Avenue, perhaps the two missing have mixed in with the crowd and head that way.

Unlike the marketplace, the religious corridor of Temple Avenue is not as crowded. Most of the people wandering the streets are worshipers and parishioners of various sects and theologies. Many men and women wearing robes or other attire ignore them as they hurry from one temple to another, not risking the punishment of being late. Vicki and Neil scowl when they scan around at the different buildings then down the street. Temple Avenue is thirteen oversize blocks with buildings large and colorful. A peek down an alleyway shows that the avenue extends in either direction by at least seven blocks though the temples are not as brilliant as main street.

Vicki and Neil step into the street and seem grateful when they find a large sign directing them to various temples in the area. They note that every building for the entire Avenue is dedicated to one immortal or other. Some are Eltis, others are their antagonist, the Tragin which causes a scowl to the sibling's features. They figure they should not have to worry about going into one of those temples. They just have to hope that Sonja's curiosity does not lead to foolishness.

Neil sees that most of the smaller temples are dedicated to Gods and Goddesses –living and dead and rubs his chin a little. Perhaps he should visit those to learn a few more tales and myths to add to his arsenal of bard tales. Vicki shakes her head and reminds Neil that they still need to find Brion and Sonja first then they will see about traveling and exploring which is their shared goal, to begin with. Neil is about to argue but ultimately agrees with his sister as they start down the avenue and into one of many temples.

Traveling merchants hark and yell at anyone who would listen, walking up and down the street carrying a large pole, many with strange items attached. The items range from dried meat or a strange and wondrous religious artifact that is trending now. A few disciples of various temples take up the offers, hungry after their day's work and curious about the artifacts.

Vicki ignores the commotion as she focuses upon a building that looked very exotic to be in this row. A closer inspection and she sees that it is the Temple dedicated to A'drianis. Neil spies the temple across from the one for A'drianis and notes that it holds large tigress statues on either side resting on their stomachs. A woman in full frontal nudity is standing on what appears to be an active volcano is carved into stone above the door along with the words Temple of Armels.

"Ok, looks like we are going to have to split up if we want to find them within the hour. I'm going to start with our original Lady of the Night's Temple," Vicki tilts her head to A'drianis.

"I'll tackle her mom," Neil thumbs towards Armels' Temple. "We meet in the center to continue down if we don't find them in either."

"Right," Vicki agrees. The two split up and walk into the separate temples.

The first things Neil notice as he walks into the building is the smell of sweet spices and the sound of soothing music. He goes through the incense smoke and spies several women performing a slow yet visually stimulating dance. The hips of the dancers are swaying provocatively, the motion carrying up their bodies and to their outstretched hands. Neil's mind flashes back to the beach where he and Brion witness Milea and Maya stretching exercises. Where they performing this dance?

The music stops bringing Neil's mind back to his current situation and the feeling of intense danger coming from the room. He flashes a sheepish grin when he sees all the women in the room glaring at him. A few of them are now armed with one weapon or other. The strongest of them stands and stretches, her large black dragon wings snap paying homage to her heritage of at least half dragonigena.

"Ladies," Neil said in a smooth tone. He sees that all the women are dragonigena.

"Are you lost," the strong woman challenges. Her voice is strong yet feminine. "What do you seek, l'vane man?"

"Actually, I am not the one lost," Neil assures. He notices the woman narrow her eyes in warning. "I am looking for two lost companions. An elf man and a little l'vane girl. Have you seen them?"

"Neither has come to our temple," the head priestess folds her arms and continues to stare down the male. "Anything else?"

"Just one more," Neil coaxes. "Ladies, you all dance divinely. I only wish I could stay and watch your stunning performance." He grins when he sees the stunned looks on a few of the women's faces. "However, I must hurry on my way. If I don't find my employer's daughter, she will surely have my head." He bows then turns and leaves the temple.

Vicki approaches the Temple of the Shiadokat with an abundance of caution due to the nature of some of A'drianis' followers. She does not want to get caught in a trap then have to pay to get out the trap. Two dark carvings of large black cats sit on either side of the door, they appear to be covering their noses in humor. Vicki is careful to cross the threshold and pause, the temple is in stark contrast to what the one would think for an Eltis of Shadows. The whole thing is made of pure white stone with sunlight bouncing from every shiny surface that occupies the area.

Vicki gawks as she scans her surroundings and then up, the open ceiling let in all the weather that Bri'al could through at them. She lowers her gaze and stares at the statue of A'drianis. Like many of her images across the globe, the Eltis is lounging upon a surface with nothing but a blanket to cover her lower nudity, her hair covers the upper part and flows to the surface she rests upon. There is a dagger held by the hand that rests upon her hip with a stray dagger next to the hand that rests upon the surface, keeping her propped up as she stares at the entrance, her eyes holding a warning within them that is captured even in stone.

Vicki looks at the Eltis' face for a long time, she feels it is familiar to her as if she'd seen it in recent days. Vicki's attention turns to see that the statue is facing a large ornate door, the image of a prowling dark jungle cat is carved upon it with the backdrop of a mountain. Different symbols upon it tell the story of A'drianis in a language that the visitor did not understand. Vicki takes care as she walks over to the door, keeping an eye out for traps as she tries the handle and finds the object locked tight.

"Damn it," Vicki whispers. "Unfortunately, Zaria's not here to help me open this," she turns to the statue. "I think..." She walks over to the statue placing her hands upon her hips. "My dear A'drianis do you know a 'treasure hunter' name Zaria?"

"Treasure hunter," a woman's voice asks causing Vicki to jump. "No, there's no treasure hunter by that name in this temple." Vicki turns then look down to see a woman no more than four feet tall looking up at her. "Hello there. Welcome to the Temple of A'drianis. My name is Opal. How may we assist you?"

"Ok, where did you come from," Vicki requests as she backs up; her hand picking up the dagger next to the statue's resting hand.

"The door," Opal points. The item is now open. "We heard you try and open the door. Figured you are a visitor." She grins.

"I," Vicki starts then clears her throat. "Actually, I'm looking for two of my friends. A preteen girl and an elf swords master. Have either of them come this way?"

"Any distinguishing features," Opal asks as she tilts her head.

"The girl has silver scales upon her left forearm," Vicki describes and step to one side then the other in a graceful fashion. "The elf has sea blue eyes and a deep baritone voice."

"Hmm... no. we haven't seen anyone like those two here," Opal features fill with concern. "Did you need us to help you look for them? I could offer you a discount on the services."

"Unfortunately, I have nothing of value upon my person right now," Vicki assures. She takes a step to the side and bows. "I will take my leave and see if I can find my charge before her mother wakes up. The Spirits know that we don't want her upset." She leaves the Temple. Opal and her apprentice both seem taken aback. How did the woman know they are trying to rob her?

The sun's rays bounce off the metals of the temples, their reflections, as well as their long shadows, indicates how much time has passed since the Dresden siblings started their hunt. The crowd of the street dies down to where there is enough room to see what is going on and spot someone from a distance.

Vicki meets her brother in the middle of the street, dodging a few vendors on their way back to their main stores to replenish stock. She informs him of the Temple of A'drianis and the attempt at a robbery. Neil crosses his arms and glances back at the temple then describe his encounter with the dragonigena of the Temple of Armels. Both reports not seeing their companions in either place. They decide to continue down the street in hopes of finding them.

Neil glances around at all the temples and sees that several of them had statues in front of them resembling the ideas of what each immortal look like. A few of the temples did not have a statue in front of them, yet the name is written above the door, and they avoided them. The siblings spread out their search down the street, going from building to building that they deem safe to investigate.

Once in a while, they would venture to those beyond the main street just in case Sonja or Brion had inkling to go into one of the lesser-known immortal's temple out of curiosity. They return to the main street with nothing to show for their efforts and time is running out.

Vicki and Neil pause in front of a large temple that looks out of place. It is formed with columns of stone dragons holding up the four corners of the structure. Other columns are placed strategically inside more to hold up the structure than to form any kind of wall. Out front is the statue of a man, life-size at seven feet tall with his hair carved to look as if it is flowing in a breeze, eyes fix on all who pass by. His facial expression is calm alert, a sword in his hand, another sheath upon his back. The clothing carved upon his is painted or stained purple.

"Temple of Kaidar," Vicki recognizes the statue. "We are officially at the end of Temple Row." She notes chanting and droning from inside of the temple.

"Ok, so we looked up and down the market place," Neil scowls. "I went inside of a brothel just in case they wondered into there. It's like they disappeared."

"Better you than me for that brothel, brother," Vicki said. "We went inside almost all the temples here. Could they have gone into the ones that every l'vane in their right mind should avoid? I sure hope not. I don't know about you. But I think we should continue searching. I'm not going to tell Milea we lost her daughter."

"I'm not either," Brion agrees causing his companions to turn. He grins at them. "Bards, you say?" He sees that Vicki has a dagger poise to strike while Neil's sword is in his hand in a flash. Sonja is ready to defend herself with her own dagger.

"With nice steady hands," Vicki concludes for her friend. "You two are very lucky." She put the dagger away.

"Where in all Ublivorion did you go," Neil demands, sheathing his katana.

"Sonja and I heard a blacksmith and went looking," Brion explains in short. "It turned out to be a poor decision. Apparently, he is paranoid about Dragons." He touches Sonja's head. "He saw our young friend's forearm. After that, we came searching for you two."

"My arm feels a little funny now," Sonja adds. "I also don't feel very good." She scowls and rubs the offended appendage.

"Can I see it," Vicki requests. Sonja takes care to hold out her arm.

The silver scales are now dull. They are turning purple towards the middle. The mark of a large man's hand is easily identified where there the arm has been constricted.

"He grabbed you right here." Vicki touches the bruise as gently as she can.

"Yes," Sonja agrees through grit teeth. "He grabbed and held me tight. It was painful then and since."

"Hopefully, that's just a bruise," Neil also examines the arm. "Where is the blacksmith?"

"We heard his hammer ringing from three alleyways back. The marketplace extends in that direction," Brion remarks. "When we were confronted, several people watched. It appears the smithy is a prominent member of the community."

"I've spoken to many prominent people in my lifetime," Neil assures. "What hand did he use?" He focuses on Sonja. Vicki tilts her head then made a sound of understanding at her brother's curiosity.

"Left... I think," Sonja answers. "Why?"

"Nosiness is all," Neil remarks with a reassuring smile. "Aside from the bruise, you seem alright. Let's get you back to the ship before we get into trouble." He places a hand upon the girl's shoulder and starts walking. Sonja follows his lead. "You know, you'll be a little taller than me in a couple of Decyars, Girly."

"Couple," Vicki scoffs. "I think she might be passing you up in a few months. She's sprouting up before our eyes, brother." She touches Sonja's head.

"With her heritage, she might even surpass me in height," Brion agrees. "Though I don't know what you would call a six foot or more l'vane warrior."

"Asai Dona," Sonja informs with a firm nod. Her friends chuckle from the frank answer. The girl beams. "I know a l'vane warrior who's about six and a half feet tall. Her name is Kiko."

"Oh," Neil focuses at his shorter companion. "Tell me more."

The evening sun is pressing the sky even though many visitors still fill Temple Avenue causing a look of surprise and concern to come to Vicki, they have been searching for each other and let the time get away from them. Sonja continues to describe her encounter with the tall I'vane woman keeping Neil's attention as he acknowledges a few of her adventures with the woman.

Vicki and Brion scan the marketplace, the latter noticing the watching crowd with a few of the members running into a back alley for some reason. Vicki sees the small group of people disappearing then spots a gypsy dealer sitting at the edge of Temple Avenue and the beginning of the marketplace. His product ranges from the religious relics she saw hanging from poles earlier to a variety of weapons and clothing from unknown origins. Brion scans the wares from a distance and decides that he does not see anything of interest for him at least.

A woman wearing colorful clothing dances into view catching both his and Neil's attention. She smiles at the group as she twirls around then shimmied towards the audience all while keeping eye contact with the tallest member. The woman dances around her audience then takes Brion by the hand, pulling him towards the vendor.

"That's one way of bringing over customers," Neil chuckles. "Shall we rescue our swords master?"

"Looks like he's having a good time," Vicki notes. The woman is still dancing around Brion. "Sure. Besides, I see a couple of daggers I'm interested in."

"No whips," Neil teases.

"Not so far," Vicki shrugs. "We'll see what he's got."

"He looks like he's got more than weapons," Sonja beams. "I want to get mom something before we leave." She jogs towards the vendor.

"Yes, like supplies," Neil agrees. "Unless the traveling armada got all of his stuff as well. If so, we will have to wait till tomorrow or travel to Oice despite Milea's objection." Vicki chuckles her agreement as they go to rescue their friend.

The gypsy vendor welcomes the trio with a show of his most pricy items. After a bit of haggling, Vicki walks away with a new set of three sharp daggers of unknown origin. Sonja is chatting with excitement about the gift she has for her mother. The small statuette is made of glass and in the shape of a phoenix with wings raised. Brion comments that it is well suited for Milea, he figured she is a phoenix anyway. Horses neigh as they stomp down the street into the marketplace. A large cart blocks the view of the marketplace from the small group until the man veers off to one of the side streets.

Neil is the first to enter the marketplace and pause along with his companions when they see a large mob people gather in the middle of the street, blocking the way back to the ports. Sonja takes a step back when she senses the angry tension emitting from the crowd. It is almost as if she has stepped into a hive of very angry hornets. Many of the townspeople hold weapons such as daggers and axes, with a few hoisting up ropes, tied in the shape of a noose.

The blacksmith, Leon, stands at the forefront of the crowd shaking his battle ax and yelling obscenities as well as half-truths about silver dragons to fan his makeshift army into a rage. Brion scowls at the man before glancing about, where are the town's watch officers or even the peacekeepers? He glances over his shoulder to see that the way to Temple Avenue is now blocked off as well.

The crowd that blocks it off is not as thick as the one in front. Neil takes in the situation in front and behind with a scowl as he focuses on the blacksmith. Even if he could kill the man, the mob will be impossible to escape. Especially since the entire opposing group is full of angry or raging orijetie. Neil takes a few steps back then places a hand on Brion's shoulder causing his friend to bend a little.

"Get to the ship. Let Milea know what's going on. I'm sure she's awake by now," Neil instructs. "We will be at the Temple of Kaidar."

"Right," Brion answers. He focuses upon the crowd to find the weakest point that he could make his way through. "Be careful, all of you."

"Sonja," Vicki whispers to the girl. "Follow me." She sees the young'un nod although her breathing is a little quick.

Many townswomen grab their children and escape the upcoming violence. Vicki turns and runs back towards Temple Avenue, ramping up to full speed within seconds with dust kicking up in her wake. Sonja whips around, drops her souvenir and follow her elder, her stride is matching Vicki within a quarter of a second as she runs next to her and towards the crowd. Neil takes a step back and turns on his heel to follow the two. He takes a second longer to kick in his speed but is already hopelessly outdistance by his sister and charge. The crowd of men they bear down on starts to back up, stunned at the apparent aggressiveness of the strangers.

Several of the men in the front release swears and move back while others in the back row drop even more unkind words and pushes forward causing the crowd to condense with the two opposing forces of those trying to get away and those wanting to advance. Vicki grunts as she leaps into the air and flips over the crowd landing a distance behind them and still running at her quick pace Sonja follows her example, landing in a crouch as she looks up to see the distance that Vicki has gotten.

Sonja takes a deep breath in then causes the dirt to explode as she launches herself after Vicki, catching up to the woman in no time. Neil did a twist with his flip, landing behind the crowd. He did a quick glance behind at the men then follow his sister and charge, ultimately kicking in his own speed so that he does not fall too far behind them. The crowd is dumbfounded by the acrobatics and speed of the three l'vanes, some of the aggressive crowd decide to abandon their mission.

"Get the silver dragon before she drives us all insane," Leon calls to his fellows. "Someone capture the elf." He points towards Brion.

A hand full of the crowd charge forward, bearing swords or daggers to capture Brion as the rest follows the blacksmith into Temple Avenue. Brion focuses his mind upon the sharp objects that are heading towards him as he places his hand upon the hilt of his own weapon. The sword hums as the weapons in the oncoming men's hands yank away from their owners.

The various items flip then point right at the surprised men causing them to stop in their tracks and stare at the items in awe. Brion charges forward with his hand still upon the hilt of his sword, the items he is controlling also lunge at the men. The merchants scream and retreat, their haunted cutlery chasing them. Brion cut a corner into the alleyway and heads straight towards the ship. As he leaves the area, the weapons fall to the ground one by one. The force holding them is fading with the retreating elf. The merchants decide to abandon the weapons, fearing they'd been cursed.

"Alright, Neil and Vicki. I'll get the lady, you two keep safe," Brion dodges a few animals in the piers. Several dogs decide to run with him. He slides to a stop when several members of the *Charred Rose* block his way. "Damn it..."

Although the streets are emptier than when they first got here, there are still people to dodge and duck around as the trio continue their headlong escape to the temple at the end of the avenue. The shouts of men and the cussing of women echo in Vicki's ears as she increases her pace. The short distance between the marketplace and the Temple of Kaidar seems to lengthen. She scowls, knowing that it is a trick of the mind. A crowd starts to gather in front of the last temple on the block causing Vicki to swear and slide to a stop several doors down. Sonja slides as well, standing next to the woman and maintaining an eye on the people that now stop them. She also hears Leon's voice behind her along with the angry words of several of his followers.

Vicki scans the group and mutters a sailor's oath when she sees Opal, the disciples of A'drianis are among the blockade. Vicki then turns her attention right to see the Temple of Alkadore with open doors and shakes her head, that temple is not a good idea. Sonja looks left to see another temple with open doors and points it out to Vicki. Neither of them knows who the temple belonged to. Vicki reasons with herself that they did not want to go to the one on the right.

An arrow lands in front of Sonja causing the girl to jump back and look up, several archers are on the rooftops of the temples and aim at her. Vicki swears when she is almost hit and, after that, heads to the temple of the left. Neil slides to a stop and unleashes a mouthful of unkind words when he sees his sister and his charge enter the Temple of Roathis. He calls out to them but it is too late for as soon as they entered, the doors slams shut.

"Oh, that is so not good," Neil said.

Instinct tells Neil to dodge and as he obeys the request, he almost trips over the arrows that had landed in front of Sonja as a new one tried to skewer him. The sounds of shouting from behind prompts him to glance back then dodge another arrow as he swears and continues down the street. Arrows follow him as archers keep missing him even though they had a perfect aim and soon he is ripped of range. Members of the blockade start forward as Neil pushes on, increasing his speed. He is going to force his way through the crowd to avoid the arrows and hopefully arrive inside of the temple of Kaidar.

"Stop him," Leon shouts.

Many in the crowd meet the l'vane halfway to his destination; the movement prompts the archers to stop shooting to avoid killing a member of their town. Neil did not notice the good fortune as he dodges a variety of people losing his vest in the process as he skillfully avoids capture. Several minutes later, he dives into the Temple of Kaidar. His footing slips on the polish marble causing a slew of obscenities to fall from Neil's lips. He loses his footing and rolls down the remaining three stairs into the grand hall.

Several warriors hop out of his way allowing him to crash into the wall. Neil sprawls out his legs and arms to stare up at the ceiling. The large golden dragon that is painted above appears to dance around and laugh at him. The room is still spinning in his head. The sour look of an old man peering at him from above causes Neil to become aware of his surroundings. Slowly, he sits up and focuses on the old man. Short of stature with a long white beard and a tattoo for hair, he would have been a funny sight if not for one thing.

"Sensei," Neil is slow to stand and bows to the shorter man. "I apologize for interrupting your class. It is a bit of an emergency."

"Truly. As fast as you were going, I figured that out," the old man agrees. His voice old yet still booming. "Are you alright? Anything broken?"

"Just my pride for right now," Neil assures and rolls his shoulders. "If I don't get my sister and young friend out of Roathis' Temple, I will soon have a broken neck." The news causes the old man to scowl.

"Sensei," a student rush forward. "Leon, the blacksmith, wants to know about the man who came into this temple. Apparently, he is wanted for bringing a dragon to the city."

"The moron wouldn't know a dragon if it bit him on the arse," the Sensei grumbles, "Tell the dumb ass that we will handle the l'vane male." He instructs. "And that he needs to be more sensitive. Kaidar is a Dragon Eltis as is the rest of his family."

"Yes," the student bows and hurries back to the door.

"Roathis, eh," the Sensei turns his attention back to Neil and rubs his beard. "You and your friends are not Reformers or training as such are you?"

"By the life that I breathe, my sister nor I will ever take that path," Neil assures. "No, my young friend is a girl. She is at least half l'vane though that shows the most. I believe her other half is Silver Dragon due to the scales upon her left forearm that I am told the blacksmith unfortunately saw."

"I see," the old man strokes his beard as he digests the information.

"I really need to get her out of there. Her mother will be very upset if she finds out she's in that place," Neil pleads.

"Her mother? Who are you and those you are looking for? Let's start there," the old man sits down.

"I am Neil Dresden," Neil introduces. "My sister is Vicki our young charge is called Sonja. Her mother is Milea Sirus of Selvast Forest. And believe me, she is the real deal."

"Yes, you are in some deep shit, my boy," the Sensei rubs his beard and appear to stare at his guest. "I am Sensei Zeroun the Strong. How long do you have to find Miss Sonja?"

"Considering I have an elf friend who is carrying a message for Lady Milea," Neil admits. "Not long at all. He should be at the ship by now."

"Then we have to help you find her before all Ublivorion breaks loose," Zeroun said with confidence. He turns to his students. "Warriors of Kaidar! Listen Up! We have to help this l'vane find a young lady in less than an hour. Neil Dresden will describe the situation to you." He steps to one side to allow Neil to move forward. All the warriors line up to hear their assignment.

"It has been long since I've visited the Warriors of Kaidar," Neil addresses with pride. "Each time I had a dilemma. It is no different now. I seek my sister. She is l'vane, three inches taller than myself. Her hair is darker than mine by a little bit. She is also extremely dangerous, approach with caution." He admits. "With her is a girl, preteen. She is also l'vane with the scales of a silver dragon on her left forearm. Both ran into the Temple of Roathis. I'm hoping to get in and get out before it's too late for them."

"Sir Neil, do not worry about your sister and friend. We will get them before they are harmed," a warrior promises. He places his hand upon his heart and bows a little.

"Hykaidar," The rest of the warriors exclaim before they depart the room. Zeroun beams with pride.

"Neil, do not fret. We will have them before nightfall," Zeroun assures. "Go relax a bit." He placed a hand upon the man's shoulder.

"Nightfall is not soon enough," Neil reminds. "From my calculations, Brion has already reached the ship." Zeroun takes a step back and rubs his beard in thought.

CHAPTER TWENTY

A Mother's Fury

Darkness fills the entire temple, the shadows upon the wall glare at the intruders that dare enter this unholy place. Both unwilling intruders sense the evil oozing from every stone of the building. Torchlight flicker and bounces off the walls in an ill attempt to lighten the place, the slow swirls and flickers imitating a dance untold victims perform before the inevitable death.

The smell of blood permeates the entire room from the large bowl that sits upon an altar in the center. Many ghosts are literally chained to the item, unable to be free of their last days. The floor is clean at least and made of marble, similar to the ceiling which makes both extremely slick. The walls are stacked stone that is sanded smooth, eliminating many cracks with windows high in the air.

Sonja pulls on the closed doors with all she is worth yet the items refuse to budge. They had slam shut seconds after she and Vicki realize they should not be in this temple. A mistake that Vicki knows will haunt her for the rest of her life and prays that it is as an extended life. She did not want to end up like many that enter this temple.

Many of the victims' spirits float aimlessly about seeking a way out. None of them seem aware of the living that is now captured in the room with them. Both Sonja and Vicki turned their attention to a hall leading to the back when they hear a strange moaning emitting from that direction. It is unclear if the person is in pain or in pleasure. Judging from the environment they found themselves in; Vicki guesses it is both.

"The doors are not going to open," Sonja finally admits through the strain of her efforts to free them. "I don't like this place." She turns back to the room and takes in the sights. "No... not at all."

"Easy," Vicki encourages. "I am not in love with it myself. This is the Temple of Roathis. A bad place for us both. I am sorry I led us in here."

"You were panicking and so was I," Sonja reminds. "Don't be so hard on..." She pauses when she hears footsteps. "I don't think we are alone."

"So, I noted," Vicki agrees and fingers her dagger.

The tension in the room increase to an alarming level as the unknown host came closer to the main hall. Vicki sees the spirits all flee to a part of the room they could hide, a few of them whimper when they discover they could not get out. Sonja focuses on the hall across from them when she feels something big and terrible is heading their way.

At first, the footsteps sound as if someone is walking through mud. The sucking and splatting of each step cause Vicki and Sonja to ease closer together. The footsteps soon became more normal, echoing against the empty chamber as a strong negative vibe fills the room. The silhouette of a figure dances upon the walls in the torchlight. The shadow resembles a woman at least her head and torso yet from the waist down, she is full of tentacles with a few of the wiggling things lining the sides of her body.

The shadow stretches as an audible sigh escapes the unknown woman walking towards the room. The wiggling tentacles on the sides of her body begin to shrink down, absorbing into her body. Vicki and Sonja brace as the shadow moves forward and the woman walks into the room. She is as tall as Vicki, her blonde hair falling as it may and thankfully cover her abundant breasts. Voluptuous, she is wearing a very thin veil as clothing. Her orange-colored eyes scan those at the door and catch Sonja's attention. The girl swears under her breath when she sees that the whites of the woman's eyes are blue-grey.

"Well, well, well," The woman coos. "What have I gotten here? Guests? Or new recruits? Perhaps a few sacrifices?" Her eyes and voice seem chipper as she speaks.

"I would say none of those," Vicki remarks. "My kind woman, can you let us out? We intruded accidentally."

"What," the woman laughed. "Me? Kind? That is your first folly. Thinking I would let you out is another." She places a hand upon her abundant hip. "I, Roathis, am never kind."

"Oh.... shit," Sonja mumbles to herself. She takes a couple of steps back as she did. Her mind races, she needs to contact her mother but has no clue as to how.

"You can't be Roathis," Vicki said. "Roathis is dead. She was killed ten generations ago."

"By the blade of Kaidar. Yes, I know. I remember the cut so well," Roathis agrees. "That warrior was quite a sight to see, no wonder he killed me. Straight through the heart. Up and out of the left side then across the neck, severing my head." She motions to the different locations. "I avoided Oswind, he is after all my uncle. Until I was returned to life as I have been for centuries. Through a sacrifice." She rubs her body. "Although this one needed a little work, it will do for now. However,...." She looks up at Vicki then Sonja. "I think I will exchange for one of you."

Sonja takes several steps back, her breathing a little quick when she sees a grotesque image cover the woman that stalks them. The girl scans her surroundings then spots an open window several feet up. Bumping Vicki out of her stupor, she points to the escape route. Vicki calculates the height and material of the wall to the window then pulls two large and sturdy daggers that she purchased from the gypsy.

Roathis pauses, unsure what to do when someone suddenly becomes aggressive. The metal from the daggers gleams in the half-light of the temple as Vicki turns her back on the approaching woman to crouch down, signaling to Sonja to hold on. Sonja hesitates but climbs onto her friend's back, making sure to secure herself in a way that would not choke her.

Vicki stands, feeling the weight of her passenger, she did a quick recalculation, shifting her weight a little then jumps straight up. She clears the height of the doors before slamming her daggers into the wall. With the added weight of Sonja, Vicki slides down causing a few swears as she places her feet on the wall and engage all her muscles. She finally stops a foot and a half down from where she landed. Sonja exhales in relief then looks around to find a way to free her friend of the added weight. She finds what she is looking for about twenty agonizing feet away from the landing point. Vicki starts to climb up to a window, her efforts slow going as she repeatedly stabs the wall to inch to her destination.

"Get to the crags, and I can climb," Sonja shifts her weight a little to get a better, yet gentle, grip on her friend.

Vicki glances over to the items the girl points out and studies them. The 'crags' are elongated, with at least four holes in them, two used to be eyes and the other two nostrils of a very large crea-ture, perhaps a dragon. Several of the long and sharp teeth are still in the skull and holds them to the blacked wood beam. Vicki scowls when she sees a shadow cover at least one of the skulls, seeing it is a weeping dragon before it disappears.

"Those aren't crags, those are dragon skulls," Vicki points out and starts towards her destination.

"They are stuck on the wall, so they will help regardless of what they are," Sonja assures. "We need Mom. That woman re-ally is Roathis."

"How can you tell," Vicki asks as she moves towards the win-dow. It is up on the left wall.

"Grandma told me how to detect other Eltis," Sonja insists and watches as they creep ever closer to jumping distance.

"Can we get Grandma here," Vicki requests, she slips a little but maintains a good hold upon her weapons and the wall.

"No, but mom and my aunt should be able to handle her," Sonja said. "Just a little more."

"Let's hope that both of them are recovered enough from Reis and Claries," Vicki scowls. "Almost there, get ready to jump."

The sound of metal stabbing into stone echoes in the temple and reflects in the burn that Vicki fells in her muscles from the effort of the climb. Sonja keeps an eye on the destination and calculates her jump. She needs just a few more feet to clear the distance. Roathis watches, humored by what she considers a small fly that is crawling across her wall. If it is not for the elite jumping skills of the adult l'vane, she would have thought the woman useless.

Roathis rubs her hands together, waiting patiently for her quarry to crawl over a hidden pit. Several minutes will pass before Roathis got what she wants. With a simple wave of her hand, the wall Vicki has been climbing on disappears. Both Vicki and Sonja cuss as they began to fall. Vicki instinctively reaches out and grab hold of a ledge. Her other hand reaching for Sonja, but it is too late. The girl cries out in fear as she falls into the pit below. Roathis cackles in glee before she turns her attention to Vicki.

"Sonja," Vicki hollers.

"Oh, come now. Make this a little easier on yourself," Roathis offers. Dark green light illuminates her form before condensing into a ball within her outstretched hand. She grins as she tosses a dark ball of light towards the woman.

"Oswind's Beard!" Vicki moves to avoid the light then again when another is sent for her.

"Oh, you're a quick one," Roathis cackles as she sends a half dozen in a row.

The dark balls of light speeds towards their destination, a hissing sound emitting from the items as the group elongates into snakes. Vicki drops several obscene words and leaps up towards the dragon skulls, her hand grabbing hold of the first horn she could. She hauls herself up and hurries across her path. Crackling reaches her ears as her route crumbles. Vicki concentrates on the exit and on the last skull, she jumps, grabs hold of the window ledge, and hauls herself out of it. Roathis snaps her fingers in disappointment, she would just have to make do with the girl.

"Oh well," Roathis said. "This will prove interesting. I've not had a victim this young before." She saunters back into the hall.

A strong wind blows from the oceanfront, reminding of the proximity to the sea. Vicki runs her fingers through her hair as she notes the setting sun in the distance and her predicament. She has to find her way back to the ship, but first, she has to get down off of the top of the Temple of Roathis without getting killed.

Taking a few breaths in and out, Vicki decides to try and jump to the other temple and climb down the long-braided column they built for it. She is about to take a step forward when her foot slips. Cussing, Vicki turns and try to grab hold of the stone but her grip slips. A strong breeze pushes her out past the temple.

Vicki cries out in surprise and fear as she plummets down to the alleyway the sound of which is cut short as she lands harsh enough to knock herself unconscious.

A warrior of Kaidar hurries down the alleyway when he hears the crash landing and focuses on the large heap in the center of the way. He gasps when he sees the unconscious woman and runs to her side. Bending down, he examines her and expresses words of relief when noting that she is still alive. But she landed awkwardly, hitting her head upon the ground. The spot where her head hit starts to swell even as he finishes making sure nothing is broken. He lifts her and heads straight back to the Temple of Kaidar.

"Sensei," the warrior calls out. "Sensei, hurry. I found one of the girls." Zeroun runs into the room trail closely by Neil.

"Vicki," Neil shouts out. "What happened?"

"I found her in the alley. She looked like she fell from high above," the warrior explains in short. "No sign of the little girl." "She must still be inside," Zeroun scowls and straighten.

"Get Vicki to the healing room and place her in front of the statue of Kaidar. Summon Petra from the Temple of Illandere, tell her we have a very touch and go patient that needs her help. We will have to form a plan to invade the Temple of Roathis to retrieve the girl."

"Yes," the man bows and carries Vicki out of the room.

"At this point in time. We might have to wait for her mother," Neil informs with a scowl. "And I will pray that she is in a good mood."

"You and me both," Zeroun slaps a hand on Neil's shoulder.

Seagulls cry out as they circle the boat but did not land on it, the slithering of various ropes spooks the birds them enough to keep a curious eye on the ship at a distance. Milea stands at the stern, stretching as the evening draws near, the ocean breeze stirring her hair a little causing her to smile. According to Zaria, Sonja has been gone all day with their new friends to explore the huge marketplace as well as Temple Avenue.

Milea gently pushes her hair back as she ponders the time. If Sonja and their friends are not back in a few minutes, she will be going to locate them. The task may be more difficult than she imagines since Tenze has one of the largest markets in all Bri'al, the entire town echo with the harking of merchants. Milea smiles at the thought of her daughter's effort to see the entire marketplace in one day.

"A marketplace city," Maya chuckles a little, standing next to her sister. "Sonja is in utopia. The girl loves to shop."

"I know," Milea agrees. "I'll have to search for them in a minute." She leans on the rail. "I'm not sure why they didn't wake us up."

"I gave them a warning not to," Zaria informs and sits on the rail next to the twins. "Night is approaching through. I can go see if...." She pauses when her senses detect a presence. "Oh, don't be stupid." She growls a warning to the person climbing the ship.

The ocean spray kisses the twins as they turn to the port side of the ship. The sound of male grunting is heard above the sounds of the port. Zaria stands up from her seat when Brion hauls himself onto the ship. He is a little disheveled as if he just escaped a very harsh battle. He has a few cut wounds on his arms and legs, his shirt is ripped from either a weapon or from being grab. Milea scowls when she sees his condition and the fact that he is alone. Maya looks beyond Brion and sees a crowd of people heading to the *Charred Rose*.

"Brion, what happened," Milea asks. "Are you alright? Where are Sonja, Neil, and Vicki?"

"Milea," Brion acknowledges. "Glad to see that you and Maya are awake. There is a slight situation at hand."

"What's going on," Milea requests, raising an eyebrow.

"Anything to do with the *Charred Rose*," Maya adds.

"No, milady. Those idiots tried to capture me," Brion informs. "Sonja, Neil, and Vicki are being chased by a mob. It started with the blacksmith noting the dragon scales upon Sonja's arm. It is his belief that she's going to drive the city insane. We were surrounded. Vicki took Sonja and made a break for Temple Avenue. Neil followed them and said they will be in the Temple of Kaidar."

"Hold up," Maya raises her hand to stop the rapid dispensing of information. "How in all Ublivorion would Sonja drive a city insane?"

"The first sign of Sorshana's attack is a liege of silver dragons," Milea explains to her twin. "Then the harp comes."

"I didn't notice the silver dragons at the temple. That, in itself, is insane," Maya rubs her temples. "Kaidar is mother's oldest child."

"The temple dedicated to him would be a safe haven," Zaria informs. "You look like Ublivorion, Brion. What about everybody else?"

"Sonja has a large bruise on her left arm, where the scales are," Brion recalls. "The blacksmith grabbed her, but I made him let her go. The man is still alive. Unless Neil or Vicki remedied that."

"I see," Milea said. "I am going to the Temple of Kaidar. I'll be back. Stay here, Brion." She walks to the port side of the ship. After a small debate in her mind, she just hops down.

"Come on. Let me see if I can stop some of those wounds from flowing," Maya places a hand upon Brion's shoulder. She notes Zaria turn all the sudden to stare into the distance. "What's wrong?"

"Oh, Great Halls of Ublivorion, no way? Not that," Zaria objects. "I'm going after Milea." She hops off the ship and hurried after the sorceress.

The halls of the Temple of Kaidar are silent except for the moans of a woman as she wrestles with the nightmare of her last wakened moments. Neil places his hands together and rests his chin upon his thumbs as he watches his sister writhe in the memories from her ordeal. His expression speaks volumes of worry, especially with the swollen knob on the side of her head, which did not bode well. Vicki's body tenses and relax as she continues her dream, her hands flex as she battles her invisible foes. Every muscle in Vicki's body tenses up. Neil jumps to his feet when his sister cries out in her sleep and sits up.

Vicki opens her eyes and looks around with a rapid, panic breath as she tries to take in her surroundings. She turns to the statue of the grinning dragon and gasps. She jumps to her feet and pulls the dagger from the Temple of A'drianis out of her belt. Neil holds up his hand to make sure those next to him did not accidentally end up dead despite their worry for the woman.

The dagger in Vicki's hand is trembling, her nightmare still fresh in her mind and she is perhaps still living through it. Neil decides to wait a minute then bravely ventures towards his sister in a slow and silent way. Zeroun watches the l'vane he hosted and notices the stalking almost cat-like behavior Neil exhibits approaching his armed and apparently dangerous sibling. The old man leans back a little as he realizes that he is not looking at simple seafaring folk.

"Vicki," Neil says to his sister. The woman whips around, weapon posed to toss. She pauses when she sees her brother. He exhales in relief. "You have a nasty bump on the head, are you alright?"

"Neil," Vicki acknowledges her brother then once again face the statue. "Ok, it's not moving."

"Not as far as I know," Neil said. "That's a representation of Kaidar."

"Sonja and I needed his help to," Vicki says then tenses up. "Gods, we have to go into Roathis' temple and get Sonja! She fell down a pit..."

"Slow down, Vicki," Neil offers. "You're not going anywhere. Not in your condition. That bruise on your head is not a good sign. I am happy you woke up."

"Neil," Zeroun catches the attention of the siblings. "We need to prepare for Lady Milea's arrival. I'm sure she will be here shortly."

"Right," Neil said. Zeroun turns and leaves the room. "Sonja is still in Roathis' temple?"

"Yes, and Roathis herself is there," Vicki informs. "We defiantly need Milea to help with this one."

"This just went from bad to worse," Neil said with a frown.

Two dozen warriors practice their skills, tossing one another around the room oblivious to the guest that saunters her way into their mist. Milea avoids the practice room and walks into a waiting hall, careful to pay her respects to the resident Eltis by leaving a gold coin on the altar in front of the door. Milea enters the hall and relaxes at the bright light and warm citrus smell that envelope her senses.

The wind swirls around and moves the large tapestries upon the well-kept walls. She stops and decides to study a few of the tapestries, in awe that all of them depict a man that is very similar to Oswind except he has white hair and a little bit more muscular build. He wears a dark blue outfit the shirt open revealing his chest and a trickle of golden scales. He is pictured walking or standing in an attack pose, his hands glowing a light blue color as he focuses upon the room. His chin hosts a small patch of black hair, and he is grinning as if he is a mischievous boy.

Milea makes a slight nod of her head in silent understanding and moves onto a second tapestry and sees the same man this time meditating with his sword across his lap. A third shows the man standing with one hand upon his sword, the other across his chest. Behind him is the largest golden dragon Milea has ever seen and next to him is a creature that looks to be a cross between a lion and a dragon.

"I guess that's Kaidar," Milea muses, studying her brother. "Interesting."

"At least it is what we think he looks like," Zeroun said. Neil and Vicki sands with the shorter man. "Greetings, milady. Welcome to the Temple of Kaidar."

"It feels very welcoming," Milea smiles. "Perhaps I should have come here to meditate and recharge. It feels very comfortable here." She focuses on her companions. "Neil, Vicki. Where is Sonja?"

"The short answer, milady," Vicki takes a deep breath in. "Roathis has her."

The quiet of the room turns from welcoming to forborne. It is as if some angry life-force has appeared into their space. The warriors pause in training when they feel the change, many of them hurrying to find arms just in case they are being attacked. A few men scout about trying to locate the cause of the atmosphere change. Zeroun takes a step back and focuses on his guest, something is defiantly stirring in this woman that he is not expecting. Neil and Vicki keep their position despite the tension yet remain vividly alert.

The air in the room starts to become heavy as Milea closes her eyes and a spark of energy illuminate around her form. The red light is pushing to go outward but is pulled back in by the sorceress. The warriors finally locate the source of the tension and head into the room with Milea then pause when they see their Sensei standing in front of the threat. Zeroun looks up at his students then shakes his head to tell his students to not interfere. The young warriors are confused but obey their teacher's request, backing down yet remaining inside the room.

"What," Milea asks slowly, her eyes opening once again. "How did it happen?"

"Perhaps I should tell you the how a little later, milady," Vicki offers. "Please note it is my fault and not that of my brother's. I accidentally took a wrong turn and Sonja followed. Sonja really needs to be rescued now. When I say Roathis has her, I really mean that it is Roathis herself."

"I see," Milea takes a couple of breaths to calm herself down. "Vicki, it looks like you had a concussion. I think you and Neil need to stay here until I return." She turns and walks toward the door.

"No way, milady," Neil jogs until he stands in front her. "Believe me. I know you are upset and have a right to be. But you are no match for Roathis and the leagues of warriors, mages, and others that may be between you and your child. Let the Warriors of Kaidar help you. I am sure he would approve."

"That's right," Zeroun agrees. He stands next to Neil, facing the agitated woman. "Besides, the Warriors of Kaidar look for any excuse to whoop the cowards of Roathis' ass."

"Then they better not slow me down," Milea growls. She stalks past the men.

Neil takes a deep breath in and out before hurrying after her, at least he would be able to take care of some of those that bar the paths into the dark temple. Zeroun calls to his pupils to gather as many of them as they could, this is an exercise in saving a life. The students all shout to one another with what they are embarking on, causing a bit of excitement to buzz from the ranks.

Vicki decides to trail after the group since the entire temple clears out and head towards the impending battle. She did not want to be left in the temple alone, perhaps because the statue freaked her out when she woke up. She swears it moved and talking to her yet no one else can see or hear it. Vicki shakes her head a little, she will have to talk to Maya about how to ward off such entities. As she leaves the temple, the statue of the dragon turns to watch her go.

The animals of the day are retreating to their homes for the night. Some squeal in terror when they sense the tension in the air warning them that something big and dangerous is approaching. Zaria feels the thickening of the air and guesses that Milea is upset. She decides to focus on the temple knowing that since the doors to Roathis' temple closed and the chanting going on inside, she could figure out why Milea is angry.

Mayhap Roathis has one of the girls, and that chanting meant one thing, she wants a new body. Zaria turns when her senses inform her to do so and face the oncoming threat. She faces Milea and the small army that follow a few steps behind the woman and places her hand upon her hip. Milea pauses when she sees the stance from the now shorter woman and takes a deep breath in.

"What happened," Zaria asks then sees Vicki standing among the group. "I think I know, Roathis has Sonja, right?"

"Out of my way, A'drianis," Milea warns.

"Not until you calm down, you know better. Fighting while angry will cost you," Zaria scolds. "In this case, it will cost you dearly." She feels the sun starting to slip closer to the horizon, giving her a bit of an advantage.

"I will calm down when I have my daughter back," Milea assures and is about to walk pass but is push back gently by her own shadow. "Shiadokat..."

"I am not going to let you go in there and kill yourself and your child, at least breathe a little and calm down to the point where you don't have steam coming out of your bloody ears," Zaria scolds. She notices that Milea grips her hands into tight fist, the right is glowing and usually meant she is about to bring her blade out. Zaria rolls her shoulders a little as the shadows grow a bit longer.

"Excuse me, ladies," Zeroun walks past them.

A large group of young men and women follows the old man as he heads to the stairs bringing a bit of a surprise to Milea, she is not expecting so many warriors on her heels. She takes a quick look back to see that many more are anticipating the next move or a signal to attack. Milea turns back to the door when she senses a powerful presence outside of her own.

Zeroun approaches the closed doors to the Temple of Roathis purposefully, placing one strong step in front of the other. As he stomps the ground, he creates small cracks in the stonework in both the steps and the street. He is Zeroun the Strong, and he is not going to let a little thing such as a fortified door stand between his warriors and the rescue of a little girl. The Sensei stops a foot from the door and squats down, holding out his hands a little as he takes a deep breath in, a menacing look gleams across his eyes.

"Hykaidar," the old man shouts as he jumps and kicks.

The door flies completely off its hinges, slamming into a few surprised worshipers inside of the temple. Zeroun lands and stands strong as his students echo his battle cry and run into the building to engage their enemy in combat. The worshipers of Roathis stand in surprise as the Warriors of Kaidar flood into their sacred hall and engage them in combat. Neil turns to his sister and notices that she shares his look of surprise. Shaking out of his stupor, Neil rushes into the structure with Vicki on his heels.

Milea blinks her own surprise until she notes that Zeroun is now bent over and swearing at himself. Left hand on his back, his right is resting on his knee while he leans against the side of the threshold. A few of his students would pause and check on him. He waves them away and tells them battle well by their Sensei. Although he is in obvious pain, he let his followers know that he is fine. The sight brings a smile to Milea's lips much to Zaria's relief.

"That is so much better. Now you may go and commence to kick Roathis' backside," Zaria bows and takes a step to the side. "I will go scout ahead." She disappears into the shadows. Milea watches her leave before walking towards the temple, noting the large number of warriors that still want to get inside to battle.

"Zeroun, are you well," Milea asks the old man, pausing to do so.

"I'm fine, fine," Zeroun assures. "Just go make sure the little girl is safe." He holds his back. "I've got something for the back at the temple."

"Thank you," Milea smiles and kiss the old man on the fore-head. She then starts into the temple. Zeroun straightens and watches her leave. He pauses and wiggles his backside a little. He feels better.

"That lady can give me a kiss any time," Zeroun admits.

The sensei retreats to the Temple of Kaidar, just in case, the authorities decide to show. He calls to those that did not get inside to follow him back so they would not cause a scene. The students, though disappointed, obey their Sensei and head back to the Temple of Kaidar.

CHAPTER TWENTY-ONE

A Powerful Foe

The stench of blood and decay hit her sense of smell and is the first thing to alert her mind followed by the sound of secular chanting. Sonja's eyes snap open, remembering the last event that happened before she went unconscious. The vision of their unholy host, sound of the pit, and Vicki calling her name are vivid in her mind. Sonja lifts her head to take in the view around her and sees an abundance of bloodstain statues of various evil creatures above her. Sonja stares at the statues for a little while, wondering if the creatures are bird or reptile. The sight of men kneeling or bowing as they repeatedly chant a strange language causes the girl to scowl and try to sit up. The strain of chains upon her arms and legs alerts her that her predicament is defiantly a bad one.

Sonja turns her head to take in all her whole situation and pause when she sees Roathis sitting on a throne and watching the proceedings, her gaze of anticipation has a trance-like effect upon her. Whatever clothing she has on is sparse if there at all and very ill fitting. Curious, Sonja turns to the other side to see a bird that resembles a peacock with a crown upon its head. She scowls at first since she recalls it not there when she looks before then her features twist into shock and recognition. It is a living version of the creature she saw drawn on the floor in Orin's castle. The beast's eyes are glowing red, and it is obvious that he is aroused.

"What the," Sonja said. She then scowls, remembering Vicki's explanation of the events she is an unwilling participant of. "Oh, I think not!"

Sonja pulls upon her chains, the stones and metal groan as they try to keep her in place, the sound of which cause the worshipers to stop their chant. The girl arches her back up then slam it down and pulls even harder on her restraints, a deep growl emitting from her as her silver scales start to glow. The chains holding her arms shriek as they give way, scattering shards everywhere and catching Roathis as well as her followers by surprise. The peacock jumps up to try and avoids the wild chain. His luck runs out as he is brought down when Sonja uses her new weapon to slap it to the ground. The bird lands on the floor with the chain wrap around its neck, squawking helplessly before Sonja pulls back and snap the head off.

The body of the bird stands up and dances around a little then falls once it realizes the head is gone. The beak of the bird opens and closes once, and then no more, black blood oozes from the deceased bird. While they are distracted, Sonja manages to snap the chains around her midsection and get to her feet. The chains on her legs prove to be thicker than those she just finished breaking. Sonja bends down to try and break them then looks up when she sees that the worshipers are moving in to try and restrain her. Sonja takes the dangling chains that are still attached to her arms and starts flaying them around.

"Stay back," Sonja commands as she whips her chains around.

The men charge forward and are slap with the sharp edge of the broken chains, many of them hitting the ground holding their eyes and screaming at their sudden blindness. Sonja whips it around like a tornado, whirling it so that she could keep her captors at bay as she figures out how to get free from the rest of the altar. One man manages to grab hold of a lock of the chain and pull on it. Sonja jerks then yank back, hard, pulling the man into the stone and knocking him out.

Two more men grab the now lack chain and cause the metal to glow as they pull. Sonja swears as she is yanked to her knees. The other chain is taken up by two more men and tug upon pulling the girl onto her rump then her back as Roathis stands from her throne and stalk over to the altar. Sonja growls and pulls, dragging the men a few inches yet they hold the chains steadfast. The chains whine but did not break this time much to her dismay. The wounded men whimper as they crawl out of the area, careful to avoid their angry idol. The lighting in the room dims ever so slightly, unnoticed by all as the angry woman glares over the child.

"I do not know what you are, girl," Roathis growls. "But you have killed a sacred animal to me. For that. I will kill you."

"If you do that, you'll have more than just Oswind to worry about," Sonja retorts, growling back at the woman. "Let me go."

"You are very astounding, girl," Roathis said with a sneer. "I would not worry too much about Oswind. He won't even see you as I devour your soul."

"I don't like you," Sonja sneers. The shadows darken, even more, spreading from the ceiling down but did not catch the attention of either one.

"You are humorous," Roathis places her hands upon her hip. "Do something about it then, child. I'd like to see you try."

The room plunges into absolute darkness catching both Roathis and Sonja off guard. Immediately afterward, a large claw slaps into Roathis, sending her backwards and into a solid object, perhaps a wall or pillar. Sonja's chains squeak as they are unlocked, freeing the girl as the remaining worshipers drop the chains and flee in the darkness. Their cries are cut short when the shadow silences them. Sonja feels her body lift off the altar and push towards a part of the room she could not see as she hears Roathis get back to her feet.

The shadow then leaves Sonja and goes after the woman, lifting Roathis and tossing her into another wall follow by several claws. Roathis blocks the blows then let out an angry sound as her body starts to glow. Sonja sees the woman in the darkness and swears as the Roathis cast a strong illumination spell, lighting the entire room, and causing all shadows to disappear.

The creator of the shadow drops a boat load of unkind words as she falls to her knees a few feet from Roathis. Sonja swiftly picks up speed and tackles Zaria out of the way as Roathis brings down her hand to strike the shiadokat. Sonja and Zaria roll out of the way at least ten yards then return to their feet at the same time facing Roathis. Zaria's hostile gaze at the vile woman is short lived as several dark light balls are sent their way. Sonja gasps and moves out of the way follow closely by Zaria. Both are still together for now.

"Any bruises besides the arm," Zaria asks in haste.

"My backside and I think I hurt my leg or head when I landed," Sonja informs just as fast. "Move!" She jumps to one side, Zaria to the other as Roathis unleashes another dark ball spell. It explodes, causing the altar to turn to dust and the body of the peacock to ashes.

"No," Roathis shouts. She then growls and turns her attention to Zaria. "A'drianis...." She sneers the name.

"Roathis," Zaria answers in the same tone. "Looking a bit plump this time around, are we?"

"I'm going to KILL YOU," Roathis roars as she cast a strong dark light spell towards the woman.

Sonja drops a few learned unkind words as she rushes forward and tackles Zaria out of the way of the spell. Both once again hit the ground and roll with Zaria getting to her feet first. The spell whips around and heads toward them again, this time Zaria is the one to get them to safety. The thief swears when the spell once again changes directions. Roathis cackles when she sees Sonja shift to stand in front of the shiadokat and brace for impact. Zaria grabs the girl's belt and is about to haul the child and herself out of the path once again when the spell stops and shrinks into nothing more than a pulsating ball of energy.

All humor leaves Roathis as she sneers at Zaria, her mind reeling with the abilities of the Shiado that she is familiar with, none of them yield the powers to do what is happening now. Footsteps alert all in the room of another party that is about to join the ranks causing all to shift their attention to the open door. A strong energy fills the room as the entity near, causing Sonja to shift a little uneasy and Zaria to place a hand upon the girl to reassure her.

Milea walks into the room, a small red glow barely seen surrounding her form as she briefly meets the eyes of Roathis then takes in the situation in the room. Sonja shifts, a little nervous, as her mother takes a position in front of her next to the dark ball of crackling energy hovering in the room. Milea inhales deeply then slowly release the breath as she once again meets the gaze of the strange voluptuous woman staring at her.

"Sonja, Zaria. Please find the Dresden siblings and meet me back on the ship," Milea instructs.

"Bring the lights down, and I can take everybody out of here," Zaria hints. "As well as give Roathis a bit of a cat scratch on the way out."

"You wish," Roathis growls. "I will snap you in half, A'drianis."

"You wouldn't find me to do so, Soith," Zaria snorts. "Ready?" She looks at Milea.

"No... I'm not going anywhere... yet," Milea said. "Do not tally." She insists, her voice a little forceful.

"Going," Sonja chimes, and high tails it out of the same door her mother entered the room.

"That girl can move," Zaria notes and follows the preteen.

Roathis glare after the shiadokat then focuses her attention back onto her new opponent. She studies her and
assumes her senses are fooling her. Roathis starts to walk,
with caution, to the left and sees her opponent stand patiently
in one spot. The woman is alert enough to follow with her
eyes and turn of the head. Milea watches her opponent as the
woman paces around. A slight look of disbelief comes to
Milea's features as she takes in what her senses are telling her.
This woman is something she never wanted to meet in her
lifetime.

Roathis is a product of a Tragin and an Eltis which brings
up

an important question. Who are her parents? Roathis continues to move about as she comes to her own conclusion
about the red-haired woman that invade her space, yet she
feels her senses are still toying with her. She senses that this
woman is a sorceress, that is true, yet she is just about as powerful as an Eltis. No mortal has reached this power for several
generations, and the last to do so has been dead a very long
time. Roathis pauses and stares at Milea, scanning her more
than once as she formulates her question.

"What are you," Roathis challenges, tilting her head in curiosity.

"Obviously not the same thing you are, thank the old ones,"
Milea answers. She glances at the large pile of rubble that
once was a table before returning her gaze to Roathis. "Why
did you have my daughter tied to the altar?"

"I wanted a new body," Roathis answers with a shrug. "I am Roathis, the devourer of souls. I take the body and eat the soul of the one the crown peacock marks. The body becomes mine, the soul... dinner."

"I see. You really are half Tragin," Milea concludes.

"And you are fascinating," Roathis remarks. "I wonder how much of your power will I retain once I have devoured your soul and taken your body."

"You cannot do that unless your minion 'marks' me, should such a remote thing happen. Besides, you cremated your peacock," Milea reminds. "Here, let me show you how you did it."

The energy level in the room reaches an alarming rate as Milea slap the dark light ball back at Roathis catching the woman off guard and causing her to take several steps back. In her curiosity, she has forgotten about the spell and swears when the dark light explodes back into its full strength then collides with her. Roathis hollers in anger as she reabsorbs her work and sends a second spell aim directly at Milea. It goes half way then reverse right back at her. Roathis dodges this time landing on all fours and growling as her body shift into a creature that is half wolf, half dragon.

Milea takes a single step back as she looks up at the twenty-foot creature and notes the height would be twice that should she rear to her hind legs. The body of the beast is covered with blonde wolf fur to protect her back, white and green dragon scales cover her legs and stomach. Milea sees the swishing of the very long and thick tail showing agitation. A tuft of hair is proofed up on end aiding in displaying Roathis' agitation. The beast growls as steam comes from her blanketing the sorceress. Milea blows the fog away with the aid of a mystical breeze.

"Bitch," Roathis snarls, steam, and black flame flicker from her snout.

"I would call you the same," Milea retorts, backing up a little. "However, in your current state, it may actually be a compliment."

Milea retreats, walking backwards as she keeps an eye on the dragon wolf. Her back touches a very sturdy stone column causing her to mentally swear as the beast stalks closer to her. Roathis claws dig into the floor to create grooves in otherwise impenetrable stone. The ears of the great beast shift a little and focus along with the eyes on her prey. Bright red light burns within the pupils of the large orbs right before she lunges forward with the intent to snap the woman in one gulp. Milea dodges, jumping onto the head of the beast much to Roathis' surprise.

A howl of anger escapes Roathis as she shakes her head and tosses it feverishly. Milea cusses a few times as she manages a climb to the hairy back of the beast. The sorceress drops a second set of unkind words as she grabs the blonde fur when Roathis starts to buck and turn, twisting in the air with barks and bellows of frustration. Roathis emits a sound of frustration as she bounces, hops then runs run around the room, bucking and kicking to get the woman off her back. Milea bears down and holds on as best as she can. Her grip slips a little causing her to slide back. She bites back her words as she reestablishes her grip to prevent falling off the galloping beast.

Roathis stops running and starts to wiggle, standing on her hind legs as she twists agitatedly to get the pest off her back. Milea holds on tight, refusing to let go then gasps when the dragon-wolf falls to her side rolls. Milea jumps off the beast, landing a distance away in a slight crouch and stands when she sees that Roathis is rolling her way. Milea tumbles to one side then gets back to her feet just in time to face her rising opponent.

"I'm going to grind you in my teeth, slowly," Roathis growls as she stalks the short distance to her opponent.

"I've had worst nightmares to deal with than that," Milea assures, backing from the creature. "There is no Wolf Eltis or Tragin that I am aware of." She is once again back to a column.

"Foolish mortal," Roathis cackles. "The sacrifice I am using in life was a wolf changeling, a Waere from the land of Solis. She was gullible enough to think that, in marking and killing herself she would be immortal. As I consumed her, she figured out the truth and regretted her decision."

"What in all Ublivorion have you gotten yourself into, Milea," the sorceress scolds herself.

The muzzle of the dragon-wolf draws back the skin revealing several large teeth, dripping with plenty of saliva. Milea is quick to cast a teleportation spell. Her body fall into a rain of golden dust as Roathis snaps at her. Instead of contacting flesh, which is expected, Roathis bites through the column she thought she trap Milea on.

The sorceress reappears behind her opponent as Roathis spits out the column and sneezes twice from the dust. Milea scans the room and spies a link of chain upon the rubble. She glances behind to see Roathis turning. Milea hurries over to the rubble and grabs the longest piece of chain she can find. Roathis snarls, her eyes flashing in her anger as she lifts her large head up high then lowers it with a mighty bellow.

Black flames escape from Roathis mouth and make a beeline straight for the sorceress, burning a deep hole in the floor as it careens to the destination. Milea cussed, dropping the chain as she holds up both hands casting a spell to divert the flames and shield from the effects. The fire hit the shield and arches to the ceiling, bouncing once more and screaming back towards Roathis, slamming upon her rear end. The dragon-wolf howls in pain and anger as she bucks then rolls to put the flames out, knocking down a few more columns resulting in a small quake as the stability of the room became compromised.

Milea quickly picks up her chain as Roathis return to her feet and charges madly towards her. The sorceress holds her ground as her opponent nears, the links on either side begin to multiply at a rapid pace to lengthen and strengthen the metal. Roathis opens her mouth wide allowing Milea to place the chain within the front of the mouth then disappear before the maul could snap shut. Roathis raises her head and is about to spit out the chain only for it to quickly wrap around her muzzle. Milea once again appears on Roathis' back this time with a rein of chains that she tugs to tighten the links around the dragon wolf's mouth and hold it completely shut.

"That takes care of the maul," Milea says with a bit of pride.

Surprised by the event, Roathis once again jump, buck and wiggle to get the woman off her back, her gurgle howls and cusses barely heard. With an angry sound, she starts to run at top speed, the walls and columns in the room whirl by at break-neck speed. Milea grips both the chain and the wolf's fur as she holds on for dear life as she calculates the seconds before Roathis will once again roll. Milea did spot a solid wall that Roathis is galloping towards.

The dragon-wolf then turns away from it as she continues to try and shake the sorceress off. With a snarl and a mighty tug, Milea forces the galloping beast to turn her head to face the wall once again. Milea makes sure they are head on to the wall then cast a spell of darkness. The lights go out so fast that Roathis did not have time to make out the wall now. Milea jumps from the back of her mount and levitates as Roathis careens forward and comes to a sudden halt as she rams into the wall. The head first impact causes the entire room to vibrate and the wall to fall onto the downed dragon-wolf, burying her. Milea takes care as she lowers to the ground and dust her arms off, breathing a little quick from her ordeal.

"That," Milea said then takes a step back when the wall begins to move. "Time to go."

The winds increase to tornadic strength, stirring anything that is loose inside of the room. Milea casts her teleportation spell making a quick swirl-like motion to fade from the room. The winds die down as Roathis bust free from her prison with a mighty roar, once again in her human form. She glares at the spot she senses the sorceress disappears from and concentrates to bring the woman back from wherever she traveled.

A sound of anger and frustration echoes in the chambers as she could not bring the mortal back from her destination. Roathis sneers as she glares across the room to the staircase, convinced that A'drianis assisted the woman, especially with the darkness. With her hands flexing ever so slightly, as if she wants to choke someone, Roathis turns and heads to a back room. She vows to deal with A'drianis once and for all.

Sonja and Zaria finally reach the top of the stairs, a little winded from the long climb to get out. Once they exit, they pause with slack jaws at the activity. The room is full of flying bodies as well as the sound of hardy battle cries and fists smacking against flesh. The various cries and unclean words echo throughout the halls of the dark temple along with several stray spells or spears launch at each other. Sonja dodges, ducks an opponent then tosses him towards a wall and looks about.

Several men cry out in either pain or victory as they battle their enemy win or lose. It is mostly the warriors of Kaidar that are victorious although a few of their lesser fighters did end up hurt. Zaria ducks then punch the man that is after her. He doubles over and falls to one side, holding his groin. Both Sonja and Zaria spot Vicki at the same time.

Although she is doing well, she did not appear to be in top condition for this battle. Sonja then notes Neil not too far from his sister. He appears to have been recently separated from her and is trying to get back to her. The l'vane man decapitates his enemy in his frustration then puts his sword away and once again resorts to hand-to-hand combat.

"I'll go help Vicki, you go and do something with Neil," Zaria instructs.

"Ok," Sonja answers and hurry to her destination.

Metal crashes against metal creating sparks from the forced union and small flames that are put out by the multitudinous amount of stomping feet that fill the room. Neil growls and tosses the man he is fighting against a wall full of spikes and seems pleased when the victim is skewed upon them. An angry shout behind him causes Neil to turn and grab his katana's hilt. His opponent falls all the sudden. Sonja grins at her friend causing Neil to let out a sound of pure joy and hug the girl despite the obvious danger they are in. Zaria takes care of a few of the men that corner Vicki and receives the same warm reception from the woman.

A handful of the Warriors of Kaidar note the reunion and the shouts from the town watch that is heading their way. The hand full of senior warriors made a call to their fellows to retreat and the Warriors of Kaidar oblige almost as fast as they attacked. Neil and Sonja joined the hasty retreat of the warriors, blending in with them as they pour out the door. Vicki follows her brother with Zaria keeping up easy to make sure that the woman makes it safely out of the dark temple.

The warriors all hop over the double doors that are destroyed when they were kicked off their hinges. A few lands on the doors to make sure the ones underneath are still unconscious. Once they clear the threshold, the Warriors of Kaidar as well as those they assisted scatter, their trails disappearing in the dust. The worshippers of Roathis exit their temple to peruse their enemy but find them long gone. Neil picks up his pace towards the marketplace with the girls easily keeping up with him.

"Sonja, are you alright," Neil asks barely slowing his head-long run into the marketplace.

"I'm ok. Mom's not happy though," Sonja said. "We all might be in trouble."

"Not comforting," Neil admits. "But I'm just happy that you're alive, Kiddo."

"Alive and not Roathis," Sonja remarks and hops over a group of frightened cats. "She's evil."

"Very much so," Vicki agrees. She slows down as her vision begins to blur. "How far to the ship?"

"Not far. Hold on," Zaria said.

As the group runs past the temple of A'drianis, the shadows fold upon them briefly. The sound of dirt changes to that of wood as the shade is released just as fast. Neil swears and slides right off the pier into the water making a mighty splash. Sonja slides but manages to jump and catch hold of the side of the ship, hanging onto it so she would not end up as wet as Neil. The girl then climbs up the side to get to the deck just in case her grip slips. Vicki is relieved that she slows down enough to stop at the edge of the pier. She bends down with her hands upon her knees to keep the world from spinning out of control. A'drianis reverts to Zaria as she stands next to Vicki and assists Neil out of the water.

"Ok, how did we get here so fast," Neil demands.

"We had to get here before Milea did," Zaria said.

"Ahoy," Maya calls and waves from the deck. "Welcome back, everybody." Neil looks up and waves at Maya, figuring she is the one that teleport them to the ship.

"Is Milea back yet," Zaria asks, pulling herself up onto the deck. She is followed by Neil and Vicki.

"Not yet, I'm sure she will be any minute now," Maya assures. "Vicki, you've got a nasty bump on your head."

"I'm feeling a bit tired too," Vicki agrees.

"No sleep for you until we figure out what damage that bump has done to you," Maya scolds. "Go and sit by Brion, he's been a little nervous since he's been back." She watches as Neil and Vicki go to sit with Brion. "Sonja, what happened?" She turns to her niece.

"Let's wait till Milea gets back," Zaria suggests. She gazes into the distance toward Temple Avenue. "Come on, Milea. You got three more minutes."

The night sky is clear and twinkles with the light of the stars. The moons seem to dance in the veil of the night with one full and the other half way. Their position reminds Sonja of two eyes, one wide with wonder the other half close with sleepiness. The girl smiles at her thoughts as the winds start to rustle her hair. Neil senses the winds and scowls, standing to look out at the seas and note that there is no storm for miles and the water is moving very gently.

The winds explode to a gale force prompting all three of the companions to drop unhealthy words as a mystical tornado spin in the middle of the ship. Maya folds her arms as red lights reach for the sky. The dark sorceress stands in front of the weather phenomenon unaffected. The winds blow out, rustling the hair and clothing of everybody on the deck as Milea appears upon the ship. She lowers her arm and takes in her surroundings, noticing first the solemn group of three standing near the sleep cabin.

"From that power surge I felt, I thought you might have exploded," Maya said, approaching her twin. Milea turns and faces her. "How do you feel?"

"I'm fine," Milea informs simply. "Roathis is a pain."

"Whoa, wait... Roathis," Maya asks. "What in Ublivorion were you doing with Roathis?"

"A brief skirmish," Milea admits. "I managed to escape before she tossed the wall off of her."

"You battled that seed of evil herself," Maya scolds. "By yourself. Are you out of your damn mind?"

"At the time, I was a little upset," Milea meets her sister's gaze, "and you need to calm down, sister. I am still a little agitated and am not very tolerant of a scolding right now."

"Alright," Maya takes a deep breath and lets it out. Her shoulders relax a little. "I am just concerned, Milea. Roathis is more than just a pain in the ass."

"Oh, trust me she's a powerful pain," Zaria assures. "Apparently she just got back not too long ago, so all of her abilities didn't wake up."

"That's good," Maya said in relief. "Milea. Don't be too hard on the group."

"I won't be," Milea says and scans them thoughtfully. She folds her arms, returning her gaze to her sister. "My concern is Sonja. She was chained to Roathis' altar." She watches as Maya rein in her initial reaction.

"Ok. I'll take a look at the girl," Maya relents as calm as she could.

"Thank you," Milea said as her shoulders relax a little more. She makes her way over to the trio. She is stopped when Sonja hurries over and give her a hug. Milea gently brushes the girl's hair before she crouches down and looks her in the eye. "Go see Maya. She needs to take a look at you."

"Yes, Màthair," Sonja mumbles. She lowers her gaze and walks to her aunt.

Maya brushes Sonja's hair and tells the girl to relax while she takes a deep look into her. The girl shifts a little then did as she is instructed to, staring into her aunt's eyes. Maya speaks softly as she searches for anything that would indicate that Sonja is affected by the altar. She is relieved when she finds nothing but concern creeps in as she notices the girl has something awakening inside of her. Maya makes a curious sound bringing Zaria over to have a look as well. Milea returns her gaze to the trio and studies them from afar until she decides to go and check on them, especially Vicki since she is the worse off of the three.

A warm breeze surrounds those aboard the *Lady of the Night* as Neil stands and uses his fingers to comb back his wet hair, his clothing still clinging to him from his surprise dunk in the ocean. Other than that, he is fine and the best fit out of the trio. Vicki groggily gets to her feet, feeling the effects of the battle and her concussion as her body nearly gives out. She is steadied by her worried brother and pats his shoulder in reassurance. Brion rises from leaning against the rails and takes a couple of steps forward, clearing his throat to defend his companions from the sorceress.

"Brion, it's ok," Milea said. "I am just here to check on you. All of you. You seem to have a few cuts upon your arms and legs. I see Maya tried to wrap them for you."

"Safe to say that Lady Maya is not good with healing," Brion offers with a kind grin. "Though I do appreciate the bandaging." He motions to the tied cloth around his arm and thigh.

"Magical healing, no," Milea gently touches his chin and smiles at him. "She's more a dark enchantress; curses and the like are more her speed." She removes her hand and turns to the next person. "Vicki, I see you have a nasty hickey."

"Not sure how far I fell after escaping from the window," Vicki remarks. "I..." She pauses when Milea touches the sore spot.

"Relax Vicki," Milea said softly. "I am not angry at any of you. I am just very grateful that you are all still alive. Unfortunately, I did not see the blacksmith that started this mess."

"Hrmm," Neil muses, he almost forgot the blacksmith as well.

"Brion, Vicki, Neil. I want to thank all of you," Milea said, removing her hand, "for bringing me the message on time and for giving me information about my opponent. If you did not tell me that she is really Roathis, I would have gone in with a different approach." She pauses and clasps her hands together, bowing slightly to the group. "Neil, I appreciate the insight to involve the Warriors of Kaidar. The many battles that I may have been involved in, I would still be there and who knows what would have happened to Sonja."

"You are welcome, milady," Vicki said. She absentmindedly touches the spot previously sore. The hickey and soreness are both gone. "I... thank you."

"Least I could do. Go rest," Milea said. "Neil, what time are we going to set sail in the morning?"

"An hour after sun up," Neil answers. "The *Dragodu* is now prowling."

"Very well. Zaria, can you make sure they do not find the ship," Milea asks.

"Easy enough," A'drianis' voice echoes in the night. "Sleep tight all. Do not worry about a thing." She chuckles mischievously.

"That's worrisome," Neil points out.

With a sigh, he decides to go to the helm to stand under the stars. Milea flashes a smile and a slight nod of her head then goes to the bow to speak to her sister and daughter.

"So now what," Vicki asks of her brother as she and Brion approach. Several stars twinkle overhead.

"I'm glad that we didn't end up a mess," Brion remarks. "I think I can guess when Milea found out about Sonja. Maya's eyes widened like saucers, and she turned to the marketplace. My guess is that she sensed her twin's mood."

"She might have felt it. I think the entire city did. Neil and I saw it firsthand," Vicki informs. "Her eyes closed; you saw a faint glow about her. The room's air became warm, the tension, very high." She shakes her head. "Let's just say, it is impressive and a warning to those around her." She places a hand upon the wheel. "All because the blacksmith being stupid."

"The blacksmith definitely caused quite a stir," Neil rubs his chin then scowls. "I'll be back in about a half hour." He picks up his katana and leaps off the portside of the ship.

The wood barely makes a sound as Neil lands on the docks. He ties his katana on his waist and travels to the empty marketplace. Those that guard the streets are walking around lazily as if they are not happy to be up and didn't pay attention to anything. Neil easily avoids the men by hopping up onto a tent top and waiting patiently. Once they are gone down the street, he leaps off of the tent and continues his way.

The quietness of the streets is interrupted by the banging of a hammer against metal. Neil passes the alley until he hears the sound then doubles back and disappears into the gloom. A'drianis shakes her head, figuring that either Neil or Vicki would go take care of the blacksmith. Milea notes Neil's departure from her vantage point then smiles a little. She has decided to take care of the blacksmith in the morning but feels that this is somehow a better way of dealing with him.

"Bards my eye," A'drianis scoffs to herself. She is standing in the crow's nest to keep a vantage point for the night.

"It appears that Neil is going to go talk to the blacksmith," Milea observes, approaching Vicki and Brion. "Will he be alright?"

"Neil's fine," Vicki dismisses the concern, "if he needs help, the blacksmith will scream for it." She watches Sonja get shooed into the sleep cabin by her aunt. "I think the little tyke reminds Neil of home. He gets attached to those who remind him of such things."

"She's a ball of energy," Brion acknowledges of Sonja. "I'm glad she's alright."

"As am I," Milea said with great relief. "Vicki, would you mind coming into the cabin with me? Sonja has a few questions about I'vane that I cannot answer."

"I'll do what I can," Vicki said. "What do the questions involve?"

"Mostly 'where' and 'how' questions," Milea said and places a hand upon her shoulder. "I'm sure you can handle it."

"Good night, ladies," Brion said to the women as they walk away. "I'll sleep on deck."

The ringing of a hammer echoes into the night driving many dogs to bark in anger at the noise level. Many of the villagers are so use to this and the very well-versed obscene words that accompany from the blacksmith's forge that they stay asleep for the most part. Leon growls and slams another sword into the fire, angry that it did not turn out the way he wants it to. The metal heated up slowly, as the flames start to die back from the lack of wood and air.

Angry and impatient, Leon throws his hammer onto the table and starts to go into his home. Perhaps his wife will be easier to heat up than the obvious cheap metal that he has purchased from a foreign source. He vows he will never use the man's metal ever again and will demand his money back as soon as he sees him at first light. Leon reaches for the door only to pause and take three steps back. Neil walks out of the doorway causing the man to be surprised at first then angry when he recognizes the intruder.

"What in Ublivorion are you doing here, boy," Leon demands. "You're trespassing."

"Shhh... or you'll wake your child," Neil warns. "My sources tell me you are the origin of the hoopla that happened during the day." He seems calm and good-natured. However, there is something deadly about his eyes.

"Out of here, boy. I've no time for you," Leon sniffs and grab Neil with his left hand. "Get out of here before I spank you."

"Same hand you grabbed my young friend with, most convenient," Neil said.

An owl shrieks somewhere in the village as Neil breaks free of Leon's grip. The blacksmith cusses and picks up a weapon with his left hand eager to kill at least one of the creatures he hunted today. Neil grins and back up to avoid the swing, then duck left and right. The I'vane is now standing next to the forge, quickly bringing the flames up as he stomps upon the billows. Neil once again artfully dodges the blacksmith and tosses in a piece of wood for the furnace.

Leon yells and lunges forward, stepping on the bellows and causing the flames to rise even higher. Neil is once again standing in front of the furnace and with a quick glance note the white-hot piece of metal within. Leon charges his opponent, determined to take his head off. Neil moves one side and brings out his weapon, swinging it twice. The blacksmith's weapon and the hand that holds it fall to the ground creating a bloody pool. Leon screams in pain, falling to his knees and holding his wounded limb.

Neil continues to move, picking up a pair of tongs and grabbing the white-hot sword from the furnace. In one swift motion, he slaps the flaming metal against the open end of

Leon's arm, searing it close. The smith's high pitch screams of pain break through the night, alerting all his neighbors for blocks around. Neil drops the now cooled weapon taking a couple of steps back then jump straight into the air, disappearing into the darkness. Leon stays upon his knees, holding his wounded arm while people gather around. Many of his neighbors either cuss or faint upon seeing the sight.

"Who did this to you, Leon," a merchant demands of the blacksmith. "Say something, who did this?" The blacksmith whimpers a sob as he rubs the nub that used to be his hand.

The sounds of concern people fill the night air with many of them combing the different stands and neighborhood in search of the one who wounded the blacksmith. Neil grunts as he finishes climbing up the side of the ship and hauls himself onto the deck. He turns towards the marketplace noticing the merchants and the security guards running around in a madden manhunt. They shout in anger to each other as if trying to figure out whom or what might have attacked the smithy. Many of them claiming it may have been ghosts or spirits of the three they chased earlier in the day.

Neil chuckles a little inwardly as he picks up a cloth and cleans his blade. He swings it twice and sheathes it as he turns to go rest. He ends up jumping at the sight behind him. Milea smiles at the man then nods her thanks to him as she walks pass towards the sleep cabin. She pauses to check on Brion noting that he is sound asleep, his wounds healing nicely. Milea then stands and look over her shoulder at Neil with another nod of 'thank you' to the l'vane man before she walks into the cabin. Neil utters words of relief to know that the sorceress is no longer angry, an education he will not forget.

"Tough night," A'drianis asks from the shadows causing Neil to turn to the source as he pulls his blade. He sees nothing. "How's the blacksmith. I think I heard him screaming."

"Nothing a little medicine could not fix," Neil said cautiously as he looks about. He did not see the owner of the voice. "Zaria. Are you alright, you sound a little different?"

"Nighttime air in my lungs," A'drianis chuckles. "Get some rest, Neil. No one will find the ship as long as I'm around." She purrs the statement. "Just friendly warnings if you go into the sleep quarters. Maya is sound asleep and will possibly send you to shake hands with Oswind before she fully awakes. I'd not go in there where I you."

"Oh, I see," Neil rubs his chin. "I'll take my nap at the helm." He sheathes his sword.

A'drianis watches as Neil finally sits down with his back against the post of the wheel, facing out to sea as if staring at his destination. Neil draws one knee to his chest, the other drops to the side with his sword resting next to it. He lowers his head and takes a deep breath in, slowly letting it out as his head drops a little. The angry shouts of the townsfolks soon start fading as they give up searching for their quarry tonight.

A'drianis stretches and cloaks the entire vessel in a shadow of darkness with a little grin. The ship is, after all, named the *Lady of the Night.* Still, in her vantage point of the crow's nest, A'drianis sits back and ponders the happenings of the night as the other ships groan in a light wave that caresses the docks. She jumps out of the nest landing as silent as a cat on the deck and heads toward the bow of the ship.

"Hmm," A'drianis muses. "Blacksmith is going to recover and tell them what he saw…. I'll just have to make sure they can't follow us out, eh?" She pauses when she reaches her destination and looks down at the figurehead. "Keep an eye on things while I'm out. I shan't be long." She folds the shadows upon herself.

Several ships rock in the gentle current of the ports left unattended and to their devices. Thin clouds cover up the twin moons casting a darken shadow upon them all as A'drianis reappears standing on the deck between all the ships. She looks left then right and grins as she goes over to one of the closest ships, walking straight to the hull above the water as she uses the shadows as a surface. The water lick at the bottom of her feet, yet she keeps herself from falling as she pulls a single nail out of the board of the ship.

A'drianis wait and is pleased to see the wood still bends to the shape of the hull and is held in place by glue and age. She chuckles to herself and raises her hand causing all the nails that hold the legion of ships together to exit their holes and float like a perilous cloud above the docks. A'drianis walks back to the solid footing and stands there a moment as she ponders where to put them. Her eyes light up as a mischievous feline-like grin plasters her face when she thinks of the perfect location for her prize catch and disappears in a wrap of shadows.

A'drianis reappear just outside of the Temple of Roathis and stays back in the shadows so that she cannot be seen or sensed. The doors to the temple are still open prompting a little bit of curiosity to come from the shiadokat. She creeps up the stairs and peeks into the main room. There is no one in this part of the temple, all the worshipers are chanting somewhere down the hall. Nearly bursting with excitement, A'drianis once again takes cover in the shadows and pushes her prize into the main room with the flick of her wrist. The rusted and old pieces of metal tinkle as they land, filling up the floor. The sound of which causes the chanting to stop.

"Perfect," A'drianis purrs and disappear as several members of the temple come into the main room and shout in surprise.

CHAPTER TWENTY-TWO

The Storm Returns

Predawn lights up the sky with pink and lavender hues to highlight the small thin clouds that drifts by. A'drianis sits in the crow's nest and stretches as she once again reverts to the form of Zaria. A large grin plasters her face as she jumps down to the deck, eager to watch as the townsmen discover the little secret, she has in store for them. She turns as Brion exits the hull, he awakened earlier to search out the maps and bring them up to the deck. Neil grumbles as he stretches, loosening stiff muscles as he did not move at all last night and slept in a seated position.

The captain looks up as Brion calls to him and both sit down to study the maps, ignoring the door as it opens allowing Maya, Vicki and Sonja to exit. Neil ponders over the routes. He ends up settling on one that is the shortest and lest hazardous than he navigated and recent days. The one thing they will have to worry about is a band of pirates known to hunt the seas. Vicki peaks over her brother's shoulders then takes the charts away from him to look at them as Neil announces his route to the masses.

"Not so sure about this route, brother," Vicki said. "There is a spot here that is a ship's graveyard. With the storm antagonist out there, are you sure we can avoid this? Sereas come with the storms in ship graveyards."

"Oh, don't worry. I can avoid that area," Neil promises. "We will be leagues away from it and you'll not even notice."

Vicki gives her brother a doubtful look as he runs his fingers through his hair and smiles at her. Sonja shouts out as she spies the approach of several Warriors of Kaidar heading their way. The young men are running at top speed with each carrying a large sack upon his back. Sonja and Vicki decide to hop down to land upon the docks to greet the travelers as the trio of warriors arrives. Neil gives in to his curiosity and jumps off the ship, landing next to his sister. Zaria yawns and stands at the port side to keep an eye on the group as well as the townsfolks, expecting an event any minute now. Maya sits on the rail and looks down with a smile. She watches Sonja approach one of the six-foot men and touch his arm.

"Warriors of Kaidar," Neil addresses the young men. "You seemed very eager to get to us. What do you bear upon your back?"

"Sensei told us to bring you supplies," one of the warriors offers. He places the pack upon the dock. It makes a thumping sound.

"We have water, dried meats, cheese, and a few hardy vegetables in these bags. Please take them," a second warrior said.

The third warrior smiles down at Sonja as she touches his arm and seems a little shock that the muscle is real. He flexes it prompting Sonja to move back, the reaction causing the young warrior to laugh a little. Maya smiles at the transaction, her mind wonders a little as she wonders what her sister would say or do in this situation. Maya grunts a little when Zaria gently bumps her to get her attention. The dark sorceress turns to the shiadokat then redirects her attention out to the marketplace.

Maya's features go from calm to a mask of shock as she sees the streets of the marketplace filling up fast with armed and angry residents. Maya swears, perhaps the blacksmith has regained enough of his senses to tell the townsfolks the identity of the one that harmed him. Maya shakes her head, wondering why Neil didn't kill the man. Zaria scratches her neck and yawns when she sees that most of the angry mob is carrying weapons of wood or iron. The rest are armed with nooses and torches as they march straight for the docks. Maya speaks a quiet prayer as she turns her attention back to the docks, noticing that the entire group is unaware of the danger that approaches.

"I see," Neil said. "Tell Sensei, thank you. We appreciate the gift." He picks up a bag and grunt. It is three times heavier than what he expects it to be. "Strong boys."

"Shall we take them on board for you, Sir Neil," one of the young men asks with a look of concern in his features.

"I got it," Neil waves the concern away. The bag he lifted disappears along with the rest of them. "What the...?"

"I did that. Hurry up and get back on the boat," Maya calls down. "We have a large mob on our hands. They are headed this way." The shouts and curses of the mob reach the ears of those on the dock.

"Oswind Teeth," Neil swears as his attention goes to the marketplace.

"The last person whose smile I want to see right now," Vicki climbs aboard the ship at a quick speed. Neil did the same.

"Sonja," Maya calls to her niece. "Hurry Up!" She did not see Zaria merely smile watching the crowd draw ever nearer.

"Thanks, guys, for being part of my rescue," Sonja said the group of warriors. "I hope we see each other again someday." She beams a shy smile at the group.

"Perhaps when the world is a little safer, milady," the first warrior said. His companions either grin or blush from Sonja's words. "Do you need a boost back onto your ship?"

"No, I got it," Sonja said. "Take care!"

The shouts of the townsfolks echo as the numbers increase in size and volume. Sonja takes a step back then jumps up and with a backflip, lands on the deck of the ship. The group of warriors applauds her efforts then waves as the Lady of the

Night unfold the sails and catch the winds. The ship lifts anchor and turns while Sonja waves back at her rescuers then watches as the men turn, picking up speed to hightail it up the pier. Zaria takes a step to stand next to the girl and watches as the men avoid the mob by going through or over a majority of them. The acrobats of the Warriors of Kaidar did not deter the mob with heavy footsteps echoing as they reach the docks.

"Too bad your mom is asleep, kiddo," Zaria places a hand upon Sonja's back. "I think she would have been proud to hear those words from you."

Seagulls and other birds cackle in the sky above as Neil calls out orders to the ship, Brion at the helm to help steer. Vicki secures various areas as the ports start to shrink behind them, the *Lady of the Night* ramping up to a nice pace. Sonja grins up at Zaria then follows the shiadokat's line of sight to the docks when she hears a soft snicker emit from the woman. The villagers still shouting and swearing all climb aboard their ships and untie them from the port.

The pursuing vessels get a sizable distance from the docks then start to sink under the weight of the villagers. Several more ships did not make it out as they fall apart before starting, the nails and glue that held them together, gone. The tone of the swearing changes to screams and bitter language that is still recognizable to those aboard the *Lady of the Night* as the ship continues to distance from Tenze. Neil gawks at first then laughs out loud when he notices the many villagers swimming back to shore or curse at the departing vessel. Sonja gawks then turn to the shiadokat as the woman makes a sound of satisfaction.

"Yep... all in a night's work," Zaria stretches. "I'm going to take a nap."

"Well deserved," Maya applauds. "Sleep tight, shiadokitty." Zaria waves at the nickname and goes into the sleep cabin to get some rest.

The open ocean beckons as the sails spread to maximum capacity, capturing every inch of wind that hits them to speed the ship to her destination. Tenze port is soon a dot on the horizon behind them as the *Lady of the Night's* figurehead points towards home. A sound of delight lifts from the wood as if it is singing merrily upon the breeze it creates. Vicki breathes in deep and slowly lets it out as she extends her arms. The winds caress her a little. She turns when Sonja makes a sound of joy; having open one of the three bags the Warriors of Kaidar gifted them.

The girl is doing a little jig as she discovers the first bag is full of darkened dragon fruit. The second bag is a vessel to carry a large amount of water, enough to get them home if properly proportioned. The third and last bag holds a great deal of jerky as well as back up flasks of water, just in case. Sonja takes one of the fruits over to her aunt as Neil rummages through the bag of the jerky. Maya turns when her niece calls to her and then makes a gleeful sound upon seeing the darken dragon fruit. The fruit is larger than what she remembers from the Temple of Light in the boiling seas and deeper in color. Maya bites into the item and mumbles her approval of it. Sonja grins and turns to go awaken her mother but pauses when Maya cautions her.

"Your mother spent a great part of the night trying to communicate with Keela with no success," Maya warns. "In truth, she just drifted off to sleep just a little while ago."

"Right, I'll take the bags downstairs to store them," Sonja acknowledges the warning.

"That's my girl," Maya agrees and brushes back her niece's locks. She lollygags to the bow of the ship, nibbling her snack as Sonja does her chore.

The morning fold to the afternoon without incident as the *Lady of the Night* hums in the sunlight. Neil sends his sister to the sleeping cabin to rest and takes the wheel in her steed. A few dolphins and baby sea dragons play in the large wake of the ship, jumping every once in a while, to provide a show to Sonja. The girl cheers from the crow's nest at the acrobatics of the ocean creatures. Brion sits down upon a rope and watches the ocean and is pleased to note that his sea sickness is under control. Thunder resounds from over the horizon in the direction of travel.

Neil frowns at the weather; the storms have not been kind upon the seas of late. Maya folds her arms and mutters a few unkind words at the storm sensing something very wrong about it. Lightning flashes as the dark green and black clouds roll into view. A small tingle goes down Maya's spine resulting in an involuntary shutter as she shakes it off and frowns even more. The sensation is what she feels when a Tragin is around, but where would it be? She stares at the storm a little more. Brion stands and begins to coax the ship to prepare for the change in the weather. He shouts up to Sonja and is acknowledged by the preteen as she shimmies down the mast to get on the deck. Maya mutters a few more words as she turns from the bow and head to talk to the captain.

"Neil," Maya relocates to stand next to the captain, "is there a way to avoid this approaching storm?"

"It depends on how big it is," Neil said. "We could try sailing around it, or we could drop anchor and wait it out."

"No.... dropping anchor would be a mistake," Maya turns towards the bow. "I'm going to wake up the others."

The winds whistle a little as Neil turns the wheel to the left, the direction is obeyed by the ship. Maya nods as she comes to an understanding and starts down the stairs, perhaps she and Milea can combine their abilities to muster enough wind to get them out of the encroaching weather.

A powerful shock to her system brings Maya close to her knees as she grips the rail leading down the stairs. She looks up just in time to see a pair of beautiful eyes glare back at her from the distance in front of the bow. Maya swears as she descends to the main deck and the eyes flash.

The sky goes from blue to a raging storm instantaneously with a strong wind slamming into the Lady of the Night. The ship moans and groans in surprise as it struggles to keep upright in the gales. Neil unleashes his strong knowledge of obscene words at the sudden appearance of the storm. His muscles strain as he tries to turn the wheel to get out of the weather. A strong gust of wind knocks Brion down and slides him across the deck until he finds something to keep him from going overboard. Sonja helps him stand up. Rain begins to pour in bucket loads turning the deck into a slippery arena in seconds.

"This is what happened before," Sonja calls out to her aunt.

"Go get your mom up," Maya shouts back over the roar of the thunder. "Neil, what do I do?" Sonja makes her way to the sleep cabin from the middle of the deck.

"Stow away the main sails," Neil shouts as loud as he could through grit teeth.

The wheel battles Neil as it tries to turn in a direction, he knows to be bad. It leads to the ship graveyard that he promised his sister he would avoid. Maya goes to work with the ropes and jumps back when they snap at her. She chastises the rope with a few angry words then once again grabs it and yanks. The item almost pulls her off the deck yet she manages to keep grounded. Brion follows her example, pulling down on various ropes to draw up the sails and store them. Sonja reaches her destination and holds tight as the ship tilts to one side. The *Lady of the Night* groans from the attack of the weather leaning over to the left side.

Inside the sleeping cabin, the tilt of the ship becomes very acute causing Vicki to fall from her cot with a thump and an obscene verbal expression of surprise. She gets to her feet as the lantern in the room jumps off the desk and crashes up on the floor, spilling oil. It is followed by the desk sliding across the floor. Zaria cusses when she is tossed from her cot by the violent churning of the ship. She manages a semi graceful landing as she scans her surrounding, trying to take in everything at one time. She gasps in surprise and jumps to get out of the way of the desk as it slides in her direction. It goes under her and Zaria lands not so gracefully upon her backside as the ship once again rolls, making the ground very unstable.

Milea, still in her cot, opens one eye and grumbles in annoyance at being awakened. Her mind snaps to alertness when a cot flips in her direction. She raises a shield, bracing as the cot smacks it then goes over her and into the wall behind her. Milea stands as her cot follows the one that she avoided and almost lands upon her rump when the ship rolls again. All furniture in the room scrapes and fly as the tilt of the ship once again flips. Milea cusses as she dodges to the left and pushes a cot away from her. Zaria jumps over the small mirrored desk and makes a more graceful landing although she still stumbles due to the instability of the boat. Vicki catches and tosses the cot that attacks her and then dodges a second. Groans of effort echoing from the wood are drowned out by the deep rumble of thunder.

"What in all Ublivorion is going on," Milea demands.

"Mom," Sonja calls, bursting into the cabin. The wind tries takes the door off. "Something's wrong, we ran into another storm."

"What," The three women all exclaim at the same time.

The ship shifts again as Milea leads the trio out onto the deck. Thunder roars and the churning sea greets them as a blast of wind smacks into the newcomers. Rain transforms the dry clothing into nothing but dripping rags as Zaria gawks at the transformation. The shiadokat makes a strong exclamation when a powerful tingle rides down her spine at the same time a lightning bolt smacks the ocean next to the ship. Milea also feels the sensation and swears as she goes to assist her twin in taming the ropes.

Vicki makes her way to the helm to assist her brother and finds him battling both the boat and the elements. A wave rams into the side of the ship, leaning it over stops just short of rolling. Brion holds onto the rope, swearing at the closeness of the water then hesitates in his language. The faces of several beautiful women smile back at him from within the water, their eyes glowing as he tries to make sense of the situation. The Lady of the Night whines as it straightens up then seems to protest when the backside of the ship is lifted by another wave.

The sudden sharp angle makes those on-board stumbles to the bow of the ship rapidly. Milea grabs hold of a rope then catches Sonja to prevent them both from traveling further to the bow. Vicki swears until her arm is snared by Brion and pulls her closer to his form so that she can grab the rope that he is holding on to. Maya, holding onto her rope, snags Zaria by the back of her shirt before either could take a tumble over the rails. Maya's grip slips causing both to cuss and panic as Zaria snags another rope. Maya continues to hold onto the shiadokat.

The ship rolls over the wave and straightens back up as another wave slams into the starboard side, turning the vessel into a different direction. Water gushes over the deck taking all spare ropes and anything else that is not tied down with it. Neil cusses when he sees his katana is among the casualties of the storms, taken into the ocean. Soft laughter is heard upon the howling winds as he focuses his attention on getting the ship as well as the passengers out of the hurricane and not follows his prized possession into the drink. A giant lightning bolt barley misses the ship and slaps into the ocean resulting in a spray of electrified water to rain down upon the group. The resulting surprise is cover by the roar of the thunder.

"You will not escape, pest," A voice whispers upon the wind. Milea, Maya, and Zaria all hear it. *"Not this time."*

The winds pick up speed and the ship is cascading into the unknown as Maya searches her memory about the voice then freezes in place in fear as she makes an unexpected realization. At the same time, a large green lightning bolt careens toward the ship aiming straight at the dark sorceress. Maya did not see it as her eyes widen and her breath quickens from her discovery and did not hear her sister call her name.

Milea swears and erects a shield around the entire ship to deflect the bolt. The lightning connects to the barrier, knocking Milea to her knees and pound upon her. She lets out a frustrated sound as she pushes back, forcing herself to stand and deflect the bolt out into the sea. The lightning shrieks as it slams into the water just behind the ship.

"Maya are you alright," Milea gently shakes her twin. Maya blinks out of her trance. "This storm is like the first one. I think it's the same Tragin. The one that interrupts the communication in the fig forest."

"That's not a Tragin," Maya corrects, her breathing quick. "I think it's..." her voice is drowned out by the roar of thunder.

The storm increases in rage as Neil drops a drunken sailor's oath and orders all sails to stow, hopefully minimizing the effects of the winds. The winds whip around and shred all the sails upon the ship before it could happen. Vicki calls to Sonja to assist in getting the tangle rags tied down so they do not wrap around those on the ship and toss them into the ocean. Brion and Zaria both stumble as the ship tilts again and turns in an odd direction.

Neil battles to once again right the course away from the dreaded destination. An angry sound echoes upon the winds as waves of the ocean toss the Lady of the Night in all directions, confusing those onboard as the sky now looks the same all over. Neil searches for a sign of their location and finds nothing but angry sea. Three more waves hit from different locations, turning the ship to a now unknown destination as the hurricane's strength increases again.

"We have to calm the wind," Milea said to her twin.

"Our antagonist is a lot stronger than either of us right now," Maya protests. "The winds have gone mad, the only thing we have remote control over is the ship."

"Then help me try and guide the ship," Milea retorts.

The strong winds shove the ship in the new direction as the twins dodge various debris to get to the helm of the ship. As they arrive, Neil unleashes words his mother would not want to hear when the wheel breaks free and turns in several directions. Milea steps forward and grabs hold of the item and fights as it twists in protest. Maya also grabs the wheel on the other side of her sister, feeling the *Lady of the Night's* displeasure of the change in captain. Milea and Maya combine their energy and efforts to turn the wheel and the boat in the opposite direction of travel.

Lightning hisses through the sky and strikes the ship, the force of the blow slams into the twin sorceresses and sent them backwards. Maya swears and snags hold of a rope before she could go over the edge and instinctively grabs her sister's hand. When she did not feel any reaction, Maya turns to see that Milea is now unconscious as she took the majority of the mystical blow. With another set of unkind words, Maya pulls her sister into her arms and lifts her upon her shoulder to carry her to shelter as Neil manages to capture the wheel and point it in a direction he hopes is to safety.

"What happened," Zaria inquires as Maya sets Milea down.

"That lightning bolt is actual a powerful spell," Maya explains. "I think our antagonist aimed for Milea more so than me."

"Who the hell is powerful enough to knock Milea unconscious," Vicki inquires bluntly.

"Her name is otherwise a curse but mom calls her Urchaid," Maya answers.

"By my mother's soul," Zaria's eyes widen when she hears the news.

"Incoming!" Brion shouts above the noise of the storm.

A large wave lifts over the ship catching the attention of the women. Vicki stumbles backwards and falls upon her rump as the wave comes crashing down, washing over the deck. Maya grabs hold of her sister and then the handle of the cabin door to keep them both onboard. She keeps her language to herself when she feels small hands grab at her, trying to yank her off the ship. Vicki and Zaria both express swears when they too feel as if someone is pulling on them. The ship pushes through the wave and further onto the path into deeper and darker waters. Brion is not caught under the wave but is out at the bow of the ship and sees the ship once again change direction and several strange items on the horizon. He pauses when he hears female laughter above the winds.

"Am I hearing things," Brion asks. "Sonja?"

"I hear it to," Sonja answers. "What would be singing upon the ocean?"

Thunder sounds like evil laughter as the storm beat the ship mercilessly making the enchanted vessel groan in misery. A sweet melody drifts over the ship's noise and mingles with the wind. It grows in volume until it is heard above the crashing of the thunder and waves. The music surrounds the ship, wrapping it into a smooth and deadly grip. Neil shakes his head as he feels strange affects upon his mind, as if someone is trying to take it over.

A wave slams into the ship's bow, shaking him out of his stupor as he once again holds tight to the wheel. The music once again surrounds the ship as Neil once again relaxes and enjoys the melody. Brion also feels the effects, lowering his arms as he stares straight at the sea. In his mind, he sees someone he treasures coaxing him to her arms just beyond the bow of the ship.

Sonja grumbles at the annoying sound as she securely ties her mother to the sleep cabin's door and a hook just above it meant to carry a torch. Vicki assists with one of the most advance knots she knows to assure that Milea does not slide into the ocean while they are busy keeping the ship afloat. Zaira perks up when she hears the faint music upon the winds and scowls. Her other senses are full of the sights and smells of the storm so she could not pin point any source for the apparition.

"I hear singing..." Zaria speaks to those around her. She turns in time to see Neil abandon the helm and walk to the front of the ship. "Great Gates of Ublivorion!! Vicki!!"

"What," Vicki stands up then pauses when she hears the music. "Sereas!" She cusses up a good streak. "Sonja, make sure that those knuckleheads don't jump ship." She refers to both Brion and Neil.

"Right," Sonja shouts.

Neil and Brion both march to the front of the ship as they obey the call of the Sereas to join them in the sea. Both are lost in their own fantasies, seeing those they desire upon the waves instead of the deadly churning ocean. Sonja uses her daft speed to get to the mast, grab and yank on a few ropes and ripped up cloth then hurries over to Neil first and ties the rope upon his waist. Then to Brion and repeated the exercise of tying the rope around his waist. The girl yanks on the rope and pulls the two entranced men backwards, aided by the rain soaking into the deck so that she can tie them to the main mast. She loops the rope twice and then repeats her knot skills once again. The rope holds, stopping both men in their tracks and keeping them away from the bow of the ship.

At the same time, Vicki gets to the helm of the ship to take the wheel. She hesitates a little when she sees that the wheel itself is twisting and turning with a mind of its own. A determine look crosses Vicki's features as she grabs it with all her strength. She didn't have time to speak any obscene words as she is flipped over to one side and forced to let go.

Vicki rolls out of the way then stands as she blinks in surprise from the impromptu lesson. She studies the wheel for a moment and rolls her shoulders before taking hold of it once more. The item tries to break free again but Vicki manages to keep it under control and plants her feet to prevent from being tossed a second time. The *Lady of the Night* groans in protest as it fights a little, unhappy with the new helmsperson and the storm.

"This ship has lost its mind," Vicki snarls her words.

"Vicki, tell us what you need," Maya calls from the lower deck.

"Anything you can to keep us afloat," Vicki instructs.

The thunder booms in rhythm to the Sereas' song as if keeping in time with them with the volume increasing as they call to the men aboard the ship. Neil strains at his rope, but it did not break. Sonja looks up and gasps when she sees a set of jagged forms in the distance.

Lightning confirms her view, and she calls them out causing Vicki to swear and yank on the wheel, barely turning the ship in time to avoid the rocks. A groan escaped the *Lady of the Night* as it scraps upon the rocks but did not get punctured, the sound of it like nails scraping against a slate board and causes the hair on Vicki's neck to stand on end. The Sereas intensifies their song; the rhythm goes up and down the musical scale, forming a circle of melodious madness.

"For the love of all, will you shut up," Vicki shouts to them. That causes the Sereas' to laugh.

"I detest humored dead sea folks," Maya grumbles.

A purple swirl of light erupts from Maya as she brings up her mystical gifts to combat the attacking Sereas. The ship rocks back and forth violently, breaking Maya's concentration as she drops a profanity. She takes a step back and releases several fouler words when a large wave comes right at the ship. Maya erects a shield to cover the entire boat as the wave slams into the vessel. The force of the water sends the dark sorceress to her knees, yet she holds strong until it stops pounding on the shield. She rolls her shoulders a little sighting that it did not feel good at all. Maya then turns the shield into several nested circles surrounding her as she readies for battle.

The storm did not disappoint as several bolts of lightning are toss at her from the clouds. Maya sends the items in all directions and then reflects the last, and largest, one back from which it came. A sound of surprise or pain echoes a little on the winds then a deep growl of discontent as Maya smirks a little. The ship bucks a little causing all to hold on and Maya to once again loose her concentration as she works on keeping on the deck. Zaria let her dissatisfaction of her muted abilities be known as she looks out ahead and notices there is a very unpleasant surprise for them.

"Ships," Zaria announces. There are an unprecedented number of sunken ships ahead, their bows sticking up from the waters. "We're in a ship's graveyard!"

"What in Ublivorion were you thinking, Neil? I told you to avoid this place, bro," Vicki growls as she pulls on the wheel again.

The *Lady of the Night* just misses the wreckage, once again scraping by as the passengers hold on tight. The enchanted ship screams in pain as hidden sharp edges of the sunken vessels slit into the sides. Vicki does not give a thought of the reaction that Neil will have should they live through this event. Instead, she concentrates on keeping the ship on as steady of a course as possible.

The Sereas song increases in both volume and intensity being joined by the wails of the restless ghosts of fallen sailors.

Vicki shakes her head and is able to prevent crumbling to her knees from the intense pain she experiences with the ghosts. Sonja did fall to her knees and to her rump as she holds her head and shakes it to rid of the sounds of the ghosts. Maya is quick to casts a circle of purple symbols pressing them out to surround the ship. Wood and water hiss as the ruins are burnt into the hull right before the vessel sparkles.

The ghosts yowl as many of them let go and Maya turns her attention to the Sereas themselves. The creatures grin evilly at the dark sorceress and try to drill their song into Maya's mind. Their taunting irritates Maya as she pushes back at the Sereas and literally causing the beast's head to explode. The Sereas reels a little then grows a new head with a more powerful voice. Zaria holds her ears from the intensified musical storm but to her dismay, the melody is now embedded inside of her mind. Vicki gets back to her feet and blocks the music as she hears the roar of water over the music. Maya turns to the front of the ship when she hears the sound and takes a step back from what she witnesses. They are headed to a large mountain of rocks and the water appears to be flowing up.

"What in Ublivorion?" Maya shouts. "Vicki we've got trouble!"

"I see it," Vicki calls back. She yanks upon the wheel yet it does not respond. "Damn It!"

The intensity of the lightning flashes is dwarfed by the roars of the thunder that mix with the Sereas's laughter and song. The giant boulder that the ship careens towards begins to actually grow out of the sea at a very fast pace. Maya swears as the stones reveal a strange creature instead of rocks as first thought. Water spills off the edges of the large creature as it moans, the sound heard loud and clear over the Sereas. The head seems made of rock and pointed like the tip of a tall mountain. Enormous hollow eyes light up as seawater pours from them creating the effect of the strange beast crying. It has no nose but a very large toothless mouth which the ship is making a beeline for.

Maya is the first to unleash unorthodox words and is followed by the rest of her aware companions at the sheer sight of the strange sea-monster. The Sereas song changes, hinting towards harsh notes of anger. Their song is drowned out as the rock creature roars and widens its mouth to present a deep and unescapable cave.

Vicki grits her teeth to prevent any more swearing as she once again yanks on the wheel, it did not respond but instead the ship rushes forward on course for the cave. A large wave of water slams into the back of the *Lady of the Night*, plunging it forward as well as causing the ship to squeak in surprise. Maya stumbles back and accidentally trip over her twin, falling to the floor. Milea groans and opens an eye, fighting against the entity that keeps her asleep.

"We're going to get swallowed," Sonja shouts the obvious.

The announcement makes Milea sit up immediately then holds her pounding head with both hands in order to nurse her headache. A deep rumble exits the cave as it sucks in the water and the ship jump in speed being pull along with the liquid. The storm and Sereas worsen, their music incorporating the emotion of rage within the melody.

The Sereas that Maya decapitated wails as she dives at the ship with claws extended. A blue lightning bolt slams into her, disintegrating the creature. In the next instant, The *Lady of the Night* is inside of the cave creature's mouth. The sounds of the Sereas and the storm die out as the beast close its mouth. The ship seems to accelerate even more as it goes down into the dark caverns.

Vicki now faces a new battle as she grimaces and keeps tight to the wheel in order to control the ship in an attempt not to hit one of the side walls. Neil shakes his head then takes in his surroundings with a sound of shock as he tries to determine their location. He turns his gaze to Brion and sees the same confusion. Neil snaps his rope to free himself as Brion uses his sword to do the same. The speed of the ship increases threefold when the pitch of the downslope steepens considerably. At one point it appears they are heading straight down, the bow pointing towards a pool of water.

Milea and Maya both see a pair of eyes watching them from the water. They are silver-grey surrounded by pools of dark blue, a voice whispers from the pool yet they did not understand it. The noise of the ship and the environment drowns out the words as well as much of the hope for conversation. Vicki makes sure she is heard above the noise as she calls for everybody to hold on as the ship skips over the middle and starts to go up an incline. Water pushes the ship forward as if trying to get it up the slope, at a quick rate. A rumbling sound causes panic or concern to settle over the group. More water pushes at the back of the ship causing it to start hydroplaning, the keel above the water instead of in it.

"Vicki! I see daylight," Sonja announces from the front of the ship.

"That's not a comforting thought," Vicki points out.

The ship races to the end of the tunnel with more and more water pushing it along. When it exits, it leaps into the air several feet then come crashing back down onto the ocean. Vicki glance behind them to see the cave several leagues away shaped like the rock creature that swallowed them in the graveyard. She is not sure if it is another head or if it is the hind part of the same creature. Vicki then turns to see that the ship itself is still intact as well as all of those that are on the ship with her. Sonja announces that land is rapidly approaching them capturing Vicki's attention.

"How do we slow this thing down? Does it have a dragger," Vicki shouts.

"Yes," Milea manages then holds her head.

"Just point," Maya instructs. She notes the direction of her sister's finger.

"Got it," Neil said. He and Brion hurry to the direction indicated.

"Hold on to something," Vicki commands as her own grip tighten on the wheel.

The wind whistles by the ears of the entire crew, the ship's sounds are unheard above the rush of the water. Brion and Neil drop the anchor, and both immediately take hold of the rail of the ship. Maya and Milea follow the example as the metal hit the seafloor. Zaria sits against the cabin wall and tells Sonja to do the same and is please when the girl quickly obeys the command. The ship jerks several times as it slows down, the anchor catching then releasing different rocks and crevices along the way.

A large dragon head peeps out of the water once the ship careens past him. He gawks, taken aback by the speed of the ship before a determined look crosses his features. The dragon dives down and goes after the anchor. The ship continues to skip along until the line is snagged.

The *Lady of the Night* jumps off the water but did not go anywhere. It slammed back down creating a large splash. All aboard, not tied down, are thrown to the deck. Vicki pulls herself up with the help of the wheel as the dragon once again peeks out the waves. He grins and goes back into the water quietly.

"All on deck," Vicki calls out. She watches as various companions got to their feet.

"Sonja, Milea, Zaria and Maya, ahoy," Milea manages as she pulls herself to a seating position.

"Neil and Brion, ahoy," Neil said. He is massaging the back of his neck.

"Ok, what happened," Brion asks rubbing his wrists. "I remember a storm."

"I remember that," Neil agrees. "Then waking up in an earthen tunnel."

"We were attacked by the same Tragin as the storm before," Milea answers. "My head is killing me." She holds her forehead.

"Our attacker is no Tragin, sister. She is Roathis' mother," Maya corrects gently. "Mom calls her Urchaid."

"What? Are you sure," Milea asks as her attention snaps to her sister, taken aback by the information.

"Oh yes, quite," Maya attests her knowledge. "I've run into her a few times. She is imprisoned, thankfully, but that does not stop her from using a few of her abilities."

"There's a beach ahead," Vicki spots. "We can see what damage the storm caused when we get there."

"Damage," Neil perks up. He notes the broken beams and ropes, as well as the scratches along the deck. "What in Ublivorion? Vicki! What were you doing?"

"Keeping us alive, brother. You wandered into a ship graveyard! Ya nutcake," Vicki scolds. "Sereas come with the storm there, you know that. Besides, didn't you promise not to go there when we set sail from Tenze?"

"Damn it, Neil," Neil scolds himself. "Sorry, sis. Thanks for saving our skins."

"You're welcome. But you have to talk to your woman," Vicki steps away from the wheel and sits on the stairs leading to the helm. Her brother plops down next to her. "She defiantly does not like the touch of another woman."

"My woman," Neil asks.

"The ship," Vicki remark.

"So... Where are we," Brion requests, interrupting the siblings for now.

"Don't know. We were sucked in and spat out," Vicki informs. "I think we can let the anchor up now. We need to get to that beach."

"I'll get it," Brion offers as he goes to the back of the ship to retrieve the item. Sonja goes to assist him.

Home Again

The winds once again fill the tattered sails of the *Lady of the Night* pushing the vessel towards the beach a distance away. Neil takes over steering the ship as his sister watches the approach from her seat upon the stairs. Brion sits down next to Vicki and observes the twin sorceresses as they assess their destination. Milea stands up with the assistance of her daughter and holds onto the rail to balance as she studies the approaching shoreline. Zaria balances on the very tip of the bow with her arms folded and her senses taking in all of the sights, sounds and smells of the landscape.

Maya cups her twin on the shoulder then they both pause upon feeling a familiar presence washing over them. It is as if someone is giving them a welcoming hug after a long and hard journey. Sonja goes back up to the crow's nest to get a good look at the landmass and gasps as a look of jubilation spread across her features. The trees that she could see are tall, almost as if they are holding up the sky. The trees themselves sit upon a tall, sheer, cliff with about a mile of beach between it and the sea. Zaria smiles as she spies a figure standing upon the beach waving. The shiadokat waves back then turns to the ship to make the announcement.

"Mom, I think Aunt Frey is on the beach! We're at Selvast," Sonja announces before the shiadokat could say a word. "We're home!"

"Aye, Sonja. That's her," Zaria chuckles. "You've got keener eyes than I thought."

"Sucked in and spat out, eh," Neil grins at the announcement.

"That's what happened," Vicki assures, joining her brother at the helm. "But I think something powerful is behind it."

"And this also concludes our adventure," Brion said, a little sadden as he goes to stand at Neil's side.

Sonja does another whoop of joy as she climbs down from the crow's nest to be at her mother's side as they wave to the figure on the beach. Vicki pouts a little as she watches those that she remembers as clients and not family. She places her hand upon her dagger belt as good memories fill her mind. Neil pats the wheel of the *Lady of the Night* and is rewarded with the warming of the wood and a groan of happiness from the ship. Brion sees the woman in the distance drawing ever nearer as the ship speeds to the shore. The welcoming lady waves again and yells a greeting barely heard above the ocean sounds.

"I'm going to miss them and this journey," Vicki said, "the good times and even the bad."

"I'm sure we will be missed as well," Neil assures as he hugs his sister. "It has been a long trip."

"Where are you two headed after this?" Brion inquires.

"Depends," Neil shrugs and releases his sibling to retake the wheel. "If they send you home, we might join you. That will be interesting." He chuckles when Brion rolls his eyes and smiles.

"Be glad to have you. Both of you," Brion cup the shoulders of the Dresden siblings. "Then my twin and I can drive you crazy next." He laughs when Vicki holds her head.

"I hope not identical," Neil said.

"Oh no, my sister is not identical to me," Brion assures. "Not sure if mom would have liked that."

"I guess this is the year we run into twins." Vicki speculates as they witnessed Maya hug Milea, happily. The red-haired woman grins a weary response.

"I think you're right," Neil boasts. "What better way to start off than helping out legendary twins."

"Why thank you," Brion puffs his chest with pride. "I didn't know my sister and I are legendary."

"And he's already starting," Vicki shakes her head in good humor.

A large sea-hawk cries out in triumph while circling the sky as if to reflect the excitement from those on land and ship. The bird calls out once more as it flies close to the ship, canting its wings to avoid colliding with the sails. Zaria feels the bird's wings brush her as it flies past, elevating its flight pattern as it flies toward the interior of the forest. Not long after the bird's departure, the *Lady of the Night* sails into the safety of the southern Selvast Forest harbor slowing down to get as close to the beach as possible.

Neil takes a step back watching the wheel turn and the sails change in order to slow the ship down and maneuver the ship. The *Lady of the Night* makes a soft sound as it bumps up against the shore, sails lift and the anchor drops. Sonja did not wait for the ship to stop moving as she jumps down, landing upon the moistened sand of the beach. The girl did a jig and starts to run to the approaching figure.

"Sonja," Milea calls to her daughter. She nods when the girl slides to a stop and turns around. "Mind your manners."

"I think she's just excited about being on solid ground," Maya admits.

The twins watch as Zaria jumps off of her vantage point and lands close to the teen's location. The shiadokat shakes a little then stands from her crouch and places a hand upon the girl's shoulder to speak softly to her. Neil swings out from the ship and is followed by his sister as they disembarked in a similar fashion as the island several days ago. Brion hops off and lands at the same time as the l'vane siblings except he is much closer to the ship. Maya lights up with jubilation upon seeing the Dresden sibling's disembarking then jumps a little when Milea touches her shoulder. Milea shakes her head as they both disappear from the ship. They reappear standing next to Sonja as the rest of the crew line to the same spot. The preteen shifts a little with nervous or excited energy.

The welcoming woman smiles as she finishes her approach to the group and pauses to study them. The woman draws herself up to a height as well as her build equal to that of Milea and focus her light green eyes upon the Dresden siblings first. Her marble color hair, fused with the colors of white, grey and light brown, shift as she then focuses on Brion briefly. A set of grey ears, similar to those of a horse, peeped from underneath her main as she listens to the various whispers of the group. Neil jumps when a portion of her hair moves. He soon realizes that it is a tail also similar to a horse. She shifts one of the shoulder straps of her green toga as her attention turns to the twins.

"Maya, welcome home. I am glad you are safe," the woman said. She smiles when Sonja hurries over and hugs her. "Yes, I miss you as well my little trouble buddy."

"Glad to be safe," Maya agrees with a respectful nod of her head. "We ran into some storms along the way."

"I know," Frey smiles. "Mother made sure you came through this last one alive though." She turns to those she does not know, humored by them. "I did not know I am such a fascinating creature."

"What," Neil blinks, unaware that he is staring.

"Yes well," Brion clears his throat. "You are quite an enchanting lady in such an enchanted place." He assures and bows a little. "Brion Kaiser of Cathalian."

"I am Vicki, this is my brother Neil," Vicki introduces.

"Dresden," Neil adds as he too bows. "We are hired by Lady Milea to help retrieve her sister, Maya."

"It looks like you've done this task and came to Selvast safely. I am Frey, the Eltis of Healing and a Guide to Selvast Forest," Frey smiles as she turns. "If you think I am a fascinating person, wait till you meet my mother." She starts to walk towards the cliff. Sonja takes her hand and walks with her.

The sounds of hidden birds echo in the forest as the strangers, and their hostess meanders down the path to the center of the forest. The many sights and wonders provide interest for the newcomers as they traverse it. Frey waits patiently as the three new friends satisfy a curiosity or two then continue down the way.

Brion studies the species of trees that he is walking through, noting that they are like the ones in Cathalian yet three times or taller and wider than the ones back home. He also takes note that the trees are evenly spaced as if they are planted in a garden whereas the ones at home are wild woods, and grow as they see fit. As Brion is studying the flora, Neil takes in the fauna quietly watching the wildlife in the forest, catching a glimpse of a white unicorn every once in a while.

A group of unicorn foals playfully bounce around a clearing as their grazing mothers stay close to the tree-line. One of the lookouts snorts a warning to those passing by, bringing up the heads of the grazers. Once they know of their discovery, the shy unicorns lift their heads then tails and trot out of sight into the deeper woods. Vicki watches as the unicorn trot out of sight then hesitates when she spots a black unicorn stalking the path within the deep shadows of the woods. This unicorn is taller and more muscular than the ones that fled. The eyes flash red then back to coal black. Zaria pauses with Vicki and sees the beast clearly, assuring her cohort that the unicorn is not going to harm them, she hopes.

Vicki stares at Zaria briefly then returns her gaze to the shadows. The black unicorn is now gone, as if it never existed. The noises of the birds of the forest increase in volume as they drew ever nearer to their destination causing Zaria to fidget with nervousness from the sounds. The shiadokat recollects the various items she needs to disclose to the Guardian of Selvast forest and did not know how well she is going to take the breaking news.

Especially the news of the Eye of Gaunt which Zaria figures will turn the forest itself on its head. Zaria mutters a little as she dreads to tell of the return of Roathis and the survival of the Underak. Out of all the news, the shiadokat thinks that the survival of this family of necromancers will be the cold icing on a very unappealing cake. Zaria makes a few quiet sounds of displeasure from her memory, which one did she miss to bring this hell around?

The sounds of the forest are not the reason for Maya's nervousness as she keeps glancing towards the northern half of the woods. The woman shakes her head and continues to walk, wrapping her arms around herself as if she is cold as she something tugs at her from that direction. Although she feels it, she refuses to respond to it as horrible memories still haunt her during her unfortunate time in Northern Selvast Forest.

Unlike the woods they walk in now, the North is haunted and cursed with the blood of numerous powerful beings. It is twisted like a nightmare that any weaker person would never wake up from. Maya shivers and then once again shakes her head as she rubs her arms trying to forget her time there. Milea notes her sister's frigidness and places a reassuring arm around her twin.

Maya leans against her sister for both support and warmth as they round a corner.

The noisy flock of birds did not settle down nor did they disburse as the group travels prompting Vicki to look up and around in wonder. She sees no evidence of the singing birds in the many tangled branches of the trees but feels they are following them. Vicki tilts her head as she turns her attention back to the sides, still taking slow strides with her group. a ball of fuzzy light floating to her prompts Vicki to pause as stare at it. The ball meanders through the large trees and onto the path to hover in front of the curious woman and bobs up and down playfully.

Vicki studies the ball, wondering if it is a ghost or some other spirit that she has yet to come into contact with. The ball of light did not behave like a ghost that she is aware off as it starts to shift and stretch its form. Vicki takes a step back and prepares for conflict. The ball of light pauses in its movements. It bobs up and down a few more times then decides to leave in a hurry, fleeing into the deeper woods. Vicki relaxes as she watches the ball of fuzz escape and then turns to see Frey staring after the ball of light. The Eltis' features are stern as if she is scolding someone at first then lighten up when her gaze falls upon Vicki. Frey smiles at the question in her guest's eyes.

"That is a sprite, Vicki. Not a ghost," Frey assures. "Sprites of Selvast forest know better than to bother guests of the Guardian."

"So, no ghost in the forest," Vicki asks

"As far as I know of, no," Frey assures.

"That's true, at least not in this part of the forest anyway," Milea acknowledges.

"Ghosts are in the North," Maya shutters. "Do not go there. That place is evil."

"You sure you'll be ok here," Zaria requests.

"I'm fine as long as I don't go north," Maya confirms. The trees shift ever so slightly, unnoticed by the traveling group.

"As long as you are in this woodland, you have a mighty guardian and she will not let anything happen to you, remember that" Milea assures, placing a hand upon her twin's shoulder and pauses when she sees the clearing ahead. "And here we are."

Through the trees is reveal an enormous clearing with a large spring sitting just off to the side. Beautiful flowers dot the landscape to complement a variety of rock and stone. Light from the sun kiss the trickling waterfall of the spring and lift the spirits of the flowers as well as the travelers. The sounds of the birds have stopped in the immediate area. Their distant calls could be heard coming closer to the clearing as the group pauses. Frey walks into the clearing to look around and relax as she turns to her guests. She waves to them to come in as the birdcalls start to increase again.

Maya is the first to walk into the area and relax, sensing the powerful protection within the space. The sun reflects off Milea's hair as she follows her sibling, the beams of the sunlight enhancing the flame effects of the locks. Sonja jogs into the clearing staying back from the spring, excited about being here. Her body seems to bounce, unable to control a large amount of energy within. Frey's look of concern catches Milea's eye causing the sorceress to turn then make a sound of understanding.

"Neil, Vicki, Brion. It's ok," Milea coaxes her companions to come into the clearing. "You are in the safest spot within Selvast Forest."

"Ok, I'll go in first," Vicki volunteers. She walks into the clearing and pause. "It feels comfortable here."

"I thought I the foolhardy one," Neil grumbles as he follows his sister. "It does feel good. A little abnormal but not threatening. I like it here." Brion is next as he comes into the clearing. His attention goes to the ground.

"The ground has a few tracks I've not seen before," Brion crouches down to study the dirt. "I'm going to guess that this is a unicorn." He touches a cloven hoof print.

"That would be a safe deduction, Lord Brion," Frey offers and smiles when the elf jumps back to his feet. He did not expect the Eltis to be crouching next to him.

"Uh, apologies," Brion offers. Frey smiles and goes to stand near Milea and Maya.

The last person to hesitate to come into the clearing is Zaria as she debates which she'd rather face. Staying in the shadows that she feels are safety or going into the clearing and potentially facing the wrath of a Mother Eltis. Zaria quietly decides to stay in the shadows for right now, not sure if she is ready to face such a force of nature. The branches above the shiadokat start to shift and move, allowing an abundance of sunlight to flood the area. Zaria perks up and looks behind and beyond, noticing that the sunlight is now saturating every bit of shadow she has available to her.

With a grumble, Zaria walks into the clearing and stands with the group, pouting a little. Neil sees the reaction and is about to inquire as to why she hesitated. His curiosity becomes lost when he hears the sound of hooves upon soft dirt. Brion also notices the lighter and softer steps sound as if they are made from a deer. Vicki, on high alert, turns her attention to the path that appears next to the spring. Neil places a hand upon his sister's shoulder when he too notices the path and stares at it intensely as he listens to the increase bird chatter.

"Whatever is coming this way does not seem to have the birds worried," Neil notes as the happy songs continue to resound.

"Those aren't birds," Sonja whisper to her friends. "Those are fae folks. They are excited."

"Why," Brion asks then looks around when the bird noises increase after he spoke.

"That's one reason," Vicki chuckles as the noises increase again.

"It appears that we have a new audience," Neil playfully boasts as the noise goes a level higher.

The songs that echo in the forest and clearing soon start to fade into silence and is replace by the sound of the rushing spring. The sudden halt in activity returns Neil and Vicki to high alert as whatever causes the faes to become silent is very close. It is hard to distinguish if the forest residence's silence means that the creature is friendly or very deadly. Brion informs his companions that the creature that comes this way disappeared along with the songs of the fae. He glances over at Milea and sees that the sorceress is relaxed and compose prompting him to rest his guard assuming that whatever is coming is not a danger. He bumps Neil and motions to their employer causing the l'vane man to return the nod and relax, whispering to his sister to do the same. Vicki is hesitated but eventually obliges her brother's wishes.

Zaria turns to see the trees behind the group shift a little as they open onto a different path. The shiadokat grumbles and turns then jumps a little as a woman steps out of the path next to the springs into the clearing. She is dress in a similar way to Frey with a green and white toga, yet her hair is black as night and fell gently to the ground, combining with a white horse's tail that shifts back and forth. Black horse-like ears stand at attention as she listens to the fast heartbeats of her guests. She scans the group with dark silver-gray eyes, the whites of which are baby blue. Standing at seven feet tall, she towers over those that come to visit, the muscle definition in her arm suggests that she may still be a warrior of sorts as well as a mother.

Milea is the first to bow to the woman follow by Maya, Frey, and Zaria as they paid their respects to the Eltis. Taking the hint, Neil, Vicki, and Brion do the same which seem to please the woman. Sonja, unable to contain her excitement, did a whoop of joy and runs over to hug the woman before Milea can stop her. The embrace causes the tall Eltis woman to smile and stroke the girl's hair even as Milea shakes her head and mutters under her breath a little.

"Mother," Frey straightens as did the rest of the group. "Milea has returned with Maya, and it appears she has found Zaria as well. With them are their guides Vicki and Neil Dresden and Brion Kaiser." She introduces, respectfully.

"I see," the woman said, her voice raspy. She then looks down at Sonja, catching the girl's attention. "You need to learn a little more protocol, young one." She scolds and listens as Sonja blushes as she apologizes. "It is forgiven." She brushes the girl's head again and approached the group, easily breaking Sonja's grip. "Milea, Maya. Both of you look worn." She notices of the twins immediately.

"We are extremely worn, mother," Milea bows her head. "The entire voyage took its toll on me."

"The attack on the Temple of Light and the return voyage wore me out," Maya admits and rubs her arm a little. "I need a good meal, a nice hot bath, and a week's worth of sleep."

"You will get those, in time," Keela assures. "I am eager to hear of your journey, but right now, I must thank the ones that made it possible." She turns to the waiting, and silent, trio.

"Ok, so how do we address a Mother Eltis," Brion challenges his friends quietly as the woman approaches.

"I am going to go with my gut and call her Lady Keela," Neil opts.

"Good gut," Vicki pats her brother's belly. All straighten when Keela arrives in front of them.

"Neil, Vicki, Brion," Keela addresses to the trio. "Do not look so nervous. I will not harm you."

"We are just in awe at being in such a beautiful and powerful presence, my Lady Keela," Neil bows. Vicki and Brion follow his example. The words and gesture cause Keela to smile.

"You have my gratitude. All of you," Keela assures them. "Were it not for you, I do not think Milea would have reached her twin in time. I sensed her hunter, and he has many allies. I, however, cannot ask you to continue. I will provide you the reward that Milea promised as well as transport to whatever destination your travels were taking you before my daughter's urgency. Name your reward, and it shall be yours." She watches as the trio glance at each other in surprise. Neil clears his throat and bows.

"My Grand Lady," Neil chooses his words. "It is a high honor for me at least to have such a gift. The trip, however, has taken its toll and I believe I need rest before I can ask for such a gift."

"I share the same thoughts as my brother, milady," Vicki said. "The last storm, I think I might have injured myself." Keela scans the group one at a time and notes that they did sustain a little injury on their journey.

"I see. Then you can rest here. Frey will tend to your injuries," Keela glances over to her child. Frey bows and straightens. "And I apologize for contributing to your injury. However, my desire to get you out of there took presidencies. I sensed my annoying sibling the first time and shocked me. This second time, I was more prepared." She turns from the shocked sibling. "And you, Brion?"

"For travel, Lady Keela, I want to return to Cathalian. However, not at this present moment. I want to spend at least a few more hours with my new friends. In the morning, when they leave so shall I," Brion said, with respect. "As far as a reward, my lady, I would ask that my original home, Solis, is freed from its current influences."

"Those are," Keela asks in a gentle way. Her attention is focused upon the elf with ears facing completely forward. The tail is swaying just a touch indicating she is in an agreeable mood for now. She also decides she like the sound of his voice.

"I do not know who they are, but I am aware of Jasmine Underak," Brion said. Zaria cusses as Keela blinks in surprise.

"Underak," Keela interrupts the elf and arches an eyebrow. "I thought they were all dead. Tell me..." She turns towards Zaria. "What is this one doing alive?"

"I thought they were gone too, all of them," Zaria contends, shifting with nervous energy. "But this woman is an Underak, I saw her with my own eyes as she wielded the same magic as her ancestors."

"I see," Keela said then calms herself. "Brion, with an Underak in their mists, it will be more difficult to fulfill this wish. Yet not impossible. Have a little patience, and it shall be done in time."

"I understand, my lady," Brion accepts. "There is also a man name Loca of Garad."

Loca did die, that I know," Zaria asserts. "Well, with the Underak alive I guess it's just a matter of time before she returned him." She grumbles.

"We will discuss matters momentarily, Zaria," Keela scolds. She takes a deep breath in and closes her eyes to regain her calm. When she opens them again, she turns to her daughters. "Milea, Frey prepare a place for our guests to sleep tonight. Zaria and Maya come with me." She walks to the path she exited.

"I thought you were my friend," Maya pouts towards Zaria.

"Hey what do you think I feel like," Zaria asks as they follow the woman. "She's my aunt you know."

"I know," Maya agrees. "But she's my mother. I think that's a bit more trouble." They disappear into the woods.

"Milea," Neil rubs his chin, "are you sure you're not an Eltis?" He notes the woman muse the question before smiling at him.

"I'm as sure as I can be," Milea chuckles. "Though Maya and I may have a few minor abilities similar to an Eltis." She admits. Frey scoffs much to Milea's amusement. "My twin sister and I are adopted. We were raised by Keela. My whole life. Maya for a portion before she was stolen." She starts walking again. Her guest keeping up.

"I am Keela's daughter by blood," Frey informs. "Milea and Maya are my older sisters. I have one more, but I've not met her."

"That is Ilandere," Vicki said. "This is getting more and more interesting."

"I did not mean to cause trouble," Brion said as he ducks a low hanging branch.

"No trouble. Except maybe Zaria. But Maya is not in trouble," Milea assures. "Mother just wants to know what they saw and heard at the temple. She will be coming for me next."

"Me too," Sonja runs her fingers through her hair. "Grandma is in a good mood today."

"She is," Milea agrees, "for now at least. Once Zaria is finished, who knows? But right now, we have a forest full with fae to keep at bay."

Filter sunlight caresses the travelers as they head down a second path into the great woods. This time, there is no accompaniment of the birdcalls, although they are still being followed. Milea pauses a little near a clearing to examine it from a distance, judging its suitability. She quietly speaks a few words of discontent, not liking it and moves on as the branches above shake a little as if a group of squirrels is playing among them. Vicki pauses to look inside the clearing briefly seeing nothing out of the ordinary for a forest then follows Milea.

A pattern begins to form among the trees as the group takes in the surroundings. It is as if the trees themselves are columns and walls and they are walking in a giant palace made from the woodland. Vicki hesitates a little and looks down at the green grass and imagine it as a carpet then through a few trees into a clearing and sees that it is more like looking outside at a garden on the left side of the path. On the right side, they seem to be large rooms and are the ones that Milea concentrates on as if she is looking for a suitable guest suite. Vicki turns her gaze up at the canopy of leaves and branches, noticing how they cross neatly creating a ceiling from the elements. The wind rustles the foliage a little but did not shake them loose.

"This is a first for me," Vicki said as she makes a small circle. She continues to walk with her friends. "I've never been to a palace made of the forest in this manner."

"I am thinking the same," Brion agrees. "Some of the halls in Cathalian have columns of stone shaped like trees." He assists the women over a larger root. "For fae, we have my sister. That's quite enough." He admits.

"You're saying your sister is as mischievous as a forest fae," Neil inquires

"I could easily call her one of the Fae Queens," Brion assures. "In charge of mischief, southern region." He smiles at memories.

"So that would make you a King or High Prince of Fae," Frey said and glances at him. "I think you'd fit the bill."

"More like King of 'Stuck in the Mud'," Brion waves the title away. "That's what my sister would say." He makes a slight gesture to Neil. "That's the ruler right there."

"At your service," Neil bows playfully. Frey smiles at him. "And you and your sisters, my beautiful lady, could pass as one of the Queens."

"Those words are truer than you know, Sir Neil," Frey beams a bright smile "We are at our destination."

A few actual birds sing out as Milea saunters into the clearing, looking about as she makes sure everything is in order. The grass low, more a carpet than vegetation and in the center is a large round stump, the tree long since gone. Around the stump are several small boulders that pose as chairs for seating a large group of people.

Milea motions her head in approval and glances around the perimeter of the clearing, taking in the seven large and comfortable mattresses that line the area. She folds her arms patently as the mattresses move away from the trees and towards the table, leaving lots of room to walk around the entire clearing. Milea smiles, pleased at the work as she returns to her companions, ignoring the golden dust that erupts from all around her. The dust settles when she walks out of the 'room' and into the 'hall.'

"Because you are new to the forest, we will all stay here for the night to include Maya and I," Milea said. "I think Mother has something planned for us all after we have rested. You will rest comfortably tonight, unlike the ship's first night."

"That's good," Vicki beams a little and enters the clearing. Her expert eye spots several niches around the clearing. "Where do those go?"

"There are five places to have privacy," Milea explains. She and the rest of her party enter the space. "Each has a spring for bathing, should you choose, and I know you will not be disturbed." "They will not be," Frey agrees. "Please, everyone, relax. Including you, Milea. You've had a long trip and Mother will be summoning you soon."

"You are right, I am going to need to relax before I face the tempest," Milea's shoulders relax as she goes to sit upon one of the beds.

Milea smiles as she watches her guests explore their surroundings. Sonja sits down upon the forest floor next to her mother and stretches a little to try and relax. The sorceress strokes her child's hair as she recalls the journey, they have taken over a short period of time. Sonja has grown in leaps and bounds to include the discovery of various abilities. Milea turns her attention back to Vicki and Neil as she pounders the ability as well as something that has been on her mind since the rescue.

"Vicki, Neil," Milea calls to the Dresdens. "I've an inquiry for you. I recall the reactions to the Harp of Hestor by you both during our trip. Do either of you have an interest in it?"

"I don't want to add it to my collection if that's what you're asking," Vicki said as she sits down on the bed across from Milea.

"Our mother's family has some history with King Hestor," Neil adds, sitting next to his sibling. Brion decides to sit on the floor and play a game with Sonja.

"Let me explain," Vicki offers.

Frey sits down on the bed next to Milea as Vicki folds one of her legs under her and begins her tale. Hestor was a king that craved power above all things. In his corrupted mind, he felt that his kingdom was not under his full control as he desired. Desperate to change this, he enlisted the assistance of the malevolent Goddess Alkadore. Two things were given to the king, a crown and a harp.

Using the crown, Hestor was able to control anyone in his kingdom to do as he pleased. The harp was used to conquer his neighbors and bring them under his command as well. Time, however, would be Hestor's greatest enemy as old age caught up with him and he died. his spirit did not go to the other side as Alkadore had other plans for the mad king. Instead, the king's spirit was trapped inside of the crown that bears his name. The crown is cursed with the opposite effects, instead of the user controlling the masses, the user is controlled. Only the descendants of Hestor are able to use it as it is intended. Hestor's accursed harp still has the same effects as it brings the targets of its current master under control.

"I will assure you that there are no more descendants of Hestor," Vicki says, confidently.

"I think Zaria said earlier that the harp was destroyed by Ilandere," Neil said. "Well, she had assistance with that in the form of d'haradune spell-song writers. Vicki and I are descendants of one of them by way of our mother. Her name was Nair."

"Sorshana's target would be dragons," Milea leans her head back and stares at the ceiling. "Not surprising as she herself is a dragon. I am at a lost, should I add this fuel to the fire that is already started by Zaria and Maya?"

"Might as well let her know," Frey volunteers. "It is best to do so now or suffer the wrath of the gods if mother finds out later."

"Hm..." Milea flops backwards onto the mattress and continues to stare at the ceiling.

The forest birds serenade in hopes to brighten the mood of the three that they entertain. Maya takes note of the group of fae children that laugh and play in the branches of the trees as their parents call to one another to travel to the clearing that they just left. The fae clears out and the path turns from bright daylight to twilight yet still somehow inviting.

Keela pauses when she reaches her destination and takes a good look around as she continues to a place she could sit comfortably. Maya walks into the destination and hesitates; it is of an old ruin that she recognizes. She cranes her neck taking in the entire area and figures it out, this is the place that she and Milea played and sheltered in when they were children. Now, the house has fallen apart from age and slight neglect yet the yard still yields the pretty flowers they planted long ago.

Zaria stretches and changes back into A'drianis as the shadows allow the transformation. She also senses that if she tries to use them to escape, the punishment will be very harsh. With a pout, she follows Maya over to the ruin as Keela sits down on the part of the wall that collapsed and offers her guest to sit across from her. Maya and A'drianis glance at each other as if debating what is going on. They hesitantly take the offered seating. It is within arm's reach of Keela which cause the shiadokat to shift a little as if a child in trouble.

"It is troubling and odd that one of the more powerful Temple of Lights was attacked so wantonly yet you, my daughter, are the only survivor," Keela focuses on Maya. "The news of the Underak is also not setting well with me, A'drianis. However, I will let you two decide who will speak first, but I will hear from both of you."

"You first, cousin," A'drianis offers.

A calm wind blows through the trees as Keela faces her child, giving her complete focus. Maya grumbles and shifts a little then takes a deep breath and explains what she saw at the Temple. Keela arches an eyebrow when Slone is mentioned along with his entourage. She then glanced over at a nervous A'drianis when Jasmine Underak is brought up as well as the fight that Maya had with her. Maya continues with Nul, and the Harp of Hestor, describing the song that precedes the inevitable battle. Keela keeps her gaze upon the shiadokat, a few of the items mentioned should have never resurfaced. A'drianis shifts under the gaze of the powerful Eltis, not sure what will happen to her once they are done.

Maya pauses to think about the events at the temple, describing the battle she had with the entranced warriors that were supposed to be the defenders of the sacred halls. Then Maya recalls fleeing into the library where she met with a mage that wields the Eye of Gaunt. The mentioning of the Eye brings Keela to her feet, a look of shock and anger comes to her features as the forest darkens around the small clearing. Those birds and fae that are close by flee to safety, unsure of what the Guardian of Selvast Forest is about to do. Although the shadows are deep enough to escape, A'drianis finds that even if she wants to run, she cannot. The shiadokat fidgets from the powers radiating off the Mother Eltis.

Keela takes a few breaths in and sits back down as the space lightens up. Maya wisely decides to pause until Keela settles down and asks for her to continue. Maya then informs her mother of the battle with Jasmine right after she survived the blast from the Eye and her attempt to teleport out. Keela listens as her daughter conclude with the results of the teleportation and how she survived until Milea found her. The Eltis requests that Maya describe the Eye of Gaunt and she is displeased with what she hears.

"I see," Keela said. "It is an original. The first time that we faced an Eye of Gaunt, many perished at its gaze. This current threat is the second most powerful Eye. But how did they get it? My sister has been locked away with Gaunt's eyes for many millennia."

"Ok, so she gouged his eyes out," Maya asks, confused by the statement.

"Armels and I killed the one hundred eyes Tragin, Gaunt, before history was named such," Keela explains. "Our sister is Gaunt's lover and quite upset that we killed him. Her real name is a curse so I call her Urchaid." She crosses her legs. "Urchaid took his eyes and swore revenge against us."

"The first eye was destroyed when Tildri defeated it, right," A'drianis said as if to clarify her memory. "So how come both Milea and Maya survived a blast from that thing?" She places both hands upon her mouth when she receives a single look from her aunt. An eagle cries out from above the treetops.

"Both," Keela raises an eyebrow after a small silence. "I am not aware of Milea's run in."

"Um... we're twins," Maya offers an explanation. "Milea said she was hit at least twice and both times had to come straight home."

"No, there is something more," Keela ponders. "Milea did not tell me she faced an Eye of Gaunt. Only that she battled the councilman, Brandon."

"That's the jerk that controls the Eye," Maya blurts out. She shifts when she notices that Keela is very quiet now. The Eltis slowly closes her eyes as if to rein in her immediate reaction.

"Maya, you may go," Keela said opening her eyes once more. The whites are a darker shade of blue. "Follow that path, and it will lead you to your sisters. When you get there, tell Milea I want to see her." The tone of her voice is very stern. A small growl is within the words though it is not anger at her children that she is feeling.

"Ok," Maya hops to her feet and leaves. A'drianis mumbles a few swears as she stays put.

The sounds of the woodlands become livelier and more vibrant the further she travels from the ruins. Maya takes a deep breath in and slowly releases it as she walks through the large trees and notes the distance of the sounds. Sunlight filters through creating a warming magical effect upon the grass and provides a little smile upon the woman's lips as she moseys down the enchanted lane.

A strong force slams into Maya's mind causing her to hit the ground. She shakes her head and looks up. Fear replaces the pleasant mood she once enjoys. The trees are twisted, black ooze flows from their evil branches with red eyes glaring at her from the shadows. Maya gets to her knees and panicked, looking about. How did she return to Northern Selvast forest? She looks down at the grass, it is green. She knows the grass in the North is red or deep maroon.

"Come on Maya, you're still in the right space," Maya encourages. "Don't do anything rash, he wants you to do that. Relax."

She breathes deeply and closes her eyes, reining in her panic. When she opens them, she sees the beautiful rich woods. The leaves rustle with the small breeze blowing through.

"Alright, Milea. Where are you?" Maya stands as she hears familiar laughter and follows the sound.

Frey's light laughter fills the clearing as she listens to the many stories that Vicki and Neil clarify with Milea. Sonja fidgets as her mother braids her hair, needing to burn a little energy so she can settle down at night. Milea ponders the tales as she finishes her task, and sits back a little. Sonja springs to her feet and decides to go climb one of the trees. Milea watches her daughter briefly then turns to the Dresden siblings and admits that a few of the stories are true, with a little exaggeration perhaps by the bards creating the lore. Maya enters the clearing and makes a beeline to her twin. Milea watches her sibling sit down. Maya is rubbing her arms as if cold.

"Are you alright, Maya," Brion asks, concern in his words and actions.

"I," Maya shutters a little and rubs her arms. "I'm fine. It's just some memories as I walk the path." She assures and exhales a little as she turns to her twin. "Mom wants to see you."

"Zaria's still there," Milea observes with a worried expression. "That is frightening. How is mother?"

"I think she might be a little upset," Maya warns before placing her hands on her hips. "You did not tell me that you did not inform mother of the Eye of Gaunt." Her twin's expression changes twice.

"I didn't know what it's called until Zaria said the name on the ship," Milea defends, crossing her arms at chest level.

"Well, I told mom," Maya admits. The twins study each other in silence for a few seconds.

"I see," Milea relents and stands up. "I will return."

"Mom, should I come too," Sonja asks, dropping from her perch in the tree.

"No. I think I will go by myself this time," Milea assures. "Behave until I get back." She walks out of the clearing via a different path. The forest rustles as she uses it to move closer to her destination.

"Lady Frey, can we go to the ship," Neil requests. "I want to retrieve my mandolin." He stands and rubs his legs a little.

"Music to sooth the savage Eltis," Maya asks with a gentle chuckle.

"If it helps," Vicki stands up and dusts her backside. "I'll get my flute, and we can try a duet."

"So, not only do you sail ships, fight Eltis, and do acrobats. But you are a traveling ensemble as well," Frey tilts her head at the trio. "You three are very busy."

"Not me," Brion said, "them." He nods to the Dresden siblings. "I'm only fulfilling a debt."

"Keep sticking around, and we will get you integrated yet," Vicki clasp Brion's shoulder. "We can start by teaching you how to play the mandolin."

"Not mine," Neil shakes his head.

"Come with me. I shall take you to your ship quickly," Frey assures. "And then perhaps you can sing one of those songs you had for my sister. It would be interesting to hear."

"As you wish," Neil agrees.

"I'll stay here," Brion offers. Sonja sits next to him. "Do you understand the bird chatter?" He asks the girl as Neil and Vicki leave with Frey.

"Uh huh," Sonja listens. "They like your eyes, Neil's chest and Vicki's rear end." She summarizes. Maya laughs in good humor from the girl's filtered translation. Brion places his hand upon his chin, thoughtful.

The birds harmonize their merry serenade as they fly through the trees. The sight and sounds are, however, more distant from the cabin ruins than normal. Keela stands with her back to the path, contemplating what she learned from both Maya and A'drianis on the journey to and from the Temple of Light. The Eltis' breathing pattern is shallow, suggesting that she is irate from much of the news.

A'drianis shift a little as she awaits Milea's arrival. The shiadokat will not be dismissed until Keela hears what Milea has to say. A'drianis hopes that her aunt does not summon Oswind, that will not bode well for any of them. Keela's ears shift back, listening to the approach of the person she awaits.

Seconds later, Milea walks into the clearing and pauses when she notes that her mother's back is to the path she exits. Keela turns to look at her child noting the woman bow and straightens to lock gazes with her. A bit of pride did fill Keela's heart when she sees Milea hold her ground despite the fact that her mother's eyes display displeasure. The Elder Eltis turn her gaze to the seat next to A'drianis in a silent invitation to sit down. Milea follows her mother's line of sight then walks over and sits down in the seat indicated. Milea crosses one leg over the other and places her hands upon her knee awaiting the questions.

"Milea," Keela once again facing the woods, "tell me about your journey. Start from a beginning."

"I will start from when we left Churn," Milea offers. "It is after I hired Neil."

The forest once again rustles with the breeze, perhaps a rainstorm is brewing above the canopy. A'drianis grumbles and fidgets, trying to remain calm in the presence of the obvious danger, silently admitting that it is not working. Milea recalls the events of Lybrinthia Bay and the first storm she and her companions ran into. The details of the weather event interest Keela enough to turn around to face her child and sit down when Milea describe King Orin and his many wives. The sorceress elaborates on Yabura and how the Tragin behaves, thus her life is spared for now. That causes Keela to fold her arms and close her eyes yet her ears continue to listen.

The *Dragodu* has the elder Eltis to once again focus on Milea as A'drianis adds her own take on the ship. Both admit to hearing the rumor of the ship being destroyed by Ra'jil, yet it is still persisting, perhaps resurrected by either Jasmine or their antagonist. The crimson dragon, Etan, induces the right eyebrow of Keela to tick up as she listens. She has not heard about him in many centuries, yet he still lingers after his daughter's death. When ask, Milea confirms that the crimson dragon's daughter, Uzuri, is also still attached to Bri'al.

"Both are deceased Eltis. They are trapped in this world," Keela scowled. "The girl was killed by Urchaid. That is why she dislikes what she sensed from the ship. Continue."

Nodding, Milea turns to A'drianis who describes the fish people and is please when Keela grins a little being humored at the events. Both then describe their take on the Temple of Light and what they saw when they first arrive. They go into great detail about the graveyard they walked into inside the Hall of Ilandere. Milea mentions a book that Vicki received from the dead head priestess, Nadine. Keela sits back when she heard the description of the article. It is torn in half, the pages appear to be blank, but they know better. Milea informs her mother that Maya looked at the book and sensed it is cursed with 'ever sleep.' Keela reassures that she will see the book later on tonight.

Once again A'drianis squirms when Jasmine's name is mention as her cousin details the escape from the Temple. Milea informs her mother of Reis and Claries, the twin Eltis and the island the *Dragodu* chased them to. Keela recalls that the Eltis twins are dead she saw their attacker kill them both on the field of battle. Milea sees her mother's mind is occupied with thought thus skips the details until she got to Tenze. Keela lowers her gaze and stares at her daughter she says one name.

"Roathis," Keela asks interrupting Milea. "You battled her?" She turns to A'drianis. "Is she at full strength?"

"As far as I can tell, she was not," A'drianis offers. "She is now in the body of her latest victim. Funny thing is, this victim is nothing that Roathis herself would have chosen."

"Roathis has taken the body of a young female wolf Waere," Milea informs. "According to her, the young woman committed suicide because she falsely believed that it would grant her immortality."

"I see," Keela acknowledges. "Why did you battle her?"

"Vicki and Sonja had unwittingly run into the Temple of Roathis while getting away from a mob," Milea recalls the explanation given to her. "Vicki escaped, but Sonja was captured and tied to Roathis' altar."

"How is she now," Keela asks.

"Her arm is bruised from the incident that sparked the battle," Milea informs. "Maya looked her over to make sure. So far, she is well."

"Good," Keela crosses her legs and place a hand upon her knee, imitating her daughter. "The book that found in the Temple of Light. Where is it? I'd like to see it."

"It's aboard the *Lady of the Night* the last time I saw it," Milea said. "I can retrieve it once you are finished with me, mother." She bows her head in respect.

"A'drianis," Keela glances at her niece. "Retrieve the book once we are done here. I've a feeling that Maya may need Milea's assistance by now."

"Of course," A'drianis bobs her head. "I... could get it now." She starts to stand up.

"No," Keela informs. "There is one more I need to speak to, and he may have questions for you both." She stands and walks to the woodland once more as A'drianis sits back down, pouting.

"Oh no, don't tell me," A'drianis mumbles as Keela stretches and pause just in front of the woods.

"Oswind," Keela said the name.

The sound of it is like a vat of cold water going down A'drianis' spine. She did not want to hear that name in the contents of this conversation. The birds quiet their song as a slight wind moves through the trees heralding the one Keela' has summoned approach. A'drianis grumbles a little upset as she senses the presence of a very powerful Eltis drawing near. Milea keeps herself calm, yet she too did not count on Keela to summon her mate, at least not this soon. The air grows cool as a handsome man fades into sight, sitting on a cushion of air as he admires the woman who summoned him from behind.

Just like his painting, Oswind is a tempting yet deadly man. He continues to scan the back of Keela's form with an appreciating eye, oblivious to the two that share his view for right now. His mind recalling many times he'd seen Keela without her current outfit or the curse she bares. Oswind's hearing finally detect the heartbeats of two others in the clearing with him and stand up from his seated position to face them. Milea stands along with A'drianis and bow to the man in respect. Oswind has a confused look about his features as he studies the two women sitting at the ruin. What has happened this time around? Last time he was summoned with both Milea and A'drianis around, one or both had triggered a deadly series of unfortunate events.

"What have you two triggered this time, daughter? Niece?" Oswind requests of both women in his charismatic deep, smooth voice.

"It's not what we triggered, father. But what we happen to run into," Milea answers truthfully as she sits back down. "In rescuing Maya from the Temple of Light in the Boiling Seas, we uncovered many things that, perhaps, should not have been discovered."

"Those things and people are what we are in trouble about," A'drianis said cryptically and retakes her seat. "And Milea is not one of those in trouble."

"Eh," Oswind asks as his look of confusion becomes even more so.

"Oswind, love," Keela said his name, catching his attention. "Why did you let one of the Underak survive?" Oswind appears stunned before he scowls.

"The Underak are all dead, right," Oswind turns towards A'drianis. The woman lifts her hands as if helpless.

"Not all of them," Keela turns to look at him. "One of them was missed, either you or A'drianis missed them. For both of you, I hope that she is the only one. The Underak is a woman, and she tried to kill our daughters."

"Let me assure you, my love, that the Underak are all gone. I know because they are all rotting in the bowels of Ublivorion as we speak," Oswind argues. "This woman that you speak of may have found a book or legend of their existence or obtain similar abilities to the Underak through depository means just to claim the legacy. But I will guarantee that she is not an

Underak." His voice is firm in his convictions. His eyes begin to reflect his displeasure.

"Milea and Maya would not lie to me, Love," Keela said with confidence. "And A'drianis knows better,"

Keela notes her mate's silence and the fact that the clearing is becoming colder. Frost begins to form on the trees and grass as Oswind's mood worsen and Keela contemplates how to break through to him. The colder it got, the more closed-minded Oswind will become; however, she knows that he needs to be informed about what is happening just as much as she did.

"Anything else," Oswind demands, his voice a little deeper indicating he is no longer in a good mood.

"Yes. The Eye of Gaunt," Keela said in an even tone.

"That thing is no longer in existence," Oswind growls, interrupting his mate. "The others are locked away with Urchaid."

As Oswind's grip on his staff tightens, the temperature continues to drop with even a little blue snow trickling down from the trees above. Milea exhales and notices her breath upon the atmosphere. She and A'drianis glance at each other, unsure of how long they will be staying until they are able to get up and leave. That, in itself, will be a dangerous thing as it has the potential of disrespecting Keela. Both seem to turn their attention back to the couple as they ponder their predicament.

"If that is your belief. You will learn the truth in a matter of time," Keela remarks. She is weary of arguing with him. "Maya has been struck once by it and survived. Milea, struck twice. I quizzed them at separate times. They both describe the same object to me."

"There is no one out there powerful enough to handle an Eye of Gaunt," Oswind grounds out. "Not unless they are blessed by Urchaid. She is locked away." He insists.

"She caused two storms that I am aware of. Those two storms almost killed our children," Keela interrupts. She glances at her silent audience. "Milea, A'drianis go. I will see you momentarily. A'drianis, remember the book."

"Of course," Milea hops to her feet and bow.

The silence of the clearing is interrupted as Milea crunches through the frozen vegetation and head down the path that A'drianis is already going down. The two meet up with each other and exhale in relief then separate with one heading back to the clearing and the other to the ship. as the cold from Oswind's mood starts to spread into the woodland. In the clearing, Oswind steps until he is within one foot of his mate and glares into her eyes, obviously upset at the information he receives.

Keela remains where she stood, unafraid as she locks her eyes with his deep dark blues. She notices that it is now im-possible to distinguish the pupils from the whites because of his agitation. Keela cast a powerful shield around her hand and lifts it to touch Oswind's cheek. The move surprises him, causing some of the agitation to go away and his shoulders to ease. Oswind closes his eyes and takes pleasure in the simple, muted touch from the woman he loves. He bends to kiss her. Keela to stop his advances by taking a step back and turn to walk a few more feet from him, creating a little distance then face him once more.

"While I am agitating you," Keela said and places a hand upon her hip. "Roathis is returned along with her son, Slone. I swear that relationship is awful."

"No one is powerful enough to bring Roathis back to life," Oswind growls.

"Except the Underak," Keela said. A slight film of ice forming over her hair "I will let you think about it. I have to go and make sure Sonja is well. She was captured by Roathis and chained to her altar."

Keela turns and walks away. Oswind lets out a long, and low growl before disappearing with a brilliant red bolt. The sky roars with thunder.

CHAPTER TWENTY-FOUR

Quest for the Eltis

The hidden audience remains hush as they listen as the bard that visits them played a beautiful tune upon his instrument. The music is mellow and echoes in the woodlands, bringing curious visitors from far and wide. Frey sees the shadows have lengthened turning her mind to concern as Milea has not returned let alone A'drianis. Brion cleans his sword, humming to the delightful and catchy melody.

Vicki makes the decision to let her brother go solo for this song as she stretches out on one of the beds. She exhales at ease in the forest as she studies the branches above at the beautiful integrated patterns. Sonja plops down next to Vicki and points out various animal shapes in the canopy. One particular shape, a unicorn, begins to move among the trees much to Sonja's amusement. Vicki gawks at it then enjoy the entertainment figuring out that the enchanted forest is just as playful as it is mysterious.

"That is fascinating," Vicki observes with awe. "How is it doing that?"

"I never figured it out," Sonja grins. "But I am always delighted by it, even when I was younger."

"You have some very strong connections to the spirit world, Vicki, to see the forest's playfulness on your first visit," Maya observes as she brushes her hair out.

"It's one of many gifts that my mother gave me at birth," Vicki sits up. "During the voyage, Milea said that we were going to pick up someone with a similar gift. I guess that's you?"

"Indubitably," Maya nods as she finishes her grooming. "It takes a while to learn it, but I will give you a starting stone, both of you, to help you out. Lessons can come later, when you are ready."

Two small rocks start to glow then levitate off the ground. The items then travel to Maya's open palm and land. Maya cups the stones in both hands and shakes them a little then relax and speak quietly to them. A burst of energy erupts from the stones before she releases them and levitates them over to Vicki and the now sitting up Sonja. A silver chain entwines around the stones, decorating them as well as providing a means to carry them. Sonja reaches to touch the floating object then gasps and catches it as if falls. Vicki catches her stone as well, feeling that it is warm and very light unlike what she expected. The stone is also purple and has a small glowing ruin in the center of it.

"Wow, this is beautiful," Vicki said. "This will keep the ghosts at bay?"

"It is a training mechanism to assist in that, yes," Maya smiles. "The ultimate goal is for you to have the power to do so within yourself."

"I think we have a visitor," Brion announces. Maya perks up and turns to the path.

The bird chatter increases a little as Milea enters the room. She is alone bringing a little worry from Maya for their cousin. She had hoped that A'drianis and her twin arrive at the clearing together and that the shiadokat is not stuck with Keela. Sonja gets to her feet and goes over towards her mother to hug her, glad that she is alright.

Brion is first focused on Milea then his eyes see movement behind the sorceress. A woman standing four feet tall peeks into the clearing from outside. He tilts his head noticing that the small woman is well developed, large colorful wings grace her back. She might have passed as a winged elf yet her ears are much longer and double as antennae. The woman sees she is discovered and disappears in a rain of golden dust. Brion then glances over at Frey. The Eltis is focused upon the entrance.

"How did it go," Maya asks of her twin as she sits down.

"I informed her of Roathis," Milea admits. "She is not pleased with the return. Then she called Oswind."

"Yikes," Maya's features reflect a combination of emotions. "Oswind's summoning's never a good thing when it comes to Roathis. Or anything for that matter."

"I agree with all my heart on that statement, sister. Mother is asking Oswind a number of questions." Milea rubs her legs down. "She is still talking to him when we took our leave. Zaria has gone to retrieve the book off the ship. Mother is curious."

"Oh good... I think," Maya said.

"Oswind's not going to come here, is he," Neil asks, overhearing the conversation. "I do not want to meet him this early in life."

"If he's curious enough he might," Milea answers. "Don't worry. He's got his hands full with Keela right now."

"Their conversation may take some time," Frey said. "I suggest that you all rest for the evening. I will bring dinner to you when it is ready." She stood and left the clearing.

"Keeping curious naked women at bay is hard work I suppose," Brion observes.

"Curious what," Neil scans his surroundings and see nothing of the sort. "Stomach pains playing havoc on your mind, Brion?"

"No, I saw a few as we walked through the forest," Brion said. "One more peeked into the clearing when Milea walked in. They are curious but did not approach once they saw Frey."

"They are faes," Milea said of the beings. "And faes know better..." She frowns her displeasure at the golden dust that rain down on the clearing as a large group of faes disappear from the branches. "I think they are enchanted by your voice, Sir Brion."

"And Neil's skills with the lute," Maya agrees.

"They like Vicki as well," Sonja informs. "But I think it's more the males than the females that like her."

"Not sure how to dissuade fae folks," Vicki voices her thoughts. She jumps when several large trays of fruits, vegetables, nuts, and cooked meats appear on the table at the center of their clearing "What's this?"

"Dinner," Sonja announces and goes to the meal. "Alright!" She did a little jig before sitting down to enjoy the meal.

"Dig in before she really gets started," Milea offers her guests. She smiles when they take her advice.

"I'm going to miss this," Neil smirks, sitting down.

The hours of laughter and mischief soon wane as the group settle down for a night's rest. Neil found the material he is on more comfortable than any mattress in all his travels as he sleeps soundly. Milea is in a very deep sleep and is closest to the entrance. Vicki and Brion are also in a deep and restful sleep. Sonja fidgets in her sleep a little as Keela sits upon her bed. The Eltis touches the preteen to make her stay still long enough to scan her. Keela then uses her free hand to feel the girl's forehead and speak in a soft voice to her.

When Sonja did not react, Keela seems at ease. The time the girl spent on the altar did not affect or change her in any way. She brushes the hair from Sonja's face and then takes up the arm, noticing that it is still bruised from where the blacksmith grabbed her. That thought brings a frown to Keela's features as she then brushes the scales. She tilts her head with a little curiosity when they glow from within then go back dormant. Sonja shifts a little in her sleep to turn onto her side and rub her arm then go back into her deeper slumber. Keela stands up from the bed and focuses on the whole preteen, the girl will be going through changes very soon. Hopefully Milea is ready for them.

Keela then crosses her arms and turn her attention to Maya. Despite the comfort, Maya is tossing and turning perhaps the vile Northern Selvast Forest is calling to her. Keela glares in that direction, eager to take care of the threat yet she knows she will have to be more powerful than her current form allows. With a snap of her tail, Keela approaches Maya and sits on the edge of the bed at the same time the woman sits up gasping for breath. Maya looks bout noting her location then fold her legs to her chest and rock back and forth. Keela studies her daughter with mixed feelings inside, most of them eager to destroy the person that kidnapped and harmed her child.

"He still haunts you," Keela asks bringing attention to herself. Maya swallows and tremble. "Hunts you?"

"Yes," Maya agrees. "Sometimes when I sleep, I feel him clawing at my mind. Threatening me then taunting me. I..." She chokes. "I don't want to go back. I don't want to remember..." She shutters.

"You will never return to him, my daughter," Keela assures. "How he hid you from me for so long?" She shakes her head. "No, you will not have to worry with him. But I feel you will have to face your memories one day. You will need to be strong enough to do this."

"That's why I went to the Temple of Light a year ago," Maya reminds. "To become strong enough but..."

"The temple is not the only means, Maya," Keela touches the woman and notices that her skin is cold and covered with sweat. With silent uplifting words, she pulls Maya into a gentle hug. "Sh... you're going to be fine..." She rubs the woman's arms as if to warm her up.

"I cannot stay here much longer," Maya whispers to her mother.

"I know you cannot," Keela said softly. She turns when she hears her niece approach. "A'drianis, do you have the book?"

"Finally," A'drianis grumbles. "The bloody ship didn't want me to take it. I had to wait till total darkness to get into the hull." She hands the book half to her aunt.

Owls hoot as Keela accept the book, noting that it is indeed bound by a powerful spell or curse. The trees part above revealing bright moonlight with a beam of illumination condensing around Keela and Maya. The Eltis turns the book over and flipped through the pages in thought. Her ears shift forward and back as she studies the document. Maya is focused on the book at first until she sees movement out the corner of her eye. She stands up when she sees that her companions are no longer in the same clearing as she and her sister.

In fact, they are in the first clearing they came to in the forest earlier in the day. The water of the spring splashes gently as it continues merrily down the rock face. Keela closes the book and stands, facing Milea's bed and finding that her stronger daughter is still asleep. The sight has Keela smile a little, the woman is very tired from her journey yet her trials have yet to begin.

"Mom, where are Vicki, Brion, and Neil," Maya asks.

"Frey is keeping an eye on them," Keela assures, "They are safe. Right now, I've a quest to discuss with you and your twin." She pauses. "A'drianis."

"I'm here, I'm here," The Shiadokat grumbles.

She jumps down and lands in a crouch. Afterward, she sits down on the ground and makes a few chuff-like noises to show her slight discontent. Keela rolls her neck and shoulders then turn to the sleeping sorceress once again.

"Milea," Keela calls the woman's name gently. She watches as the sorceress's hand flex a little. Her mind is in a deep and hard-won sleep. "Milea, wake up. It is important." The woman turns to her back.

"I'm going to move over there," Maya edges towards the spring. It is behind Keela and far away from her awakening sibling.

"I'm going with you," A'drianis gets to her feet and follows her cousin.

"Milea, last chance," Keela warns, remaining in the same place she started. Milea takes a deep breath in and opens her eyes. The woman then exhales, stretching. Her hands and feet reaching in opposite directions. "I know it is late. However, I must speak with you, Maya and A'drianis. It is about the rising storm."

"I'm up," Milea answers, her voice sleepy. She sits up and yawns, stretching again. "I'm up..." She repeats and gets to her feet. She shakes her head to rid it of sleep. "What's wrong?" Her voice is clear, she is fully awake now.

"I have gone over the information that you gave me," Keela informs, taking her seat on the rock next to the spring. "All of you. It has me concerned This," she holds up the book half, "has added to it. This is the Book of the Eltis. A book that will locate your sleeping siblings. Ilandere, Kaidar, and Tadious." She makes a positive gesture when her daughters sit on large boulders in front of her. A'drianis sits down next to Milea on the ground. "This is half of it. You will need the other half to find them."

"Where are we going to find the other half," Maya asks. "Back at the Boiling Seas?"

"It will not be there," Keela guarantees. "This book is purposefully torn apart to keep my children sleeping."

"Why," Milea asks, tilting her head much like her daughter.

"After the Great War, the Eltis were deemed evil and dangerous," Keela explains. "Especially the House of Drackor."

"That's us," A'drianis informs. "A group of powerful Gods and Goddesses got together and made judgment and punishment. Lead by Alkadore."

"There is a lot of bad blood between Alkadore and us. It will come out in time," Keela admits. "However, we are the ones to defeat Tandon when they had the original Eye of Gaunt. The Eye itself was defeated by Tildri eventually," Keela hands the book to Milea. "However, I digress. Your quest, my daughter, is to wake up your siblings. I do not know where the other half of the book is at, and I can guess that Oswind does not know either. To find it, you will have to go to the Fáidh of Desitana."

"Oh no, not her," A'drianis groans and holds her head. "She's crazy."

"But she knows where to find the book and how to find your cousins," Keela reaffirms. "Milea?" She looks at her daughter.

"I accept the quest, mother," Milea takes the book and places it on her lap. "How long do I have to complete it?"

"This quest will take you all around Bri'al. Do not rush your-self unless it is necessary," Keela cautions. "Take Sonja with you, it will be a world lesson for her. A'drianis, you have no choice."

"I know," A'drianis pouts.

"Maya," Keela turns to her silent daughter. "You will be accompanying Milea on the quest. Perhaps during it, you will build your courage for you have a great amount." She smiles when Maya meets her gaze. "Your courage even impresses this old Eltis."

"Thank you, mother," Maya bows her head respectfully.

"Relax all and rest well," Keela stands along with her children. "I will see you off in the morning. Before which, I will be rewarding your friends. I have a feeling I know what I will provide them as a payment for assisting you."

"Thank you, Mother," Milea bows. The forest shifts as she straightens. She is once again in the clearing with her companions and sister. "Well, I knew that was coming."

"Handwriting on the wall," Maya agrees. "What's the plan?"

"The Fáidh of Desitana is on Pirate Island last I know," A'drianis sits back down on an empty bed. "We can start there."

"Maya also needs to rest," Milea rubs her chin. "And I have to wake up Ra'jil. Damn." She paused and thought about her course of action. "Ok, first stop will be Dorma after I get another few hours of sleep."

"Sleep is the best plan of all," Maya agrees and lays down. "I'll try not to have nightmares this time." She closes her eyes and let out a shaky breath. Her eyes open when she senses her twin lay down behind her, their backs facing each other. "Thank you, sis."

"That's what I'm here for," Milea retorts. "Just don't wake me violently."

"I'll levitate to the private chambers if I have too," Maya admits. "Teleport if it's urgent." She smiles when her sister chuckle.

The night yields to day as the sun's light filter through the trees and Frey walks into the clearing in order to rouse her charges for the day. The younger Eltis smiles when she sees that she did not have to awaken them after all. Vicki stretches as she yawns and sits up, the night being very restful to her especially after sleeping in the cots on the ship as the other bed they had on this trip. She sees her brother and traveling buddy are the only other souls left in the room. Apparently, Milea and the others are early risers and Zaria simply a night prowler.

Frey studied the trio, remembering the condition they came in just one day prior. Vicki did have concussion yet Milea had healed it as best she could in her exhausted state. It was enough so that Vicki would survive the trip to Selvast or someplace where she would get more complete healing. Frey turns to the elf to see that he is moving a little. Brion's wounds did get a little infected from whatever battle he endure but are now completely healed. She figures the blades that cut him were anything but clean.

Frey then looks to the luckiest of the trio, Neil. He did not suffer much damage, just a few bruises on his arms and around his chest area. Frey figures that Neil is extremely resilient and tough-skinned. The younger Eltis notes Vicki finishing her morning stretches. The l'vane woman then turn and let out a soft swear, jumping a little at the Eltis' silent presence.

"Good morning, Vicki," Frey greets. "Mother asked that I come and retrieve all of you. I think it's time you told her your wishes."

"I... ok," Vicki faces her companions. "Neil, Brion, get up. It's time to go. Come on lazy bones."

"Tired bones are more like it," Neil grumbles as he sits up and stretches. He stands and rolls his back a little. "Brion."

"I hear you," Brion waves as he sits up, drawing one knee to his chest. He places his elbow on it with a smirk. "This has turned into a little more than an adventure."

"You're telling me," Neil agrees. "I'm almost saddened that it came to an end."

"Bri'al is a big place, brother. We will have more adventures," Vicki assured. "Just not as interesting as this one." She noted Brion standing up and stretching. "Besides, Brion invited us back to Cathalian with him. Might as well start a new adventure there."

"Plenty of adventures back there," Brion promises. "Trust me, you will not get bored." Frey grins at the three as she faces the 'hall' of the forest.

"Mother is waiting for you on the beach with Milea, Maya, Zaria, and Sonja," Frey informed. "I am instructed to guide you there. We do not want the fae folk to become mischievous. That would turn into more than an adventure." She starts walking down a path. The trio follows her out.

The ocean washes over the sand as gulls circle around, watching those upon the beach. The *Lady of the Night* sways back and forth with the waves and a gentle breeze with gleams of light bouncing off the polish wood. Keela leans against a tree as she gazes out over the beach and those that are occupying it right now. Unlike the area where the ship landed, this beach is level with the forest, so there is no hazardous cliff to climb.

Keela smiles at the memories of chasing the twins and catching them as all three of them tumbled down that cliff. She was angry at them that day, but still happy they were alive and unbroken. The sound of laughter echoing upon the beach brings Keela back to the present as she watches Maya skillfully avoid her niece in a game of catch. Every time Sonja got near, Maya fade from sight and appear just out of reach. Zaria sits on the beach and takes a deep breath in, stretching as the last bit of shadow depart with the sun rising higher in the sky.

The fires of the morning sun reflect in Milea's hair as she stares at the ocean, lost in her thoughts on her new mission and how long she expects it to be. This mission is one full of surprises, ranging from the new friendships she's obtained with Neil and his crew to the strange promise of Reis. Milea folds her arms across her chest as she turns her attention to the horizon contemplating, perhaps she needs to gain more intelligence on Tandon as she travels the globe, it will become very helpful in either avoiding them or countering them in the upcoming future. Milea pushes her hair away from her eyes as the wind plays with her mane joyfully.

"Coin for your thoughts, cousin," Zaria asks, standing with the woman.

"My instincts are telling me that there is more to this quest than simple awakening," Milea said. "I am going to go with my original goal of awakening Ra'jil first. Then I will go to Pirate Island. I will talk to Maya. She can keep an eye on Ra'jil as she relearns her strengths. That will keep both of them healthy."

"Even with Amadahy around," Zaria asks with a curious look as she glances up at her cousin.

"I will hope that Amadahy has the good sense to leave them alone," Milea admits with a strong amount of doubt in her voice.

"The trip to Pirate Island will not take long, and we can return before Amadahy becomes bored."

"Sounds like a plan," Zaria chimes.

At the tree line, Keela's ears once again move as a smile comes to her features, overhearing the conversation of her daughter and niece. Milea is still concern about Maya's health. Apparently, being hit by the Eye of Gaunt takes a lot out of a sorceress, and she needs to recover. The thought cause Keela to search her memory. She scarcely recalls Tildri's battle with the Eye but did remember Tildri having a sister that could also resist the Eye. The sister died before Tildri's final battle with the Eye of Gaunt. Keela looks from Milea to Maya in thought.

Maya will be the closest to being reborn of Tildri, but unlike the heroine of the past, Maya is not jealous or backstabbing of her sister. The twins support each other and Keela would not have it any other way. The Mother Eltis returns her mind to the present when she senses Frey's presence and snaps her tail as she faces those whom her youngest daughter guides. The younger Eltis bows, takes a step back and goes to the side to witness the accounts of the beach. A smile and a little bit of laughter come from Frey when she sees Maya dodge Sonja with a cheerful sound. The girl whips around and goes through her aunt's image again.

"Neil, Vicki, Brion. I trust you slept well," Keela queries the trio as they draw near.

"It's the best rest I've had in a long time, my lady," Vicki assures.

"I'd have to agree," Brion said.

"Hey, what's wrong with the ship," Neil demands. He grins from the side looks of both companions. Vicki even rolls her eyes. "Alright, I too had a great night's sleep. I don't think I heard a thing."

"That is good," Keela smiles at the mischief. "Brion, to free Solis of its grip, we have to awaken my children. They are locked beyond this realm. Milea sails to Pirate Island to find a means to free them. I do not know of one. The Fáidh there will be able to assist." She turns towards the siblings. "Vicki, Neil. Have you decided on your reward and path of travel?"

"I am simply a traveling bard now, milady," Neil said. "I have no home or family other than Vicki. I will accept any reward you see fit." He bows his head a little.

"And you Vicki," Keela requests calmly.

"I seek a song," Vicki said a little soft then clears her throat. "Mother talked about it a lot before her untimely demised but never taught it to us. She called it the Dragon Song. It had the power to create and destroy. I am curious as to what it sounded like."

"I know of this song. It has many different parts to it. Sung in a language all too old for many in this realm. The

D'haradune, speaks it fluently," Keela informs and smiles. "I detect that you and your brother are at least half D'haradune."

"Mother was D'haradune," Vicki agrees.

"There are two in this realm that know this song," Keela pauses and appear thoughtful. "Three. The King of Deltor, his daughter Jaide and of course, my daughter Ilandere. The last knows the song in its entirety. I do not know where King Darimus or his daughter are at. They are in hiding since Nul has taken Deltor. However, Milea is going to find her siblings. When she does, I will mention your interest. Ilandere is always eager to teach anyone willing to learn."

"Thank you, My Lady," Vicki bows.

"Your reward, Neil," Keela said as lifts up her hand and it starts to glow, "I have a feeling you are more than just an ordinary bard. I see it in your eyes. Thus, I know what to present to you. Accept it as my blessings."

A ball forms in front of Neil causing him to take a step back and place his hand upon his hip. He releases a bounty of unkind language when he remembers his sword is not there. Keela's ear twitches, a knowing smirk crossing her features as the ball expands to a sword. It then shapes to a fine katana blade before solidifying. Neil gawks at the blade that floats just a few inches in front of him.

The metal shimmies in the light of the morning sun with a very detail design of an eastern dragon running the entire length of the blade. The golden handle and small guard are the tail of the creature. A sheath for it appears upon the l'vane man's hip. Neil, awed, takes hold of the blade by the hilt and swings it a couple of times. It is light, sharp, and durable. Taking a deep breath, Neil places the sword in its home.

"My Lady, thank you. I am truly ecstatic about this gift," Neil kneels down, bowing his head lowly. "I will keep it close."

"Then I am pleased," Keela smiles before walking over and touching his head gently. "Arise Neil." She takes a step back and turns to her next guest. "As for you, Vicki. I've something I think you will like. It is also my personal favorite." A hint of mischief on her voice as she causes a ball to appear in front of the l'vane woman.

Vicki instinctively takes a step back from the glowing orb, her hand going to her dagger. Keela watches as the sphere grows into a long bullwhip. Vicki blinks in surprise, how did the Eltis know what weapons she and her brother prefer and are professionals with? The whip is black with a thick dark grey handle. A belt appears upon Vicki's waist complete with a means to hang the whip. Vicki takes hold of the weapon and pauses, it feels warm as if it is alive. When it did not wiggle, she figures it is safe. She cracks the whip once then rolls it up and placing it on her hip.

"Thank you," Vicki manages and knees similar to Neil. "It is an honor."

"It is one of the most versatile of weapons," Keela said and assists Vicki to stand. "In my youth, I had to use it against Oswind to keep him at bay." She whispers the words to the woman and wink before stepping away.

"Remind me not to anger you," Brion teases. He didn't hear Keela's last statement which amuses the Mother Eltis. Vicki chuckles.

"I only use it to keep overly zealous men at bay," Vicki retorts, patting the weapon.

"Like I said," Brion reiterates. He pauses when something appears in front of him. "What?"

"It would not be right for me to exclude you, Sir Brion," Keela said. She folds her arms as lightning flashes overhead and slams into the ball in front of Brion.

The sphere takes on the properties of the lightning as more bolts continue to strike. A broadsword stretches from the ball, lightning careens up and down the blade. The hilt is golden and in the shape of a dragon, a dark blue jewel in the center of it. The blade is a lighter shade of blue and alive with electricity. It crackles as it solidifies, lightning still shooting out occasionally. Brion studies the weapon before he gathers the courage to take hold of the hilt.

A bright light erupts from that embrace, catching the attention of those on the beach as well. Vicki and Neil both cusses and move back a few steps away from their friend. Frey turns and squints when she sees the lightning surrounding Brion. Milea whips around and covers her eyes when she sees the light. Zaria turns then hiss and covering her eyes as she falls to her knees. She growls and peeks through her fingers at the new and obvious threat to her sight. Maya hesitates when the light erupts and did not see Sonja's charge. The woman grunts as her niece tackles her with a triumphant cheer. The light dies down revealing that Brion is still in one piece as he blinks to clear his own vision from his experience. Keela smiles at the elf, she figures he is something more than he pretends to be.

"What you have, Brion, is the blade of my son, Tadious," Keela informs. "This blade harbors a portion of his powers since he forged it. He is a Storm Eltis. The blade and this knowledge will come in handy."

"I. see," Brion kneels. "Thank you. I will keep it close."

"I know you will," Keela agrees and assists him to stand. "A warrior of your caliber rarely breaks his word." She bows her head briefly in respect and steps back.

"I think you caught the attention of a lot of people when you took that sword, Brion." Zaria points out. "That's quite a beacon." She along with Milea are now standing close to the group. Keela decides to go stand with her children and watch her guests.

"I agree," Neil said. "Milea, I hear you are going to Pirate Island?" He addresses the woman.

"I am," Milea agrees. "I am about to leave. But I had to come and thank you for helping me with the Temple of Light one last time."

"Hmmm," Neil rubs his chin in thought. "Pirate Island...?" He appears to be contemplating a little bit.

"Full of monsters, creeps, and well... Pirates," Vicki muses as she fingers her new whip.

"Could be dangerous," Brion sheathes the sword and folds his arms. "Not sure that I would forgive myself if something should happen to the Ladies."

"I see," Milea places a hand upon her chin. "Zaria, do you know where Pirate Island is at?"

"Well," Zaria begins then pauses as she seems to get the hint. "No. I do not. I thought it might have been just around the corner."

"Then I think we may need a guide," Milea hints. "Neil, Vicki, Brion. Can you please guide us to Pirate Island?" She smiles when Keela rolls her eyes. The Eltis returns the smile, enjoying the mischief.

"I don't know," Neil rubs the back of his neck as he fringed thinking about it. He is smacked on the back of the head by his sister. "Sure, hell why not!"

"Besides, we know a shortcut," Vicki adds. "Let's go, Brion. While we are at sea, I'll teach you how to carry a tune" She walks to the ship.

"Does it involve ancient dragons, overly zealous kings, or any such matter that we just went through," Brion challenges as he keeps up with the woman. Neil follows after them.

"It involves two legendary sorceresses, a legend in the making little girl and legendary thief," Neil informs. "All riding together on a ship made from a legendary forest to aide a legendary Eltis."

"And we can add that legendary sword of yours," Vicki reminds.

"Which means that we are now legends," Brion smiles.

"Alright," Maya watches the trio board the ship as she approaches her family. "What did I miss?" She sees that Keela is humored.

"I think Neil enjoyed our company so much he decided to stick around," Milea remarks.

"Oh?" Maya raises an eyebrow. "I guess he likes trouble."

"Double with you two," Zaria hints and hurries after the trio. Sonja runs to catch up with her.

"Be careful my daughters. I look forward to your return," Keela said as she hugs her twins. "Like it or not, Neil, Vicki, and Brion are now a part of this brewing storm. I believe it is for the better. You will need their talents."

"I think you are right, Mother," Milea agrees.

"Please be safe," Frey said to her sisters. She watches as Milea and Maya go towards the ship. "Mother, will they be alright?" Frey asks as the *Lady of the Night* lift anchor and faces the sea, sails un-furrowing.

"I foresee a lot of adventures for your sisters, Frey," Keela stares after the ship. "Some will be more thrilling than others. They will return, and they will have one more to their number."

"Ilandere," Frey asks as she and her mother head into the forest once more.

"Yes, Ilandere will be with them. But so will a powerful other," Keela predicts, her ear twitching a little. "I've a feeling that the one the twins have rescued will be awakening soon. And she is a force to be reckoned with."

The *Lady of the Night* skips across the ocean heading into the kiss of the rising sun with Neil setting the course for the northern tropics once more, this time going to the island of Dorma. Milea indicates she needs to stop by the island nation before she goes to Pirate Island. Apparently, there is someone important she wants to check on before they start a new adventure.

Milea leans forward on the rail at the bow of the ship. She knows the voyage that is underway now will be a long and intense one. Especially once they have visited the Fáidh of Desitana. Vicki calls out to Sonja, teaching the girl the various tricks of the ropes. Neil watches with a bit of pride as he steers the ship to her destination. Brion holds onto a rope and watches as a sea dragon peeks at them from a distance. He grins and waves at the old man of the sea.

"What are you thinking about," Maya sits on the rail next to her sister.

"The path ahead," Milea answers, straightening until just her hands rest upon the rails. The ocean parts before the ship with ease. "About how to awaken Ra'jil? As well as the fact that you still need to recover from the Eye of Gaunt."

"I'm fine, but I see your point," Maya hops down and turn to the sea. "Dorma. That's in a jungle, right?"

"It is," Milea agrees. "Not so much hot as it is humid." Her sister frowns catching her attention. "What's wrong?"

"My hair is going to hate that place," Maya grumbles the obvious. Milea laughs at the comment. "Seriously, do you know how hard it is to keep this mane tamed?"

"I have a red one just as long as your black, sister," Milea reminds. "I also spent years in Dorma. I know." She smiles when Maya grumbles. "Anyway. I'm going to ask you to stay in Dorma to keep an eye on Amadahy. She will, no doubt, become curious when I wake up Ra'jil."

"Yes, I already heard her talk about testing the Legendary Pirate Queen when we brought her to Dorma," Maya recalls. "What did you want me to do?"

"I know that Ra'jil will eventually lose her nonexistent temper and accept one of many challenges that Amadahy will spew forth," Milea requests and leans again. "Just try and make sure that Ra'jil is recovered before it happens."

"Sounds simple enough," Maya said. "I get a tropical vacation while you go and wrestle with pirates." She rubs her chin, musing the situation. "Hmm... maybe I want to watch the pirate wrestling."

"Well. I think Neil was a pirate once. I could wrestle him," Milea offers, straightening once more to turn towards the cabin and start to walk.

"No. I think he'd enjoy that way too much," Maya shakes her head, keeping step with her sister.

Milea laughs once again as they join their companions near the helm. Dolphins and baby sea dragons play in the wake of the *Lady of the Night* as the ship continues a speedy journey towards Dorma.

www.ingramcontent.com/pod-product-compliance
Lightning Source LLC
Chambersburg PA
CBHW070259310726
48976CB00005B/1489